THE MORTALITY IN LIES

Scott Gibson

For Colleen

"There is a taint of death, a flavor of mortality in lies."

— *Joseph Conrad, <u>Heart of Darkness</u>, 1899*

Part 1

"Imagine, Madame, a circle into which I place a certain number of officers suspected of a crime; by means of successive elimination the circle shrinks more and more. Then, finally, one name alone remains in the center of the circle; that of your husband."

— Major the Marquis Armand Du Paty de Clam, speaking to Lucie Dreyfus, October 1894

Chapter 1

London, 12 August 1898

Welles was unpleasantly surprised to discover that he could not conceal the gun on his person. The club livery was unsuitable to the task; the waistcoat was too tight, the jacket lapels too low. He tried slipping the gun into the waistband of his trousers, but it was no good. The jacket did not cover the grip, which stuck out for anyone to see. He had a long walk before him, from the butler's pantry through the lounge, into the foyer and, from there, up the stairway to the hall of private dining rooms. He would pass dozens of people on the way, both members and club staff, and someone was sure to see it. He might just as well carry the damned thing in his hand.

He almost lost his nerve. But he had come too far to turn back now. He had prepared a tray with a decanter of brandy and three glasses. Now he took an ice bucket from the shelf and peered inside. It might just be big enough. He put the bucket on the tray, then placed the pistol in the bucket. He covered the bucket with a towel. The towel bulged slightly over the grip of the gun and it looked odd, but it would have to do. He took a deep breath, lifted the tray to his shoulder and passed through the doors into the lounge.

It lacked a few minutes of midnight and there were perhaps twenty members seated in the comfortable leather chairs arranged about the lounge in small groups. Two gentlemen stood at the bar to Welles's left, their backs to him. The barman gave him an odd look, but he ignored the man, moving through the room as quickly as decorum permitted. It seemed an eternity; but the members took no notice of him and then he was through the doorway and into the foyer. The entrance to the Travellers Club was to the right and the porter was there, seeing someone out. While the man's back was turned, Welles moved down the hall and mounted the stairs. His luck held; when he reached the upper landing there was no one in sight.

He stopped at the door and took a moment to catch his breath. The polished wood of the door glowed in the warm light of the gas lamps that lit the hallway. He heard a faint murmur of conversation coming from the room. He leaned closer to the door, straining to hear, but could make out nothing. He cursed himself for a fool. At any moment someone might enter the hallway and see him with his ear pressed to the door. He would lose his chance. Quickly he shifted the tray to his left shoulder, opened the door and stepped into the room.

Three men sat at a large dining table in the middle of the room. He recognized Lord Salisbury at the far end of the table, flanked by the two others. The dinner service had been cleared away and the three were enjoying brandy and cigars. Welles pulled the door closed behind him, then lowered the tray to the table beside the door. As he did so, he saw one of the men, the one seated to Salisbury's left — a younger man than Salisbury, with ginger hair and beard — take note of him.

"We have brandy already. Be so good as to leave us to enjoy it."

Welles did not reply. His back to the men, he bolted the door. This action did not go unnoticed; behind him, Welles heard a chair being pushed back. He reached under the napkin, took hold of the pistol and turned to confront the three men.

Ginger Beard was in the act of standing, so Welles pointed the gun at him. The man stopped half-way to his feet, his torso bent forward slightly, his hands on the arms of the chair supporting his weight. The room was dimly lit, and Welles hoped that none of them could see that his hand was shaking. He could feel his heart pounding throughout his body, resonating like a drumbeat in his ears. His throat was dry. He swallowed and managed to find his voice.

"Please don't call out, gentlemen. I am not a violent man and I don't wish to use this, but I have come to a desperate pass. I beg you to believe that I will shoot you if I must."

This opening was met with silence. Welles gestured to Ginger Beard with the gun.

"Sit down, please."

The man hesitated.

"Do as he says, Geoffrey," said Lord Salisbury.

Slowly, the man lowered himself into the chair.

"Who are you?" demanded Salisbury, glaring at him from the far end of the table.

"My name is Welles, sir, Percival Welles. Do you know it?"

"I do not. You're not a waiter. How did you get in here?"

"As it happens, I'm a member; getting in was the easy part. As for this," Welles said, indicating the livery, "I stole it. The cupboard wasn't locked. I'm afraid you'll find the club rather relies on its members to obey the rules."

"I shall have to speak to the club secretary. What do you want?"

"I have business with you, Prime Minister," said Welles. "I am — or rather, was, until recently — an employee of Sir Reginald Hull. I imagine you do know that name?"

It was plain from Salisbury's face that he did.

"If this is a matter of state, then it cannot concern these gentlemen," Salisbury said. He addressed his companions: "You may go."

"No," Welles shook his head. "They will stay. For this conversation, I want witnesses. I have learned that much, at least."

With the gun he indicated the two men.

"Who are you?"

Ginger Beard opened his mouth to speak but Salisbury raised a hand to quiet him.

"These are gentlemen of my acquaintance," he said. "I see no need to introduce them. I very much doubt that you will shoot me if I decline to name them."

"I'm afraid I must insist." Welles looked at the other men. "I will know your names."

"For my part, I don't care if you do," said Ginger Beard. "I am Geoffrey Bingham, a solicitor." He attempted a smile, managed only a grimace. "You may have need of my services before this night is done, sir."

"I will bear that in mind."

Welles turned his attention to the third man. He was older, of an age with Salisbury, but in every way his opposite in appearance: Short, thin, clean-shaven, and possessing a full head of gray hair, unusually long. He wore it brushed back from his forehead and it fell to his shoulders. His grey eyes met Welles's own.

"My name is Lawrence," he said. "William Lawrence." Nothing more.

Salisbury drank a bit of brandy — his hand was quite steady — then took up his cigar and leaned back in his chair.

"Would you like to sit, Mister Welles?" he asked, coolly. "Or will this be brief?"

Welles was glad of the offer. The gun was getting heavy and it would help to rest it on the table. He chose a chair opposite the Prime Minister, sat. He lowered his arm to the table, keeping the gun pointed at Salisbury. The latter put the cigar to his mouth. The end glowed brightly, then he pulled it away, blew out a puff of smoke.

"Now, Mister Welles," he said. "What can I do for you?"

"You might well ask what I can do for you, Prime Minister. I have come to offer you something."

"Give it to me, then, and be gone."

"I wish it were that simple. I need something in return."

"Ask, then. Perhaps I can save you some time."

"I should like you to betray your country," said Welles. "I imagine you will decline. I hope to convince you otherwise."

"And how do you propose to do that?" Salisbury turned to Lawrence. "He is a madman. Do you not think so?"

"The gun is a good indication," Lawrence replied.

Welles waved the pistol at them to regain their attention.

"I have a story to tell, Prime Minister. I fear it is rather long and will take some time. Are you gentlemen comfortable?"

Salisbury waved the cigar in the air. "Get on with it, man."

"Very well. My story begins some two years ago, when I went to Paris at the request of Sir Reginald. He sent me there to meet a man. I first laid eyes on the traitor Esterhazy on the lower platform of Monsieur Eiffel's great tower. I say traitor, but in truth I did not think of him that way, I suppose because he was not betraying my country on behalf of his, but his own on behalf of mine. I see now that it is these fine distinctions that constitute the moral code — if I may call it that — of the profession upon which I had only recently embarked."

Chapter 2
Paris, April 1896

The doors of the east elevator opened, and a score of ladies and gentlemen spilled out onto the first platform of the tower. The platform was well-lit and open to the air, an iron lattice deck in the shape of a square with a hollow center. The outer perimeter of the square was lined with shops, restaurants, even a small gallery. Some passengers made their way to the center, to stand at the railing and marvel at the view of the base of the tower more than two hundred feet below them. Others drew their heads back and gazed up, their eyes drawn by the insistent curve of the cast-iron lattice to the top of the tower, dimly visible against the night sky, a dizzying nine hundred feet above them.

Welles recognized Esterhazy in the crowd. He'd been shown a photograph of the man; it was a good likeness of his face, capturing the deep-set, dark eyes, narrow jaw and pointed chin and the sweeping mustache. But as he watched Esterhazy turn and walk towards the Restaurant Brébant, he saw now what the photograph had not revealed: Esterhazy was not a physically impressive man. Of medium height and slight build, his excellent evening clothes could not conceal the droop of his shoulders, his narrow chest or the bulge around his waistline. Welles knew that Esterhazy was not quite fifty years old, but the man looked ten years older. His hair was still dark, with little gray in it, but when he removed his hat and coat and gave them to the *maître d'hotel* at the door, Welles could see the bald patch at the crown of his head.

Count Marie Charles Ferdinand Walsin-Esterhazy was the descendant of two aristocratic families, the Hungarian Esterhazys and the French Walsins. He had inherited both titles and, to go with them, a crumbling chateau and a mountain of debts. The family was Army by tradition — his father had been a general, his uncle another — but Esterhazy had managed to advance only to the rank of major, albeit a major assigned to the General Staff.

Welles watched Esterhazy enter the restaurant, then studied the crowd. He had been warned to take care not to be noticed when meeting with Esterhazy, but now, truth be told, he was not entirely sure what he was looking for and as a result felt rather silly. No one seemed to have taken any note of the Count's passage. Welles wondered if he would even be able to tell if the man had been followed. He shook his head, then walked quickly around the platform to the restaurant. He gave his name to the *maître d'* — along with his own hat and coat — and was shown to Esterhazy's table.

The Count had chosen a table on the small terrace, in a corner away from those with the best view. It was early to dine by the standards of Parisians and the evening was cool, so the terrace was not crowded. The nearest tables were all empty. Esterhazy saw Welles approaching and stood to offer his hand.

"Monsieur Welles?"

"Indeed, sir, Percival Wells, at your service."

"A pleasure. I am Esterhazy."

He spoke English, perhaps in deference to Welles. He gestured to the opposite chair and they sat. The *maître d'* distributed menus, then bowed and retreated. Esterhazy took up a menu and studied it intently. Welles pretended to do the same. In fact, he was more interested in the other diners on the terrace than the fare on offer at the Brébant. He scrutinized them carefully over the top of the menu, but again had to admit he was stumped. None of them looked as if they might be agents of the French government; but then, how would he know?

Esterhazy lowered his menu, whereupon the waiter appeared at his elbow. Welles thought his French was good, but Esterhazy unleashed a burst of French too rapid for him to easily follow, then handed his menu to the waiter. The waiter turned to Welles and, before he could speak, took his menu, bowed, and departed. Esterhazy smiled.

"I have taken the liberty of ordering for us both," he said. *"Veloute de champignons. Filets de sole au beurre e citron.* And *pave de boeuf en croute a la moutarde.* I hope you do not mind, Monsieur Welles."

"Not at all, sir."

The sommelier approached and presented a bottle for Esterhazy's approval. A corkscrew was applied, a taste poured. Esterhazy sipped, then grunted with satisfaction. The sommelier filled both glasses, wiped the lip of the bottle, placed it on the table between the two men and left. Esterhazy raised his glass.

"A toast, Monsieur Welles. To a successful collaboration."

Welles nodded, raised his own glass. The wine was exquisite. He looked at the label. It was a red Bordeaux from the Medoc region; an expensive vintage.

"If we are to be collaborators," he said, "perhaps you should call me Percy?"

"As you wish. Percy. And you may call me 'Count'."

Esterhazy smiled, making a joke of it, but Welles noted that he did not offer an alternative.

The waiter returned bearing covered dishes. He placed one before each of the men, then whisked the covers away to reveal the soup, as if performing a magic trick. He bowed, retreated. Esterhazy applied himself to the soup with enthusiasm. Welles tasted his, a cream of mushroom; very good, but in truth he had little appetite. He was more than a little anxious about this meeting and found himself preoccupied with the handful of other diners on the terrace. He glanced at them frequently, trying to determine if any seemed to be watching. He forced himself to eat some of the soup, but for the most part only dipped his spoon into it and stirred it about. When Esterhazy finished, he put down his own spoon.

Esterhazy broke the silence. "Is this your first visit to *la tour*, Monsieur Welles?"

"No," Welles replied. "I came to Paris for the opening, at the exposition of 1889."

"I see," he said. "And tell me, what do you think of it? You know that many of my countrymen find it repellent?"

"I do, but I cannot agree with them. It is large, of course, and dominates the city in an unsettling way when you first see it. At the same time, I must say I find it rather graceful."

Esterhazy nodded. "Graceful. Yes, that is precisely the word. Despite the hard reality of the iron, there is more air than substance. I have read something on the matter which may interest you. Did you know that if you melted the tower down into a pool of iron constrained by the dimensions of the base, the puddle would be only a few inches deep?"

"Indeed? Remarkable."

"Monsieur Eiffel has said so himself. I confess that, like you, I admire the tower. Do you think that makes me a traitor to my fellows, Monsieur Welles?"

The Count smiled at his own joke.

"Percy, please," Welles admonished. "It is my impression that as they have become accustomed to the tower, most Parisians have also come to admire it, as you do."

"How can one not admire such a monument to the ingenuity of man?"

The waiter returned to clear away the soup. The two men waited in silence. When he had gone, Welles spoke.

"Did you often meet with Captain Hawthorne in restaurants, Count?"

"No, not often. Occasionally, I would say. Captain Hawthorne felt it would draw unnecessary attention."

"I quite agree with Captain Hawthorne. We must be careful."

Esterhazy waved a hand dismissively.

"But you are a journalist, my dear Percy, not a soldier. A private gentleman, with no ties to your government. And two gentlemen may dine together; why not? Is this not the reason you are here in place of Captain Hawthorne? Because we may be seen together without arousing suspicion?"

"Yes, quite right. Still, perhaps in the future we might meet in more discrete surroundings?"

Pointedly, Welles looked around the terrace, his gaze settling in turn on each of the other tables, calling to Esterhazy's attention how public a place it was. The Count looked thoughtful, then nodded.

"Very well, Percy, it will be as you say."

At that moment the waiter reappeared bearing covered dishes. He performed his trick again, revealing the sole. He refilled both glasses and vanished as quietly as he had appeared. Esterhazy took up his fork and knife. Welles did the same, but without enthusiasm. The fish was a little dry, and his poor appetite not equal to it.

The Count finished his fish, washing it down with the rest of his wine. The waiter appeared and refilled both glasses. The bottle was empty. Esterhazy asked for another. The waiter cleared the table and departed. Welles glanced around at the terrace, then took an envelope from inside his dinner jacket. He placed it on the table, slid it across the surface to Esterhazy. The Count picked up the envelope and slipped it into his jacket. The sommelier arrived with the wine and fresh glasses. He opened the wine, Esterhazy repeated the tasting ritual, then the sommelier filled their glasses and left.

"We should meet face to face only when it is necessary," Welles said. "That is, when you have something for me, or I have something for you. I have made a list of possible meeting places. The list is in the envelope. I've assigned a code to each place. We can arrange a meeting with a simple note. You need write only the date, the time and a code which indicates the location."

Esterhazy nodded. "Yes, very clever, Percy. Do we post the notes to each other?"

"No. Posted letters may sometimes go astray, wind up in the wrong hands. I have established a kind of post office of our own, a tailor's shop in the Rue Volney. The address is in the envelope.

When you wish to arrange a meeting, put your message in a plain unmarked envelope. Take it there, give it to the proprietor, his name is Barre. Tell him it is for me. He will hold it until I collect it."

"Yes, I see. And if you have a message for me?"

"I will do the same. You should make it a habit to visit Barre's shop every week. It would be helpful if you employed the man, to give yourself a reason to go to his shop. He's a decent tailor."

"All right," said Esterhazy. "But what if someone were to read these notes? Perhaps this Barre fellow himself?"

"I think it unlikely; I'm paying him well not to read them. But, even so, he would find only a date and a time and nothing else. Only you and I know the codes for the locations. Never leave any other message for me, only date, time, location."

Welles nodded at the envelope in Esterhazy's pocket.

"Can you memorize the list?" he asked.

Esterhazy made a face. "I'll try, Percy. But I'm really not good at that sort of thing."

Welles sighed. "Put it in a safe place, then. Not your office. Home would be better. Hide it if you can."

The beef arrived, was revealed. The two men ate in silence for some time. Then Esterhazy put down his knife, took a drink of wine.

"But suppose I need to see you and the matter is urgent?" he asked. "What then?"

"In an emergency you can send a *petit-bleu* to my office. My address is also in the envelope. But again, conform to the protocol. Date, time, location code. Nothing else."

"And if the urgency is yours? What then? Will you send me a *petit-bleu*?"

Welles smiled. "I know how to find you, Count Esterhazy. Leave that to me."

Esterhazy nodded, returned to his plate. Welles picked at his food. He really had no appetite at all. Looking around, he saw that the terrace was beginning to fill up with diners. It would be best if he were to leave soon. He had done what he needed to do. He said as much to Esterhazy as the Count was refilling both their glasses. Esterhazy looked disappointed.

"Very well," he said. Then: "There is one other thing, Percy. A small thing. I hesitate to bring it up."

"The money?" Welles asked. "It is in the envelope. The amount as agreed."

Esterhazy smiled, shrugged in the French manner. They made small talk over the last of the wine. Welles was about to take his leave when Esterhazy abruptly stood and wished him a good evening, offering his hand. He rose to take it and Esterhazy pulled him closer. With his free hand, the Count slipped a small fold of papers into Welles's jacket. It was clumsily done, and Welles looked around at the nearby tables, but no one seemed to have taken note. He sat and watched Esterhazy leave. As he was congratulating himself on a successful first encounter, the *maître d'* arrived with the bill.

Later that night, sitting at the desk in his office, he opened the envelope Esterhazy had given him. Inside was a handwritten copy of the minutes of a meeting of the *quatrieme* bureau, the division of the General Staff devoted to transport and communication. Esterhazy's unit. He leafed through the several pages quickly. Most of the matters discussed seemed routine, and he found little of interest save perhaps one paragraph near the end:

Thibet to sail by end of April in support of Marchand mission. Colonial Office confers highest priority to mission. 4th Bureau staff to support mission requests without delay. Conflicts to be referred to the office of the Chief of Staff for resolution.

Welles could make little of it. *Thibet* was a ship, surely. Marchand? Could be a man's name, or a place. He shrugged; perhaps they'd make more sense of it in Whitehall. He took a clean sheet of paper and began his report.

Chapter 3

London, 12 August 1898

The three men had listened without interruption to Welles's tale of his first meeting with Esterhazy. Now Lawrence spoke.

"You say Sir Reginald sent you to Paris to meet this Esterhazy fellow, Mister Welles?"

Welles nodded.

"Why would he do that? What was your connection with Sir Reginald?"

"You gentlemen may be aware that the Foreign Office often makes use of men like me — journalists working abroad, I mean — to gather information or undertake the odd errand?"

Welles paused, but no one replied.

"I had been of some service to Sir Reginald in that capacity," he went on.

"And this was another such *errand*?"

"No. It was a more permanent arrangement. Sir Reginald offered me a position with the Foreign Office. Well, perhaps not a position as such. Nothing so formal as that. He wanted me in Paris. I was to go there, to live and work as a journalist. He called that *cover*, a way of disguising my true purpose."

"And your true purpose was this Esterhazy fellow?"

"Yes," said Welles. "Sir Reginald needed a control, someone who runs the agent. I was to meet Esterhazy regularly, convey instructions, collect the intelligence he provided and pass it on to Whitehall."

"A moment, please." This from Bingham. "Who is Esterhazy, exactly?"

"An officer in the French Army, assigned to the General Staff. And a spy, working for us these past four years."

"You say you had been of some use to Sir Reginald," said Lawrence. "Presumably that's why he offered you the job. But why did you accept it?"

Welles shrugged.

"A fair question, one I have asked myself in light of all that has occurred," he said. "Sir Reginald gave only a vague description of what I might be asked to do. The work would not be dangerous, he said, and it should not take up much of my time. I would be expected to continue my own work as a journalist, so that no one would know my true purpose. He could pay only a modest salary, but he thought it would be adequate to the needs of a gentleman living in Paris. Of course, the Foreign Office would also pay any expenses incurred in carrying out their instructions."

"And you accepted knowing no more than that?"

"Yes," said Welles. "I can only think that it was because the offer so accorded with my own desires. I had for some time been considering the idea of establishing a news syndication service on the Continent. I would rely on free-lance journalists rather than chasing after stories myself. Paris was the perfect location for such an enterprise, and I confess I love the city. The impediment was money. I am not a wealthy man, gentlemen. I have some small income, sufficient to my needs, but hardly enough to launch an enterprise of this nature. I had all but given up on the idea and now here was Sir Reginald, offering me the funding I needed in return for what he said would be a modest expenditure of my time. So, I suppose it must have been that. In any event, I found myself agreeing on the spot."

"You say you went to Paris in 1896," objected Salisbury. "Yet Esterhazy had been our spy, according to you, for two years before that. Who controlled him before you arrived?"

"I was given to understand that a certain Captain Hawthorne — your military attaché — performed the service. Sir Reginald told me that Esterhazy had approached Hawthorne at an embassy reception in the summer of 1894 and surreptitiously passed him an envelope. On later examination, this proved to contain a handwritten copy of a General Staff memorandum on the dispatch of an infantry regiment to Tunisia and a scrap of paper upon which was written the name of a popular street cafe near the Place de la Concorde, along with the date and time of a proposed rendezvous. Hawthorne kept the appointment. Over a coffee Esterhazy declared his view that France and England shared a common enemy in Germany, that it would be best for both nations to cooperate and that he was prepared to personally undertake that cooperation even though his countrymen had not yet arrived at his conclusions on the matter, with full confidence that eventually they would. As a way of acting on this conviction, he offered to provide Hawthorne with such French military and government secrets as came his way, asking in return only that the British government assist him in meeting the inevitable financial costs one might expect to incur in such an endeavor."

Salisbury snorted. "What did Captain Hawthorne deduce from this?"

"No doubt the same as you: That Esterhazy was in financial difficulty and looking to derive an income from selling his country's secrets. We pay him, gentlemen."

"Then you did not believe he was motivated by his affection for Britain, or his enmity for Germany?" asked Lawrence.

"No, I do not say that. I suppose I thought it the case that his political views and his financial needs were conveniently compatible. You gentlemen may not understand this, but a man in my role comes to feel a certain paternal interest in his charge. One assumes responsibility for the agent and finds it difficult to think ill of him."

"It is hardly surprising that you feel kinship with this traitor," offered Lawrence. "As you said, your own reasons for this association were every bit as mercenary."

"Quite so," said Welles, agreeably. "May I go on?"

"A moment, please," said Salisbury. "You recount your meeting with Esterhazy in some detail, Mister Welles, though two years have passed. You are embellishing, are you not?"

Welles shook his head. "No, sir. As it happens, I am possessed of what I have been told is an unusual ability to recall such things. Even as a youth, I had it. I remember everything I see and hear with great clarity. I have only to look at a document and it is as if I have captured a photograph of it in my head. It is a trait which has served me well in my profession; in both of them, I should say."

"Remarkable!" said Bingham. "But tell me: What is a *petit-bleu*?"

"Within the city of Paris," Welles replied, "the postal service employs a system of underground tubes powered by air pressure — *pneumatique* tubes they are called — to move messages rapidly between one post office and another. One may go to any post office, write one's message and the address on a small slip of paper and give it to the postal clerk. The message is placed in a cylinder, which is then inserted into the appropriate tube and instantly sent to the post office nearest the address. From there, a bicycle carrier delivers the message to the intended recipient. The slip of paper is a pale blue and the message is thus called a *petit-bleu*. May I proceed with my tale?"

The last was addressed to Salisbury. The Prime Minister exchanged a look with Lawrence, then nodded.

"Very well, gentlemen," said Welles. "I must tell you now of the circumstances by which I met Georges Seigneur, who will come to play a major part in this story."

Chapter 4

Paris, May-July 1896

Welles habitually breakfasted at a cafe on the Rue Anjou, a short walk from the office he'd taken on Boulevard Haussmann. The little square of greenery of the Place Louis XVI across the street from the cafe was a favorite of the nannies and governesses from the stately homes surrounding the park and when the weather was fine — as it was today — he liked to sit at a table on the sidewalk where he could hear the laughter of their charges at play.

He had good reason to be pleased with himself. He had established a routine of visiting Barre's shop twice a week and had already met the Count three times to collect documents to send on to London. Only yesterday he'd received a cable from Sir Reginald, who pronounced himself very pleased with the material. Still, Welles was troubled. His clandestine work was proceeding in a satisfactory fashion, but he could not say the same of his more conventional one.

He had for some weeks been trying to hire an editor for his news service, someone local who could help him recruit journalists and acquire stories to sell. He had many acquaintances among the journalists of Paris and he had thought it would be a simple matter to convince one to join him. To his chagrin, he had found no takers. The free-lance journalists were, to a man, reluctant to give up what they saw as their freedom; and those employed by the Paris press were not inclined to abandon the security of their positions. He had written a few stories himself and managed to sell them to his normal clients in London and Paris, but this was no different than what he had been doing before.

In desperation, he had placed an advertisement in the papers and even put up a notice at several post offices. From this effort came a flood of letters, nearly all of them useless. Among the few possibilities, the most promising was one Georges Seigneur, an independent journalist with an ambition to be a news editor. Seigneur had enclosed in his letter clippings of several published articles, all recent. They were very good and, together with his letter, conveyed the kind of insight, skill and acuity Welles was looking for. His only reservation was that he was surprised he had not met Seigneur before and that none of his acquaintances had mentioned the man. Still, with no other prospect in sight, he had written at once to arrange a meeting.

Welles put down the paper he was reading and looked at his watch. He was to meet Seigneur this morning and it would not do to be late. He paid the bill, folded his paper under his arm and set off towards the Boulevard Haussmann. He turned right onto the broad avenue, walking east to the next intersection. On the north side of the street was a single building, six stories high, running the entire length of the block. The building had the majestic stone facade, uniform rectangular windows and leaded roof marked by dormers typical of the Empire style. At the second doorway he turned into the lobby. From her counter near the doorway Madame Hebert called out to him.

"*Bonjour, Monsieur Welles. Comment allez-vous?*"

"I am well, Madame, and you?" Welles replied in his passable French.

"Very well, Monsieur. I did not see you go out this morning."

From the tone of her voice Welles knew it was a question. He had long ago learned that the concierges of Paris liked to know what their tenants were up to. In addition to the office on the first floor, he had taken a garret on the sixth. It was small and the rent was ruinous, but he liked the convenience.

"I went out quite early," he said. "Has the post come yet?"

She made a face. "*Oui, Monsieur*. More letters for the *Service des Informations*."

She passed Welles a thick stack of envelopes. He took them, glanced through them.

"I'm expecting a Monsieur Seigneur this morning," he said. "Georges Seigneur. Any moment now, really. Can you please send him up?"

"As you wish, Monsieur."

He climbed the broad stone stairs to the first floor, reaching a tiled landing where there were several offices. Each had a wooden door inset with a frosted glass panel with the name of the business or proprietor painted on the glass. The one on the second door read '*Service des Informations*' and, in smaller print below, '*P. Welles*'.

He unlocked the door. The main room was large and open, with enough space for several people to work. One corner of the room had been partitioned to create a smaller office, reached through a door with an inset frosted glass panel. There were two other doors off the main room; one led to a washroom and the other to a small kitchen. The building had at some point been fitted with gas, and the suite was equipped with gas lamps on the walls, but the two large windows fronting onto the boulevard let in plenty of light, so Welles didn't bother to light the lamps.

He had only one desk with two chairs. At first he'd put his desk in the smaller office, with the idea that others might work in the main room; but after a few days working alone in the gloom, he had one morning looked out into the sunlit main room, taken off his jacket, rolled up his sleeves and dragged the desk out into the light. His typewriter was in the center of the desktop, flanked on one side by a small stack of office files and on the other by a ream of paper. An armoire against the interior wall of the office served as a filing and supply cabinet and a coat rack by the door was his closet. The walls were papered in a faint floral pattern but were otherwise bare.

He hung his hat on the rack, laid the post and paper on the desk, crossed the room and opened a window to let in some air. In the kitchen, he filled a kettle and lit the gas. He made coffee, then placed the pot on a silver tray. He added two cups and saucers, spoons and a bowl of sugar. He was carrying the tray to the desk when he heard footsteps on the landing, followed by a knock at the door.

"Monsieur Seigneur? *Entrez-vous, la porte est ouverte,*" he called out, arranging the things from the tray on his desk. He heard the door open.

"Monsieur Welles?"

It was woman's voice, speaking English with a pronounced French accent. Startled, he looked up, saw her.

"I beg your pardon, Madame," he began, but at the sight of the lady his voice trailed off. In the awkward silence that followed he could hear a carriage passing in the street below. He opened his mouth to speak, but no words would come. Finally, his visitor broke the silence.

"I am Georges Seigneur. You are expecting me, Monsieur?"

Belatedly Welles recalled his manners, bowed. "Madame Seigneur. A pleasure." Then, unable to contain himself: "What the devil are you wearing?"

She laughed, a pleasing sound. "Do you like it?"

She was dressed as if for riding: A tight-fitting double-breasted jacket with full sleeves over a white blouse; riding trousers tight at the waist, full in the leg and gathered just below the knee; and calf-high tight-fitting leather boots. Her hat was shaped like a small turban and adorned with an ostrich feather. She was quite tall, nearly as tall as he was, and slender, with long legs; and without meaning to, Welles found himself noticing how the tight jacket emphasized her narrow waist and the slight curve of her body above and below. When he again met her eyes, he saw immediately that she had observed the direction of his gaze.

Her own eyes narrowed, her smile vanished and, deliberately, she struck an exaggerated pose: one hand on her hip, the other arm extended out to the side, palm facing out, chin lifted high and face turned up to the ceiling. She held the pose briefly, turning slowly to the left and then the right. It was as if she had said *go ahead then, look at me, damn you*. Welles felt the heat rising in his cheeks, and he knew in that instant that he must seem a vulgar fool.

"Forgive me, Madame," he said. "Please, do sit down."

He held the chair and she sat. He took his own chair. He resolved to say something sensible, and instead said: "I'm afraid I was expecting a man." He knew it was the wrong thing to say before he had even finished saying it.

"Yes," she said, dryly. "How very rude of me, Monsieur. Here I am, a woman!"

She did not smile. She had short auburn hair with a natural curl and wide-set eyes over broad cheekbones. Her nose was rather long, a Gallic nose, and when viewed in profile it traced a smooth line that joined without interruption the graceful arc of her eyebrow. She had a strong jaw and her chin came to a point, and now she seemed to thrust that chin forward. She was, Welles thought, about thirty years old.

He took a deep breath, unsure how to proceed. Everything he had said and done so far had been wrong, even offensive. He shifted miserably in his chair, looked down at the papers on the desk, hoping for some inspiration. None came. He looked up, met her gaze, but found he couldn't hold it. He looked away, blushed again. At last, she seemed to take pity on him.

"It is a bicycle suit, Monsieur Welles."

"A bicycle suit?"

"Yes, a bicycle suit. One wears it to ride."

"Have you come on a bicycle, then?"

"I have not," she said. She smiled at his confusion. "It is only that I like to dress this way. Don't get me wrong, Monsieur. I adore a well-made gown for the right occasion, but for work I much prefer to wear trousers. So, I do. They are very nice, quite stylish, I have a good tailor."

Welles was at a loss for words.

"Did you know it was against the law?" she asked.

Welles shook his head.

"It is, I assure you. In Paris, a woman may not wear trousers in public, not without the permission of the police. Not since the revolution. Can you imagine that?"

He shook his head again. She leaned forward.

"How would you like to have to go to the police, Monsieur Welles, and ask them if you may wear trousers?"

Welles realized he was shaking his head yet again. *I'm an idiot*, he thought.

"I expect I would refuse," he said.

"Yes, I rather think you might. I did go, once, to see what they would say."

"And?"

"They told me I might be arrested. They did not seem particularly certain about that, mind you. Almost as if they felt they had to wait until the moment to decide what to do. I had a notion to test them, but then they changed the law."

"Changed it?"

"Yes, three years ago. The new law allows that a woman may wear trousers, but only if she is 'holding a bicycle handlebar or the reins of a horse.'"

She laughed and to his surprise, he found himself laughing with her.

"You must find it difficult to sit in a cafe while maintaining a firm grip on your handlebar," he said.

"Yes, precisely! I am afraid I rather stretch the law when it comes to that. I don't even own a bicycle. I have found that *les gendarmes* are," she paused, searching for a word. "Reluctant? Yes, reluctant to arrest me."

"Yes, I think they would be," Welles said. Belatedly, he asked: "Will you take coffee?"

She nodded, thanked him. He poured two cups. While he did so, he gathered his thoughts. He had been searching for a polite way to dismiss her as quickly as possible, but now he reconsidered. The unease with which his oafishness had infused their meeting was now quite dissipated and it was entirely due to her effort. She was a woman, to be sure, and a striking one, but for the first time in the conversation he was intent on what he could sense of the mind behind her eyes.

"Sugar?" he asked, placing the cup before her. She declined. He sat, stirred his own coffee, took a sip.

"Shall we talk about the position, Madame Seigneur?"

"Mademoiselle. But please, you must call me Georges, everyone does."

"Is your name really Georges? I thought it must be a *nom de plume.*"

"No, it is my real name. I am named for my father. He hoped for a son." She made a wry face. "Like you, Monsieur, he was expecting a male, and got me instead."

"He named you Georges?"

"No, that was my mother. My birth was difficult and afterward, when she knew there would be no more children, she insisted. He suggested Georgette, but my mother was never one for half-measures."

You must take after her, Welles thought.

Aloud, he asked her how she had come to be a journalist. She said she had tried other occupations. She had studied law — her father was an attorney — but found in the end that her gender was an impediment to practicing it. For a time, she worked as a teacher, but found it dull, stifling work and she had no patience with children. She had a friend who wrote for *Le Temps* and it occurred to her that here was an occupation where her sex would not matter. This, she said, turned out to be only partly correct. No one would hire her, but she found them willing enough to buy her work and credit her by name; and she came over time to build a reputation which kept her busy and her work in demand.

"It is a compromise," she said. "I can work, even enjoy a modest success, but only so long as I hide who I am. There is no hope for more. I read the work of my colleagues and I see what I would do to improve it. There are stories I would pursue with all the resources a paper can bring to bear, but those stories go untold. No paper will hire me to manage their newsroom or edit their copy. They will buy my stories because my work is good and because they can pretend to their readers that I am a man, but they will not have me in their office, Monsieur."

These words provoked in Welles a profound sense of injustice. He had read Georges' work and thought her to be an accomplished journalist and writer; yet she was thwarted in her ambitions because of her sex, which after all was nothing more than an accident of birth. He resolved at that moment to give her the chance no one else had.

"If we are to work together," he said, "you must call me Percy."

From the look on her face he understood that she'd held little hope that this interview would turn out differently than any of the ones before, and he liked her even more for the courage with which she'd carried herself through it.

"Come," he said, "let me tell you what I'm trying to do."

***

She came to work the very next day, arriving on a hired cart bearing her desk, chair and typewriter. From the start she all but took over the office and Welles gladly made room for her. From her network of acquaintances, they began to receive a small but steady stream of copy. They quickly developed a routine. They reviewed submissions together each morning and decided which of them to buy. Georges would edit the ones they chose for the Paris papers and, if any were suitable, Welles would in turn produce an English version for the London market. Side by side, they banged away at typewriters in the warm light of the morning sun. In the afternoon, Georges carried stories around the city, offering them to the editors with whom she usually worked, while Welles went to the telegraph office to wire stories to the editors he knew in London. In this way they began to establish a reputation and as spring turned to summer each day brought more submissions to their door.

Welles found that working with Georges was a singular experience. True to her warning, she always wore trousers. Her preferred fashion was simpler than the bicycle suit she'd worn to the interview: Long wool trousers and, invariably, a white silk blouse. Both were nominally made in the style of a gentleman's clothes but tailored to suit her slender form. On the first day he discovered that she smoked and, when reviewing a submission, she had the habit of stalking around the office with the story in one hand and a cigarette in the other, reading the text aloud and punctuating each point by stabbing the air with the cigarette. She seemed to contain a charge of electricity, like a Leyden jar, so that if you were to touch her the resulting discharge might knock you off your feet. She was always in motion, as if driven by the need to make up for all the time she had lost to foolish prejudice.

Thus, it was something of a surprise when Welles arrived late one morning in July to find her standing at the window in a kind of brooding silence. She did not turn at the sound of the door and made no response when he wished her good morning. She was wearing her jacket, a sort of tweed thing not unlike a man's shooting jacket. It was already too warm for it and he deduced that she had been standing at the window from the moment she arrived, having in her distraction neglected to remove it. She stared out the window, deep in thought and perfectly still except for the hand that occasionally brought the cigarette to her lips. When she did not respond to his second attempt at a greeting, Welles hung his hat on the rack and crossed the room to stand behind her.

"Are you all right, Georges?" he asked.

When she still did not respond, he placed a hesitant hand on her shoulder. She started, brushed away the hand and turned to face him. She crossed her arms, one hand still holding the cigarette, and looked him directly in the eye, and for the first time he realized that she was as tall as he.

"Percy," she said. "Good morning. I'm sorry, I was quite distracted."

"Good morning, Georges," he said. "Is there something wrong?"

"No," she said. "I mean, yes, but nothing to do with you."

"What, then?"

She brought the cigarette to her lips, inhaled, blew out smoke, her free arm still clasping her body.

"It's nothing, really. Something to do with my father. With a client of his."

"A client?" he asked.

She did not reply. Instead, she resumed staring out the window, apparently lost in thought. Welles extended a hand, then thought better of it. Her reaction when he'd touched her before did not invite a repetition. He turned away from her, went to the kitchen and busied himself making coffee. When he looked up, she was there, in the doorway, arms folded across her chest, leaning against the door frame.

"Percy," she said, "have you ever heard of Alfred Dreyfus?"

"Dreyfus," he said, placing cups on the tray beside the pot. "Army officer, right? The one who got caught selling secrets to the Germans?"

"Yes. I met his brother last evening. Mathieu Dreyfus. He came to consult with my father, then stayed for a drink. After he left, I asked my father why he'd come. He said Mathieu wanted to engage him."

Welles lifted the tray, turned to face her. "Engage him? To do what?"

Georges took the tray from his hands. He followed her as she carried it to the desk. Over her shoulder, she said, "He wants to prove that his brother is innocent."

Chapter 5

Paris, July 1896

Georges lived with her father in a town house on the western end of the Ile Saint-Louis, near the bridge of the same name which joins it to the Ile de la Cite. Welles arrived shortly before seven in the evening, in accordance with Georges' instructions. He rang the bell and waited, trying to understand how he had, against his better judgment, come to agree to her proposal. As a journalist, it would not be unusual for him to involve himself in the story of an Army officer who had betrayed his country; but as the man who secretly bought secrets from another such traitor, it struck him as madness to link his own name with that of Dreyfus. He felt sure that Sir Reginald would not approve. But Georges was nothing if not persuasive and she had worn him down.

The door opened. A butler took his hat and cloak, then led him up the stairs and into a large room; a library it seemed, though furnished for entertaining as well. The windows offered a splendid view of the cathedral and he was admiring the sight when his hosts entered.

Georges introduced him to her father, and they shook hands. Monsieur Seigneur had a thick shock of white hair and, though he was not tall, his shoulders were broad and his chest deep, so that the impression he gave was one of physical power. Seigneur offered him a drink and Welles said he would take a whisky. Georges asked for one as well.

They made small talk in English. Seigneur spoke it well, though with a strong accent, and it sometimes took a moment for Welles to understand what he had said. Seigneur asked him about his business and Welles tried to explain the idea of a news syndication service, but he could see that Seigneur had no real interest in it and was only trying to be polite. Georges tried to keep the conversation going, but with little success, and they had lapsed into an awkward silence when the butler showed Mathieu and Lucie Dreyfus into the room.

Mathieu was perhaps forty years old, a gentleman of medium height and a trim, athletic build. He had dark hair and a mustache and blue eyes that gave Welles an appraising look as they shook hands. His sister-in-law Lucie was tall for a woman, nearly as tall as Georges and, like Georges, she had auburn hair, although hers was a shade darker, and she wore it pulled tightly into a bun at the back of her head.

Mathieu joined them in a whisky. Lucie took a sherry. Georges suggested they sit, gesturing to an arrangement near the window. The Dreyfuses sat together on one sofa; Welles joined Georges on another. Seigneur took a chair between them.

They spoke in French. After some pleasantries the conversation turned, inevitably, to Alfred Dreyfus. Lucie corresponded with her husband, now imprisoned on Devil's Island, and she reported that, despite his ordeal and a recent bout of fever, he remained in good spirits. Welles could follow the conversation well enough and was content to listen. Gradually, he came to understand that the others — the Dreyfuses, Georges and her father — accepted as given that Dreyfus was innocent; that he had been wrongly imprisoned. His own knowledge of the affair was hazy at best. Although it had been a sensation at the time, the trial had been conducted almost entirely in secret and few could say with any certainty what Captain Dreyfus had done, how he had been caught, or how his guilt had been proved to the military judges of the tribunal. Welles was intrigued and at a suitable moment, he spoke.

"I cannot imagine how awful this must be for you," he said to Lucie. "How long has it been?"

"Nearly two years, Monsieur. It began in October of 1894."

"How did it begin, Madame?"

Lucie Dreyfus looked to her brother-in-law Mathieu, who gave an almost-imperceptible nod. She gathered herself, as if preparing to lift a great weight, but without further hesitation she recounted the events of that fateful October.

Their ordeal began with a knock at the door of their home, early one Saturday morning. It was messenger with a summons for Captain Dreyfus; he was ordered to report to the Chief of Staff the following Monday. Alfred and Lucie were puzzled by the message but not alarmed. The Captain enjoyed a reputation as an excellent officer, and both assumed that a meeting with General de Boisdeffre could bring only good news. Alfred was in good cheer when he left early Monday morning for the meeting.

At around eleven o'clock, Lucie said, she heard a knock at the door and opened it to find three men, one uniformed and two dressed in civilian garb.

"Who were these men? Did they give you their names?" asked Georges.

"The man in uniform was an officer, a Major Du Paty. I knew him, not well. He is on the General Staff, like Freddie. He introduced the other men; said they were policemen. I don't recall their names."

Major Du Paty told her that her husband had been arrested. He would not say why. He presented her with a warrant, after which he and the two policemen searched the house. They seemed mainly interested in documents and took away most of the contents of Alfred's desk. As they left, Du Paty warned her not to speak of the matter to anyone.

Alfred never returned. For two frantic weeks she heard nothing more. Then, one day, a journalist turned up at the apartment seeking to confirm a report that Alfred had been arrested for treason. The next day, several papers printed a story to that effect, though none mentioned Dreyfus by name. Desperate, she petitioned Du Paty for permission to tell Alfred's family what had happened. This request was granted. She cabled Mathieu, who arrived a day later.

"The first thing I did was to arrange a meeting with this Major Du Paty," said Mathieu. "We met at his home. He would tell me nothing of the case, saying only that Alfred's guilt was certain. I asked to speak to Alfred. I told Du Paty that Alfred could not lie to me, and if I were to speak with him, we would know the truth of the matter."

"How did Du Paty respond?" asked Georges.

"He declined. His behavior was extraordinary. He said if I were to speak to Alfred it would be war."

"War?" asked Welles, baffled. "What did he mean by that?"

Mathieu shrugged. "I took him to mean that he and I would then be at odds. He is a strange man, taken to dramatic pronouncements of that sort."

The butler announced dinner. They moved downstairs to the dining room and arranged themselves. Wine was poured and the soup served all round. They ate in silence for a few minutes, then Mathieu took up the story again.

Having achieved nothing with Major Du Paty, he said, he had hired an attorney, a man named Demange. It was not until December — a full two months after the arrest — that Demange was permitted to meet with Alfred, or indeed to see any of the evidence against him.

"Demange said they had nothing," Mathieu said. "No evidence linking Alfred to treason. Only innuendo. They said Alfred was consumed by gambling debts. Alfred, who could not abide a casino. They said he kept several mistresses and needed money to keep them well, but no mistresses were named. They claimed that Lucie's mother told a friend that Alfred and Lucie were divorcing, which is a complete fabrication."

"Was there no substantial evidence at all?" Welles asked.

"There were affidavits from two hand-writing experts. They referred to a document. The *bordereau*, they called it. Both men swore that Alfred was the author."

"What was the nature of this *bordereau*?"

"I cannot say. It wasn't included in the case file. Du Paty told Demange that it was a military secret; that we were not permitted to see it. In any event, we were pleased by what we had learned. If this was all the evidence they had to present, then it was clear they had the wrong man. They would never convict Alfred on such nonsense. Demange said that if Alfred were not a Jew, they would surely not have arrested him. We came to the first day of the trial with every confidence that Alfred would be exonerated."

"You were at the trial?" Welles asked, surprised. "I understood it was conducted in secret."

"Not at the start. Lucie and I attended, along with others from the family. But on the first day, when Demange began to ask questions about this *bordereau*, the officer commanding the panel stopped the proceedings and cleared the courtroom. He said it was a question of national security. Only Alfred and Demange were permitted within the courtroom for the remainder of the trial."

Mathieu's knowledge of the trial was therefore second-hand, given to him later by Demange. The lawyer had dealt quickly with the allegations of gambling and affairs, demolishing them as entirely groundless. Then, under his skillful cross-examination, the hand-writing experts contradicted each other and even their own testimony. Major Du Paty was called and testified that Alfred was guilty, but according to Demange his testimony offered nothing beyond what had already been said. The court adjourned for the day. The following day the government surprised Demange by resting their case.

With no real evidence to contest, Demange called a series of witnesses to attest to Alfred's good character. He later said he was sure the jury — a panel of seven military officers — were both disdainful of the prosecution's presentation and impressed with the witnesses he called. He was confident that Alfred would be acquitted of the charges.

However, at this point something unusual occurred. Despite having rested their case, the prosecution now asked permission to call another witness, one who had not previously been identified. Demange objected, but the judge allowed the witness to be called, even though no explanation was given for why he had not been called before, or indeed why he was being called now. The witness, a Major Henry, representing the counter-intelligence bureau, took the stand. Henry testified that he had been alerted to the existence of a spy on the General Staff and had, through his investigation, determined that the spy was Captain Alfred Dreyfus. As he said this he stood and in dramatic fashion, pointed at Dreyfus and shouted his name. In cross examination, Demange pressed him for an explanation of how he had arrived at this conclusion, but Henry declined to elaborate, citing the need to maintain national security. It seemed to Demange that the members of the jury were unduly impressed with Henry's testimony. Still, he remained confident that Dreyfus would be acquitted.

In fact, Mathieu noted, there was so little evidence against Dreyfus that the entire trial lasted only three days. It ended on a Saturday afternoon, whereupon the jury withdrew to confer on a verdict. Two hours later, they reconvened and to Demange's consternation pronounced Dreyfus guilty of treason.

Mathieu's tale was interrupted by the arrival of footmen, who cleared the soup. The fish course was served, more wine poured, then Mathieu resumed.

"I was shocked," he said. "Demange as well. He could not understand what had occurred. He said it was a singular event, like nothing he had seen before in his career."

"What did you do then?" asked Georges.

"We appealed the verdict, of course. But the appeal was denied." He looked at Lucie, continued. "At this time there was much talk of the death penalty. This was foremost in our minds, that they might kill Alfred. I had no thought for anything else. Then something happened." He paused, looked again at Lucie.

"Because he had been convicted, there was to be a ceremony," she said. "A degradation. Do you understand?"

She looked at Welles, who shook his head.

"An officer convicted of such a crime must be publicly humiliated," she explained. "Reduced in rank. Expelled from the Army. Shamed. Early one morning Freddie was paraded into the Place Fontenoy. He was in full dress uniform, wearing his sword. The staff of the War College was assembled to bear witness and a large crowd had gathered around the square. We stood in the crowd. The people around us shouted, called him *traitor. Jew.*"

Lucie's voice caught. Her eyes were damp, and she fumbled for a handkerchief. Welles was mortified.

"I beg your pardon, Madame. I did not mean to dredge up such awful memories."

"*Mon dieu!*" she exclaimed, angry at her own tears. She wiped her eyes in the shocked silence, composed herself, continued.

"First an officer stood before Freddie," she said. "He removed Freddie's cap, threw it to the ground. One by one, he tore the buttons from Freddie's jacket. Then came the epaulets, the braid, even the stripes on his trousers; all torn away. Freddie bore this in silence, playing his role with dignity. On cue, he drew his sword and presented it to the man, who took it and broke it across his knee. Freddie told me later that he had filed the sword, so it would break easily. It was the same with the buttons, the epaulets, the stripes. He had cut most of the threads fixing them, so they could be easily stripped from the uniform. He said it was his duty."

Welles shook his head at this.

"But here is the remarkable thing," she said. "They made him march around the square in his tattered uniform. It was supposed to be his moment of shame, but he would not be shamed. Instead, he began to shout. *Vive la France! I am innocent of this crime! I swear that I am innocent!* Over and over he shouted these words. The people in the crowd, who had been jeering throughout, now fell silent. As Freddie marched around the square, proclaiming his innocence for all to hear, it seemed to me that many of the people were impressed with his dignity and bearing. And I noticed a change even in the attitude of the officers around him. They expected him to confess, you see. That is the way of a scoundrel;

once he is unmasked, he always shows himself to be a scoundrel. But not Freddie. Even when there was nothing to be gained, he proclaimed his innocence. Even as France condemned him, he professed his love for France. When we learned later that day that he would not be executed, would instead be sent to Guyana for the rest of his life, I knew that he had raised a doubt in the minds of his persecutors."

"You believed they were unwilling to execute him because they were no longer certain of the verdict?" asked Georges.

"Yes, I believe that."

"If they doubted the verdict, they would surely have reexamined the case," said Welles.

"Perhaps," said Mathieu. "But it is the nature of institutions that they cannot admit their mistakes. Instead, they sweep them under the carpet. It would be profoundly embarrassing for some men, important men, if the verdict were to be overturned. So instead, they sent Alfred away quickly. We were permitted to visit him only once more, a week after the degradation. He was calm, defiant, unbending in his claim of innocence. Four days later, he was gone."

"Have you never believed he was guilty?" Welles asked Mathieu. "Not even for a moment?"

"No, never. I know my brother. He is a patriot, he loves France. I thought from the beginning the charges must be a mistake. And when I saw him, spoke with him, I was certain. We are very close, and we have never been able to conceal anything from one another. It was not a question of convincing myself he was innocent. It was a matter of convincing those who do not know him as I do. As we do."

He reached out, took Lucie's hand.

"I have devoted my life to freeing Alfred," he said. "More than that. Our fortune — mine, and that of both our families — is committed to that cause."

"What can be done?" Georges asked.

"The only hope is to find grounds for an appeal," said Seigneur.

"I thought that an appeal had already been denied," said Welles.

"Quite so, and that is the difficulty," said Seigneur. "It is why I have asked you here, Monsieur Welles."

Welles did not know what to make of that. He looked at Seigneur, who in turn looked at Georges. Welles turned to her. She met his eyes, a half-smile on her lips.

"My father thinks that for an appeal to succeed, we must bring some pressure on the government."

"Pressure?"

"We must gather public support for an inquiry," said Seigneur. "Enough to force the government to act."

"What has that to do with me?" asked Welles.

"We are journalists, after all," said Georges. "We can write about the injustice."

For an instant Welles thought he would refuse. He understood now that this was why Georges had asked him to come; that she had intended from the start to draw him in to the affair. But all eyes had turned to him and he found he could not bring himself to decline.

"Yes, we should like to help," he said, addressing Mathieu. "With your permission, of course."

"I would be pleased to have your assistance," replied Mathieu. "If there is anything you require, I am at your service."

The footmen returned to clear their places and serve the roast. The interruption was timely. Seigneur, sensing the mood of his guests, took advantage of the opportunity to ask Welles a question about his syndication service. Mathieu expressed a desire to hear more about it. In this way the subject was changed, and they passed the remainder of the dinner in more general conversation.

When the Dreyfuses had gone, Welles joined Georges and her father in the library. He sat beside Georges on the sofa. Seigneur did not sit; he seemed restless, even agitated, and he wandered aimlessly about the room. Welles lit a cigarette for Georges, and another for himself. He dropped the match into an ash tray, and when he looked up, Seigneur was standing behind a chair, hands gripping the back, as if he were standing at a lectern.

"There must be more evidence," he said without preamble.

"What do you mean?" asked Georges.

"I do not doubt that anti-Jewish bigotry played a role in this case, but the decision of the court was unanimous. I cannot believe that all seven officers convicted a man on such weak evidence; that not one of them was free of this abominable prejudice. It can only be that they were shown evidence not presented in the court."

Welles considered this. "You may be right," he said. "Neither Alfred nor Demange ever saw the *bordereau*. If it was too secret for them to see it, there may be other things that were kept from them."

"It would be a travesty to convict a man on evidence he was not permitted to see. It makes a mockery of the very idea of justice. If we could establish that Dreyfus was convicted on evidence not shared with the defense, on that fact alone I believe an appeal might succeed."

"If there was secret evidence, what can it be?" asked Georges.

"We don't need to know what it is. It would be enough to show that it exists. That would form the basis of a new appeal."

It occurred to Welles that there might be a way to confirm the existence of secret evidence, but he did not voice that thought. Instead, he offered a note of caution.

"Suppose there is such evidence, and it shows Dreyfus is guilty? After all, it was enough to convince the jury."

Welles could see that neither of them were pleased by this line of thinking, but they had no reply. On that sober note, Welles took his leave. Georges accompanied him to the door. She took his arm as they descended the stair and made no move to release it until the butler had brought his things. At the door, she turned to face him.

"You didn't like my suggestion that we help," she said.

"I was surprised by it. That's all."

She stepped close, her face a few inches from his own.

"I'm a woman, Percy. I'm not a Jew, but I know what it is to be judged unfairly; to be held back, prevented from doing what I want to do because of who I am. What I am."

She spoke softly, but her eyes belied the calm of her voice. He saw that she would not be dissuaded.

"Yes, of course you're right, Georges. It's an interesting story. If nothing else, it ought to sell papers."

She held his eyes a moment longer, then leaned forward and kissed him on the cheek.

"Good night, Percy. Thank you for coming."

She turned towards the stairs. Welles lingered in the doorway a moment, unable to turn from the sight of her long, lean form as she ascended. Then the butler thrust his hat into his hands and closed the door behind him.

Welles looked at his watch. He had some distance to go, so walked quickly up the street in search of a cab.

***

The coach dropped him in front of the Cafe Americain on the Boulevard de Capucines. It was shortly before midnight and the after-theater crowd filled the cafe and overflowed onto the sidewalk, where tables had been set to accommodate them. Welles had to detour into the street to reach his destination: An elegant wood-and-etched-glass door surrounded by an elaborate brass scroll-work frame. The door was unmarked, but as he approached it opened to receive him and a doorman waved him into the *Cercle de la Presse* — the Press Club. Welles showed his membership card; the man offered a quiet greeting and took his hat. He crossed the lobby, noting that the dining room was still quite busy, then climbed the long, curved stairway to the second floor.

He paused in the doorway of the card room and immediately saw Esterhazy. The Count was seated at a table with four other players. A larger group of members stood watching the game. They were playing *chemin de fer* and Esterhazy held the bank, playing against the other four. He won the hand, looked up from the table and saw Welles. He gave no sign of recognition, but with his eyes indicated the door to the lounge. He began dealing the next hand of cards and Welles left the group.

The lounge was a large comfortable sitting room with a bar at the far end. There were upholstered chairs and couches arranged in intimate groups about the room and banquettes along one wall. These latter were u-shaped, with dividers that ran all the way up to the ceiling, so that they afforded some privacy for the occupants, especially given the dim glow of the gas lamps lighting the room. Welles chose the banquette farthest from the door. When seated, he could only be seen by someone standing at the bar. A waiter came to take his order, returned a moment later. He placed a bottle and two glasses on the table, then left Welles alone to wait.

The Press Club of Paris was a casino, the only one in the city. It prospered despite a legal and social regime which was inimical to gambling, in large part because the owners had hit upon the idea of disguising it as a club for members of the press. Though anyone could join, journalists could do so at a significant discount. By this stroke of genius, the owners muzzled the criticism which the Paris papers would surely have leveled at any similar establishment. The membership boasted professionals from every reputable occupation, and not a few dukes and princes.

Esterhazy appeared about twenty minutes later and slipped into the banquette opposite Welles. From his pocket he withdrew a small stack of thousand-franc plaques, placing them before him on the table. His eyes sparkled in a face flushed with excitement.

"My dear Percy! How are you this enchanting evening?"

Welles smiled. "I'm well, Count, though not as well as you. I gather you've had a good streak. I hope I didn't interrupt it."

Welles had found Esterhazy to be a great believer in luck, both good and bad, and knew that it would not be beneath the man to blame Welles for any change in fortune. Happily, it seemed that tonight Esterhazy was winning and in correspondingly high spirits, and the Count dismissed the interruption with a friendly wave of his hand.

Taking advantage of their momentary privacy, Welles took an envelope from his jacket and passed it across the table. Esterhazy exchanged it with another which he, in turn, passed to Welles. The envelopes disappeared into their respective pockets. Welles poured brandy. Esterhazy raised his glass, drank it in one gulp. He put his empty glass on the table.

"If you'll pardon me, Percy, I'll get back to the game."

He gathered himself to leave, but Welles stopped him with a hand on his arm.

"A moment, please," he said.

Esterhazy sat back, eying Welles with curiosity. Somewhere between the Seigneur house and the Press Club, Welles had come to a decision.

"Our masters have asked for something. The Dreyfus dossier."

"The Dreyfus dossier?" Esterhazy was surprised. "Why should they want that?"

"They didn't say. If I had to guess, they want to know how he was caught. I can see how that might interest them." Welles shrugged. "Who knows why they want what they want? Can you get it?"

"I don't know."

Esterhazy leaned forward, across the table between them, bringing his face close to Welles's.

"I'm not even sure who has it," he said. "It should have been Colonel Sandherr. But the poor chap died last week. I can hardly ask him for it."

"I understand it was a Major Du Paty de Clam who led the investigation, collected the evidence."

Esterhazy blinked. "Du Paty? He runs the operations bureau."

"Perhaps you could approach him?"

Welles knew as he said it that this was an absurd suggestion. How could one officer ask another about the contents of a secret file? What possible reason could he offer, without raising suspicion? He could see that Esterhazy had little enthusiasm for the idea. The Count held his eyes for a long moment. Then, to his surprise, Esterhazy nodded.

"Very well, Percy. If London wants it, then of course we must try. Let me give it some thought."

He stood, collected his stack of plaques, returned them to his pocket and left without another word.

Chapter 6

London, 12 August 1898

"Good God!" Lawrence interrupted. "Esterhazy would be mad to expose himself by asking questions about a secret dossier. It was daft of Sir Reginald to even suggest such a thing."

"Sir Reginald made no request," said Welles. "The idea was mine."

"Why ever for?" asked Salisbury. "The Government could have no conceivable interest in the Dreyfus dossier. Your suggestion to the contrary was pure nonsense."

"Indeed, but it was the best I could come up with in the moment. I wanted the dossier for myself."

"For yourself?"

"For Georges, rather."

"You hoped to help Georges prove that Dreyfus was innocent?" Lawrence asked.

Welles shook his head.

"I had no great hope of that," he said. "I thought it more likely that the dossier would contain proof of his guilt. I was moved by my meeting with Dreyfus's wife and brother, but they gave me no real reason to believe he was innocent."

"If the case was as they described it, there was even less reason to believe him guilty," objected Bingham.

"Perhaps," said Welles. "But I assumed there would be more in the dossier. If it contained evidence of his guilt, I could put the matter to rest."

"And if there was no more evidence?"

"In that case, his conviction was unfounded. That would be a sensational story. But in either case, there was nothing to lose by asking Esterhazy to get the dossier."

"Nothing to lose, save perhaps an asset belonging to Her Majesty's Government," objected Lawrence. "One you were bound to safeguard against exposure."

Welles shifted in his seat.

"I didn't think there was much risk," he said. "I had come to know the Count well enough to understand that he would undertake nothing he believed would put him in jeopardy. If he could not get me what I wanted without exposing himself, I felt sure he would not try."

"Even if the risk were small," asked Salisbury, "why should you ask him to take it? What could you possibly stand to gain that would justify it?"

Welles had no reply to this. The question hung in the air between them. In the end, it was Lawrence who supplied the answer.

"You were in love with the girl," he guessed.

Salisbury looked at Lawrence, then Welles. Realization dawned in his face, then was quickly replaced by a look of exasperation. He leaned back in his chair, rolled his eyes.

"You were in love with her," Lawrence repeated.

"Yes," said Welles. "I wanted to help her."

"Help her? If Dreyfus was guilty, as you believed, how could you help her? Or do you mean you wanted to impress her?"

Welles said nothing.

"You were willing to risk Esterhazy to impress her. To help her, as you put it."

"You think me a fool," Welles sighed. "You're right, I was a fool. Am a fool."

With some difficulty, he used his free hand to take a case from inside his jacket, place it on the table, open it, and remove a cigarette. He put the cigarette in his mouth, then took a box of matches from his pocket, drawing one match from the box. He looked from one man to the next.

"Have a care, gentlemen."

He put the gun down, struck a match and lit the cigarette. He shook the match out, dropped it, and recovered the gun.

"Where was I?"

"You were being a fool," offered Bingham.

"So I was, Mister Bingham," Welles nodded agreeably. "If anything, I'll wager none of you have any idea how great a fool I was. No matter; I will explain my folly in good time, and then you will know it as well as I do."

"I know it already," said Salisbury. "It is quite late, Mister Welles, and my patience is not infinite. I have little interest in your profession, and even less in your— " He paused, searching for the right phrase. "Your domestic arrangements."

"I would not trouble you with them, sir, were it not that those arrangements, as you call them, are what put me on a long and treacherous path which has led me to you."

Salisbury batted this away with a wave of his hand.

"Spare me your riddles, sir. Can you not make your meaning plain?"

Welles regarded him coolly. Either the Prime Minister was genuinely puzzled, or he was an excellent actor. Welles suspected the latter, but it hardly mattered. His course had been set before he had even entered the room and he was resolved to see it through as he had planned.

"I mean to, Prime Minister," he replied, "but you must let me tell my story in my own way."

Salisbury's face hardened. "Must I? Must I indeed? I tell you, sir, that I have no more patience for these theatrics. I don't believe you will fire that pistol. If you were to do so, it would only bring help on the run, to your ruin. And if I call for help instead, what can you do to stop me? Better yet; how can you stop me from taking my leave?"

Salisbury gripped the arms of his chair and made to rise. As he did, Welles raised the pistol, cocked the hammer with his thumb, and aimed at the Prime Minister's head.

"I beg you to believe that I will shoot you, sir. I have killed one man already, and I am wanted for the death of another. What can it matter if I kill three more? If you do not take me for a desperate man, then you are mistaken, and it will be the last mistake of your life."

Welles's heart was pounding, his breath short, and he found it difficult to speak. His hand was unsteady, and the gun visibly shook as he struggled to hold it on target. Perhaps it was this unsteadiness of hand that decided Lawrence. The latter reached out a hand and gripped the Prime Minister by the arm.

"Careful, sir," he said. "You may be right that this fellow won't shoot us. On the other hand, he might; and if we must choose between being shot and listening to his tale, I choose the tale."

"Hear, hear," seconded Bingham.

For a moment Welles thought that Salisbury would ignore his companions: and perhaps the Prime Minister thought so as well, but then reason won out. Salisbury settled back into his chair. He looked at Lawrence's hand on his arm. Without comment, Lawrence withdrew the hand. Welles lowered the gun to the table. He took a deep breath, trying to calm himself.

"I thank you both for your prudence," he said, nodding to Lawrence and Bingham. "May I go on?"

"One moment," said Bingham. "This Dreyfus fellow. I've heard the name, but I confess I don't really follow continental politics."

"Dreyfus is a French officer and a traitor," said Lawrence. "He was unmasked some years ago, as I recall, and now languishes on Devil's Island. He has recently become something of a *cause celebre* among the socialists in Paris, who say he is innocent, that he was wrongly accused and convicted. That he was framed for this crime by the Army."

"Why should the Army frame an officer for treason?"

"Because he is a Jew," Welles said. "Jews are not widely loved in Paris. And he is an Alsatian as well, so for many Frenchmen he is almost a German. He was tried in secret. The evidence against him has never been made public. You gentlemen know how the papers can be when they lack facts to print. Any decent man would have been sickened by the naked appeals to prejudice which passed for reasoned opinion at the time. No trial could have been fair in that climate."

"But earlier, you said you thought Dreyfus was guilty," said Bingham.

"I did think that," Welles replied. "It was a question of which explanation was the simpler one. Should we believe that the French discovered evidence of a traitor, found the traitor, and locked him up? Or should we believe that the French found evidence of a traitor and, rather than finding the traitor, framed another man for it, leaving the traitor free to continue his treason against France? Why would they do that?"

"Who can say why the French do what they do?" said Lawrence. "But, tell me, Mister Welles: Is Dreyfus the reason you are here? What can the matter have to do with the Prime Minister?"

Welles smiled, shaking his head.

"That would be telling the tale out of order, Mister Lawrence. Patience, please. May I continue?"

Chapter 7

Paris, August 1896

A few days after their dinner with the Dreyfuses, Georges presented him with an article she had written. She had cast in in the form of an interview with Mathieu and Lucie Dreyfus. It was a good piece, he conceded, and he allowed himself to be convinced to have it published in *Le Temps*. At Georges' urging, he sent it around to the London papers, and the *Daily Chronicle* ran it as well. Several Paris papers published follow-up stories, but all of them made clear their certainty that Dreyfus was guilty. There was no response from the government. Welles, who had never wanted to be associated with the affair, was relieved when the story quietly died.

He had not reckoned with her determination, however. When her opening shot disappeared below the water without leaving so much as a ripple, the effect on her was profound. She withdrew into a kind of brooding melancholy. She said little, and when the needs of their work required her to speak, she was brusque and impatient; so that he, in turn, was reluctant to draw her ire. He realized not only that she had expected the story to spark a revival of the debate about the affair, but that she had become committed to the belief that Dreyfus was innocent, a victim of ugly prejudice and injustice. At first, he tried to ignore her mood, certain that it would pass. Every day brought new submissions to review, new pieces to edit and place. He felt sure that the routine would soon bring her out of it. He was wrong. As the days passed, she grew more distant.

One afternoon, when it seemed to him that they'd passed the entire day in silence, he could stand it no more. He suggested that they follow up on some of the loose threads Mathieu had noted. Georges was amenable, and they agreed on a course of action. He would see Major Du Paty, the officer who had led the case against Dreyfus. For her part, Georges would seek an interview with the military attaché at the German embassy, a Colonel von Schwartzkoppen. It was generally believed, though never confirmed, that he had been the recipient of the secrets Dreyfus peddled. There was no good reason for the colonel to grant an interview on the matter; but he had a reputation as a man who preferred the company of beautiful women and Georges was keen to try.

Welles first tried to meet Du Paty at his office at Army headquarters but was told the major was not available. He left a card, with no real expectation of a reply, so was surprised when later that afternoon the postal messenger brought him a *petit-bleu* from Du Paty, inviting him to call at his home the following morning. This he did, mounting the steps of the house just before ten and knocking on the door. A servant let him in, led him through a grand entry hall to the library and left him there to wait. Welles passed the time idly reading the spines of the books, occasionally taking one from the shelf to examine it more closely. He was looking at one when Du Paty entered the room. The major was not in uniform, but no one who saw him would mistake his occupation. He was, Welles thought, something over forty years old, with a stiff, upright posture and an aristocratic bearing. He'd lost a good deal of his hair and sported a clipped mustache, though his cheeks and chin were clean-shaven. He had piercing eyes beneath a strong brow, eyes which first focused on the book in Welles's hands, then fixed him with a withering look. Welles mouthed a chastened *pardon* and returned the book to its place.

"Major Du Paty? I'm Percival Welles. Thank you for seeing me."

He offered his hand and, after a slight hesitation, Du Paty took it. The major's grip was not strong, and the handshake was brief, as if Du Paty were wary of the physical contact.

"A pleasure, Monsieur Welles." Like Welles, Du Paty spoke in French. "Will you take coffee?"

Welles accepted, and the major pulled a bell-rope near the door, then directed Welles to a group of chairs around a low table. Welles took one and Du Paty sat across from him. A servant entered, placed a tray on the table between them, poured coffee and left without a word.

"Cream? Sugar?" Du Paty offered.

Welles declined. The major took both, then lifted the saucer bearing his cup with one hand and stirred the coffee with the other. His posture when seated was no more relaxed than standing; he sat straight and upright, legs close together before him, knees bent at ninety degrees, feet flat on the floor. He rested the saucer on his left knee, holding it steady with his left hand, and raised the cup to his lips with the right. He smacked his lips with appreciation, returned the cup to his knee, and addressed Welles.

"You are a journalist, Monsieur?"

"I am," Welles replied.

"For what publication? Your card, it says *Service des Informations*. What is that?"

"I'm independent. Free-lance, we would say in English. My business is to syndicate news; to take one story, something of broad interest, and place it with several newspapers in different cities. Different countries. For now, we're concentrating on Paris and London papers, but we intend to grow."

"You write these stories yourself?"

"Some we write. Some we buy, from other journalists."

The major sipped coffee while considering this, then nodded.

"A sensible idea. I applaud you. But, tell me: Why are you here? How may I be of service to you?"

Welles had considered several deceptive approaches and rejected them all. He would play it straight.

"I'm interested in the Dreyfus case," he said. "You may have seen one of our reports recently, in *Le Temps*. An interview with his wife and brother. As they tell the story, it is a miscarriage of justice. But that is one view, a view which is, perhaps, not entirely objective. I hoped you could tell me the other side of the story."

"There is only one side to the truth, Monsieur. Dreyfus is guilty. I have said so. The officers of the court, they have said so. What more need be said?"

Welles leaned back, crossed one leg over the other.

"May I smoke?"

Du Paty inclined his head. Welles took his cigarette case from his jacket, offered it to Du Paty, who declined. He took one for himself, lit it, placed the case on the table before him.

"I understand you had charge of the investigation," Welles said. "Can you tell me how you came to be involved?"

"To begin, Monsieur Welles, you must tell me why I should answer your questions."

Welles shrugged.

"I'm only after the truth. Some people claim Dreyfus is a scapegoat. I've told that story. Now I want to tell your story. If, as you say, Dreyfus is guilty and the evidence is clear, I will report that. Perhaps in this way we can be of help to each other?"

Du Paty gave him a long, appraising look, then seemed to come to a decision.

"I will tell you what I can," he said. "You understand I must be discrete? You may not use my name. And there are some things I cannot tell you even then."

Welles indicated his agreement to these conditions.

Major Du Paty drank the last of his coffee, placing the saucer and cup on the table.

"We were in possession of a document which had been passed to someone in the German embassy," he began. "It contained secret information, military information, the nature of which could only be known to an officer on the General Staff. I was assigned to lead the investigation."

"Why you, if I may ask? Why not someone from the intelligence service? You are in operations, are you not?"

Du Paty sniffed. "The document was uncovered by the counter-intelligence section. They are an independent group reporting directly to the Chief of Staff, General de Boisdeffre. The general himself asked me to take it on. "

"But why should he do that?"

"The incriminating document, the *bordereau*, it was hand-written. As it happens, I am an expert in handwriting. It is a hobby of mine. When the matter was brought to the attention of the Chief, he naturally supposed I would be well-suited to identify the traitor. And as the head of the operations bureau, I could act with broad authority to conduct the investigation. He gave the matter over to me to pursue, with the aid of the counter-intelligence section."

"What is this *bordereau*?" asked Welles. "How was it discovered?"

"It is a list of military documents of a sensitive nature. It seems clear that it was provided along with those documents, as a sort of digest, though we never recovered any of the others. As to how we discovered it, I am unable to tell you that. For reasons of security."

"I understand. But tell me, how did you proceed?"

"The document was unsigned, but the nature of the information being provided was a kind of signature. These were secret documents, technical in nature, and each would have been available only to an officer in the appropriate bureau or section. But each from a different one, you see? We knew we were looking for an officer of the General Staff who had, at different times, been assigned to each of those *bureaux*. We searched the personnel files for officers with the right background. This led us to Captain Dreyfus. His career on the General Staff was a perfect match for the author of the *bordereau*."

"I see," said Welles. "What did you do then?"

"Dreyfus is not really French, you understand. His people are German, from Alsace. Jews. Naturally we were suspicious. I compared samples of his handwriting, from reports in his file, to the *bordereau*. To my eyes, they were written by the same man. But we had to be sure, Monsieur. Somewhere there was a spy, betraying France. He must be found, identified beyond any doubt. That was my view. To that end, I contrived a test."

"A test?" Welles lit another cigarette.

"I summoned Captain Dreyfus to a meeting on some trivial matter. I pretended to have injured my hand, so that I was unable to write. I asked him to write something for me. Naturally, he agreed. Can you guess what I had him write?"

Welles shook his head. Du Paty leaned forward slightly, as if confiding a secret.

"I dictated to him the contents of the *bordereau*."

From the look of amusement on Du Paty's face, Welles understood the man believed he had executed a stroke of brilliance.

"Very clever," Welles agreed. "What did he do?"

"I could see right away that he was the guilty man. His hands shook as he wrote, a clear indication that he recognized the words. And when he had finished, I compared his writing to that of the *bordereau*. The hand was the same. Dreyfus was the traitor."

"I see." Welles inhaled a long breath of smoke, held it a moment, then expelled it. "What did you do then?"

"We arrested him immediately. It was necessary to prevent him from betraying us further. We hoped he would confess, but he declared his innocence. So, we set out to build the case against him. Now that we knew he was our man, it was simplicity itself to find the evidence of his crimes. His debts, a consequence of his gambling and affairs with several women. He had need of money, more it seems than he had at his disposal. The pro-German statements he'd made as a young man. Secret trips he made to Germany. And other corroborating evidence. He denied it all, but in the end the Court was convinced."

At this Du Paty, who had been leaning forward and speaking with animation, pulled back and resumed his erect posture. Welles smoked, allowing the moment to stretch, then spoke.

"I understood that the hand-writing experts at the trial disagreed on whether the *bordereau* matched Dreyfus's hand. And they found no evidence of trembling in the copy he wrote from your dictation."

Du Paty waved a hand at this.

"This is the nature of *experts*," he said, dismissively. "One can always hire one man to dispute what another has said. But my judgment is not for sale, Monsieur. I have seen the handwriting, and I tell you it is the same. I saw Captain Dreyfus as he copied down my words, and I say he shook with fear. He is the traitor."

"But it is true, isn't it, that the other things — his debts, the trips to Germany and so on — they were disputed at the trial?"

The major's eyebrows shot up.

"Disputed? Certainly, they were disputed. What do you expect from the accused, that he acquiesces to the facts aligned against him? We are not so easily fooled, Monsieur."

"Of course not. You said there was other corroborating evidence?"

"Indeed. When we arrested Dreyfus, he was conveyed to prison in a carriage, escorted by Major Henry of the statistical section. There, in the carriage, he offered Henry money for his freedom."

"Did he?"

"Yes. And his brother, Mathieu, he made the same offer, to Henry's superior. The family is quite wealthy — they are Jews, are they not? — but there is not enough money in the whole world to buy France's honor."

Welles blew out smoke, leaned forward to stub out his cigarette.

"You say you searched the personnel records to find officers with access to the documents listed in the *bordereau*," he said. "Was Dreyfus the only possibility you found?"

"There were six officers with a similar background."

"How many of them were Jews?" Welles asked. "Besides Dreyfus, I mean?"

"None of the other men were Jews. There are not so many Jews on the General Staff."

Welles detected no note of irony in the major's voice, saw no change in his expression.

"You understand how that might seem to some people? Here are six suspects, only one of them is a Jew, let's accuse the Jew?"

Now Du Paty smiled.

"You have it the wrong way around, Monsieur Welles. It would be unjust to blame someone, even a Jew, for a crime he didn't commit. But tell me: If you are looking for a traitor to France and you have several suspects, then where do you begin if not that man among your suspects who is the least French? We tested Dreyfus first, of course, this is only logical. If he had passed the test, we would have tested the others."

Welles did not reply. The two men regarded each other as the silence stretched. When it began to be uncomfortable, Du Paty looked away.

"I have very good relations with intelligent, artistic, and scholarly Jews," he said, "but there are some situations in which persons who are not incontrovertibly French ought not to be placed. Now," —he took his watch from his pocket and examined it— "I fear I have no more time, Monsieur Welles. I will show you out."

In the entry hall, as they waited for the housekeeper to bring Welles's hat, Major Du Paty called his attention to the half dozen paintings adorning the hall: dark and heavy portraits of men, encased in elaborately carved, gilded frames. Du Paty regarded them for a moment in silence — reverently, it seemed to Welles — then turned to him.

"These are the faces of my ancestors, Monsieur. Before them I declare that I have weighed all the evidence, that I have searched for the truth. Dreyfus is guilty."

Du Paty said this as if he thought it ought to settle the matter. For his part, Welles judged that the remark needed no reply, so he simply thanked Du Paty for his time and took his leave.

He went from there directly to the office, where he found that Georges had not yet returned from her own visit to the German embassy. While he waited for her, he replayed the conversation in his mind. What had he learned from the man? Du Paty was certain that he'd found the right man, but the evidence he'd recounted was unimpressive and he had revealed nothing Welles had not already heard from Mathieu's account of the trial. Except for the bribery attempts; if what Du Paty said was true, it was certainly damning. On the other hand, Welles thought, such a claim — without any other witnesses — was easy to make whether it had happened or not.

Georges arrived shortly after one o'clock. She sat across the desk from him and listened without comment while he recounted his meeting with Du Paty. When he had finished, she seized immediately on one point.

"There were six suspects, but they settled on Dreyfus from the start. These other men, they were never investigated."

"Indeed," said Welles. "The same thought occurred to me."

"The real spy must be one of those five. We must find out who they are, Percy! If we knew that, it would be a simple thing to track him down."

He made a face. "I don't see how we can, Georges. Major Du Paty won't tell us. It could be in the sealed file, part of the investigation record, but it may not even be there. Perhaps the Dreyfus dossier contains only the evidence they accumulated once they'd settled on him. And we don't have the dossier in any event."

"Major Henry," she said. "From the counter-intelligence section. He was part of the investigation from the beginning. He would know."

Welles shrugged. "Perhaps. But why would he tell us? By all accounts, he was the strongest witness at the trial, the man most responsible for convicting Dreyfus. He would have nothing to gain by casting doubt on the case."

"Still, we must try, Percy."

She leaned forward, extended her hands across the desk. Her eyes met his. He could see that she was committed to this cause, and more; that she wanted to know that he was committed as well. He hesitated. He knew that if he were to take her hands now, to agree to try, he would have to see it through, no matter where it led. He felt sure London would not approve. Still, he reached across the desk, took her hands in his. She gripped them tightly.

"Yes, we must try," he said.

"Do you believe he is innocent, Percy?"

Her eyes were on his, and he felt that she was examining him for any sign that he was not committed to the cause. He chose his words carefully.

"I think he may be," he said. "I had doubts about the verdict after hearing Mathieu and Lucie tell their story. What I learned from Du Paty today did nothing to allay them. If anything, it made them stronger. The man is an egotist, and he makes no secret of his feelings for Jews. Ask him for evidence, he replies that you must believe him because he is a Marquis."

She rewarded him with a warm smile. She squeezed his hands once more, released them, sat back in her chair. He offered her a cigarette, took one for himself, lit both.

"How did it go at the embassy? Were you able to see von Schwartzkoppen?"

"Yes, with some difficulty," she said, rolling her eyes. "He is well guarded, by a woman. I think perhaps she trained soldiers before she came to Paris. A Prussian sergeant concealed in an ill-fitting dress. *Does Fraulein Seigneur have an appointment?* No, she does not. *The colonel is very busy today, perhaps the Fraulein could make an appointment for another day?* No, she wishes to see the colonel today, and she is quite happy to wait. The sergeant does not expect this, the defenses are strong. She draws back, gathers strength, probes another part of the line. *Could the Fraulein explain the nature of her business with the colonel?* Yes, she would be delighted to tell the colonel all about it. Alas, the enemy is well entrenched. The sergeant withdraws. We sit, on opposite sides of the room, each pretending not to notice the other."

Welles smiled. He could well imagine the woman's consternation, faced with Georges' determination.

"What happened then?"

"I sat for about an hour, across from the closed door of his office. Then, at last, the door opened. The colonel emerged, gave me a long look, spoke to the woman, looked at me again, went back into his office, closed the door. Five minutes later, the door opened. The colonel appeared, looked at me again, asked the woman to come into his office. Another five minutes, the door opened, the woman came out. She marched stiffly across the room, stood in front of me. *The colonel will see you now, Fraulein.*"

Welles laughed at this. A striking young woman, dressed in Georges' unusual style, who refuses to say why she's come? Certainly, the colonel would see her.

"What did you tell him?"

Georges shrugged. "The truth. I am a journalist, interested in Dreyfus case. All Paris knows that he, Colonel von Schwartzkoppen, is the man to whom someone gave our secrets. Can he confirm that the spy was Captain Dreyfus? Will he discuss the case with me?"

Georges leaned across the desk to stub out her cigarette in the ash tray.

"He denied it, of course," she went on. "He is a military officer and a diplomat, not a spy. He has never met Captain Dreyfus, has never received any secrets from him. He has nothing at all to say about the man. I was in his office for more than an hour, and he never wavered from that line."

"That long? What did you talk about?"

"He talked about Paris, what he liked about. The art, music, people. The night life. How much he preferred it to Berlin. The rumors of his involvement with Dreyfus have put him in some difficulty, he said. He has only just avoided being recalled."

As she spoke, Georges rose from her chair, walked slowly across the room to the window. Welles turned in his seat to watch her as she continued.

"He asked me about myself. Who I was, how I came to be a journalist. How I could dare to dress as I do. It was, he said, quite shocking, though he admitted he liked it."

She lapsed into silence, standing at the window, her back to Welles. He waited for her to continue, but she didn't; instead, she seemed to be watching something in the street below.

"So, he told you nothing," Welles prompted.

"Nothing about Dreyfus," she replied. After a pause: "He asked me to have dinner with him."

"Dinner?" Welles was dumbfounded, could think of nothing else to say.

"Yes. Tomorrow night." Georges turned from the window, looked across the room at him. "He was very charming. I accepted."

Chapter 8

Paris, August 1896

Welles stood in the shadow of a doorway in the wall across the street from the Seigneur house. It was late, nearly eleven o'clock, and he had been standing there for more than an hour, racked by indecision. He wanted to stay, to see Georges emerge, follow her to her assignation; and he wanted to go, to flee before she could see him standing there. Jealousy and shame fought to control him. Just as it seemed shame had won out, a carriage pulled up to the front of the house, the light of the carriage lanterns briefly illuminating him as it passed by.

Alarmed, he drew back into doorway, pressing his body against the wall. She emerged from the house dressed as he had never seen her before, in a jet-black gown adorned in gold embroidery in the form of branches of leaves and flowers trailing down her long body. The dress was worn off the shoulders, exposing her long neck and, he thought, far too much of the pale skin above and between her breasts. It was tight to her body through the waist and hips, where it flared slightly, running to the floor and then some, for as she descended the steps from the door of the house, he saw that she trailed a good deal of it on the ground behind her. The butler took her hand — she wore no gloves, and her arms were bare — and helped her into the carriage, and then she was gone.

He wanted to follow her, had planned to follow her, but it was already late, and he had another engagement. He hid in the doorway until the carriage was out of sight and the butler had gone back into the house. Then he emerged, turned right and headed for the Pont Philippe to cross the river to the right bank. Ten minutes walking brought him to the Place du Chatelet, where he passed the theater and entered the Brasserie Zimmer, climbing the stairs to the bar on the second floor.

Le Zimmer was a new establishment, one that pretended to cater to artists and writers, though to Welles's eyes it was frequented by the same upper-class ladies and gentlemen one found in the many stylish new brasseries and music clubs popping up around the city. A set of double doors connected the upstairs bar to the adjacent theater, so the bar was crowded with theatergoers refreshing themselves between the second and third acts. Welles spotted Esterhazy in evening clothes near one end of the bar. He managed to catch the Count's eye but did not approach him. Instead, he pushed through the crowd and found a seat on a sofa near the back of the room.

A young woman approached, dressed in what he took to be the pajamas of some Arab or Persian princess, and offered him a glass of champagne from the tray she carried. He accepted, took a cigarette from his case, lit it, placed the case on the small table before him. He had finished the cigarette when an usher appeared in the doorway of the theater carrying a bell. The man struck the bell with a small silver hammer, calling the theater attendees back for the second act. The bar emptied quickly and, as the last of the theatergoers passed through the door, Esterhazy approached, holding an unlit cigarette of his own.

"I beg your pardon, Monsieur," he said. "Do you have a match?"

Welles stood, took a match from the case, struck it and lit the cigarette. Esterhazy nodded his thanks. The princess arrived with more champagne. They each took a glass and Esterhazy sat, quite naturally, in the chair opposite Welles, with his back to the nearly empty room.

"My dear Percy, how are you?"

"I am well, Count. And you?"

"Quite well, thank you."

Esterhazy turned in his chair to look around the room, then produced an envelope from his jacket and placed it on the table. Welles picked it up and gave him one in return. When both envelopes had been put away, out of view, Welles drank the last of his champagne. He started to rise from the sofa, but Esterhazy stopped him with a gesture.

"There is something of interest for you there," he said. "Do you recall asking me about this Dreyfus matter? Some weeks ago, I think."

Esterhazy turned to check the room again, then leaned forward.

"As I told you then, the Dreyfus dossier is sealed," he said. "The only copy is in the files of the counter-intelligence section."

"Ah. Out of reach, then."

"Perhaps." Esterhazy smiled, a mischievous smile. "You know that Colonel Sandherr, the commander of the section, died last month?" Welles nodded. "They've appointed a new commander, a Colonel Picquart, but he has not yet taken over. Major Henry has been minding the shop. I know Henry well, we were at *l'École* together."

The Count was enjoying himself, Welles could see, so he adopted an expression of rapt attention.

"I thought I might be able to get something about Dreyfus from Henry, so I went to see him late one evening at his office. Henry is a good officer but not a stickler for the rules. I found things were rather lax. This is a secret section, you understand. Perhaps the most secure office in headquarters. But I found the door was unlocked and the reception desk unmanned, so of course I went in. It was the same inside. No one was at home and the door to the file room was unlocked."

Esterhazy paused, sat back, sipped champagne.

"You didn't," Welles said.

"Oh, I did, Percy, I did. I went in. It took only a few minutes to find the Dreyfus dossier. I couldn't take the file, mind you, and I didn't have time to copy it. I did what I could; I wrote up a catalog of what was in the file."

Welles was speechless. Esterhazy had run a tremendous risk; one he should never have taken. One Welles should never have asked him to take. Still, it seemed he'd gotten away with it. He took a deep breath.

"What do they have on Dreyfus?" he asked.

"There was the *bordereau*, of course. And some of the things which were made public at the time of the trial. Letters from his lovers; and from his creditors."

"Is that all? Hardly worth the risk, then."

Esterhazy shook his head.

"No, Percy, that's not all. There were other letters. One to the German military attaché, von Schwartzkoppen, from the Italian military attaché which mentions '*the scoundrel Dreyfus*' and some material Dreyfus supplied to the Italians about harbor dispositions in Nice. Another letter from the same man, thanking Schwartzkoppen for passing on material supplied by '*our friend Dreyfus*'. It seems Dreyfus was working for both the Germans and the Italians. And we intercepted a telegram between the Italian Embassy and their Foreign Ministry in Rome, apparently a warning: '*Dreyfus has been arrested. Precautions taken, our emissary warned.*'"

Welles felt he'd been struck a sharp blow. *Dreyfus is guilty*, he thought. His meeting with Du Paty had left him doubting the fact; the man's prejudice was plain to see, and he'd offered nothing of substance to support the charge. But this? This was concrete evidence that Dreyfus had spied for the Germans; and, apparently for the Italians as well.

"Why was none of this mentioned at the trial?" he asked.

"Sources and methods, my dear Percy. They must be protected. These are private letters between agents of foreign governments here in Paris. I can't imagine how we intercepted them, but if they were to be made public then the Germans would know we have a source with access to them. We might very well lose that source."

"Yes, of course," Welles said. "It seems a strong case after all."

"More than enough for a conviction. And even more now. There are letters to Dreyfus in prison."

"Letters?"

Esterhazy took another cigarette from his case, offered one to Welles. Welles struck a match, lit both. The Count nodded his thanks, continued.

"He gets mail, more than you might think. Some from his family, but also from supporters. He seems to have a lot of supporters. Socialists. Jews. Even some admiring women. We review everything, of course, as we do the letters he sends from prison. Some time ago — I think it was a month or so after he arrived at Devil's Island, so that would have been early last summer — there was a letter from Berne. A German fellow, a Herr *Wiess* or *Weil*, the signature was quite hard to make out. The letter seemed innocent enough, family gossip for the most part, but there was something odd about the feel of the paper. It was stiff, as if it had somehow gotten wet and then dried again. We had the chemists examine it and they found a hidden message."

"Hidden? How?"

Esterhazy laughed. "Invisible ink. Can you believe it?"

"You're joking."

The Count shook his head. "It is true, I assure you. The message was from a confederate. He wanted to know the location of some documents Dreyfus had hidden before his arrest."

It took a moment for this to sink in.

"Then he was expecting Dreyfus to reply? From a cell on Devil's Island?"

"Yes, that is what surprised us. There have been several more messages, all from this same *Weiss*. The content of the letters makes it clear that there is a conversation happening between the two of them. But, you see, we have never detected any reply from poor Captain Dreyfus. None of his letters use invisible ink or any other secret method we can detect. Somehow, we don't know how, he is able to communicate with his allies. We've searched his cell, of course, but found nothing."

Welles tried to collect his thoughts.

"Dreyfus is guilty, then," he said.

Esterhazy tilted his head to one side.

"Did you think he was innocent, Percy?"

"I wasn't sure. From what I heard about the trial, the case seemed weak. Then I spoke to Major Du Paty."

"You've spoken to Du Paty?" Esterhazy's face registered surprise.

"Yes," Welles said. "I met him as a journalist. He agreed to talk with me about Dreyfus. He left me with the very strong impression that Dreyfus was singled out because he was a Jew."

Esterhazy considered this, then nodded.

"I don't doubt that, Percy. Jews are not much loved in the Army, especially among the officers of the General Staff. You understand, we're a priggish bunch; for us what matters above all is family, class, faith. A German Jew like Dreyfus, the son of a shopkeeper? He would simply not do, never mind that he was by all accounts an excellent officer."

Esterhazy said this without any hint of malice, as if he were only explaining the foibles of his fellow officers.

"But, my friend, the one thing does not preclude the other" — here he put a hand on Welles's shoulder — "It's possible that both things are true: That Dreyfus was singled out because he was a Jew, and that he was, in fact, the guilty man."

He was right. Welles nodded.

"Who knows, maybe we drove Dreyfus to it," said the Count. "It can't have been an easy life, to be the only Jew on the General Staff."

Welles nodded again, trying now to hide his disappointment, but Esterhazy detected his mood.

"Did I do right, Percy?" he asked. "Isn't this what London wanted?"

"You did marvelously well. But listen, you must be more careful. I'm sure London will be happy with this, but I'm not sure they would approve of the risk you've taken. I won't tell them how you got it. We should keep that between us."

"As you say, Percy." The Count finished his champagne, made to rise, then stopped himself. "Oh, there's one other thing. Do you recall that Marchand business?"

"Marchand?"

"Yes, Marchand. I'm sure I must have mentioned it before."

Esterhazy paused, expecting a reply.

"Sorry, I don't recall it," Welles said. "Can you refresh my memory?"

"A ship left Marseilles in April, bound for parts unknown. The *Thibet*? Part of some larger operation, but that operation is a secret. No one will say where they're going, or what they're doing. The whole thing is being run out of the Colonial Office. The officer in command is an up and coming Colonial Infantry man, a Captain Marchand."

"Something that came up in a meeting? Yes, I remember now. What about it?"

"The *Thibet* made port in Dakar. She took on men, one hundred fifty native troops. *Tirailleurs*, native soldiers from Senegal. Then she departed again."

"Departed for where?"

Esterhazy shrugged. "It's a mystery. But I've given you a copy of the manifest."

With his eyes, Esterhazy indicated the envelope in Welles's pocket.

"The manifest? How did you come by that?"

"I'm fourth bureau, transportation and communications, my boy." Esterhazy got to his feet. "They sent it to me so I can pay the bill. *Adieu*, Percy."

Outside it had started to rain. Welles hailed a cab, gave the driver his address. The lobby at Boulevard Haussmann was dark and quiet. He climbed to the top floor, let himself into his flat, lit the lamps. The apartment was modest: a small sitting room, a separate bedroom, and a bath. In the sitting room there was a table and two chairs, a couch, a coat rack, and a bureau.

He removed his jacket, hung it on the coat rack to dry. He took the envelope Esterhazy had given him from the pocket. He carried it to the table and opened it, spreading the pages on the table, smoothing the creases.

He read the summary Esterhazy had written of the Dreyfus dossier. It was as the Count described it, proof that Dreyfus had been spying for the Germans, and for the Italians as well. He'd asked Esterhazy to try and get this in order to help Georges, but now that he had it, he wondered why he had bothered. He couldn't give it to her, he realized, without explaining where it had come from. When she asked why an Army officer would have provided him with details about the contents of the Dreyfus dossier, what could he say?

He set the summary aside, took up the next page. As was his habit, the Count had meticulously hand-copied the manifest of the *Thibet*, going so far as to draw the lines separating the columns on the original form. She had sailed from Marseilles on the 23rd of April, carrying one passenger — a Lieutenant Andre Durand — and thirty tons of supplies.

Welles flipped through the pages, running his finger down the center of each. The ship was carrying arms: rifles, pistols, machine guns. Even some light cannon, he saw. Not enough arms for one hundred fifty men. There would be more shipments, he supposed. And the *Thibet* carried other things. Tents. Field uniforms. Boots. Supplies for an expedition of some kind, he thought. But to where? And why so heavily armed?

He looked at the first page again but could find nothing about the ship's destination. Then he noticed another curious thing: Nearly everything had been packed in uniform crates of just over sixty pounds each. Was that so they could be more easily loaded on board the ship? Welles didn't know.

He wondered now why Esterhazy had decided to pass this on. The ship had left Dakar at the end of June. Whoever this Marchand was, he'd long since received his men and his cargo, and whatever he meant to do, he'd probably already done. He shook his head. Perhaps London would know what to make of it.

He took two envelopes from the top drawer of the bureau. He put the *Thibet* manifest into one; he would take it to the Embassy tomorrow, have them put it in the next diplomatic bag to Whitehall. The Dreyfus summary he put in the other envelope. He sealed both envelopes. The one for the embassy he put into the top drawer of the bureau. The other envelope he held in his hand, looking around the flat.

The chairs. They were made of carved wood, with a round seat and oval back, both upholstered. He lifted one, turned it over. A thin sheet of plywood hid the springs of the seat. With a knife he pried the wood loose. He slipped the Dreyfus envelope into the space between the board and the springs they concealed, then hammered the board back into place with the hilt of the knife. That done, he righted the chair, sat in it, testing it.

Satisfied, he went to the bedroom to prepare for bed. He removed his shirt, hung it inside the armoire and went to the bathroom, where he washed his face in the basin. He took a towel from the bar, then walked out of the bedroom and into the sitting room, drying his face as he went. He considered a drink, rejected it.

He turned down the lamps and was halfway to the bedroom when he stopped, cocked his head. He'd heard a footstep in the hallway. Then there was a knock at the door. It was so unexpected that he was gripped by a momentary panic. The knock came again, softly. He thought it must be Madame Hebert; who else could it be at this hour?

He donned his shirt, then unlocked the door, opening it a few inches. The hallway was dark. He could just make out a cloaked figure, the hood raised to hide the face. The cloak glistened in the dim light spilling from the bedroom; it was wet from the rain. The figure pressed forward and he took a step back, alarmed. Then he detected a familiar scent.

"May I come in, Percy?"

It was Georges, her voice soft, almost a whisper. He looked into the hall behind her, then stepped aside to allow her to slip into the room. He closed the door and locked it. He turned to find her standing in the middle of the room. She'd thrown the hood back, was unfastening the wet cloak. She removed it, draped it over the back of a chair. Underneath the cloak she wore the black gown, the one he'd seen earlier that evening when she left for her engagement with von Schwartzkoppen.

"Georges," he began in a hoarse whisper, "what the devil are you doing here? You shouldn't —"

She stepped forward quickly, placed a finger to his lips to silence him. The she took hold of his upper arms, pulled him towards her, kissed him. The smell of her fragrance enveloped him and for a moment he was dizzy and thought he might fall. Then he felt a rush of heat. He put his arms around her, crushed her against his chest, kissed her.

Later, when they were lying together in the dark sharing a cigarette, she told him she had wanted to come to him almost from the beginning; that she had only held back because she thought he might be outraged by her behavior, might even reject her. That he might be too English for such an affair. Welles smiled at the suggestion.

"We have a reputation for prudishness, but it is only a facade. English ladies and gentlemen do what ladies and gentlemen have always done, Georges. What matters is that they try to be discrete about it, to avoid scandal."

"Then you are not very different from Parisians. I'm glad."

"Still, we must be careful," he said. "I don't care about my reputation, but I won't see yours harmed."

"Oh," she said, "did you think there would be other times?"

He stiffened, held his breath. She felt his reaction, lifted herself to look him in the eyes, her smile barely visible in the darkness. He let his breath out, relieved. She took the cigarette from his hand, put it to her lips. She lay back on the bed. The tip of the cigarette glowed, illuminating her face and upper body, lying nude beside him. She held one arm behind her head, as a pillow, her back arched, eyes looking up into the darkness. She blew out smoke, and the hand with the cigarette moved, came to rest on her belly.

"I saw you tonight, you know," she said. "Across the street from the house. What were you doing there?"

He flushed with the shame of it and was grateful for the darkness.

"I'm sorry, Georges," he said. "I don't think I can really explain it."

"Did you follow me?"

"No."

"You were jealous," she said.

"Yes," he said. Then: "Will you see him again?"

"Max? Yes, I think so," she said. "He's good fun. When we met in his office, I was quite surprised by the way he responded to me. He seemed to take me seriously, as if I were a man. No, not a *man*; an equal, I should say. It was unusual, like — how do you say it? An attraction?"

"You may do as you like, of course."

The tip moved to her face again, glowed. In the dim light, she turned onto her side, facing him. Her eyes were bright and, he thought, amused. *Laughing at me.*

"Oh, Percy, you silly fool. I thought he was attracted to me. I thought I might charm something from him, something useful. So, I put on that ridiculous dress."

She lowered her arm, held it across her body, covering her breasts. It was, he thought, the first show of modesty she'd made since she knocked on the door.

"As if he might have a look down the front," she went on, "and then blurt out the name of the spy."

Welles found it difficult to breathe.

"And did he?"

She laughed again.

"No, of course not," she said.

"You learned nothing, then?"

"Oh, I did learn something. Max is an amiable dinner companion, witty and attentive and full of charm. It was great fun, but gradually I came to understand that he was entirely

uninterested in me as a woman. I think if we were to try again —
to woo him, I mean — you will have to be the one to try."

For a moment, he was confused. Then he understood.

"Do you mean to say…?"

"Yes, I rather think so," she said. "So, you see, Percy, there's no
reason for you to be jealous."

He made no reply. The cigarette was nearly finished. She
reached across him to the ash tray on the side table, her skin warm
where it touched his, her breasts pressed against his chest. He felt
her hair on his face. He breathed deeply, intoxicated by the smell
of her.

"I mean to show that Dreyfus is innocent," she said.

She pressed the cigarette end into the ashtray, turned her face to
his, lying atop him now.

"I shall need help, I think," she said. "Will you help me?"

"Help you?"

"Yes. Help me find the truth. This is important to me; I can't
explain why. I don't know myself. I only know that I must do
something."

She had spent her life being constrained by her sex, chafing at
the bit she had been born wearing. He found it easy to understand
how she might feel kinship with Dreyfus, a man singled out for
suspicion, perhaps for no reason other than that he had been born
a Jew. Only Welles knew better. He thought of the document
hidden in the chair, only a few steps from where they lay. He
wanted to tell her about it, show it to her, explain that Dreyfus
was, after all, guilty of the crimes of which he'd been convicted. He
would make a clean breast of it, tell her about Esterhazy, of his
work for the Crown. Perhaps she would understand, forgive him
for having deceived her.

"Will you help me?"

He felt her breath again, warm against his cheek. With one hand
she reached down, grasped him. Her hand was warm, and he felt
himself react to her touch. She shifted her hips.

"Yes," he said. "Of course I'll help."

Chapter 9

London, 12 August 1898

"Around this time Georges and I became lovers," Welles said.

That was surely enough, he'd not share with these men any part of those interludes, the details of which still haunted him, came to him in the night in place of sleep.

"And you agreed to help her free this Dreyfus fellow," said Bingham. "I confess, sir, that I do not understand you. You have only just told us, not half an hour ago, that you were sure the man was guilty. What changed your mind?"

Welles shrugged. "Why, nothing, Mister Bingham. I was sure he was guilty. I agreed to help Georges because I did not have it in my power to refuse her. When I look back on how it was then, it seems to me that I had been drawn into a small circle of people, bound to them by a tangle of obligations. There was Georges, to whom I owed the faith and dedication of a lover. There was Esterhazy, to whom I owed my help and protection for the risks he was taking. And there was Sir Reginald. Although he was far away in London, I felt his presence every day. To him I owed the duty of a trusted employee. Those three made up my entire world, and I sought to be true to them."

"But you were not true to them."

"No. How could I be? The obligations were at odds with each other. To protect Esterhazy, I lied to Georges about what I knew of Dreyfus. Lied even about who and what I was. To be true to Georges, to help her as a lover should, I involved myself publicly in the Dreyfus matter, which could only serve to draw attention to me and to connect me, however obliquely, to the matter of espionage; something which could do neither my employer nor my charge any good."

Bingham did not reply to this. Welles looked at the other two men. As he told his story, Welles had been looking for any hint of a reaction from Salisbury or Lawrence. Just now he had seen it clearly. *They have taken the hook,* he thought. *Now to set it firmly.*

He coughed once, cleared his throat.

"Story-telling is hard work, gentlemen, and I find I'm thirsty. Will none of you offer me a drink?"

"Forgive me, Mister Welles. We have forgotten our manners," said Salisbury. "Will you take a brandy, sir?"

"With pleasure, Prime Minister."

Salisbury nodded to Lawrence, who stood, picked up the decanter, glanced about the room and, seeing the clean glasses on the tray Welles had brought, raised his eyebrows. Welles nodded assent, whereupon Lawrence crossed the room to fetch a glass. Welles kept the pistol trained on him as he approached the door, but Lawrence simply took a glass and brought it to Welles. He placed it on the table and poured. As he did, Welles spoke.

"It seems I have discovered a subject which is of interest to you gentlemen."

"And what might that be, Mister Welles?" Lawrence asked.

He finished pouring, returned to his own seat, taking the decanter with him.

"Captain Jean-Baptiste Marchand," said Welles.

The name clearly meant nothing to Bingham. Lawrence, on the other hand, shot a glance at Salisbury. The Prime Minister hesitated, then seemed to come to a decision.

"Yes, Marchand," he said. "An interesting fellow. What can you tell me about him?"

"About Marchand? Not much, I'm afraid. One of those intrepid soldier-explorers one reads so much about. Something of a hero in the French colonial service. Why do you ask?"

"Where is he?" asked Lawrence, his testiness undisguised. "Where is he going? What does he mean to do?"

Welles felt a rush of relief. He had come on a gamble, a roll of the dice that depended on two things: That Salisbury did not yet know what Marchand planned to do, and that the Prime Minister desperately needed to know. He took a mouthful of brandy, savored it, buying time before answering. He must proceed with care. Everything depended on the next few hours.

"I do," he said. "Indeed, I have come here to tell you precisely that."

"Get on with it, then," said Salisbury.

"I shall, sir; only, you must let me do that in my own way. I want something in return, as I said from the start."

"Name your price. Let us haggle now and make an end to it."

"No, sir. I think my way is better. Better for me, better for you. If I were to name my price now, you would not grant it, and then you would get nothing from me. I give you my word: If you will listen to my tale, then I will tell you what I want; and, if you will agree to give it to me, I will tell you what you want to know about Marchand."

"Maybe he knows nothing at all about Marchand," said Lawrence to Salisbury. "Just the name, and the things he's already told us."

"What of that, Mister Welles?" asked Salisbury. "How can I know you even have anything to sell?"

Welles sighed.

"Very well. I would of course like to tell the story in my own way — a writer's prerogative — but as you insist: Gentlemen, I must now acquaint you with a certain Andre Durand, late of the French Colonial Army."

His eyes took on a look of concentration. After a moment, he began to speak as if he were reading something from a book.

Chapter 10

The Journal of Lieutenant Andre Durand

Tuesday, 22 April 1896
On board the Thibet
Marseilles

Captain Marchand came to see me off. All day I have labored at the docks, supervising the workers as they load our equipment. They are a good gang and know their business. Still, it was dark when the last crate was secured in the hold. I spent the better part of an hour below, inspecting their work. Some crates contain ammunition and explosives; it would not do for anything to break loose during our passage. But everything was in order, and I dismissed the gang with my thanks.

From the wheelhouse I watched them leave. We lie alongside a pier near the edge of the port, one normally reserved for naval vessels. No other ships are at present using this pier; the closest one is several hundred yards away. There is no moon tonight, but arc lamps strung along the pier make pools of bright light in the darkness, through which the workers walked to the gate at the end of the pier. My eyes were thus drawn to that gate when a carriage arrived and discharged a single passenger. The figure lingered a moment alongside the carriage, then spoke with the guard and was waved through the gate. He walked along the dock towards the ship, and it was only when he stepped under one of the arc lights that I realized it was the Captain. He was not in uniform, but I could never have mistaken him; he is very tall, though quite thin, and by habit grooms his dark beard into a fork which stood out quite clearly in the harsh light of the lamp. I waved to him and, after a moment, he saw me and returned the wave.

I met him at the top of the midships gangway. He took me by the shoulders and embraced me as he might a brother. I was surprised by this. Among our small band, I am the one officer who has not served under him before. Still, I was pleased, and more so when he spoke to me, when he called me Dédé, a nickname my friends often use but one I didn't realize he even knew.

He wanted to speak privately, so we went to my cabin. It is small — only a cot, a small desk and chair, and a washstand — and I have found that if I stand in the center of it, I can touch both bulkheads and everything it contains. I offered him the chair, but he waved me to it and sat on the cot. He asked me about our preparations, and I was happy to report that everything was in readiness for our departure tomorrow on the morning tide.

'Kitchener is at Wadi Halfa,' he said. 'He's been given command of the combined Anglo-Egyptian forces.'

He told me this in a matter-of-fact tone, but it is the worst news he could have delivered.

'How strong is his force, Captain?' I asked.

'You must call me Paké-Bô, Dédé. Everyone does.'

Paké-Bô, I knew, is the name given to him by the colonial tirailleurs of Senegal. They gave it to him to honor his bravery. I'm told it means 'piercer of forests' in their tongue.

'As for Kitchener's force,' he said, 'we don't know the strength. Nor do we know for certain where he's going. Probably Dongola.'

For a moment I thought he had come to tell me that the mission had been canceled before it had even begun. But only for a moment, for he went on.

'We shall accelerate the timetable, Dédé.'

He took a packet of papers from inside his jacket and opened them on the desk, flattening the creases with his big hands.

'You will proceed to Dakar as planned, only now I will sail before the end of June. I should join you in Loango by the first of August at the latest. You must be ready by then.'

I confess I do not see how it can be done. True, I have more than three months, but nearly half of that time will be spent on board the Thibet. I said as much.

'If any man can do it, you can, Dédé,' he said. 'Captain Mangin will join you in Loango; he's an Africa man, knows the natives and their ways. But listen. You'll be on your own in Dakar. You must find Corporal Dialike there. I've cabled the Colonial Administration; they'll help you find him. Let him pick the men. You can trust him to manage that, and other things besides. You have enough money?'

Before I had left Paris, they sent me with a clerk to a room containing only a table and a chair. On the table was a small fortune in franc notes. The clerk had waited while I counted it, then asked me to sign a receipt. With obvious pain, he told me the money was now mine to take and left the room. The money was in a leather valise, underneath the cot where Marchand sat. I told him as much.

'I was going to give it to the Thibet's captain to lock in the safe,' I said. 'Then I met the captain, and saw the safe, and thought better of it.'

He laughed at this, a full-throated laugh, and my spirits were much lifted.

'Spend it carefully, Dédé!' he admonished. Before I could reply to that, he laughed again. 'In short, my friend, you've got to work quickly, surmount all difficulties, overcome the impossible, and not spend a centime. Nothing to it.'

Now it was my turn to laugh. This was Marchand's reputation. He would ask you to do the impossible, and make a joke of it, and his enthusiasm and confidence would win you over to the idea, so that you would go and do the thing which could not be done. Or, if you were not convinced, he would go and do it himself, and bring you along with him so you would know that, after all, it could be done.

'What could be simpler?' I asked with a shrug, and I could see that he was pleased with my reply.

He had some other instructions for me. He had arranged for a physician to join us in Dakar, and a cook. The cook would assemble other personal attendants, but I must be careful to have Dialike look them over before taking them on.

When these and other matters were attended to, he asked me if there was anything to drink. I took a bottle of brandy and two silver cups from my kit bag and poured a measure into each cup. He raised his cup, as I did my own.

'To Africa!' he said.

'To Africa!' I replied.

We both drank. Together like this, as if we were simply two friends, I felt I could speak my heart.

'Can this be done?' I asked. 'We are so few.'

'This will be your first service in Africa, Dédé?' he asked, though surely he knew. I nodded. 'When you know it as I do, you will understand. For this, fewer is better. A thousand men would die trying to walk across the heart of Africa. Too much to carry, too far. We'd need an army of bearers. Feeding them would be nearly impossible, and our efforts to do it would turn every village against us.'

He leaned forward, placed a hand on my shoulder.

'Trust me, Dédé. This is the only way.'

He took his leave shortly afterward, aiming to catch the midnight train back to Paris. At the top of the gangway, he embraced me again, bid me adieu. He started down the stairs, then turned.

'All of Africa will be ours, Dédé. We will make it so, you and me. It is a story you will tell your grandchildren.'

Afterward I found it difficult to sleep. At dawn I returned to the quarterdeck. The arc lights were extinguished and in the early light I saw members of the ship's crew approaching as they returned from their leave. Before long the two stacks began belching black smoke, and I felt the throb of the engines. We slipped our moorings and eased away from the dock. We moved at one-quarter power through the busy harbor and into the open sea. The captain called for half power and we turned southwest, making for Gibraltar and the Atlantic.

Chapter 11

Paris, September 1896

London, 3 September 1896
Dreyfus Has Escaped!
Fugitive May Be in the United States

It is reported that Captain Alfred Dreyfus has escaped from Devil's Island and may now be in the United States. The news of his escape was brought here by Captain Hunter, of the British merchant steamer Nonpareil, which arrived at Newport yesterday from Cayenne, French Guyana. According to Captain Hunter, his ship encountered a small boat not far from the island, bearing the prisoner and, curiously, several of his prison guards. He agreed to take Captain Dreyfus on board and later transferred him to an American schooner, which was last seen sailing to the north. During the several days Dreyfus spent on his vessel, Captain Hunter says he became convinced of the innocence of the condemned man. In his account, he reports that Captain Dreyfus told him that no evidence against him was presented to the secret court that ultimately convicted him. It is believed that Dreyfus' escape was accomplished through the bribing of his guards, which explains their presence on the boat with which he fled the prison on Devil's Island.

The story had been Georges' idea. Welles was cool to it, but he had promised her he would help, and he could find no easy way to escape that promise. He had hoped that Mathieu Dreyfus would reject the idea when Georges took it to him. Instead, Mathieu had given his enthusiastic approval. She wrote the piece and there was nothing for Welles to do but find a London paper willing to run it. This was also her idea; she thought that a London paper would give the story more credibility, and a report from London would take longer for the French authorities to discredit.

When the news of Dreyfus's escape reached Paris late in the afternoon of the third, it caused a sensation. The following day — a Friday — every daily paper ran the story, many with their own embellishments. Some of those, Welles realized, were as fanciful as was Georges' story. *La Libre Parole*, a ferociously anti-Dreyfus paper, published an interview with Captain Hunter of the *Nonpareil* in which the Captain recounted his meeting with Dreyfus on the high seas. Welles, who knew that Hunter was a creature of Georges' imagination, could only laugh as he read the piece. Not quite so amusing was an editorial in the same edition which attributed the escape to the machinations of a secret cabal of Jewish businessmen. For good or for ill, the Dreyfus case was again the principal topic of conversation in every restaurant and salon in the city.

The authorities responded quickly, cabling the colonial administration in Guiana, and learned almost immediately that there had been no escape. They issued a flat denial on the afternoon of the fourth. As this came on a Friday afternoon, however, it did little to dampen enthusiasm and the name of Dreyfus was on every Parisian's lips throughout the weekend.

But the story couldn't hold up for long. The following Monday, a journalist from *The Times* sought out Captain Hunter, hoping to get more from him. He was unable to find any sign of the man or his vessel in Newport. Lloyd's of London reported they had no record of any British vessel called the *Nonpareil*; indeed, they said, they were aware of no such vessel flying the flag of any country in the world. By the middle of the week, the entire story was understood to be a fraud.

Still, Georges had accomplished what she intended. There was a renewed interest in the case. She was in high spirits that Friday evening as she accompanied Welles to a performance of the opera *Hamlet* at the Palais Garnier. She dressed for the occasion in a gown of black lace worn over a shift the color of her skin. She wore a cape against the weather, but he helped her off with it and draped it over one arm when they entered the lobby, so that her neck and shoulders were bare. The effect was mesmerizing, and not only to him; he'd sensed other eyes on them as they climbed the marble stairs to the box level. He left her briefly to check her cloak; then they proceeded to the box he'd taken. He offered her the seat closer to the stage, so that he could see her and the stage at the same time.

Georges seemed engrossed by the opera through the first three acts. Welles, on the other hand, was unable to concentrate on the play, and not only because he was distracted by Georges. Since they had become lovers, he'd found it increasingly difficult to account for his absences when he needed to meet with Esterhazy. Georges had supposed — quite naturally — that his nights belonged to her, and as he spent much of his days with her as well, there was little opportunity for his clandestine work. To make matters worse, he'd had a cable from Sir Reginald, one making it urgent for him to meet the Count.

Thus, in the lobby during the intermission before the fourth act, he excused himself and made his way to the antechamber of the men's room. A few minutes later Esterhazy joined him. The two retired to a corner, next to a small table, Welles standing in a position that permitted him to watch the lobby through the open doorway. They quickly exchanged envelopes. Esterhazy turned to go, but Welles asked him to stay. He took a cigarette from his case, offered one to the Count, then lit both.

"Thank you, Percy," Esterhazy said.

He exhaled a cloud of blue smoke, looking around the small lounge as he did. It was crowded with men, some coming and going, others standing and smoking.

"Rather a public place for a meeting, don't you think?"

He made a clucking sound as if to scold Welles.

"It couldn't be helped."

Welles had spoken quietly, but now his eyes went around the room, and he leaned closer to the other man, dropped his voice to a whisper.

"I've had a cable from our masters."

"Indeed?" Esterhazy likewise lowered his voice. "And what do they want?"

"Marchand. They want everything you can give us on this expedition. Where is he going, and why?"

The Count raised his eyebrows.

"I'm not sure what I can give them," he said. "The things I get relate to transport, communications. I can keep my eyes open, but what you want would come from operations."

He shrugged, that particular French shrug which suggests, politely, that the thing is impossible.

"There must be something you can do. The cable said this was *urgent and most important*. They seem to be in a bit of a state about it."

Esterhazy sighed.

"All right, if you insist. I'll need some time to think of a way. Will a week or so be soon enough?"

Welles nodded. "It will have to be. Thank you."

He had inclined his head towards the Count, the better to hear him, and his eyes had unconsciously fixed on the other man's face. Now he looked up again, through the doorway into the lobby, and immediately saw Georges. She was talking with two gentlemen, a glass of champagne in her hand and a smile on her face, but he could see that she was looking at him. He smiled at her without thinking, nodded his head. Esterhazy saw the movement and, curious, turned to look himself.

"What an exquisite creature," he said. "Is she yours, Percy?"

To Welles's dismay, the Count also smiled at Georges, nodded.

"She is my colleague," Welles said. "Nothing more."

It was not entirely convincing. Esterhazy gave him an appraising look.

"You must introduce us," Esterhazy said.

"I don't think so. Not a good idea at all."

Welles could see the curiosity in Georges' eyes. He dropped his cigarette in the ash tray on the table.

"I need to go. Next week?"

The Count chuckled, nodded. Then, as Welles was moving, he took him by the arm.

"I say, what do you make of this news about Dreyfus?"

The question was natural enough, but there was something in the tone that got his attention.

"The escape, you mean? Seems like a hoax, doesn't it?"

"Yes, a hoax," said Esterhazy. "An invention. But who invented it? Why?" He seemed genuinely perplexed.

"Newspapers do this sort of thing all the time," Welles said. "Invent a story, I mean. To sell papers."

Esterhazy held his look a moment longer, then smiled.

"Yes," he said. "Well, it's a strange business you're in, Percy." He released Welles. "Thanks for the ticket, dear boy. A marvelous opera, *magnifique*."

Georges came to meet him as he emerged from the lounge. She put one hand on his arm, leaned forward to kiss him on the cheek.

"Who is that man you were talking with, Percy?" she asked, her cheek warm and soft against his own. She drew back, eyes fixed on his.

"A man I know, not very well," he said. "An Army officer. I met him a few years ago, working on a story."

"Does he have a name, this officer?"

"Of course, my dear. His name is Esterhazy. Count Esterhazy."

At that moment, the attendants passed into the hall, ringing chimes to call them back into the theater. He offered his arm.

"Shall we? The fourth act will start soon, the madness of Ophelia. We shouldn't miss it, I understand it's the best part."

She took his arm, walked with him across the hall.

"You seemed very absorbed in your conversation with this Count Esterhazy," she said as they climbed the stairs. "What were you talking about?"

"Dreyfus, what else? It's all anyone is talking about this week. He saw me in the lobby, recognized me. We made idle chatter over a cigarette, then he braced me about Dreyfus."

"Braced you?"

"Yes, he was quite intense. Angry, even. Wanted to know why the English papers would print such nonsense. I suppose he must have thought I could explain it."

They reached the top of the stair.

"Come, let's go in,' he said.

Later, after the play had ended, they walked arm in arm along the Rue Auber. Welles had arranged a late supper at a restaurant that served the theater crowd. They had nearly reached the place when he suddenly stopped. He turned and retraced his steps to the newsstand they had just passed, took a paper from the stack, and began to read, squinting in the poor light of the streetlamps. Georges stood close to him, and he held the paper so that she could read it too.

11 September 1896
The Traitor
Dreyfus Guilt Confirmed
Proof of His Treason Held in Secret Dossier

It is revealed to this reporter by an officer of impeccable patriotism and fidelity that Dreyfus is a traitor, and that the truth of his guilt is demonstrated in the contents of a secret dossier compiled by those charged with determining the identity of the scoundrel who so cruelly betrayed France. This dossier, the truth of which there can be no doubt, contains secrets of such profound national importance that it was felt they could not be revealed to anyone other than the judges who presided over the trial, lest more damage be done than that already visited on our nation by the traitor.

Welles felt Georges' grip on his arm.

"Percy!" she said, "They have admitted it!"

"They have," he said. "What damned fool would make such an admission?"

"Whoever he was," she said, "he will live to regret it."

She slipped an arm around his waist, pulled him close.

"Oh, Percy. Now they will have to answer for what they've done."

Part 2

"I stated the other day that in consequence of these claims of ours, and in consequence of the claims of Egypt in the Nile valley, the British and Egyptian spheres of influence covered the whole of the Nile waterway."

— Sir Edward Grey in the House of Commons, 28 March 1895

Chapter 12

London, 12 August 1898

"Georges was right," Welles said. "The revelation that Dreyfus had been convicted by evidence he never saw ignited a firestorm. The trial was denounced by eminent jurists, politicians, even members of the government. Whatever Parisians might think of Germans and Jews, they can't abide a perversion of the system of justice. The following week, Lucie Dreyfus petitioned the Chamber of Deputies to set aside the verdict and order a new trial. It was everything Georges had hoped for."

"Hardly," said Lawrence dismissively. "As I recall, the Chamber took up the matter in October, then rejected the petition in November."

"But why should the Chamber have rejected the petition?" asked Bingham. He seemed genuinely exercised by the matter. "It is a bedrock of any civilized country that an accused man has a right to see the evidence arrayed against him. If Dreyfus was convicted by secret evidence, then the trial was no better than a sham."

"An excellent question," said Welles, "and one I will soon answer."

"In any event," said Lawrence, "this woman's trick resulted in little of consequence."

Welles smiled. "So it might seem. But I hope you'll grant, Mister Lawrence, that things are not always as they seem?"

"What does it matter?" This from Salisbury. "It is of no consequence to the question of Marchand."

The Prime Minister leaned forward in his chair and wagged a finger at Welles.

"Mister Welles," he demanded, "what is the nature of this journal you recited to us just now? Where did you get it?"

"It is a record of the Marchand mission, written by Lieutenant Durand. I have it from Durand himself."

"In that case, kindly dispense with these theatrics. I have no interest in this Dreyfus business, and even less in you or the nature of your personal relations. I am, on the other hand, interested in this journal. What will you take for it?"

Welles was tempted, but he knew that the Prime Minister was not yet ready to pay the price he meant to demand.

"I'm afraid it will not be so easy," he said. "I have a story I want to tell. I have another a story you want to hear. Shall we make a bargain? You will listen to the one I want to tell, and in return I will tell the one you want to hear."

"Come, Mister Welles," said Lawrence. "You're wasting the Prime Minister's time."

Welles shifted the gun so that it pointed directly at Lawrence.

"But you see, sir, this is my time, not his. Not yours. I've taken it from you, from both of you, and I'll use it as I think I must."

This was greeted by silence, a silence that stretched so long that suddenly Welles was afraid; afraid that he'd overplayed his hand and lost them. Then — to his relief — Salisbury spoke.

"As far as we know," he said, "Marchand is still somewhere in central Africa. If this Durand fellow is with him, how did he manage to give you his journal?"

"Another good question," Welles said. "Is it a bargain, then?"

He cocked his head slightly, waited.

The Prime Minister sighed.

"Very well, have it your way," he said. "Only, get to Marchand as quickly as you can."

Welles nodded. "I shall endeavor to, Prime Minister. Indeed, I shall offer a fair balance, and give you as much of Marchand as my purpose will bear. That is, I'll do that as soon as I have persuaded Mister Lawrence that he is wrong."

"Wrong?" asked Lawrence. "In what way am I wrong?"

"You are wrong to say that Georges' trick was of no consequence. It was, I venture to say, the single most consequential act of my entire tale."

Chapter 13
Paris, September 1896

Welles took a *fiacre* to the Gare de l'Est, then spent an hour losing himself in the warren of narrow streets and alleys south of the station. It was late, even by the standards of Paris, and the streets were deserted. He stopped frequently to look behind him but saw no one and heard nothing other than the sound of the gently falling rain. Confident he was not being followed, he made his way to the cafe Cheval Blanc.

Through the window he could see a solitary man — a laborer by his clothes — sitting at a table, a bottle and glass before him. Behind the bar a bartender loitered, tired and bored. There was no sign of Esterhazy.

He opened the door and entered. The laborer looked up at the sound and Welles realized with a start that it was the Count. He nodded to the man behind the bar, crossed the room and took the empty chair across from Esterhazy. The bartender brought another glass, then returned to the bar, where he polished glasses in a desultory fashion. Esterhazy poured a splash of brandy into the glass, raised his own.

"*Salut*, Percy. Sorry to get you out so late on such a miserable night."

Esterhazy swallowed the brandy in one gulp, then refilled his glass.

"Are you sure you weren't followed?" he asked.

"Yes, I'm certain," Welles said. "Has something happened?"

"I think I'm being followed," Esterhazy said. "On Monday, walking home from *L'Ecole Militaire,* a man was behind me, I think most of the way. I didn't make anything of it at the time. Then I saw him again on Tuesday. I wasn't sure it was the same man. But he was there, again, yesterday. I saw him when I came out of Barre's."

"He followed you to Barre's?"

"It's all right. I had something to pick up there, some shirts I'd ordered. It would have looked normal, no reason for suspicion."

Welles knew about the shirts. Monsieur Barre had, with poorly disguised irritation, presented him with Esterhazy's tailoring bill. He'd paid it, deeming it necessary to maintain good relations with the man and putting it down as an operational expense. The Count's finances, he knew, were in a constant state of crisis.

"A creditor, perhaps?" he asked.

"Not a creditor. Not that look at all, Percy." He smiled, a rueful smile, drained his glass. "No, something about this man makes me think *policeman.* I can't say why, it's just a feeling."

"Can you think of any reason why the police would be following you?" Welles asked.

"No."

Esterhazy poured another measure into his glass, drank it quickly. He was, Welles could see, already feeling the effects of the brandy.

"Unless it is this Dreyfus business."

"Dreyfus?" Welles was suddenly uneasy. "What do you mean?"

"They've reopened the case, you know. That new man at counter-intelligence, Major Picquart, he's reviewing all the files."

"Yes, I read about it. But what has that to do with you?"

Esterhazy shrugged.

"They know there is a traitor. If it isn't Dreyfus, who is it? That is a natural line of inquiry."

Welles produced his cigarette case, offered one to Esterhazy, then took one for himself. He lit both, shook out the match.

"What does that have to do with you?" he asked.

"Maybe nothing. But there is a certain tension in the office. Everyone is on edge. And now this man who seems to be following me."

"Dreyfus is guilty, though, isn't he?" Welles said. "You've seen the dossier. It's all very well to question the procedure, a conviction on secret evidence, but when Picquart has finished his review he'll know it was Dreyfus all along. And that will be the end of it."

The Count considered this, then nodded.

"Still, you were right to be careful," Welles said.

Esterhazy looked past him, checking the window first, and then the bartender. Apparently satisfied, he produced an envelope from inside his jacket, slid it across the table to Welles, who took it and immediately put it in his own pocket.

"So, Marchand," Esterhazy began.

"Yes?"

"He's in Loango. That's a French station in west Africa, on the coast. He arrived near the end of August, aboard another steamer. The *Stamboul*."

"What's he doing in Loango?"

"I can't be sure, Percy, but I imagine he's trying to move a hundred tons of cargo overland to Brazzaville."

"A hundred tons of cargo? What kind of cargo?"

"You remember the manifest I gave you for the *Thibet*?" Welles nodded. "There were three ships in all, each carrying similar loads. Enough to last one hundred fifty men three years in the field."

Welles considered this.

"And you think he's going to Brazzaville?" he asked.

Esterhazy shrugged. "A guess, Percy. Loango is the main French port of entry for men and supplies bound for Brazzaville."

"Why overland? Why not drop everything at the mouth of the Congo, use the river to move your men and supplies?"

"It can't be done. The river isn't navigable below Brazzaville. There are three hundred miles of cataracts between Stanley Pool and the sea. No, they'll have to carry their supplies. Hire bearers to carry them, I should say. We move three or four times that weight of goods between Loango and Brazzaville every month. All carried by men on foot. Natives."

"Incredible," said Welles, shaking his head. "But why send a company of armed men to Brazzaville?"

"I imagine they're using it as a jumping-off point. They're heading up the Congo."

"Up the Congo to where?"

"It's a long river, Percy. The second longest in Africa. And there are dozens of tributaries. They could be going anywhere."

Welles stubbed out his cigarette. He couldn't shake the feeling that Esterhazy knew more than he was telling. The Count had a habit of initially holding something back, then springing it with all the triumph and joy of a child.

"Why, then?" he asked. "You must have some idea."

Esterhazy smiled. "You're too clever for me, Percy. I can't get anything past you."

He looked around again, then leaned forward, beckoning Welles to do the same, his actions overly exaggerated, as if he were performing on a stage for the benefit of the audience in the back rows. Welles could smell the brandy on the man's breath.

"I was saving the best for last. I took the manifests to an officer I know in operations. I was a bit pushy. Made on that all this secrecy about Marchand and his damned mission was an insult. Appealed to his sense of honor as a fellow officer of the General Staff. I must have touched a nerve. He didn't give much. Wouldn't tell me where they're going. But he did tell me the reason for the secrecy."

Esterhazy paused for dramatic effect. Welles said nothing. Disappointed, the Count leaned back in his chair.

"Whatever Marchand is doing — wherever he is going — he is carrying out orders from the highest authority."

"The highest authority?"

"Yes. I'm told his orders come from the cabinet. And, Percy?" The Count paused, wanting to be sure he had Welles's full attention. "The purpose of his operation is to drive the British from Africa."

Welles searched Esterhazy's face but saw no sign that the man was joking.

"With one hundred fifty men?" he asked. "How the devil can he do that?"

Another shrug. The Count didn't know, or he wouldn't say. There was no way to be sure which. Welles collected his cigarette case, put it back in his jacket. From another pocket he drew an envelope and passed it across the table.

"I think London will want to know where they're going," he said. "See if you can find out. Nothing too risky, mind you. Leave a message at Barre's when you have something."

Esterhazy lifted the bottle, held it over Welles's glass, raised his eyebrows.

"No, thank you," Welles declined. "I should be going. You too; you ought to be home by now."

He stood, but Esterhazy made no move to leave. Welles went to the bar, laid a few franc notes on the counter. The bartender examined them, nodded.

Welles spared a last glance at Esterhazy. The man was pouring more brandy. Welles sighed, then went out into the night. It was raining harder now. He turned up the collar on his cape. A few minutes of brisk walking brought him to Boulevard Saint-Denis. There was no cab in sight, and little prospect of finding one at this hour. He resigned himself to walking, turned right and struck out in the direction of Montmartre.

Chapter 14

The Journal of Lieutenant Andre Durand

Thursday, 25 June 1896
Loango
French Congo

Loango is a disaster. We arrived yesterday and the native workers began unloading our supplies immediately, but when I went to hire bearers, there were few to be had. The Governor, Colonel De Brazza, says that the Basundi are in open revolt. Two chiefs of those people are cooperating in a kind of confidence scheme. One chief, Mayoke, will pounce on any column with a band of armed men. The other, Nganga, will arrive shortly thereafter to rescue the convoy. Mayoke and his men then withdraw, taking with them what supplies they can carry, while Nganga demands payment for saving the column. Inevitably bearers are killed in this process, with the result that few Loangans will now consent to work as bearers. For now, our supplies are simply being moved into the warehouses along the beach where, I'm told, they join another twenty-five thousand parcels waiting to be carried overland to Brazzaville.

Captain Mangin has been here for several days. He has had words with de Brazza. As the Governor, de Brazza is responsible for the flow of goods throughout the colony, and Mangin blames him for our present circumstances. But as de Brazza is also a senior officer, Mangin's words were necessarily guarded. De Brazza was unmoved. What few laborers he could muster were needed for other, more important work. Nor would he hear of compelling the Loangans to work, given the danger of expanding the revolt.

I went with Mangin to visit two villages where he tried to hire bearers, offering double and even triple the usual wages, but it was no good. They would not come. Mangin was disgusted. On the way back to the beach, I asked if we could not rely on our soldiers to begin moving some of the supplies. He shook his head.

'Senegalese are soldiers, not bearers,' he said. 'They will do what we ask, but they will not like it. They see themselves as better than bearers. Those people, they say, are born into this world with a load on their head. If they will not carry, what else are they good for?'

On the beach, Corporal Dialike has our tirailleurs well in hand. Finding no accommodations for the men, he has staked a claim to an unused section of beach and erected a neat camp. Paké-Bô was right about Dialike, he is an excellent man in all respects and the soldiers he recruited for us would be the envy of any company in France. So here we sit and wait.

<u>Tuesday, 30 June 1896</u>
<u>Loango</u>

This morning after breakfast we were treated to an astonishing sight: a small vessel steaming out of the south, being battered by the heavy Atlantic surf. She was built for rivers and, by the look of it, overloaded. It seemed impossible that she could make any headway at all, climbing up and then crashing down among the rollers, wallowing in the troughs as if she might capsize at any moment. But she came on and by mid-morning she was just off the beach, in the shelter of the breakwater.

I commandeered some of the dockworkers and we pulled her onto the sand, whereupon a man leapt from the deck into the water and waded ashore. This was Captain Baratier, another of our company. He had sailed separately from Marseilles aboard the Villes de Maranhao, to Boma, where the Congo flows into the sea. There we had been promised the use of the new Belgian railroad, to carry a third of our supplies a good part of the way to Brazzaville. But he had been kept waiting in Boma for more than a week, then was told that the railway was closed to us. No one would explain to him why. Nor could he hire bearers, as the portage market was also strictly controlled by Belgian concerns.

The Villes de Maranhao had by then departed. With no prospect of getting to Brazzaville, he had hired this riverboat, the Soyo Princess. It cost a small fortune — the boat was used for moving people and cargo in the shelter of the port and no one believed it would survive a voyage up the West African coast. Nonetheless, he had loaded his cargo and started for Loango to join us. He and Bertrand, the engineer, had spelled each other at the wheel, taking turns shoveling coal into the firebox. They could not risk steaming at night, when they could not clearly see the seas ahead, so each evening they beached the little craft and waited for dawn. It had taken six days to make the passage.

'It is no good here,' I told him, explaining that there were no bearers to be had.

To my surprise, he was not discouraged by this news. If anything, he approved of de Brazza's handling of the situation.

'We must take care with the natives,' he said. 'To demand of them what they would not willingly give would be to play into the rebels' hands. There would be more uprisings, and more time lost suppressing them. In this adventure, force is a source of weakness, not strength. It can only be our last resort.'

Mangin snorted at this, but it sounded like wisdom to me.

'What can we do, then?' I asked.

'There is a river — the Kouilou — to the north, perhaps forty miles from here," Baratier said. 'I'll take the Princess there, try to make my way inland. The Kouilou eventually joins the Niari, which I can use to get all the way to Kimbedi, within one hundred miles of Stanley Pool.'

'The Kouilou is too shallow,' Mangin objected. 'I have seen it. You'll never get that barge over those rocks.'

'Sometimes it is shallow, yes, but other times it is passable. I will try it.'

'If you are wrong, you'll be stuck on the river, hundreds of miles from Brazzaville. It would serve you right, but you'll be stuck with a third of our supplies and we can't spare them. You would need a thousand men to carry them.'

'I need a thousand men to carry them now,' said Baratier.

'Where will you find them, in the middle of that wilderness?' Mangin was exasperated. 'At least here, there is a chance. Or in Boma. You should have stayed there.'

'If I follow the Kouilou to the Niari, I shall avoid much of the rebellion. I will take some boats along. Even if I'm forced to abandon the Princess, I can load our supplies into boats, and hire men to drag them through the shallows. We should make good time that way, even with only a few men at the ropes. We will be in Brazzaville before you, my friend!'

This argument between them went on for the rest of the afternoon. I am struck by the stark difference between two men who have by all accounts served together for many years. Baratier is by habit cheerful and filled with enthusiasm; in every way an amiable companion. In contrast to his sunny disposition, Mangin is a dark fellow, quick to find fault and, it seems to me, always on the edge of anger. Nonetheless, it is clear the two respect each other.

I was so encouraged by Baratier's plan that I suggested we join him; that the entire expedition follow him north to the Kouilou. At this, Baratier shook his head, laughing.

'No, my friend,' he said. 'Mangin is right; this is an uncertain gamble, too big of one to risk the entire expedition.'

Thursday, 2 July 1896
Loango

Baratier left today, taking the Princess north in search of the Kouilou river. With him went two dozen of the tirailleurs. In addition to the soldiers, the Princess carried nearly a thousand crates — the ones she'd brought from Boma — and some longboats Baratier had been able to buy from the cargo master. He is an admirable man, I think, one who sets his mind to a thing and then does not rest until he has done it. I said this to Mangin as we stood on the beach watching the little riverboat steaming slowly north, being tossed like a cork in the heavy seas. He looked at me as if I were mad.

'He is already lost,' he said. 'I doubt we will ever see him again.'

'Perhaps,' I said. 'But he is right about one thing: we cannot sit on this beach and wait forever.'

'No, we cannot. Come with me, Durand.'

We went together to see de Brazza. There, Mangin demanded permission to form a column. He would draft bearers from the village, against their will if necessary, and send along enough soldiers to keep them under control. Colonel de Brazza refused, saying that if we were to impress men from the villages, they might join the Basundi in revolt.

'Very well,' said Mangin, 'then I shall go farther afield to find them.'

Again, de Brazza refused. He was angry now and ordered that no portage column could henceforth depart without his leave. Mangin could barely contain his fury and it was all that I could do to get him away before he forgot himself entirely.

Later that afternoon, I went to the telegraph hut and sent a cable to Libreville. Paké-Bô should be there by now. We need him here, in Loango, or we will have failed before we even begin.

Monday, 20 July 1896
Loango

Still no word from our leader. Where can he be? And we have heard nothing of Baratier and his men. I try not to be disturbed by this; even if he has met with success, it will be some time still before they can reach Brazzaville and send a cable. If, on the other hand, he has found the Kouilou impassable, he would have returned by now. I tell myself that I must take the silence from that quarter as good news. We have had little enough as it is.

Mangin has just come from de Brazza. Their war of words has continued these past two weeks, but it seems Mangin has at last won the day. The Governor has agreed that we may form a column and try our luck; he says only that we may not impress bearers into service. Mangin laughed when he told me this, saying that a bearer who has been forced is no more or less black and sullen than one who has volunteered.

'Who can tell the difference?' he asked.

I urged him to obey. It would not be wise to make an enemy of de Brazza, I said. But I see that he is not the kind of man who will listen to such advice.

Mangin has decided to lead the first column. He will take some of the soldiers with him, and as many bearers as he can find. I will remain here with the rest of the men and our supplies, waiting for our leader's arrival, and trying to arrange another column.

<u>Wednesday, 29 July 1896</u>
<u>Loango</u>

Mangin left today. He managed to assemble eighty-five porters, each of whom would bear a sixty-pound crate on his head. He took with him forty of our soldiers. He had planned to take only twenty, but when Corporal Dialike saw the bearers, he pulled Mangin aside and told him he must take more.

'You will need them, Monsieur,' he said. 'These men, they are not right. I do not like the way they look. There will be trouble.'

Mangin had another look at the bearers and agreed. Dialike went to muster twenty more tirailleurs. Mangin turned to me.

'When I am gone, you must begin to recruit bearers to form another column,' he said. 'We should be three weeks to Brazzaville, perhaps a few days longer. Less time to return, of course, we'll be traveling light. But I'll cable you from Brazzaville when we arrive.'

'Very well,' I said. Then: 'Are you sure this is a good idea? Dialike is right. I do not like the look of these bearers.'

'We must get moving, Durand,' he said. 'You remember what Paké-Bô told us? Everything depends on speed."

He is right, of course, but I cannot escape the feeling that he is making a mistake. The bearers he takes march against their will. Perhaps he takes enough soldiers to control them in normal times, but if he is set upon by the Basundi, will he have enough to manage both?

Tuesday, 4 August 1896
Loango

Paké-Bô has arrived at last! I cannot describe the relief I felt when I saw him coming down the gangway of the Stamboul. I waved to him and he came immediately to where I stood, embracing me as he had in Marseilles when last I'd seen him.

'Where are the others?' he asked, looking around.

I told him what I could: that Mangin had left a week before, hoping to lead a column overland, and that Baratier was attempting to take the Princess up the Kouilou river.

He shook his head. 'I do not think he will make it. The Kouilou is too shallow.'

'Perhaps he should have waited in Boma for the railroad,' I said.

'No, Dédé, I have just come from Boma. That railroad is nothing more than a dream, a narrow trail hacked from the jungle and the rocks in the vague direction of Brazzaville. I doubt they've laid more than five miles of actual track.'

'Merde.' I said. 'Why should they promise it to us, knowing it does not exist?'

Paké-Bô shrugged. 'Men on the ground always claim more progress than they have made. Perhaps they have taken it too far, so that the ministers in Brussels believe it is real. In any event, it is no use to us now.'

'What shall we do?'

'We have no choice,' he said. 'As long as the rebellion persists, we will be unable to move. We shall have to help the Governor put it down.'

He wanted to see the tirailleurs, so I took him to the camp. He greeted Corporal Dialike warmly, like an old friend, and despite the composed and impassive face the Senegalese habitually wore, I believe the man was pleased. They spoke about the condition of the men, and Marchand took a turn about the camp. He talked to several of the men, nodded his approval, then took his leave, saying he must go and speak with Colonel de Brazza.

Just as it seemed we might sit on this beach forever, things are
happening. A cable came yesterday from Brazzaville. Mangin has arrived!
Ordinarily I would be cheered by this, but his news was otherwise all bad.
Only one week into his trek the column was set upon by a large band of
raiders. Our tirailleurs managed to fight them off, but in the chaos many
of the bearers ran away, and a few were killed. When the dust had settled,
Mangin had lost nearly twenty of them. With no other choice, he
distributed the remaining crates among the soldiers, and they set off
again.

Two days later, the raiding party struck again. This time, the fight was
more difficult, but in the end Mangin prevailed. The raiders fled, but not
before carrying off a good part of the cargo. Mangin managed to capture
several of the raiders. He learned from them that the leader of gang was
one Missitou, another follower of Nganga. This Nganga seems to be a
kind of native priest or holy man and he has vowed to drive the white man
from West Africa. The Basundi are a fractious people, like many of the
local tribes, but they have been united under his leadership. And Mangin
has worse news: he says the rebellion is spreading to the he Bakonga
people of the Brazzaville region.

Mangin's column arrived at Brazzaville having lost two-thirds of his
bearers and half the loads they were carrying. The surviving Loangans
have refused to make the return journey. Worse, two of the tirailleurs
were killed. Our force is such that we cannot afford to lose a single man,
else even if we were to arrive at our objective, against the odds, we would
not be able to hold it for long.

The news has had a galvanizing effect on Paké-Bô. For two weeks he
has been arguing with de Brazza and sending cables to the Colonial Office
in Paris; all to no effect. Now his patience with the Governor is exhausted.
I went with him to see the port master; there, he asked to see an inventory
of the contents of the entire warehouse. He pored over the document at
length, then borrowed the master's pen and began marking entries.
Finished, he handed the inventory to me.

'Seize these crates, Dédé.'

When the master objected, he repeated the order.

'Take Corporal Dialike and as many men as you need and get these crates.'

Then he marched off to see Colonel de Brazza. I looked at the inventory; the crates he'd marked were those containing rifles and ammunition intended for the Colonial administration in Brazzaville. The master looked at me. I shrugged an apology, then went to do my duty.

Thursday, 20 August 1896
Loango

Paké-Bô did not return that evening. Three times during the night the port master appeared at our picket, demanding the return of the arms we'd taken. Three times I sent him away. In truth, I thought he had the right of it; but faced with an armed camp guarded by nearly one hundred veterans, there was little he could do. I felt sorry for the man.

I was eating my bread dunked in coffee, wondering what the day would bring, when Paké-Bô came into the tent.

'Up, Dédé!' he said, 'No time for lounging about!'

I leapt to my feet, though he smiled as he said it, and I could see he was in a good humor.

'The Governor has declared martial law. The rebels are to be destroyed, the supply lines to Brazzaville reopened. De Brazza is off to Libreville this morning, to confer with the colonial authorities there. He's left things to his lieutenant, but as I am the senior officer present, I'll not wait for that man to act.'

'Very good, my Captain,' I said, saluting him as I spoke. 'What are your orders?'

'Find Corporal Dialike. Have him break open the weapons we took yesterday. I mean to conscript every Frenchman in this compound. They will need arms.'

The surprise I felt at these words must have been evident in my face, for he laughed loudly to see it.

'Go, Dédé. Do as I say.'

Chapter 15

Paris, October 1896

Welles took two glasses of champagne from the offered tray. As he turned to give one to Georges, he heard the crowd break into a cheer some distance away. They joined the throng of spectators at the parapet. From their vantage point atop the Arc de Triomphe, they could see thousands of people lined up along either side of the Boulevard de la Grande Armee. It was a clear fall day and the afternoon sun was bright and warm. The spectators waved flags, scarves, hats; whatever they had to wave. Lines had been strung between the buildings to either side of the boulevard, at regular intervals, from which were hung thousands of flags, the tricolor of France. This had the unfortunate effect of interrupting Welles's view of the street, so that it was some seconds before his eye was drawn to motion in the middle of the empty boulevard, perhaps two-thirds of the distance to Porte Maillot.

"There!" he pointed.

Georges handed him her champagne glass. She raised the binoculars that hung around her neck. He waited as she adjusted the focus.

"It is number six!" she shouted.

The crowd around them, well-lubricated by the champagne that had begun flowing at ten that morning, erupted in reaction, some cheering, others cursing their bad luck. Georges lowered the binoculars, reclaimed her glass, and slid her free arm under his.

Together, they watched the strange contraption roll towards them, moving at perhaps twice the speed of a horse and carriage.

Welles found it disconcerting. The vehicle looked for all the world as if it *were* a carriage, the kind you might take out for a ride around the Bois du Boulogne on a pleasant day. But there was no horse in sight; indeed, there was no coachman. Instead, the box at the front of the vehicle was empty, the number 6 painted on the front now plain to see. A lone passenger sat in the carriage, dressed in an outlandish get-up: A heavy leather coat and tight-fitting cap, over which he wore a pair of goggles to protect his eyes from wind and dust. He seemed unnaturally calm, given that he appeared to be trapped in an unguided and careening carriage.

Welles leaned forward over the wall as the vehicle passed below him. He could see now that the occupant held a tiller that controlled the front wheels of the vehicle. He heard the steady coughing tattoo of the combustion engine and a faint trail of blue smoke followed the carriage. It disappeared beneath the Arch as, somewhere below, a band broke out into the stirring strains of La Marseillaise. All around him people were raising their glasses to toast the victor. He turned to Georges, smiled.

"It's a new age,' she said. "From Paris to Marseilles, and back again, in ten days. A thousand miles over unpaved roads in a horseless carriage."

"It would be faster by train," he observed.

"One cannot use a train to go where there is no track. This will change the world, *cher*."

They descended to the street. There, the winning car had come to a stop at the foot of the Champs Elysees. A huge crowd milled around a cordon the *gendarmes* had formed to keep them well back from a collection of dignitaries, uniformed Army officers and journalists surrounding the car. Welles took Georges by the arm and approached a policeman, where he announced himself as a journalist and presented his card. The man permitted them to pass within the cordon. Georges went immediately to join the group of journalists surrounding the driver, Emile Mayade, while Welles examined the car.

It was one of the four cars entered in the race by Messieurs Panhard and Levassor, who had designed and built all four. The number 6 car was a four-seater carriage with a four-cylinder petrol engine mounted in a box directly over the front axle. This engine drove a shaft suspended underneath the carriage which in turn drove the rear wheels, achieving speeds of more than fifteen miles per hour. The car was steered using a tiller mounted at the front right of the carriage and several other levers were fixed to the floor there. Welles guessed that they controlled the gearbox and the brakes. He could see the brake mechanism, a simple cast iron pad that could be brought into contact with one of the solid rubber rear wheels and thus slow the car.

It was an ingenious design and had served to defeat a field of more than thirty other competitors. Indeed, by Welles's count, two dozen cars had dropped out over the course of the grueling ten-day race. Driving the number 6 car, Mayade had won seven of the ten stages of the race, including this final one, and along the way amassed the best overall time, some sixty-seven hours for the thousand-mile trip.

He looked to the winning driver, saw that Georges had engaged him in an animated conversation. He turned to peer through the Arch, back along the Grande Armee, but saw no sign of any other car approaching the finish. He took another turn around the car and had decided to join Georges when he caught sight of Esterhazy.

The Count stood among the small group of Army officers he'd seen earlier. They were talking among themselves. As he watched, one officer gestured to the car. They all turned to look. and Esterhazy saw him. The Count did not react or give any other sign of recognition, and after a moment they turned away and resumed their conversation. Welles turned his back to the group, resumed inspecting the car.

He had not met Esterhazy since their rendezvous three weeks ago at the Cheval Blanc. He'd left several notes at Barre's, requesting meetings, but Esterhazy had failed to appear at any of them and had left no note of his own. It was not the first time in their association that one of them had failed to turn up at a rendezvous. The system was an inexact one, and prone to that sort of failure; but this was the longest period without contact between them since he'd come to Paris. He had been, frankly, worried. He'd considered the possibility that Esterhazy had been arrested. The Count had said he was being followed; by a policeman, he'd thought. But there had been nothing in the papers about the arrest of an officer on the General Staff and it was not the sort of thing that could be kept quiet for long.

To make matters worse, he had received another cable from Sir Reginald, only two days after he'd put the Marchand material into the diplomatic bag.

Urgently require more on M. Where is he now? Where is he going? What is the objective of his mission? Worth any repeat any cost to know.

He had hoped each day that he would hear from Esterhazy and be able to respond to Sir Reginald. But after three weeks with no contact, he had decided he must act; so, he'd gone early yesterday morning to Esterhazy's home. He'd meant to knock on the door but once there he lost his nerve. He stood beneath a tree at the corner for a few minutes, waiting. Then he'd realized that he couldn't very well stand there, possibly for hours, waiting for Esterhazy to emerge, at least not without attracting unwanted attention; whereupon he took to walking quietly around the neighborhood, returning every few minutes to a different vantage point from which he could see the house and the street in front of it. Even this was untenable for long; someone was sure to notice him eventually.

He had been about to give it up when, from a corner just down the street from the house, he caught sight of Esterhazy in uniform, walking in the opposite direction, presumably on his way to work. He stepped into the street and was about to call out, but then turned abruptly and walked the other way. A man had emerged from a doorway below the street level of a house midway between Welles and Esterhazy. He was dressed in plain clothes, but something about his posture as he climbed the few stairs to the street, and the way he looked carefully in both directions, immediately made Welles think of a policeman, or perhaps a military man. Walking away, Welles resisted the impulse to look behind him until he reached the next corner. There he turned, using the movement to look back, but neither Esterhazy nor his shadow were in sight.

The Count had been right. He was being followed. Welles assumed Esterhazy must have confirmed the fact himself and decided to avoid Barre's shop. For his part, Welles was inclined to agree with that decision. He didn't know who was following Esterhazy, or why, but he was not one who put much store in coincidence. Perhaps it would be best to avoid putting the man at any more risk. Only, the thought came unbidden, Sir Reginald had said it was *worth any repeat any* cost. Did that leave him any choice?

He looked for Georges, saw that she had joined the group of journalists around the driver Mayade. Slowly, he began moving towards the group of officers, stopping only when he saw that Esterhazy had taken note of him. With a slight movement of his head, he beckoned the Count to follow. Then he turned and walked away, into the shade of the Arch.

The space was crowded with spectators, some watching for the appearance of the next car while others jostled for position at the several bars arranged at the base of the monument. He waited near one, just outside of the doorway to the stairwell which took one to the top of the Arch. When Esterhazy appeared, Welles waited until the Count had seen him, then withdrew into the stairway, taking a position under the first flight of stairs. A few moments later, Esterhazy joined him. Welles could see at once that the Count was angry.

"This is madness," Esterhazy said. "I am officially under suspicion. We can't be seen together."

Welles put a hand on Esterhazy's arm, shifted their positions so that he could look past the Count through the doorway.

"Officially under suspicion?" he asked. "What do you mean?"

"I told you, they've reopened the Dreyfus case," said Esterhazy. "Apparently they made a profile of the sort of officers who could have provided the material outlined in the *bordereau*. I fit the profile."

There were six officers with the necessary background, Du Paty had told him.

"Blast," he said.

Esterhazy was one of the six. It was bad luck, the sort of bad luck that might lead to catastrophe. He needed more time with the Count; but not here. Not now.

"Very well, you should go. But listen," he went on, taking him by the arm again. "Go to Barre's tomorrow. I'll leave a note there, with further instructions."

The Count looked dubious.

"And some money, of course," he added.

A moment's hesitation, then Esterhazy nodded and left without another word.

Welles held back, watching him, but he saw no one else taking note of the man. Then Esterhazy stepped out of the shade of the Arch and into the sunlight, and he lost sight of him in the glare. He waited a few minutes, then followed into the sunlight, looking for Georges, but he didn't see her among the group of journalists. A cheer went up from the crowd behind him, and he turned in time to see a second car arriving, the number 8. This was another Panhard, a six-seater, and the group of officers quickly surrounded it. Esterhazy was with them, so Welles turned away, back under the Arch. In one corner was the race board, which detailed the results from each stage of the race. A man was entering in the results for the number 8 car with a piece of chalk. Georges stood to the side of the board, a glass of champagne in hand, talking with a gentleman who had his back to Welles. She caught sight of him and waved.

"There you are, Percy," she said. "I was looking for you when I met this charming gentleman. May I present to you Sir Reginald Hull?"

"Welles, is it?" Hull asked, turning and extending a hand. "A pleasure, sir."

***

It was late when Welles knocked on the door. It was raining now, a cold rain that had somehow insinuated itself beneath his cloak. Welles was wet to the skin and shivering when Sir Reginald opened the door, and the other man ushered him in quickly, closing the door behind him. A fire had been laid in the sitting room. Welles shed the cloak and went to stand before the fire to get warm.

"Will you take brandy?" his host asked.

Welles nodded. Sir Reginald poured two glasses, brought them to the fire, offered one to Welles. They drank.

His employer was perhaps forty years old, tall and lean. When they'd first met some years before in London, Sir Reginald Hull had seemed familiar to Welles, who had tried but could not recall when he might have seen the man before. Days later it had come to him, unbidden, the memory of a painting he'd seen once in Madrid: El Greco's rendering of the apostle Paul. Sir Reginald might have been the model. He had the same thin, impossibly long fingers; the same lean, almost cadaverous face, made narrower still by his high forehead, widow's peak and the dark goatee beard he habitually wore. It was surely a result of the similarity with the painting, but even now Welles could not look at Hull without seeing in his expression a kind of religious zeal, and he often felt that Sir Reginald was devoted to making of England a church which would last forever. He was a man on a mission and had the effect of drawing others to his cause; as Welles, himself, had been drawn.

It had been a shock to find Hull conversing with Georges, though he thought he'd managed to avoid revealing to her that he already knew the man. She had explained that Sir Reginald had approached her to ask if she spoke English, as he had little French and was hoping to learn more about the race. The three of them had chatted amiably for perhaps fifteen minutes, after which Hull thanked Georges and took his leave. He offered his hand again to Welles, using the opportunity to discretely pass him a note, which Welles slipped into a pocket as the man walked away. Later, alone, he'd read the note: *Am at the Continental. Do join me for a drink in my room. Eleven tonight. R.*

"Esterhazy has broken off contact," Welles said now, without preamble.

"When?"

"Three weeks ago. He told me then that he thought he was being followed. I didn't think it likely. I put it down to nerves, but he was right."

Welles described his visit to Esterhazy's street yesterday, how he'd seen a man following the Count.

Hull considered this.

"You saw him today, though?" he asked. "Did he give you any explanation?"

"It's this Dreyfus business. They've reopened the investigation. He says he's a suspect, he and a handful of others."

"Why should Esterhazy be a suspect in the Dreyfus case?"

"Coincidence. Or bad luck. They made a profile of the suspect based on the nature of the information that had been given to the Germans. Several officers fit the profile. Esterhazy is one of them."

"I see," said Hull. He indicated Welles's glass. "Another?"

Welles nodded, and Hull went to fetch the decanter.

"When will you see him again?"

"See him?" Welles snorted. "I can't see him. I got him to agree to visit Barre's, we can use that as a drop. But he won't meet, not while the risk of exposure is so great."

Sir Reginald made a clucking noise as he filled the glasses.

"I don't understand you, Percy. We need Esterhazy, but if he won't cooperate with us, he's no further use. Surely, he must understand," he said, then paused. He began again. "Surely *you* must understand that we're in a position to do more harm to the Count than any investigation into the Dreyfus matter. We can prove he's been spying for us."

"You would threaten him with exposure?" The idea was mad, Welles thought. "If we expose him, we get nothing from him."

"Trust me, Percy, Esterhazy has an excellent instinct for survival. He won't let it come to that."

Hull put his hand on Welles's shoulder.

"Listen," he said. "This Marchand business is altogether strange. A company of men heading off into deepest Africa, armed to the teeth? Total secrecy about where they're going, or what they mean to do when they get there? It's a mystery, and I can't abide a mystery. We need Esterhazy now. If he won't cooperate, we must use what leverage we have."

"Offer him the stick, then?"

Hull laughed.

"Yes, but offer him the carrot as well. If he helps us, we'll help him in return."

"Help him?" Welles was having difficulty following Sir Reginald's lead. "How do we help him?"

"Help him with this Dreyfus business."

Hull's grip on his shoulder was suddenly tighter. He was not smiling now.

"It should not come as a surprise to you that I know you are the author of the Count's present predicament. You, and your, ah —" Hull paused as if searching for the right word. "Your *associate*, Mademoiselle Seigneur. Your fanciful tales of escape on the high seas."

Welles looked away. He said nothing, but he knew the guilt on his face was plain to see. Hull released his shoulder.

"Sit down, Percy," he said, gesturing to a pair of chairs drawn up before the hearth.

Chastened, Welles sat.

"Ordinarily I would be pleased that you pursue your other occupation with such enthusiasm, Percy, as it makes for excellent cover. And, having met the lady, I quite understand her charms. Still, I might have hoped that you would take more care in your choice of subjects. Surely it must have occurred to you that it would not do for you — of all people — to associate yourself with the most notorious spy scandal of the decade?"

He paused, making it plain he expected an answer.

"It did occur to me."

"Then why did you do it? Reading your work from London, you seemed determined to raise a fuss about Dreyfus, get the case reopened. I suppose you must be one of those who think he is innocent? A scapegoat? A persecuted Jew?"

"No," said Welles, "there's every reason to think him guilty."

"Every reason? What do you mean?"

Welles sighed, seeing no alternative.

"I've seen a summary of the evidence against him," he said. "The secret dossier. I asked Esterhazy for it."

He went on to explain what Esterhazy had found. When he finished, Sir Reginald nodded.

"Yes, I'd say they have the right man," he said. Then: "But I wonder, Percy, if *you're* the right man for this job. You lied to Esterhazy, put him at risk over something we don't care about. I don't mind the lie so much, we trade in lies, but to risk our agent for your own private reasons? You were lucky he wasn't caught. Not that it matters, because now that you've forced the French to reopen the investigation, we've lost him anyway."

"How could I predict they would suspect Esterhazy?" Welles protested.

Then he saw the expression on Hull's face.

"It was a mistake to get involved in the matter," he continued quickly. "I see that now. I tried to avoid it, I could see the danger, but Georges..." He could not finish the sentence. "Things got out of control," he said.

"Yes, that's all very well," said Hull. "But what do you intend to do now to fix this problem?"

"Fix it?"

"You've put our man under suspicion. You say that was a mistake. Fine, we all make mistakes. Now clear him. Take the suspicion away, I don't care how you do it."

This extraordinary suggestion hung in the air between them. Welles tried to think of a response, failed. He waited, hoping that Hull would say more, but the man simply looked at him, waiting for an answer.

"Can't we just wait for this to blow over?" Welles asked. "Dreyfus is guilty, anyone can see that from the evidence. They'll review the case and, in a few weeks, decide they were right all along."

A look of exasperation came to Sir Reginald's face, and he leaned forward in his chair.

"No, Percy, we can't wait, don't you see that? Africa is ours, Her Majesty's. Yes, I know the French like to disagree and that bloody King Leopold thinks it's his personal possession, but it is ours. Egypt in the north? Ours. Kitchener has marched for Khartoum; he'll send the bloody Khalifa packing and take the Sudan back. That's the whole Nile basin, what matters in the north. Ours, Percy. In the south, the Cape Colony and the British concessions in in the region, ours. In between, Kenya and Uganda, ours. A line of British possessions, from the north to the south, cutting the continent in half. Kitchener is building a railroad behind him as he goes. Ostensibly to secure his supply lines, but when his campaign ends, the railroad will still be there. There to be extended, a railroad from Cairo to Cape Town, the whole length of the continent. Then we'll drive them all out: the French, the Germans, the Belgians. Even the bloody Portuguese. Or maybe we'll be nice and leave them a few crumbs."

"Yes, I understand," said Welles.

"Good. You see, then, why this is important? Why we can't wait? The French can read a map and they know what we're about. They don't like it one damned bit. I'd have said there's nothing they can do about it, but then you send me word of this Marchand fellow. I want to know where he's going and what he plans to do when he gets there. I need Esterhazy to find that out for me. And I need you to squeeze him until he does."

Hull regarded Welles with calculation.

"So, if you're not the right man for the job, Percy, tell me now. I hope you are. I don't want to find someone else. I don't have the bloody time to find someone else. But I can't go on with you, not if you aren't up to it."

He placed a hand on Welles's knee.

"Understand me, man," he said. "I don't even care if Esterhazy is caught out, so long as he's caught out after he's told us what we need to know. That's the business, Percy. We do what we must for Queen and country. You should understand that by now."

"I do understand it," Welles said.

"Good. It's a hard business, I know, and some men don't have the stomach for it. Do you? Are you in, or out?"

Welles understood now that his post was on the line. Not just his post; if Hull were to discharge him, he would not be able to afford to continue the wire service. He might not even be able to stay in Paris.

"I'm in," he said.

He felt a rush of adrenaline, was suddenly dizzy. He took a deep breath to clear his head.

"Only, I don't see what we can do to clear Esterhazy. Or to speed up the review, which amounts to the same thing."

Hull released Welles's knee, sat back in his chair.

"As for that," he said, "I have an idea. Tell me again about those letters Dreyfus receives. The ones with the secret messages."

Chapter 16

The Journal of Lieutenant Andre Durand

Saturday, 29 August 1896
Mayombe
French Congo

We arrived in Mayombe at mid-day today after more than a week raiding among the Loangan villages. It has been hard work, and I was pleased to see the stockade of the outpost on the hill above the village, the tricolor flying high above this bend in the Kouilou river. When we reached the village, I left Dialike to get on with the job and went in search of the district administrator. I could not find him, so I settled for a beaten copper tub I found in the supply tent and gave myself a bath, washing the dust and grime and the smell of smoke from my tired body.

Paké-Bô has sent me north overland to the river and obliged me to move along it, burning the crops and stores in each village as we went. I confess I was surprised by these instructions, but he assured me it was necessary. He meant to drive the villagers to the coast, where out of need they would be forced to become bearers in exchange for food. Burning the crops would also deny the rebels the supplies they needed, and they would be forced to fall back further into the bush before us. Thus, we weaken them and enlarge our own territory at the expense of theirs.

Dialike and I have two squads of tirailleurs. Paké-Bô has taken the rest of the men and marched east from Loango, following the supply trail to

Loudima, a village not quite halfway to Brazzaville. Mangin is marching from Brazzaville, moving west from Brazzaville as Paké-Bô moves east. I am to follow the Kouilou to the northeast, perhaps one hundred miles from the sea; from there I will bear southeast and make for a rendezvous with Paké-Bô at Loudima. The three of us will drive the rebels before us, until they are trapped between us. The Captain also hopes that, by following the river, I may find some word of Baratier and his men.

From my tub I saw the fires starting in the fields below the stockade and the wind carried to me the smell of smoke and the lamentations of the villagers. I tried to duck my head below the water, but the tub was too small, and I think I must only have looked ridiculous.

Before long the district administrator arrived, stood before my tub as if he had encountered me at my desk and began to harangue me. I was sympathetic — this was his outpost and his village — but my orders left no room for such charity and in truth the efforts of the last ten days left me little patience with the man, who reminded me of the kind of officious self-important mayor you might find in a rural town; which he probably had been, before coming to Africa. I tried to call him to order but found it difficult to do while crouching nude in a copper tub of dirty water; so, I gathered my courage, stood at attention and bellowed at the man until he quieted; whereupon he offered me a towel. I cannot say whether it was his dignity he meant to restore or mine, but I was glad of the towel.

Having thus made my introduction, I acquainted the fellow with the exigencies of our current situation while I dressed. From my satchel I produced a copy of de Brazza's order proclaiming martial law, and another order signed by Paké-Bô, charging all officials of the colonial administration to cooperate fully with the Army. I told him he should prepare to receive refugees from the villages we'd passed through, organize them into groups and march them to the depot at Loango.

He objected, of course; he had a few assistants, but no soldiers and hardly any weapons. I told him that he and his assistants were henceforth soldiers for the duration of the emergency and that I would provide him with weapons, enough food to get the villagers to the coast and a few of my men to go along with them.

I confess he took it well. Perhaps I had misjudged him. Later he produced a bottle of decent brandy and we shared it under a rare thing, a wondrous clear African night sky. Between that and the bath, I felt wholly restored; and I was further cheered by the news that Baratier had passed along the river at least five weeks before, heading upstream, the little steamboat making good time against the flow of the river.

<u>*Thursday, 3 September 1896*</u>
<u>*Kitaba*</u>
<u>*French Congo*</u>

The Soyo Princess is here. The weather has been dry and there are stretches of river between Mayombe and Kitaba that are no more than a few feet deep. I do not know how Baratier managed to get the steamboat this far. Somehow, he did, but no further. The district administrator tells me that she ran aground here perhaps four weeks ago. The rocks ripped open her bottom and that was the end of her journey. Baratier hired men from the village to help unload her, transferring the cargo into the boats he'd brought. He persuaded a few of the villagers to go with him, then set of again, dragging the boats through the river behind them.

It may be that we will encounter him when we rendezvous with Paké-Bô at Loudima. Certainly, the joke will be on us if he should arrive there before we do, for the river is passable from there all the way to Kimbedi, within a hundred miles of the Pool and Brazzaville. It will mean that his gamble was perhaps the sensible choice after all.

I found no copper tub here and have had to make do with bathing in the river, as Dialike and his men do. They were like boys at play when I found them, jumping and cavorting and making a joyous cacophony at the sheer pleasure of the cool, clean water. But when I removed my own clothes and waded into the river to join them, they became silent, even sullen. I realized that I had crossed a barrier invisible to me yet quite clear to them. Was it the color of my skin, I wonder, or merely the fact that I am an officer? I cannot say; but in any case, I made short work of my bath, then retired to leave them to their own.

These tirailleurs occupy a strange state of in-betweenness, where to the Africans of the Congo they are French, while to Frenchmen they remain Africans. For my part I find that, as soldiers, they are the equal of any French poilu, and in the time I have spent with them — on board the

Thibet, at the depot and on this march — I have found nothing about them which sets them apart from the white man save the color of their skin, and the fact that nearly all of them are Mohammedans. Though even in this they seem people to be admired, for the attention with which they approach their devotions would be an example to many a French country parish priest.

If there is one thing in them that I can find to criticize, it is the manner they adopt with the people of the Congo, who they quite obviously view with disdain and treat with a cruelty I find wholly unnecessary. I have spoken to Dialike about this, but we do not agree.

'They must fear us,' he said. 'Soon we will be alone with them in the wilderness, Monsieur. There will be ten of them for every one of us. How then will we control them?'

'We shall be armed,' I said, 'and they shall not.'

'Should they ever gather the courage to resist,' he explained patiently 'our guns will not protect us against such numbers. They will kill us in our sleep; or, if the rebels should attack our column, when we are thus occupied? Then they will kill us. Only their fear keeps them in our grip, Monsieur.'

He is an experienced soldier and wise in the ways of the dark continent. It may be that his view is a sound one. Still, I am troubled by it.

We will leave tomorrow after we have sent the villagers on their way to Loango under guard. We will abandon the river — I shall miss it! — and strike east through the bush, making for our rendezvous at Loudima. Somewhere between here and there we are likely to encounter the rebels. I hope that we do; we have not had anything like a fight on our march, having only to burn out and round up defenseless villagers and I am coming to believe it is bad for soldiers to spend too long doing such things. I feel it erodes their discipline and their sense of honor. For my part, I find no joy in it and long for a clean fight against a worthy foe, where dignity is restored to all, even the vanquished.

<u>Wednesday, 9 September 1896</u>
<u>French Congo</u>

The rebels struck us early this morning. They chose their moment well,
two hours before dawn, when our sentries were the least alert and the
night at its darkest. The attackers were armed with assegais, a kind of
short lance with a long, broad blade at the tip, suitable for throwing or for
stabbing at close quarters. It is a silent weapon and they killed two of our
pickets and wounded a third before he sounded the alarm.

Dialike woke instantly at the cry and — without waiting for my orders
— took command of our defense. We were well-bivouacked; he had chosen
a bit of high ground, made strong points of our baggage, and placed our
fires at the perimeter rather than the center, so that we could see them as
they charged the camp, while they could not easily see us. Now he barked
orders at the men, sending them to take up positions behind our bulwarks
of supplies and directing their fire at the attackers. I joined him, my pistol
drawn. I meant to stand with him, but instead he offered me his rifle and
pointed to a pile of crates behind which two of our tirailleurs crouched.

'If you please, Monsieur,' he said, 'you will join those men there. That
is where you are needed.'

I hesitated, then took the rifle, handed him my pistol and ran to the
position he had indicated.

The two soldiers were startled when I flopped down beside them —
even more so when they saw who it was who had joined them — and they
were momentarily paralyzed, staring at me open-mouthed and paying no
attention to anything else; and it was at this moment that the rebels by
chance chose to rush the camp in an attempt to overwhelm our defenses.
Of the three of us, only I saw them coming, the picket fires illuminating
the steel of their spearheads and reflecting red off the sweat of their black
bodies. Without thinking, I stood, raised my rifle to my shoulder, and
fired, working the bolt as quickly as I could.

Everything was happening at a kind of distance, and slowly, without a
sound. My first shot seemed to have no effect at all and if I had not felt the
recoil, I would have thought the rifle had misfired. I fired again and then a
third time, then saw one go down, but still they came. One savage cast his
spear, his arm moving slowly forward in a graceful arc, so I worked the

bolt again and squeezed the trigger, only this time the rifle didn't buck against my shoulder. I had fired my three shots and the chamber was empty. Still I stood there like a fool, watching the spear come towards me, moving through the air at an impossibly slow speed, or so it seemed. Somehow, it did not occur to me to move.

Something hit me hard between the shoulder blades, knocked me off balance and the spear flashed past just above my head.

'You must reload, Monsieur,' Dialike said, as he raised my revolver and squeezed the trigger.

He fired six shots, slowly and deliberately, emptying the cylinder, then crouched beside me behind the baggage and began to reload. Belatedly, I scrabbled in the dirt, searching for another clip of ammunition for the rifle. My two comrades had regained their senses and were firing at the approaching savages, shouting hoarsely as they did. Then it was silent, save for the ringing in my ears. They had run out of ammunition themselves and needed to reload. My fingers finally found the bag of ammunition clips and I grabbed one, forced it into the open chamber and worked the bolt. Dialike rose to look for more targets and I followed suit, rifle to my shoulder, but there was nothing more to do. The enemy had fled.

We counted eleven Basundi dead and four others badly wounded. Dialike examined one of the wounded and then, quite casually, shot him in the head with my revolver. Then he shot the other three. That done, he reloaded the pistol and returned it to me.

'Thank you, Monsieur,' he said, with the slightest of bows, then went to organize the men in the event of another attack.

With nothing else to do, I tended to our own wounded man. He had been on picket when the attack came and was slashed badly before he managed to parry the spear with his rifle and drive his bayonet into his assailant. He had a deep cut down one arm, bleeding badly and likely to fester. I cleaned it as well as I could, and then bound it in clean linen, tightly enough, I hoped, to stop the bleeding. Later, I saw him join the other men when the sun came up. As was their custom, they washed their hands and faces, then each man laid a small rug on the ground, knelt on it, and together they began to pray, bowing and rising as they spoke the *same words. Dialike has told me what the words mean: 'God is great. There is no god but God.'*

When they had completed their devotions, we buried our dead. The two men were washed, then wrapped in clean white muslin taken from our stores and lowered into the ground. More prayers were said. The Basundi dead we heaped into a pile, then set it alight. While the men packed their things, Dialike approached me.

'I am sorry that I knocked you down, Monsieur,' he said.

He had done more: he had usurped my command, treating me as he might any of his men. But he did not seem sorry. His eyes betrayed that he knew he had done well. I thought that perhaps he was testing me, anxious to see what kind of officer I would be. I told him the truth, that he had saved my life, if not that of every man in the column. I had examined the bodies and knew that his six shots from my revolver had been true; that each had claimed a life. He had surely broken the assault.

'You are a good man, corporal,' I said. 'You should be proud.'

'Thank you, Monsieur,' he said.

He paused a moment, as if considering something.

'You must be more careful, Monsieur,' he said, shaking his head, but with a hint of a smile. 'Allah surely loves you, but He is not infinitely patient with those who test His love.'

At this I laughed and clasped his shoulder as I would that of a friend. I feel we are bound together now, brothers in arms, the distinctions of color and faith rendered meaningless in the roar of gunfire and the stink of gunpowder.

Chapter 17

Paris, October 1896

There was a knock at the door. Welles slipped the latch, opened the door slightly and looked through the gap. He stood well back so as not to be visible from the front of shop. Monsieur Barre glared back at him, his annoyance plain on his face, and without a word shifted his eyes to indicate the figure standing behind him. Welles nodded and Barre stood aside, ushered Esterhazy into the room, then closed the door behind them, leaving the two men in Barre's fitting room.

"Thank you for coming," Welles said. "Please, do sit down."

He indicated one of the chairs, but the Count made no move to sit.

"What is the meaning of this, Percy?" he said. "You asked me to come to pick up instructions. I've come, but I can't stay long. Give me the envelope and let me go."

"I have instructions for you," said Welles. "And your money, but we need to talk first. Will you not sit?"

Receiving no reply, Welles shrugged, pulled a chair away from the wall, then sat.

"You will understand that you have placed yourself in our hands," he said. "We are in a position to do you much harm. Many of the things you've given us — things you sold to us — are written in your own hand. I have only to take a representative sample, put them in my briefcase and call on the appropriate authorities. Perhaps this new fellow Picquart would be interested?"

Esterhazy smiled, a nervous smile.

"Who is this talking, Percy?" he asked. "It doesn't sound like you. Some fellow from London put you up to it?" He shook his head. "You need me. You need what I can get for you. Just have patience. This will all blow over and we'll be back in business. If you turn me in now, you'll get nothing. We both know that."

"Indeed," agreed Welles. "But we're not getting anything now, are we? And there is no prospect of anything soon. In light of that, some people are suggesting that we might as well be done with you and save ourselves the money."

Esterhazy was silent for a long moment. Then: "Very well, Percy, I take your point."

The Count pulled the other chair away from the wall, arranged it opposite Welles's chair, sat. He took his cigarette case from his jacket, extracted a cigarette, put the case way without offering one to Welles. He lit it, waved the match to extinguish it, dropped it on the wood floor. He crossed one leg over the other, as if getting comfortable, and leaned back.

"*Nous voila!*" he said. "What shall we talk about? I think it will rain today. Do you think so, old boy?"

"Let's talk about the letters," said Welles. "The letters to Dreyfus. The ones with the secret messages."

Esterhazy's face registered mild surprise.

"What about them?" he asked, warily.

"You said your men opened his mail. Do you still have access to it?"

The Count drew on his cigarette, fixing Welles with a calculating look as he considered the question.

"Yes," he said at last. "I have not been relieved of my duties. Not yet, at any rate."

"Both the letters he receives, and those he sends?"

"Yes."

"Very well," said Welles. "I need a letter, one he has written, but which has not been sent on for delivery yet. Can you get one for me?"

"You want me to copy a letter?"

"No, not a copy. I need the original. Can you get it?"

The Count uncrossed his legs, leaned forward, his elbows on his knees.

"What's this about, Percy?" he asked.

Now it was Welles's turn to reach for his cigarette case. He took his time selecting a cigarette, then pointedly offered the case. Esterhazy ignored it, so he shrugged, put the case away.

"If you're of a mind to help us, then of course we'd like to help you," Welles said, pausing to light the cigarette. "Do what we can to end this enquiry. Quickly, if possible."

"If I get you a letter from Dreyfus," asked Esterhazy, "you can put an end to the enquiry? How?"

"Let me worry about how. Can you get one?"

Esterhazy stared at Welles a moment longer. Then he leaned back in the chair, crossed his legs again.

"I think so," he said. "He writes often enough. To his wife, his brother. A few others. Which do you want?"

"Ideally no one of prominence. Best if it is an acquaintance, better still a foreigner. But I need it quickly. Now, if possible. So, if there's nothing else, his wife or brother will have to do."

"All right, Percy," said Esterhazy. "I'll get you your letter. I'll bring it to you here?"

Welles nodded.

"Very well," Esterhazy continued. "Is there anything else?"

"Yes," said Welles. "I'll need you to put the letter back again, when I'm finished with it. When you leave this room, speak to Monsieur Barre. Place an order with him. A new dinner jacket, or a uniform, something that will require multiple visits. Have him put it on your account but tell him I'll pay. Come back the day after tomorrow for a fitting and bring the letter. I'll have more instructions at that time."

He took an envelope from his pocket, held it out to Esterhazy. The Count hesitated, then came to a decision.

"As you say, Percy," he said, taking the envelope.

***

The cab dropped Welles in the Place de Clichy. There was no rain, but the night air was cold and damp, and halos formed around the gas lamps along either side of the street. He turned up the collar of his coat and walked northeast, then east. Ten minutes' brisk walking brought him to a spot across the street from the nightclub, instantly recognizable by the bright red windmill perched incongruously between two six-story empire blocks. Cabs arrived in a constant procession, stopping in front of the doors beneath the gas-lit letters that spelled out the name and disgorging more passengers into a growing throng of men in evening attire who seemed to be waiting for the doors to open. He crossed the street, lost himself in the crowd, then worked his way through to emerge at the east edge. He continued his brisk walk along Boulevard de Clichy, counting the streets to his left as he went. When he reached what he thought must be the right one, he turned into it, then ducked into the shadows of the near wall and waited.

No one followed him around the corner into the alley. After five minutes he struck a match and peered at the name, just above eye level on the opposite wall: Cite du Midi. He blew out the match and walked quickly but quietly down the narrow, cobbled lane, finding his way by the faint light emanating from cracks around doorways or poorly covered windows. The end of the alley was in sight, a wall of brick unbroken by door or window, when he stopped in front of a particular door on the left; one marked by a sign hanging from a metal bracket protruding into the lane: *Antiquities et objets d'art, M. Leeman.* A pull-cord hung from the wall beside the door, and he tugged on it once.

A bell rang somewhere behind the door. After a moment the door was unlocked, and it opened a few inches. Through the narrow gap, a short man with a pinched face regarded him without enthusiasm.

"*Ferme*, Monsieur," he said, and began to close the door. Welles stuck his foot in the gap.

"Basil sent me," he said, feeling rather foolish as he said it.

To his surprise, however, the words had the desired effect. The man took another look at him, then nodded and opened the door wide enough for him to squeeze past into the shop. To Welles it looked like nothing so much as a pawn shop, dusty wood and glass cases filled with the detritus of broken lives. He looked in one case; it held a variety of cheap pocket watches. Behind him, the proprietor cleared his throat.

"English?" the man asked.

"Yes, English."

"And how is Basil?"

"Very well. He says to tell you the glass eye was just the right shade of green," he said, repeating the words Sir Reginald had told him to use.

The man nodded, executed a perfunctory bow.

"I am Leeman, Monsieur. And you are?"

"Smith. Charles Smith."

Leeman smiled at the absurdity of the name. "And how may I be of service to you, Monsieur Smith?"

"I am here about a document."

"I have many documents here, of every conceivable type. Can you be more specific?"

"Of course," said Welles. "But you don't have the document I'm interested in. The document I want doesn't yet exist."

"I see." The man gestured to a doorway behind the counter. "Would you care to sit, Monsieur Smith? Through here, please. Perhaps a little wine?"

Welles preceded him through the doorway into a small room, shabbily furnished with a sideboard, table and chairs. He sat. The man poured wine from an earthen jug, then sat across from him.

"Tell me more about this document, Monsieur."

"Yes, certainly. Only, first, what can you tell me about invisible ink?"

"Invisible ink? A fascinating subject."

Welles listened while the little man explained the basics of invisible inks: how different substances produced invisible writing that could be made visible in different ways. Some could be read by applying heat, while others became visible when treated with a solution, much like developing a photograph.

"The ideal invisible ink is characterized by a few attributes," he said. "The ink itself is easy to produce, or commonly at hand. When dry, it leaves little residue, so it does not mar the paper on which it has been written. And the message can be easily developed, again by means readily to hand, rather than complicated chemical compounds."

"What sort of commonplace things make a good invisible ink?"

"Oh, many things, sir. A solution of ordinary sugar will work, or of lemon juice, or the juice of other fruits. Milk. Even soap, diluted in water. And — forgive me, Monsieur — bodily fluids."

"Bodily fluids?"

"Oh, yes. Saliva will work. Or blood, in a very thin solution. And urine, again diluted in water."

"Urine?" said Welles. "You can write an invisible message with urine?"

"Indeed, Monsieur. I should say it is not ideal. There is the odor, of course, and that it forms crystals when it dries, which can be detected on the paper. And if it is an overly strong solution, it can damage the paper. For these reasons, it must be diluted to a very thin solution, else the presence of some foreign substance will be obvious to even routine inspection. A proper solution will be detectable only by close examination; though to be sure, once developed the message will be quite faint."

"How is it developed?"

"By heating the document. Permitting it to rest on the hearth for a few minutes should do it, though you must take care that the paper doesn't catch fire. Or you can press it with an iron. In a pinch, you can hold it over a candle, moving it along slowly as the message appears; though I wouldn't recommend that method if the message is particularly important."

"You have experience with making and writing messages in invisible ink of this sort?"

Leeman adopted an expression of smug satisfaction.

"Indeed, Monsieur, it is one of my meager skills."

Welles took a sip of the wine; it was strong but quite bad, sour and perhaps improperly stored. Nevertheless, he smiled appreciatively and replaced his glass on the table.

"I should like you to write a message for me in invisible ink made from urine. I will supply the text of the message, and the document on which to inscribe it."

"Easily done, Monsieur."

"The document will be a letter, written in a particular hand," said Welles. "Can you write the invisible message in that same hand?"

"It is tricky, Monsieur. One cannot see very clearly what one is writing, so it is best to write in a simple manner. But, accounting for that, it will be close enough. When do you need this done?"

"I will bring the letter soon, perhaps as soon as two or three days. How long will you need?"

"A day, sir, no more. It requires skill but, once mastered, it is a simple matter. And the urine? Will you bring that, too?"

"I'll leave that to you, Monsieur Leeman. Shall we discuss the fee?"

Chapter 18

London, 12 August 1898

Lawrence interrupted him.

"I think I see it," he said. "But perhaps you should explain what you meant to do."

"The idea was simple," said Welles. "Esterhazy was under suspicion. This suspicion stemmed from the notion that Dreyfus might not be guilty after all, a notion Georges and I had helped to create in the minds of the authorities. As Sir Reginald said, I caused this problem, and I should be the one to solve it."

"How did you mean to solve it?" asked Salisbury.

"I knew Dreyfus was guilty. I'd seen the summary of the secret dossier. But somehow, that wasn't enough for this new man at counter-intelligence, Major Picquart. Something more was needed, something which would serve to quickly convince the major that he was guilty. Sir Reginald and I discussed the letters that had been sent to Dreyfus by his unknown accomplice, the ones with the hidden messages. It was I who suggested that we forge one — like those others — and send it to Dreyfus."

"And Sir Reginald agreed?" asked Lawrence.

"No. Dreyfus had already received several such letters, and Major Picquart would surely know that. If the major had not been convinced by those letters, why would one more change his mind? No, it would not do, Sir Reginald said; but something along those lines might."

"He suggested not a letter to Dreyfus," said Lawrence, "but a reply from Dreyfus."

"Yes. He supposed that the other letters were not convincing because, despite close inspection, they had never detected any sign of a reply in any letter sent by Dreyfus. It was not therefore a correspondence between two parties, but instead done entirely at the volition of one party, someone whose motivations could not be known."

"But a letter from Dreyfus, with a secret message? That would make it a correspondence," said Salisbury.

"Indeed, sir, this was Sir Reginald's idea, and the basis of his instruction to me. I was to obtain from Esterhazy a letter recently written by Dreyfus but not yet delivered, add a secret message to it, and have Esterhazy reintroduce it into the man's correspondence. Then it would only be necessary for him to feign discovery of the message while inspecting Dreyfus's mail and hand it over to the counter-intelligence bureau."

"What was the content of this message?"

"It was purposefully vague yet damning. It directed the recipient to recover the contents of a deposit box from a bank in Berne, which would be of some importance — according to the note — to certain friends in Berlin. Neither the specific bank nor the deposit box number were indicated; the implication was that they had been communicated in a previous message."

"And the recipient?" This from Lawrence.

"We were in luck there. By chance, Dreyfus had obligingly written a letter to a distant relation who lived in Strasbourg. If not for that, we would have used a letter to Mathieu."

"Yes, that was most fortunate."

"Fortunate?" Bingham's face was a deep red beneath his beard, and his hand shook when he pointed a finger at Welles. "What kind of man are you, Welles, to do such a thing?"

"Nonsense," said Lawrence. "It was cleverly done. Clever of Sir Reginald to conceive it, and clever of Welles to carry it off so well."

Bingham sprang to his feet.

"Sir," he said stiffly, addressing himself to the Prime Minister, "I find it impossible to believe that this is the behavior of servants of Her Majesty's government, nor would I have imagined that two such gentlemen as these were in your employ."

Salisbury opened his mouth to respond, but Welles spoke first.

"I quite agree, Mister Bingham. I would not have credited it either; not, that is, until I found myself one of them. You might be surprised to learn what someone will do, under the right circumstances."

"We're not children playing at games," said Lawrence. "I say it was well done, for it served our purpose with no harm to anyone else. Or, if you insist, no harm to anyone other than Dreyfus; a condemned spy, a traitor to his country. What reason have we to worry about harm to the likes of him?"

Bingham was not persuaded. "Forgive me, sir, but I must retire. I find I have no further appetite for this tale."

Welles pointed the gun at him. "Sit down, Mister Bingham, please."

Bingham glared at him. For a moment, Welles thought he might refuse. But Bingham eyed the gun, thought better of it. Reluctantly, he lowered himself into his chair.

"I regret that you don't like my story," Welles continued, "and if it is any consolation, I don't like it very much myself. But — and I ask you to trust me on this, sir — I think you must hear it; and, when I am finished, I believe you will be glad you did."

"I hope that I will be glad as well," said Salisbury. "Thus far, I find it tawdry and tedious, with little of interest to me, certainly not enough to compensate me for the ordeal of listening to it."

"I am sorry to hear it. Nevertheless, I must go on. I trust that you, like Mister Bingham, will soon find something of value in it."

Chapter 19

The Journal of Lieutenant Andre Durand

<u>Monday, 28 September 1896</u>
<u>Loudima</u>
<u>French Congo</u>

We arrived in Loudima yesterday to find that Paké-Bô was already here. He has been very ill, a recurrence of malaria. He was taken by the fever a week ago and had to be carried here to Loudima. Nonetheless, he sent for me this morning, as soon as he had word of our arrival. I found him at work, reading dispatches and making notes, weak but in good spirits. He was half-lying on a cot, his back propped up with cushions, a wooden tray on his lap serving as a desk. He shifted the tray as if he meant to stand to greet me, but it was beyond him and he gave me a rueful smile as he lay back on the pillows.

'Dédé,' he said, 'how good to see you.'

He bade me to sit, and I perched on a small wooden box which had been left beside his cot for the purpose. He asked me about the march, and I gave him my report.

Since the engagement with the Basundi, we had encountered three more villages. At each one, as before, we burned the crops and the stored grain, then organized the villagers into a column and sent them to the coast under a light guard. It was disheartening work, made more so by a kind of brooding tension among the men. The attack on our camp had inflamed their nerves, and although there had been no further attacks, it was in our minds that there might be at any moment; so that we were constantly on our guard. We slept poorly and the men bickered among themselves over petty offenses; and they were even more rough with the villagers we encountered than they had been before.

All this I told to Paké-Bô. In truth, it never occurred to me to keep my thoughts from him. Still, I was gratified to see the look of understanding and compassion on his face.

'Yes, it is cruel, Dédé,' he said. 'But it is also necessary. Were it not for these rebellious chiefs, we would move quickly, with a light touch as we go, in the way that we planned. But that is not to be. I mean to put down this rebellion quickly so that we can get to Brazzaville and start our mission in earnest.'

His face lit up, and he smiled.

'Ah, Brazzaville, of course, Dédé, you will not have heard. We have word that Baratier is there, with most of his men and all the supplies.'

'Incredible!' I said. 'How did he manage it?'

He laughed. 'It seems they dragged their boats all the way here to Loudima; sometimes over water, but even then, hardly more than a trickle. From here the Niari deepens, so they made better time to Kimbedi, where the river bends again to the north, in the wrong direction. But in Kimbedi he was able to hire bearers at last, and in a week the march was done.'

I realized that Baratier had therefore carried nearly a third of our supplies to Brazzaville in a little over two months, without fighting his way there or making beggars of the villagers he found along the way. I said as much to Paké-Bô, whereupon he shook his head.

'No, Dédé. We could not have known he would succeed. It is the kind of trick only Baratier can do, after all, and then usually only once. Besides, it is not only our supplies that sit on the beach; they sit alongside everything intended for Brazzaville, and for the rest of the colony. Nothing has moved for months and the situation at many of our stations by now may be quite dire. We have taken on ourselves the responsibility of reopening the portage trail, of seeing that everything can be delivered. That is our duty now. We must put down this revolt and, when we have, we will need an army of bearers to clear the beach.'

I saw that he was right. With the best will in the world we could not move that much cargo along Baratier's dry riverbed. The subject was closed, and we moved on to other things. *Mangin was due any day, he said, returning with his men from Brazzaville.*

'When he is here, Dédé, we will make a plan to finish the rebellion.'

<u>Wednesday, 30 September 1896</u>
<u>Loudima</u>
<u>French Congo</u>

Today we held a council of war: Paké-Bô, Mangin and me. Already the Captain seems stronger. He asked Mangin to give a briefing. According to Mangin, the Basundi rebellion is led by the chieftain priest Nganga, who is aided in his efforts by four lieutenants: His son Nkinke, and three others, being Missitou, Mayoke, and Tensi. The rebellion is mainly among the Basundi, though the Bakonga people east of Kimbedi have recently joined them.

'But we need have no worry about the Bakonga,' Mangin said. 'I dealt with them harshly on my march from Brazzaville to Kimbedi. If we eliminate the Basundi leaders, the Bakonga will not fight.'

He pointed to the map, indicating the line of the Niari river between Loudima and Kimbedi.

'All of the leaders of the rebellion are now somewhere along here, between us and Kimbedi.'

'We must destroy the leadership to end the rebellion,' Paké-Bô told us. He addressed himself to Mangin: 'Charles, you will march from here to Kimbedi, flush them from their hiding places, and take them.' Then he turned to me. 'Dédé, you will go with him. Baratier will bring his force from Brazzaville to Kimbedi to prevent their escape to the east. They will be trapped between you.'

Mangin and I made our plans. Mangin will take one detachment and move eastward along the north bank of the Niari, while I will advance with another on the opposite bank, taking care to remain in communication with his force so that we may coordinate our movements. Dialike will march with me. We depart tomorrow.

When we were agreed, Paké-Bô shook hands first with Mangin, then with me.

'I will join you in a few days,' he said, 'and bring the rest of the men. We will put an end to this foolish revolt. Only then can we proceed with our mission, to the greater glory of France.'

<u>Tuesday, 6 October 1896</u>
<u>French Congo</u>

As I write this, we are encamped for the night a mile from our latest victims, and the stench of the fire is still in my nostrils. We now burn even the villages we find along our line of march. Not only the crops, but the huts, the livestock pens; everything we find. Inevitably there is resistance and some people have been hurt; a few even were killed. Mangin says this is necessary, to deny the rebels their base of supply and the support of the people. I understand the logic, but I am troubled at the misery we leave in our wake.

None of this is how I thought it would be. I recall the strategy Marchand related to me, many months ago in Paris when he first asked me to join his expedition. He told me his plans and I confess I did not understand. How could so few men hope to achieve what they were sent to do? I had read the accounts of other explorers of the dark continent and had formed the impression from them that moving through equatorial Africa was something only to be undertaken by an army; that one must be prepared to fight one's way.

When I told him then of my misgivings, Paké-Bô had smiled a sad smile.

'Such men have learned the wrong lessons,' he said. 'They believe it is the resistance of the natives that creates the need for a host. I disagree; it is the presence of the host that creates the resistance of the natives. If we were a thousand men — or ten thousand — we would be like a ponderous beast, eating everything in sight, and destroying the very ground upon which we marched; and every man's hand would be turned against us. But if we are a hundred, or a hundred and fifty, with the river as our bearer, we may pass without notice.'

He had spoken with confidence, and at the time his words made sense. Yet, here we are, embroiled in the very war we meant to avoid. This was not the quick, quiet movement through the wilderness we had planned, undertaken with care to avoid antagonizing the local people. Had Paké-Bô been wrong? Or was it only our misfortune that the Basundi had chosen this moment to launch a rebellion against the presence of the white man? Does it matter which is the case? For already it is October and we have not made three hundred miles of progress. Indeed, we are hardly any closer to our goal than we were three months ago.

<u>Thursday, 17 October 1896</u>
<u>French Congo</u>

We shot the rebel leaders Missitou and Mayoke this morning. There was no glory in it. We bound the two men to a tree. Corporal Dialike formed up the squad ten paces away. I gave an order and the men took aim. I gave another order and they fired. The crowd of villagers who stood watching made a sound, a kind of low moaning. Dialike walked to the tree to examine the bodies. He was not satisfied and asked for my revolver. I gave it to him, whereupon he fired a single shot into each man's head. At this, the villagers fell silent. Dialike returned my pistol, then he and the men dragged the bodies away to be burned. I went in search of Mangin to report that I had done my duty.

We had encountered the two men three days ago, moving with a large force along the north bank of the river. Our scouts detected the rebels before they knew we were there, so Mangin quickly organized an ambush along their path. At first the rebels stood their ground and returned fire, but the force of Mangin's arms — and the two machine guns he had deployed — routed them. They fled across the river, where I had laid a second ambush.

We killed many of them, took some prisoners and from these we learned they had been led by Missitou and Mayoke. Neither man was among the dead. In the confusion, they had managed to slip away. We found their trail and tracked them for the rest of the day and through the night. In the morning we came to this village alongside the river.

We searched the village, going from hut to hut, but we found no sign of our quarry. I thought perhaps they had passed through the village and continued their flight, but our tracker insisted that there was no trail to follow. The men we sought were here, somewhere.

Mangin ordered a picket line established around the village. Then he had Dialike assemble all the people together in the center, under the watchful eyes of a squad of soldiers. Mangin picked the village headman from among the crowd, took him by the arm and pulled him forward to stand in front of his people. He spoke a question to the man in a language I didn't know.

'He asks where they are, the men we seek,' Dialike whispered to me.

The headman did not reply. Without another word, Mangin walked quickly to the villagers, pulled from the crowd a young man, hardly more than a boy. Mangin drew his pistol and shot the youth in the chest. He was dead before his body struck the ground. The villagers erupted in a cacophony of wailing and keening. Dialike shouted a command, the men raised their rifles and the crowd fell silent. Mangin strode back to the headman, spoke to him again.

'He says he will shoot all the villagers, one by one, unless the headman tells him,' said Dialike. His voice was flat, with no sign that anything untoward had happened.

'Captain!' I called, sharply.

Mangin turned to me.

'What are you doing?' I asked.

He regarded me with a brief, baleful stare. Then he turned back to the headman, repeated his question. When there was no reply, he went again to the crowd, this time laying his hand on a young girl — perhaps ten years of age — and dragging her towards the headman. A cry went up among the women of the village. Mangin pointed his pistol at the girl's head. Her knees buckled and she fainted, her slack body folding in on itself as she crumpled to the ground. Mangin grabbed her by the hair, pulled her head up, aimed his pistol.

I wanted to stop him, but I could neither move nor make any sound. With his thumb, Mangin drew back the hammer of the pistol. Somehow, the sound of the hammer locking into position could be clearly heard over the bedlam of the women. He looked again at the headman, lifted an eyebrow in silent inquiry. Then he shrugged, pressed the muzzle of the pistol against the girl's head. I could see his finger on the trigger grow taut, turning white. Then the headman shouted something. Mangin *lowered his pistol, released the girl's hair. Her senseless body collapsed in a heap.*

The headman led us to one of the huts, pointed to the floor inside. Dialike called a half-dozen soldiers over, positioned them against the walls inside the hut, and then with his bayonet probed the dirt floor. He signaled to the men, they aimed their rifles, and he lifted a panel woven from thin strips of wood which lay beneath the dirt, exposing a hole that had been carved from the earth beneath the hut. There we found Missitou and Mayoke and made them our captives.

I thought we would take them with us to Kimbedi, but Mangin wanted to kill them. I drew him away from the men and we argued, but I could not change his mind. He was angry with me, so he told me I would be the one to do it, to organize the firing squad. To give the order. In the end, what could I do? I did my duty and we shot them.

Afterward I found Mangin near the river, talking with two native women. Several of our tiralleurs stood watch around them. I waited until he finished with them, whereupon one of the soldiers led them away. He turned to me. I told him that it was done; that Missitou and Mayoke were dead. Incongruously, he smiled at me, then clapped me on the shoulder.

'Well done, Dédé,' he said.

When I did not return the smile, nor answer him, it only seemed to amuse him more.

'Come, Dédé, we have only done our duty. That which we had to do.'

Still I said nothing. He shrugged.

'Very well. Go and find Dialike, tell him to strike camp. We leave in two hours.'

He told me then what the two women had told him, that Nganga himself was near, not more than a day's march from here.

'We must move quickly before he can slip away.'

I turned to go and do his bidding, but he took hold of my arm.

'You can't believe I meant to shoot the girl,' he said.

'You shot the boy,' I replied.

'The boy is different,' he said. 'You saw him. He was nearly a man and strong. In a day or a week, he'd be with the rebels. Killing him now is no different than killing him later. Not like the girl.'

I did not reply. After a moment he released me.

There is a bluff above the river here, an extrusion of rock rising a hundred feet or more, around which the Niari has been forced to make a detour. The face it presents to the river is a cliff, a virtual fortress wall; while away from the river the ground slopes steeply down to the forest floor. Here Nganga has taken refuge, in a cave about a third of the way down from the summit.

How many men are with him we cannot say; but that they are well-armed we know to our misfortune. On our first attempt to climb up the hill to the cave they opened fire on us. One of our men fell and two others went to his aid. Then one of them fell, so another ran to help. And so on. Before Dialike could get them under control, seven men lay sprawled in the hot afternoon soon. It was not until nightfall that we were able to drag them to safety. One was already dead, and another will not last the night.

Mangin and I were discussing how we might turn the rebels out from their redoubt when a runner arrived from Madingou, with word that Nkinke was headed our way with a large band of men, intent on rescuing his father. Mangin at once assembled his men and set off to intercept them, leaving me to solve the problem of Nganga.

'Get them out, Lieutenant,' he said and then he was gone.

I turned to Dialike, unsure how to proceed. Would it be best, I wondered aloud, to try to reach the cave mouth under cover of darkness? He shook his head.

'No, Monsieur,' he said. 'They know the ground and we do not. They have cover and we do not. We must wait until the morning. Then we can send up scouts, make a proper survey. Find a way up that they cannot cover from the cave.'

The advice seemed sound and I gave my assent. Dialike nodded, touched his cap and went to check on the pickets he'd set around our camp.

Sunday, 21 October 1896

Near Madingou
French Congo

The following day we found a second entrance to the cave, on the far side of the hill. I suggested that we use it to take Nganga and his men from behind. Dialike shook his head. The passage would surely be guarded, he said, and in the confines of the cave the advantage of our numbers would be nullified.

'Two good men might hold a narrow passage against a hundred, Monsieur,' he said. 'We do not enter the cave.'

Then he told me his plan. Again, it seemed sound, and I agreed.

Dialike and ten others climbed the slope to the second entrance. Keeping well out of sight, Dialike climbed above it, then scrambled across until he was directly above it. There he placed a large explosive charge in the rock above the entrance. He fixed a detonator with fuse and then climbed to the top of the hill, unrolling the fuse from a spool as he went. There he signaled to us, then bent down and lit the fuse.

The explosion brought the rock above the second entrance down, effectively sealing it. It also precipitated a fusillade of rifle fire from the main entrance. Given the range there was little danger; but as we meant to begin our own ascent to the cave, I ordered the machine-gunners to give covering fire. Sparks of bright light erupted from the rock around the entrance, and each bullet ricocheted and sent deadly splinters of rock in random directions. The men inside were forced back. It was death for them to spend any time at all at the mouth of the cave, so we were able to climb towards it unmolested.

We took up positions around the entrance, close enough to be heard, and I called for Nganga to come out. If he would, I said, I would spare him and his men. Otherwise, they would all die. I made this offer several times, but there was no reply.

We proceeded as we had planned. Dialike and the men on top of the hill began to collect brush and wood, dragging it down the slope above the cave. From there they pushed it to fall around the entrance. This provoked another burst of fire from the cave, but the machine guns quickly drove the rebels back. The work continued, until there was a great mound of scrub and wood piled around the entrance. Dialike signaled to me. I shouted an order and several men rushed up the slope to flank the entrance while machine-gun fire blew bits of wood and scrub into the air around the entrance. Then it was only necessary to set fire to the brush and wait for it to catch. The men above cut fresh branches, green with wet leaves, and dropped them onto the blaze. Great billowing clouds of smoke were sucked into the cave.

After two hours, Dialike signaled that it was enough, and he and his men came down the slope to join us. The fire burned for several hours more, so that it was late afternoon before we could kick aside the smoldering embers and, cautiously, enter the cave. The air was foul, acrid smoke and ash, and we crouched low hoping to find better, scrambling over the rock in the murky dark until we stumbled over the bodies. Some had been badly burned by the heat of the fire, and the smell of burnt flesh and excrement mingled with the smoke and ash was overwhelming. I choked, then suffered a fit of coughing. Dialike asked for my pistol and I gave it to him. He cocked the hammer, then moved from one lifeless form to the next, feeling for a pulse, pistol at the ready. But there was no need. He stood, released the hammer and handed the pistol back to me. The two of us went out into the late afternoon sunlight. I longed for fresh air, gulping and gasping in the stifling heat. Dialike seemed, as always, immune to all discomfort. He sent men into the cave to drag the bodies out, then turned to me, ready for my orders.

'Well done, corporal,' I said.

My throat was dry and sore from the smoke of the cave, so that my words were like the croak of some animal. But Dialike simply nodded. He studied my face for a moment, then met my eyes and I had the sense that something passed between us.

'You go down to the river, Monsieur,' he said. 'I will finish here.'

He was right. There was nothing more for me to do.

I went down the hill and through the camp to the river. There, I set aside my cap, removed my gun belt and blouse, and plunged my head into the cool water, meaning to wash the stench of death from my skin and hair. But it was no use; no matter how many times I ducked into the water, when I emerged the smell was still there, waiting for me. I stood, drying my face and hair with my blouse. I reached down for my cap, and *then, in the same motion, fell again to my knees, bent over at the waist, and vomited into the river.*

<u>Wednesday, 24 October 1896</u>
<u>Madingou</u>
<u>French Congo</u>

I am to take a detachment to Brazzaville tomorrow. Paké-Bô is sending me there to begin preparations to receive the bulk of our supplies. Now that Nganga is dead — and Missitou and Mayoke, and even Nkinke, for Mangin shot him two days ago — he says it will be safe to form up columns and begin the long portage to the Pool. Tensi is still at large, but the last report has him moving north, away from the Mayombe trail. Mangin has been dispatched to run him down.

I am eager to go. We have been two days waiting for the Captain. There is much to do — seeing to the injured, repairing equipment, cleaning our weapons — but as always Dialike has it well in hand. For me there has been little to do but wait; and to dwell, I confess, on the events of the past three weeks. The men sense my mood and avoid me, and the villagers are altogether terrified of us, so that my waking days are no different than my sleepless nights. I am alone with my memories. To his credit, Dialike has made some effort to be convivial, but there are limits to the fraternization which may be permitted between officers and men — to say nothing of that between black man and white — and it seems those limits are graven into his very soul. Or perhaps this is unfair to him and the fault is mine, for I have been less than a willing companion.

It was a relief to me when Paké-Bô arrived today, with his reserve force of two dozen tirailleurs. He greeted me as warmly as ever and after turning his men over to Dialike we retired to my tent. There I gave him my report. I tried to make it brief, for I did not trust my emotions to tell the tale whole, but still it took some time. He was in high spirits when I began and at first asked me the odd question; but as I went on, he grew quiet, simply letting me talk and now I cannot recall precisely what I told him. I only know that a moment came when I realized I had not said anything for some time. He looked at me with those sad eyes and shook his head.

'Dédé,' he said, 'You have only done what needed to be done.'

I wanted to tell him then what I had been thinking — that I should never have joined this expedition — but it seems I lack the courage even to do that. So, I said nothing. He took me by the shoulders, his face arm's length from my own.

'Soon it will be behind us, Dédé. We'll be on the river, on our way to our destiny, to the glory of France.'

He gave me a slight shake, then released me and took his leave, saying he had to see to arrangements for his own tent. Later, near sundown, I saw him walking with Dialike, the two of them deep in conversation. I thought to join them, but then it occurred to me that they were talking about me; that Paké-Bô wanted to hear the story from Dialike and would not welcome my company.

We dined together and it was then that he told me he was sending me ahead to Brazzaville.

'We'll begin moving things there soon, Dédé. You'll need to get a camp ready for us. We can't rely on the Colonial Office people there.'

He gave me to believe that it was an important task, but I understood that he only meant to send me away from the fight. I suppose it is a kindness and I am ready to go.

Chapter 20

Paris, December 1896

The palace which houses the Ministry of Foreign Affairs boasts two grand staircases facing onto the Quai D'Orsay, a broad avenue fronting the Seine. At night, the palace was bathed in the bright light of the arc lamps set for the occasion. From the Seigneur carriage Welles had a good view of the facade of the building, a Second Empire structure in white stone with Greek columns adorning both floors.

One by one the line of carriages drew up to the west staircase and disgorged their passengers. Ladies were resplendent in evening gowns that vied for attention with the elaborate uniforms of the officers who took their arms and escorted them up the stairs and into the palace. Their husbands, somber in black evening attire or uniform, followed behind, forgotten for the moment.

Welles remarked on it to Georges, who laughed softly. Then the footman was at their own carriage. Welles descended to the cobbled street, then offered a hand to Georges. She took it, stepped lightly onto the pavement, then seemed to glide past him, releasing his hand and offering her arm to a young man in the dress uniform of an artillery officer. The two started up the stairs without him.

Welles lingered a moment. Georges had chosen the gown with care — a sheath in gold silk, quite daring, sleeveless and revealing a good deal of her back — and the sight of her lean figure climbing the stairs on the arm of the handsome young officer drew admiring glances from the other officers awaiting their own charges. She wore black gloves to her elbows and a fur stole across her shoulders for warmth, but Welles was sure that she must be freezing with so little material between herself and the frigid night air.

She reached the top of the stairs. The officer bowed, kissed her gloved hand and — reluctantly, it seemed to Welles — retreated. She turned to beckon to him, a look of amused impatience on her face. He vaulted the stairs two at a time, took her by the arm, and they passed into the west hall; a large, open space around another grand staircase leading to the second floor. Welles spotted a waiter moving through the crowd of people, took two glasses from the offered tray and passed one to Georges. The champagne was very good, dry and quite cold. Georges drained her glass quickly and handed it back to him.

"I want to have a look around," she said.

With a flourish, she arranged the stole so that it draped below her exposed back, then set off into the crowd. It seemed to part before her, as if she were cutting her way through the sea and, as Welles watched her go, he saw the eyes of the gentlemen in her wake turning to follow her passage and he heard the whispered exclamations from the ladies on their arms. He smiled. Georges meant to shock, and he felt a frisson of pleasure that she'd pulled it off so well.

He finished his own champagne, found a waiter and exchanged his two empty glasses for a full one. Then he mounted the stairs and climbed to the broad landing of the first floor. A large globe, perhaps three feet in diameter, rested in an elaborate wood and gilded framework in the center of the black and white checkerboard floor. A few gentlemen stood smoking on the landing. The globe's frame offered a convenient level place to serve as a table, so he set his glass down to retrieve and light a cigarette of his own. He spun the heavy globe slowly until he was looking at the familiar outline of the Mediterranean Sea. With his finger he traced the north African coast, moving westward to the Atlantic, then following the curve of the coast south and east and south again, until he came to the mouth of a great river. He peered closely at it, could just make out the faint word: *Congo*.

A hand clapped him on the shoulder. Before he could turn, a uniformed arm came into view, a finger reached out to touch the globe beside his own, then moved a short distance east along the course of the river and stopped.

"He's there, dear boy," said Esterhazy.

Welles turned to see the Count in full military dress, buttons and medals flashing in the gaslight, a bewildering arrangement of colored cords looped around one shoulder and pinned to his chest by a large medallion. Welles looked quickly around the landing.

"Have a care," he said quietly. "We shouldn't be seen together."

Esterhazy smiled broadly.

"It's Christmas, my boy, and all is well in the world."

He was drunk, Welles realized. He dug an elbow into the man's ribs to get his attention, then nodded towards the doorway. He dropped his cigarette into an urn by the wall and walked away, through the doorway into the hall beyond.

He passed through two rooms full of people, then into a great hall adorned with ornate wood-and-gilt carved walls and a large chandelier hanging from the coffered ceiling. He continued through to the next room — a group of men stood around a billiard table watching two officers play — and the one after that, until he came to a hallway with a service stairway and several doors. One door led to a small pantry or closet, empty now. He waited by the door until Esterhazy appeared in the hallway, then drew the Count into the room and closed the door behind them. He stood with his back to it, one foot lodged tightly against it to prevent anyone from opening it.

"What are you doing?" he asked, unable to keep the note of exasperation from his voice. With the Count under suspicion, they had avoided all public encounters, meeting only in the fitting room at Barre's shop.

"You're not pleased to see me?"

Esterhazy tried to look hurt, but could not hold the pose, and smiled instead.

"Have no fear, Percy," he went on. "The cloud is lifted. I am once again wrapped in the warm embrace of my fellows."

"What do you mean?"

"The Dreyfus review has been closed." The Count gave a broad wink. "It seems that new evidence has come to light, evidence that shows conclusively that Captain Dreyfus is a traitor and a spy. The Army is satisfied. More importantly, the Government is satisfied. They will announce the end of the review tomorrow."

"The letter worked?"

Weeks had passed, weeks during which Welles alternated between frustration that the letter had had no discernible effect, and shame for his part in the deception.

"Yes, Percy, but only just. Do you have a cigarette, old boy?" Welles produced one, lit it for the Count. "Thanks. Where was I? Ah, the letter. Picquart didn't believe it."

"Didn't believe it?"

"No, he said it must be a forgery. That we had never intercepted such a letter before, and the timing — coming right after he'd reopened the case — was too convenient. Luckily for us, his deputy Major Henry disagreed. They went back and forth for weeks, Henry saying this was certain proof of Dreyfus's guilt, Picquart saying the opposite."

"What happened?"

"Henry convinced Picquart to take it to their superiors. Ultimately to the Vice Chief, General Gonse. He sided with Henry. Dreyfus is guilty, the letter is the final proof. The case is to be closed. I hear Picquart rather lost his temper."

"If Colonel Picquart is not convinced, will he give up so easily?" Welles asked. "Even if he's been told to close the case, he might still be watching the other suspects. Watching you."

Esterhazy barked a short laugh.

"Picquart isn't watching anybody." He paused to draw on his cigarette, then expelled smoke. "He's been removed from his post at the counter-intelligence section. Major Henry has been given the command."

Welles shook his head.

"Still, we should be careful," he said. "If Picquart doubts the letter, he could still be dangerous."

"He's finished, Percy. With any luck he'll soon be dead."

Welles felt a wave of heat rush over his body.

"What the devil do you mean, dead?"

"He has been ordered to take command of a regiment in Tunisia," said Esterhazy. "There's a war going on there, you know. Half the officers we send are killed in the first year."

The Count paused to let that sink in.

"I rather think that's the idea," he continued. "They don't expect him to return to Paris."

Welles could think of nothing to say. His mind was reeling. Why should the Army wish Picquart dead? Even if they wanted to put a lid on the Dreyfus matter, surely it was enough to remove him from any responsibility for it? No, the idea was implausible, unthinkable. It must surely be a coincidence. Picquart was an officer of regimental grade, after all; there was nothing unusual about sending him to take up a field command.

"You know, Percy, I ought to be angry with you," said Esterhazy, interrupting his thoughts. "You threatened me with exposure, didn't you? And here I thought we were friends."

The Count cast his features into an exaggerated sadness, mouth turned down at the corners, eyes half closed, head hanging. Again, though, he could not hold it and laughed.

"But I find I cannot resent you, my boy," he said. "You were right after all. I should never have cut you off; I should have asked you for help instead."

He shook his head as if in wonder, went on.

"You have got me clean out of trouble and sent Picquart to his doom."

"I did not mean to put him in danger," objected Welles. "I only thought to allay his suspicions."

The Count made a clucking sound with his tongue against the roof of his mouth.

"Well, all's well that ends well, so they say."

Esterhazy looked around the bare closet, shrugged, then dropped the end of the cigarette on the floor and crushed it beneath a gleaming black boot.

"Now we may resume our friendship, and not a moment too soon! I find the holidays have been rather a drain on my resources, if you take my meaning." He clapped Welles on the shoulder. "*Joyeux Noel*, Percy."

He took a step towards the door, hesitating so that Welles could move aside. But Welles stood his ground.

"He is where?" he asked.

Esterhazy peered at him, confused by the question.

"Earlier, you pointed at the globe, said 'he is there'."

"Ah, you mean Marchand? He is in Brazzaville."

"I thought he was stuck in Loango," said Welles. "Didn't you say he couldn't move, that there was some kind of uprising?"

Esterhazy shrugged. "Apparently he has put down the uprising himself. He's killed all the rebel leaders and reopened the supply routes. He's even clearing the supply depot, delivering everything that has been rotting on the beach for months. He's a hero, they say. I imagine there's a promotion in the works."

"How long will he be in Brazzaville?"

"Not long, I should imagine. The Belgians have loaned him a steamboat, the *Villes de Bruges,* to ferry his men and equipment further upriver. A ship really, one hundred fifty feet from bow to stern. Better than anything we have to offer him at Brazzaville. I expect he will depart for Bangui soon."

"Bangui?"

"An outpost on the Ubangi river," Esterhazy explained. "Perhaps eighteen hundred miles upriver from Brazzaville."

"The Ubangi river? You mean the Congo, surely?"

"The Ubangi," repeated Esterhazy. "They'll leave the Congo where the Ubangi joins it. From there the Congo would take them due east. The Ubangi will take them north."

"They're going north, not east?"

Welles was surprised. He'd assumed Marchand's objective must be some station or other deep in the Congo.

"At least as far as Bangui. They'll need to make several trips to move all their men and equipment. So, perhaps two months before they have everything in Bangui."

"Two months," repeated Welles. "And then where?"

The Count shrugged. "I don't know. The Ubangi turns east again at Bangui, but the river is too shallow for the *Villes*. I have no instructions for transport from there. I assume Marchand will make his own arrangements."

"He'll follow the river, surely. Where will it take him?"

"I have never been there, Percy," said Esterhazy. He smiled to take the edge off his impatience. "I'm afraid we're at the limit of my geographical knowledge. Though I imagine someone in London must have a map, my boy. Is there anything else?"

"London will want to know where he's going, and why. What he plans to do."

The smile vanished now.

"How do you suggest I find that out, Percy? I told you before, his mission is a secret, one I'm not privy to. I have only been able follow him so far through transportation orders. Once he leaves Bangui, he'll be beyond my sight."

"You must find a way. You're resourceful. I'm sure you'll come up with something."

The Count's smile returned, but it was not reflected in his eyes.

"Very well," he said with a nod of his head. "I shall try."

Welles shifted slightly, took hold of the doorknob, and opened the door just enough for the Count to pass through. He closed the door again, waited a few minutes alone in the stillness of the empty closet. Then he stepped into the hallway and turned towards the service stair. He descended quickly to the ground floor and found himself in another hallway. He chose a door at random, opened it, and stepped into the east foyer of the palace. The room was filled with people, all talking at the same time. He made his way through the crowd, searching for Georges.

He found her in the center of the palace, in a room with a long bay of glass doors which looked out onto a curved terrace above the gardens. Georges stood with her back to the doors, a champagne glass in hand, engaged in conversation with a group of young officers. She saw him as he approached.

"Ah, there you are, *cher*," she said, linking her arm in his and pulling him close.

"Where have you been?" she asked. "I looked everywhere for you. These gentlemen have been kind enough to keep me company in your absence."

"Forgive me, my dear," he said. He nodded to the young men. "My thanks, Messieurs."

There was an awkward silence; then, reluctantly, the officers bowed and took their leave.

"You're a spoilsport, Percy," she said. "I was rather enjoying myself."

"Yes, I can see that. Another drink, my dear?"

"Yes, please."

He signaled a passing waiter, exchanging Georges' empty glass for two full ones. They sipped champagne together in silence, Georges watching the other guests while Welles replayed in his mind the conversation with Esterhazy. He wanted to tell her that the Dreyfus case had been closed again — it would come as a shock to her, and he wanted to soften the blow — but he could think of no way to do it without having to explain how he knew. He tried to think of some innocent explanation, but nothing came. He had reached the conclusion that there was no way to do it when he felt her grip on his arm tighten. He looked at her, then followed her gaze to see a man approaching them.

"Monsieur Welles is it?" said Major Du Paty de Clam. He offered his hand and Welles took it.

"Major Du Paty, a pleasant surprise. May I present Mademoiselle Seigneur?"

"Charmed, Mademoiselle." He took her hand in his, bowing from the waist to press her glove to his lips.

"A pleasure, major," Georges said.

Du Paty released her hand.

"I am surprised to see you here, Monsieur," he said to Welles. "I would not have thought many journalists were invited."

"Monsieur Welles is my guest," Georges said. "The invitation was for my father, but he insisted I come in his stead."

Du Paty looked her up and down, his eyes lingering on her form for far longer than good manners permitted. Then his eyes widened, an exaggerated show of having realized something.

"But of course," he said, addressing Georges, "you are Monsieur Welles's" —here he paused, as if searching for a word— "his *associate*, are you not?"

Welles felt a flash of anger and was about to express it, but Georges tightened her grip on his arm, and he said nothing. She laughed.

"How direct you are," she said. "So refreshing, I'm sure the ladies find it quite charming. Do you have a cigarette?"

Du Paty produced his cigarette case. Georges released Welles's arm and took one. The major offered one to Welles, who declined. Du Paty extended a lighter. Georges handed her glass to Welles, then leaned forward, placing both her hands on Du Paty's own as he held the lighter. He struck a light. Georges tilted her head to one side to light the cigarette, then pulled away, expelling smoke.

"*Merci*," she said. She turned to Welles. "Percy, *cher*, I am suddenly quite starved. What time is it?"

With a glass in each hand, he couldn't reach his watch.

"Nearly eleven, I think," he said. "I've booked a table at Montorguiel for half past, if that's all right."

She made a face.

"It will be hours before they give us anything to eat there."

To his astonishment, she squirmed, plucking at the waist of her tight-fitting dress.

"And I simply must get out of this dress," she said, placing her hand to his chest and leaning close to him. "Couldn't you just make me an omelet, *cher*?"

He resisted the impulse to laugh at the expression on Du Paty's face. He knew Georges was simply trying to embarrass Du Paty.

He had never before cooked for Georges and would not be able to manage anything like an omelet in his flat.

"Of course," he said. "Whatever you like, Georges. Shall I bring it to you in bed?"

She smiled at him, blew him a kiss. She took her glass back, sipped champagne while gazing into his eyes. Then she seemed to realize that Du Paty was still there.

"Oh, dear, I thought you'd gone," she said. "Was there something you wanted?"

She faced him directly, one foot slightly forward, her chin raised, holding her cigarette high and to one side of her face, her elbow tight to her side, the other hand holding the champagne glass in front of her body.

"Indeed, Mademoiselle," he said with a slight bow, "I wished only to express my regret that you shall both have to find a new hobby."

"A new hobby?" asked Georges. "Whatever do you mean, Monsieur?"

"Why, only that the Dreyfus investigation has once again been closed, Mademoiselle. It seems the original verdict of the court was correct after all, and it has been corroborated by the appearance of new evidence that removes any doubt of the man's guilt."

Chapter 21

The Journal of Lieutenant Andre Durand

<u>Monday, 14 December 1896</u>
<u>Brazzaville</u>
<u>French Congo</u>

A runner came today with a message from Mangin. Two days ago, he caught up with Tensi and a large force of rebels near the village of Zilengoma, about forty miles north of Loudima. They fought a great battle there, one that lasted all day; and in the end Mangin was victorious. Tensi was killed, along with all his men — how else could it be with Mangin? — and as he was the last of the rebel leaders the rebellion is finally at an end.

Already supplies have begun moving from the coast to every corner of the colony. Paké-Bô says that he will rescind the order for martial law by the end of the month. His fame has increased ten-fold and here in Brazzaville he is feted at one dinner after another. He has taken great pains to give credit to us all — for that is his nature — and consequently, as the man who killed Nganga, I too am hailed wherever I go. It is almost more than I can bear, and I find I spend more and more time at the camp, working late into the night with Dialike and the men, seeing to the organization of the next phase of our journey. I sleep there most nights, and I am comforted by the sound of the men around the campfires in the evening, and the deep quiet of the African night that comes later.

There is more good news. The Belgians have agreed to loan us a steamship for the journey to Bangui. Paké-Bô says it is in recompense for the debacle of the Boma railroad. Although it is a large vessel, built for the wide and deep Congo upriver from Brazzaville, it is still far too small to carry us all in one trip, and we will likely be two months or more ferrying men and equipment up the much shallower Ubangi. If all goes well, we should be assembled in Bangui by the end of March. How we will continue from there I cannot say.

Saturday, 26 December 1896
Brazzaville
French Congo

It is nearly morning and Christmas has come and gone. I write by the light of a candle in the small room allotted to me in Government House. Martial law has ended. Governor de Brazza has returned to Brazzaville and once again taken the reins of the administration into his hands. Tonight, he hosted a dinner at which Paké-Bô was the guest of honor. When the remains of the Christmas goose had been taken away and the brandy poured all around, de Brazza made a short speech, thanking Paké-Bô for putting down the rebellion and rescuing the colony. There was applause from everyone, which erupted into cheering when de Brazza announced that he had received a cable from Paris and that Paké-Bô was promoted to major.

The party lasted until well after midnight, whereupon we three — Mangin, Baratier, and I — took our newly-minted major into the deserted lounge for a quiet congratulatory toast. We talked excitedly about the journey to come. For this brief interlude I was untroubled and felt as if I were in the company of brothers, embarked on a great adventure; but for Mangin, of course. I cannot warm to the man, and it is no secret that he has no regard for me.

Afterward, when we rose to find our beds, Marchand pulled me aside.

'Dédé,' he said, 'Baratier will take the Villes to Bangui with the first load of men and equipment. You will go with him. He will remain in Bangui, and you must bring the Villes back to collect us.'

I think he meant to convey the confidence he felt in me, that he would give me command of such a vital part of our mission. And I was pleased; though another part of me thought that he had come upon the idea as the best way to keep Mangin and me apart.

Friday, 22 January 1897
On board the Villes de Bruges
Ubangi River
French Congo

We have left the Congo river and now move up the Ubangi. As we steam north, we travel along what is effectively the border between two countries. To our port side lies the Congo of France; to the starboard, the Congo Free State, perhaps the strangest of all the colonies white men have made in this land. As Baratier explained to me, the Free State is a personal possession of Leopold, the king of Belgium. A territory of nearly one million square miles and everything in it — including perhaps thirty million natives — belongs to one man. Baratier says the Free State is a source of great wealth to the king, and the company he formed to exploit that wealth — nominally the Anglo-Belgian India Rubber Company but known throughout the Free State as simply the Company — acts as the de facto government along the Ubangi.

The change in our passage since leaving the Congo is remarkable. Whereas the Congo above the Pool is wide and deep, a great mass of brown water which flows so slowly it almost seems a lake, the Ubangi is narrow, shallow and has a strong downstream current. It is difficult to describe adequately our passage along this dark river. Like the Congo, both sides of the river are an impenetrable mass of undergrowth and great trees which rise to a thick canopy. But the Ubangi is so narrow that the trees tower above us and spread their branches and leaves over the river so that the sun is always obscured, and we journey in a kind of twilight.

The river is shallower than it should be. We have had to go carefully, and on several occasions have felt the Villes scrape bottom on the rocks beneath the water. It costs us time, time we cannot spare; and if the water level continues to drop, it may be too low even for the flat-bottomed Villes. She will be lighter when I take her back to the Pool, but once laden with the rest of our expedition she may well run aground.

<u>Wednesday, 26 January 1897</u>
<u>Giri</u>
<u>Congo Free State</u>

This morning we passed through a particularly low stretch of the river. We came on it suddenly, the first warning the lurch and sound as the Villes rubbed bottom. Baratier adjusted the throttle until we moved upstream no faster than a man might walk, then I took the wheel while he stood in the bow and with his hands pointed the way towards the deepest channel.

It was nerve-wracking work, and when we found ourselves some two hours later again in deeper water, we were filthy with sweat. Baratier clambered over the crates stacked all over the deck, looking for any sign that we were taking on water. I offered to leap into the river to inspect the hull from below, but he shook his head, pointing to the crocodiles waiting on the nearby bank by way of explanation.

'We will find a village by and by,' he said. 'That will be soon enough.'

He was right, for not a quarter of an hour later we rounded a curve in the river and spied the new wooden jetty of the village of Giri.

Baratier took the wheel and steered us to the pier. Two men — black men, naked to the waist — had heard our approach. One of them took our lines and tied us off fore and aft, while the other ran along the bank of the river, calling out to announce our arrival. A white man appeared and introduced himself as Jacob Maes, the company agent at Giri. Baratier explained that we wanted to offload some cargo onto the dock, to lighten the load so that we might inspect the hull.

Maes shouted for more laborers. In short order a team of natives were shifting our load onto the dock. While they worked under Baratier's watchful eyes, I took a tour of the village with Maes.

'Giri is a rubber factory,' he said, as we walked together away from the river and into the village.

He explained that the Company employed thousands of natives to search through the jungle to find the vines that bore the milky sap that could be made into rubber.

'The vines can be enormous,' he said. 'They grow up the trunk of one of the great trees and then spread throughout the canopy. When you find one, you tap it by cutting it with a knife. You cut it deep, but not too deep, else you might kill the vine. And you don't want to do that, do you?' He smiled at me. 'That's a death sentence, killing the vine.'

'Surely not,' I said, but I saw at once that he was in earnest.

'A single vine is worth a fortune,' he said. 'If you take care, it will produce sap for many years, even decades. The sap flows from the wound very slowly. You must catch it in a bucket, wait for the bucket to fill. The wound may close, and you'll have to cut the vine again. It takes time. When the bucket is filled, then you have to dry the sap.'

I looked around at the trees, glistening with damp. Large drops of water fell constantly from the high canopy overhead and collected in pools at every low point in sight. With each step, my feet were sinking into ground which was permanently wet.

'How do you dry it?' I asked.

'The best way is to smear the sap all over one's body, wait for the body heat to dry it, then peel it off.' He laughed. 'The natives say it is quite painful the first few times, as it pulls out all the hair from your body. Then they pack the dried rubber into a ball, fill a basket with balls and bring the basket here.'

We stopped in the middle of the village. A crude warehouse had been constructed there, with a raised wooden floor, open sides and sloped roof. Several natives were working there, taking lumpy gray balls of rubber from baskets and pressing them together to form a larger block. At one end of the platform were stacked dozens of such blocks, each about the size of a small wooden chest.

'A boat will call in a few days,' Maes said. 'Then the rubber will head downriver, eventually to Boma. From there it will be shipped to Antwerp.'

I watched the men work. The heat was stifling and sweat glistened on their bodies as they worked the reluctant rubber into the right size and shape for shipment. They worked in silence; a deliberate silence, or so it seemed to me, which combined with the heat and the damp to create a kind of oppressive stillness. One man lifted a finished block of rubber and carried it to the stacks. He lifted it to the top of a stack. The movement seemed clumsy, and I noticed for the first time that he had only one hand. I looked at the other men; it was the same with each of them.

'What has happened to these men?' I asked Maes.

'They are evidence of a fraud,' he said. When he saw that I did not understand, he explained. 'The Company relies on the village chiefs to keep order. We white men are few and must work with what we find. We arm the chiefs, supply them with ammunition. But not very much ammunition. If they want more, they have to prove how they expended what they had.'

I confess I was mystified by this explanation and said as much.

'We don't want them selling the bullets, or stockpiling them to use against us,' he explained patiently. 'If they have used the bullet to kill a man, we require proof of the death. The customary proof is the hand of the man killed.'

I was momentarily struck dumb by this explanation. Maes waited patiently, a smile on his face, as if we were discussing an ingenious method of tallying the weight of rubber to be shipped downriver.

'These men aren't dead,' I said.

'Indeed, they are not,' he replied. 'As I said, they are evidence of fraud. Some chief somewhere has sold his bullets, then taken the hands of his subjects in order to trade for more.'

'But that is monstrous,' I protested.

He shrugged. 'They are savages, Monsieur,' he said.

'They are savages? Who is it that demands the hands, then?'

'If we knew which chief it was, we would punish him. A man needs two good hands to collect the sap. When we find men like these in the bush, we have to find other work for them.'

By now I had had enough of this tour. I told Maes I needed to return to the dock. Unbidden, he accompanied me. We walked in silence for some minutes when something occurred to me. I stopped, looked back towards the center of the village. Maes looked back, too, as if trying to see what had captured my attention.

'Where are the women?' I asked. I had seen only men in the village.

'The women are in Zongo,' he said. 'When we come into a village, we take the women away. It is a way of ensuring the cooperation of the men. This is how things are done here, Monsieur.'

I stood looking at him for a long while. He was by appearance a perfectly ordinary man. No one seeing him would have guessed the corruption in his heart. I wanted to shout at him, even to strike him; but I knew that it would do no good. He would not understand my objection. He had gone beyond that kind of understanding. I turned away from him and continued back to the river. There I found the men reloading our supplies onto the Villes. Baratier told me with some satisfaction that he'd found no evidence of any leaks.

'That is good news,' I said. 'We should leave this place as quickly as we can.'

He turned to me, a question on his face. Then he saw my own expression, and simply nodded.

Chapter 22

London, 12 August 1898

Now it was Salisbury's turn to interrupt Welles. The Prime Minister slapped his hand on the table.

"How long must we listen to this sordid tale, Welles?" he demanded.

He took his watch from his pocket, examined it.

"It is now past three in the morning," he said. "Do you have something of use to tell me regarding Marchand, or don't you?"

"I do," replied Welles. "I intend to honor the bargain we made. But I must do it in my own way."

"I have heard enough. I will buy your journal, if you will only tell me the price you demand."

For a moment Welles was silent, as if considering it. Then he shook his head.

"You are not ready to pay my price," he said. "I'm afraid you will have to hear me out."

He nodded at the gun in his hand. The Prime Minister glared at him but said nothing.

"I will try to move along," said Welles, magnanimously. "Indeed, I shall move forward in time to the summer. Nothing of interest to you occurred in the intervening months."

"Nothing?" asked Bingham. "What of Miss Seigneur? How did she react to the news that the Dreyfus review had been closed?"

"As you might expect," said Welles. "She was angry, and more determined than ever to pursue the matter. I knew that it was useless, but I was quite unable to refuse Georges anything. So, we made an effort. She wrote another article, placed it with a Paris paper, but it made barely a ripple. She tried to arrange an interview with Major Du Paty, but he would not see her. She spent several weeks following him around Paris, even asking her father's acquaintances about him, but learned only what we already knew: He was an Army officer, assigned to the operations bureau of the General Staff. He possessed a minor nobility, with the country estate that came with it, and was widely thought to be something of a martinet. But she found nothing we could use as a lever to pry information from him. She renewed her friendship with Colonel von Schwartzkoppen and dined with him and his crowd once or twice a week. It meant that we could not see each other as often as we had; but in truth I was relieved, for it gave me more opportunity for my clandestine life. In the end, we accomplished nothing of use. She learned nothing from any of them, not even Max. Slowly, the Dreyfus matter faded into the background. People lost interest, and even the socialist press largely abandoned the story."

"And what was the effect of this on Miss Seigneur?"

"I think you can imagine it, Mister Bingham," Welles said. "Gradually she seemed to lose hope. In time we stopped speaking of the affair altogether. We remained lovers, but there was a distance between us now; an air of secrets kept, grievances unspoken. It was," he paused as if searching for a word. "Unsupportable," he decided. "I see now that we could not have gone on much longer; that there would have been a break eventually. The weight of suspicion — and of guilt, my own guilt — was too much. Then came the note from Picquart. That was in August of last year."

Chapter 23

Paris, August 1897

Wednesday, 4 August 1897
Monsieur Georges Seigneur
11 Quai de Bourbon
Ile de Saint-Louis

Monsieur,

Please forgive the presumption of this note; my time in Paris is limited. I should like to discuss with you a particular matter, for which I have good reason to believe you share my interest. I shall call upon you at your home, on the afternoon of Friday, 6 August, at six o'clock. Will you be so good as to receive me, and to arrange for the presence of your daughter Mademoiselle Seigneur, and that of her associate, M. Welles?

Yours most sincerely,

Lieutenant Colonel Marie-Georges Picquart

Picquart arrived promptly at six and the butler showed him into the library where Welles waited with Georges and her father. Picquart was not in uniform, presumably so as not to attract unwanted attention. Instead, he was trim and handsome in the traveling clothes of a gentleman, and he carried in his left hand a leather valise. Monsieur Seigneur introduced himself, then presented Georges and Welles to the colonel. Picquart had a regal face and an aristocratic bearing, and, Welles thought, eyes that were somehow sad. He imagined that it would be difficult to read anything in Picquart's manner that the man didn't intend you to see.

Seigneur offered refreshment but Picquart declined, so no one else accepted. They sat, Georges and her father on the couch, Picquart in a chair opposite them with his valise on the floor. Welles took a chair to one side from which he could more easily observe the other three. There was an awkward silence, as if no one knew quite how to begin. Then Georges welcomed Picquart back to Paris and asked about his tour in Tunisia.

"I must count it as a minor success, Mademoiselle," Picquart replied.

"A minor success? How so, colonel?"

"A success in that I was not killed, as no doubt I was intended to be," he said. The words should have been sensational, but his matter-of-fact delivery robbed them of any sense of the dramatic. "And minor," he went on, "as I can't say I accomplished anything else of value there."

"Intended to be?" echoed Seigneur. "What do you mean?"

"I mean what I say. I was sent to Tunisia to be killed. The fighting there is fierce, the climate inhospitable to man. Half the officers are killed within the first year of their assignment. My death was by no means certain, but I believe I'm justified in saying that certain people had hopes for that outcome."

"That is an extraordinary statement," said Welles. "Why should your superiors desire that you be killed?"

"I have come to tell you that, and more," said Picquart. "Before I begin, however, I know that you, Monsieur" —he indicated Welles— "and Mademoiselle Seigneur are journalists."

"We are," said Georges.

"And, further, I believe that the three of you are all supporters of Captain Dreyfus? That you believe him to be innocent of the charge of spying?"

"We do, most emphatically," she replied.

Her father echoed this sentiment. Picquart turned to Welles. He hesitated, then nodded.

"But tell me, colonel," he asked. "Why should you suppose that we think him innocent?"

"Because either you or Mademoiselle Seigneur was the author of the hoax about his escape."

When neither Georges nor Welles responded to this allegation, Picquart waved his hand impatiently.

"Please. I was chief of military counter-intelligence for France. If a story appears alleging that a convicted spy has escaped, you must believe that I have the means to discover where it came from, and who caused it to be published; and that I have the wit to understand why."

"I wrote it," said Georges. "I hoped to spark interest in the affair and provoke a response from the government."

"And provoke one you did. Indeed, it was that response that, in the end, sent me to Tunisia. Though I do not blame you, Mademoiselle," he said, agreeably, "as you could not have foreseen that chain of events. That I would be moved to review the Dreyfus file and become convinced myself that he is innocent; or that this conviction would lead to my death sentence."

"You believe him to be innocent!" Georges was unable to hide her excitement at his announcement.

"I do," said Picquart. "However, before I go further, I must ask you to agree to this: Our conversation today is not for publication. The time may come when I have enough to reveal to the world, but for now I hope only to advance my own investigation of the affair."

Welles looked at Georges. She nodded.

"Very well," said Welles. "We are in agreement."

"I am not a journalist," said Monsieur Seigneur, "but I understand that we are speaking in confidence."

"Excellent," said Picquart. "To begin, Mademoiselle, will you tell me why you believe Dreyfus to be innocent?"

"I have met his wife, Lucie, and his brother," said Georges, "and I have come to know them well, and from this I know that his character is entirely incompatible with the charges against him."

Picquart did not reply, and his face gave no hint of reaction to this. After a moment, her father spoke.

"I have known the family for many years, and I agree, it is not possible to believe the charges. But I am also an attorney, and I know that such assessments of character must be weighed against the evidence; and that one may find that the evidence is so strong, so overwhelming, that the character assessment must be disregarded. Indeed, I myself might be convinced by such evidence, and I am ready to test my judgment. If only there were any evidence to weigh." Seigneur shrugged. "As it is, I'm told the evidence is secret, and I know that any verdict resulting from secret evidence is inherently flawed. Indeed, such a conviction is so weak, so open to challenge, that I believe no court would agree to hide the evidence unless it was the case that the evidence, itself, could not stand up to scrutiny."

Picquart turned to Welles.

"And you, sir? You say the trial was unjust. How so?"

Welles shrugged. "I agree with Monsieur Seigneur. A conviction on secret evidence is an injustice. Beyond that, Dreyfus is a Jew, and I have good reason to believe this was a factor in the accusations against him."

He gave a brief account of his meeting with Du Paty.

"He made no secret of his view that Jews cannot be trusted," he said, "and as much as admitted that he first suspected Dreyfus for that reason. Then there was the mood of the press, and the climate in Paris at the time of the trial. Suffice it to say that I don't believe Dreyfus can have gotten a fair hearing under the circumstances."

Picquart looked from Welles back to Seigneur, then to Georges.

"Is that all?" he asked, his disappointment evident in his voice.

"All, sir?" asked Georges.

"I mean to say, have you nothing more? No direct evidence that can clear this man, or point the finger at any other?"

"None, I'm afraid," said Georges. "Did you suppose we did? Or that, having it, we would not have already used it to free Dreyfus?"

"I had hoped you had something concrete. Less circumstantial. Something more than a feeling."

Georges bristled.

"And you, colonel? As you say, you were the chief of counter-intelligence. You reviewed the matter and concluded that he was innocent. You must have something, some fact, some piece of evidence, that led you to that conclusion. Something more than a feeling, as you say."

Picquart gave a slight nod and smiled; a small, apologetic smile, as if he were awarding a point.

"Several factors serve to convince me, Mademoiselle," he said. "You know that I was not in the counter-intelligence section at the time of the trial and played no part in the investigation. When I learned — thanks to your ingenious prank — that the conviction had been founded on a secret dossier, I went immediately to the archives and retrieved that dossier. Based on what I found there I would be forced to conclude that Dreyfus is, indeed, guilty."

"Guilty?" exclaimed Seigneur. "But you have only just told us you believe him innocent."

"I do, Monsieur. Allow me to explain. Much of the evidence in the dossier consists of documents which seem to incriminate Dreyfus. Collectively, they are quite damning. But as I examined them, one thing leaped out at me: Many of them come from the same source. Indeed, it is the same source through which we first discovered the existence of a traitor."

"The source of the *bordereau*, you mean?" asked Welles. "What is the nature of this source?"

"I regret, Monsieur Welles, that I am not at liberty to say," said Picquart.

Welles made a face.

"Come now," he said, "it is something of an open secret in Paris that the spy was delivering material to the German military attaché. Is your source someone in the German embassy?"

Picquart shrugged. "As to that, you may believe what you like. But I am not here to confirm such rumors, Monsieur. What I can tell you is that my curiosity was piqued. Our source is still active, as we say, and I undertook a review of all the material we receive through it."

"And what did you find?" asked Georges.

"Something quite surprising: That the flow of secrets to our enemies did not stop when Dreyfus was arrested. Indeed, as far as I know, it continues to this day."

This revelation was greeted with a moment of shocked silence. Then everyone tried to talk at once.

"Do you mean to say—" began Seigneur.

"—It has not stopped?" interrupted George.

"Then the spy is still at large?" asked Welles.

"Either that, Monsieur, or there are two spies," said Picquart. "I could not dismiss that possibility, however remote it might seem. But let us set it aside for a moment. At the very least, the continued existence of an active spy should have been considered by the court that convicted Dreyfus. But there is no mention of it in the Dreyfus dossier. Neither is there any in the transcript of the trial."

"That is an outrage," said Seigneur. "You must report it at once to your superiors."

"I have reported it, Monsieur," said Picquart. "I took my evidence to the Vice Chief of Staff — General Gonse — and asked his permission to re-open the case."

"And what was his response?" asked Seigneur. "Did he give it?"

"Not entirely. General Gonse seemed to me disinclined to believe that Dreyfus might be innocent. On the other hand, he was alarmed at the possibility of another traitor; so alarmed that he ordered me to pursue the matter. To me, the one was as good as the other; I would pursue this new investigation and — at the same time — use it to re-examine the facts of the Dreyfus affair. As a first step, I placed a number of officers under surveillance. These were all men who had been suspects along with Dreyfus, if only because they had access to the same secrets."

"With what result?" asked Welles. He had listened to Picquart's tale with a growing sense of unease.

"Why, none, Monsieur Welles," said Picquart. "Though I was only at it for a few weeks before I was forced to stop."

"Forced?" asked Seigneur. "What stopped you?"

"Not *what*, but *who*," said Picquart. "It was at this moment that something unexpected happened. We intercepted another document, a letter which seemed once again to incriminate Dreyfus; but which is an obvious forgery."

Welles felt a stillness come over him. He fumbled for a cigarette, dropped it on the table, picked it up, lit it. From what seemed like a great distance, he could hear Georges and Picquart talking.

"A forgery?" asked Georges.

"Yes, Mademoiselle. A letter from Dreyfus himself, sent in late October of last year. We routinely check his mail, both incoming and outgoing, and someone thought there was something odd about this one. We subjected it to a number of tests, and discovered that the letter contained a hidden message, written in invisible ink."

"You cannot be serious," said Georges. "Invisible ink?"

"Yes, invisible ink. For reasons of verisimilitude, the ink was made from" —here the colonel glanced at Georges, blushed— "from a substance produced by the body. This was presumably to lend credence to the idea that the ink was made by a man in prison. The hidden message itself seemed to be part of a correspondence between Dreyfus and an accomplice. And, in truth, we have intercepted other letters, sent by persons unknown to Dreyfus and containing hidden messages. Though we have never before intercepted a reply from Dreyfus."

"If that is the case," said Welles, "then this reply would seem to confirm that correspondence. Yet you say it was a forgery. How can you know? Was the letter not written by Dreyfus?"

"The letter was genuine, Monsieur; it is the secret message which is a forgery. It was added to a letter by someone else after the fact, in a hand meant to resemble that of Dreyfus."

"But if the letter was written by Dreyfus, and the secret message resembles Dreyfus's own hand, then perhaps it is genuine?"

Welles was insistent; perhaps too insistent, he thought. He shot a glance at Georges, but she was intent on Picquart and his reply.

"I tell you that Dreyfus could not have written the secret message, Monsieur Welles. It is an impossibility, because of the conditions of his imprisonment."

Picquart turned to Georges, adopting an apologetic look.

"I regret to say, Mademoiselle, that those conditions were made incomparably worse by your hoax about his escape. You published your story in September, before this letter was written. From the time the story appeared, Captain Dreyfus has been kept sequestered in his hut, chained to an iron bed for twenty-two hours of every day. There he takes his meals, reads and writes his letters, and sleeps. He is unchained only for some exercise and the necessities of hygiene. A guard is always present inside his hut. The guard would have watched Dreyfus write the letter. The guard would have observed Dreyfus collecting his" —he blushed again, went on— "making invisible ink. He would have seen Dreyfus adding the hidden message. No. Under the circumstances, it is impossible to believe that Dreyfus contrived to do these things, and that he was not observed doing them."

Georges' face was white.

"Then my story was a catastrophe for Captain Dreyfus," she said. "Not only has it not helped him, it has done the poor man immeasurable harm."

Picquart smiled, a sad smile, and shook his head.

"No, Mademoiselle. Some good has come from it. It was the impetus that drove me to reexamine the case. Because of your story, I may yet expose the true culprit, and free Dreyfus from his barbaric imprisonment."

"I don't understand why he has not already been released," said Seigneur. "This letter proves there is a conspiracy to persecute Dreyfus. Why have you not brought it to the attention of your superiors?"

"But I have, Monsieur. Let me tell you what happened when I took the letter to General Gonse. I explained — as I have to you — why it is certain that Dreyfus could not have been the author. To my amazement, rather than agreeing that it must be a forgery, he insisted that it was proof that Dreyfus was guilty and ordered me to end my investigation. When I reminded him that there was evidence that the spy was still at large, he was not swayed. He said that it was the view of the Chief of Staff that the case be closed for the good of the Army. When I refused, he lost his temper. He said to me — I shall recall the words until my dying day — he said, *'what is it to you if that Jew stays on Devil's Island?'* And when I told him that I thought Dreyfus was an innocent man, he said *'but if you say nothing, no one will be the wiser.'*"

"*Mon dieu!*" said Georges. "He said this to you?"

"I was as shocked as are you, Mademoiselle, so I was perhaps imprudent in my reply. I told him that I would not be silent. Indeed, I said I would not take this secret to my grave. I think this must have inspired him. Two days later I was removed from my post as head of counter-intelligence and sent away from Paris. Four weeks later I was ordered to take command of a regiment in Tunisia."

"Do you mean to say," asked Seigneur, "that General Gonse — the Vice Chief of Staff — is in league with a spy? And that even the Chief of Staff himself, General de Boisdeffre, is implicated in this conspiracy?"

Picquart shook his head.

"I do not say that, Monsieur. It may only be that they cannot accept that the Army has made a mistake in this affair. It is the nature of men in their position to seek to protect the institutions they lead. So, they simply wish the whole thing away. I believe they will not be moved unless I can name the true spy and produce evidence to support my case. I have sworn to do so."

"What will you do now, colonel?" asked Welles. He had followed the conversation with increasing distress, and now he hoped to draw a line under it.

"I am in Paris on leave; I came to put my affairs in order. I had a close scrape last month — a fall from my horse — and realized that I have done nothing to make good my promise to General Gonse."

He lifted the valise onto his lap, unbuckled the straps which held it closed. From inside he drew a thick envelope.

"Monsieur," he said, addressing Georges' father, "I should like to engage your services as an attorney."

"I see," said Seigneur. "How may I be of service to you?"

"I have written a letter of instructions to be carried out in the event of my death. I should like you to accept it, and the responsibility for acting in my stead. In addition, I've given you copies of documents, photostats I took the precaution of having made before I was dismissed. These documents will be of use to you in carrying out my instructions."

He offered the envelope to Seigneur. The latter hesitated.

"May I read the letter first, before I decide to accept this charge?"

"*Mais certainement*, Monsieur. I would not have you bound to an unknown obligation."

Seigneur stood and took the envelope.

"A moment, *s'il vous plait*."

He bowed, then went to his desk, where he sat, slit the envelope open, removed a sheaf of documents, and began to read. The others sat in silence, Welles and Georges both considering the consequences of what they'd heard. At length, Seigneur cleared his throat.

"I accept your commission. I will take charge of these documents and keep them safe."

"And if I should die, Monsieur Seigneur?"

"In that case, I will carry out the instructions in your letter."

Seigneur took a folder from a drawer, placed the envelope into the folder, returned it to the drawer, then rose and rejoined them.

Picquart took his watch from his pocket and announced that he had no more time and must take his leave. They all stood and accompanied the colonel from the library, down the stairs and to the door. The butler appeared with Picquart's hat. Welles asked for his own. Georges put a hand on his arm, drew him aside.

"Will you not stay to dinner?" she asked.

"I regret that I cannot, my dear," he said. "I have another engagement."

Welles could see that she was waiting for him to say more, to explain the nature of this other engagement. Instead, he patted his jacket as if he were looking for something.

"I've left my cigarette case in the library," he said. "I won't be a moment."

He climbed the stairs quickly. The library was empty, and he closed the door behind him before crossing to Seigneur's desk. He took the folder from the drawer, laid it on the desk, opened it, slid a stack of documents from the envelope inside. He scanned Picquart's letter quickly, then flipped through the documents one by one. When he reached the last page he paused, then held his breath as he read. He hesitated a moment, then took the last page from the file, folded it carefully into thirds and slipped it into his jacket pocket. He replaced the other documents as he had found them, then retrieved his cigarette case from the table and exited the library.

Georges and her father were waiting at the door, Georges holding his hat. Seigneur shook his hand, bid him good evening, and mounted the stairs. Georges stood close to him, her eyes on his. For a moment he thought she meant to ask him where he was going; then the moment passed. She put a hand to his cheek, leaned forward to kiss him on the other cheek. Then she gave him his hat and closed the door behind him.

***

Welles sat at the table in his flat, a bottle and glass before him. The document he'd taken was in his hands, still folded. He didn't want to look at it. He laid it on the table, poured himself a whisky, drank half in one gulp. Then he stood and turned the chair over. With a knife, he pried the bottom of the seat loose, removing the envelope he'd hidden there so many months before. He righted the chair, sat, drank the rest of the whisky, and poured another. He removed the fold of documents from the envelope, laid them on the table, smoothed them with his hands.

He read again Esterhazy's summary of the contents of the Dreyfus dossier, the summary he'd found so damning when first he'd read it. It matched in every respect what he'd seen in Picquart's copy of the dossier. There was no doubt that Esterhazy had seen it.

He took up the page he'd stolen from Picquart's packet, unfolded it. It was a letter; or rather, a photostat of a letter. The letter was hand-written. There was no salutation and no signature:

Being without information as to whether you desire to see me, I send you nevertheless, Monsieur, some interesting information, viz:

1. A note concerning the hydraulic brake of the 120mm gun.

2. A note upon the organization of the mobilization of troops to the frontier, as some modifications will be carried out according to the new plan.

3. A note concerning a modification in the formations of the artillery.

4. A note relative to the plan for conquest of Madagascar.

5. The proposed new manual of artillery.

This last document is exceedingly difficult to obtain, and I can only have it at my disposal for a very few days. The copies are numbered and each officer is required to return his copy after the maneuvers. Therefore you must glean from it what you can, or copy it if you wish, and let me have it back again as soon as possible. I am just starting for maneuvers.

This could only be the *bordereau*, the infamous and treasonous communication which had begun the Dreyfus affair. He laid it on the table alongside Esterhazy's summary of the dossier; the summary that had convinced him of Dreyfus's guilt. Even now, he wanted to believe it; wanted to believe that secret dossier put the matter to rest. But he could not; not now, not having seen the copy of the *bordereau* in Picquart's file. Not having now confirmed that what he'd suspected when he'd taken the *bordereau* from the file in Seigneur's desk was surely true. The truth was evident in every line of Esterhazy's note. It could be plainly read in the crabbed style of the hand, known to anyone by the slant of the letters; it cried out from every loop and curl of the text. The man who wrote this summary — the man who'd given him dozens of other documents he'd written, documents Welles could even now see clearly in his mind's eye — that man was the same man who'd written the *bordereau*. The same man who'd sold secrets to the Germans; the man for whose crimes Dreyfus now languished in chains in the sweltering hell that was Devil's Island. That man was Esterhazy.

Part 3

"When the truth is buried underground it grows. It chokes. It gathers such an explosive force that on the day it bursts out, it blows up everything with it."

— *Emile Zola, January 13, 1898*

Chapter 24

Paris, August 1897

Welles was only just in time. Had he waited one more day, Picquart would already have departed for Tunisia. As it was, Picquart was busy and, Welles thought, not entirely happy to be interrupted. Still, the colonel showed him into his office. A servant brought coffee and, having served it, left the two men alone.

"Thank you for seeing me," began Welles. "I would not have disturbed you had I not felt that the matter was of the utmost importance. In the days since we met at the Seigneur home, I have formed a suspicion, one that has been growing in my mind until I feel it is nearly a certainty."

He paused, but Picquart said nothing, merely nodded for him to continue.

"In the course of my work as a journalist in Paris, I have come to know several officers of the French Army. Among them is a Major Esterhazy. Do you know him, sir?"

"Esterhazy?" Picquart was surprised. "Yes, I know the man. Why do you ask?"

Welles ignored the question. "Can you tell me, then, if Major Esterhazy was among the original suspects in the Dreyfus case? Those officers with the background needed to supply the secrets that were given to the Germans?"

Picquart stared at him, a look at the same time suspicious and appraising. Welles waited.

"Yes," said Picquart at last, gruffly. "He fits the profile."

"Then, colonel, I suggest to you that Esterhazy is the true culprit of the affair."

Picquart rose, crossed to the window. He stood with his back to Welles, hands clasped behind him, staring out the window, obviously deep in thought.

"Why Esterhazy?" he asked at last, without turning from the window.

"As I said, I'm acquainted with the man," said Welles. "I understand that he serves on the General Staff, in the fourth bureau."

Picquart did not reply. Welles went on.

"The fourth bureau concerns itself with transport and communications," he said. "Esterhazy would have access to Dreyfus's correspondence. He would be in the perfect position to introduce false evidence. The letters with the secret writing you spoke about."

"Indeed," said Picquart, still with his back to Welles. "What else?"

"His handwriting," said Welles. "I have seen it, and to my eyes, it matches that of the *bordereau*."

At this, Picquart turned to face him, a look of anger on his face.

"And how is it, Mister Welles, that you have come to see the *bordereau*?"

"I have seen the copy you left with Monsieur Seigneur," Welles said.

Picquart's face went red. Welles went on hurriedly.

"Seigneur is blameless, I assure you. He would not show it to me without your permission. Nevertheless, I have seen it. I took it to examine, without his permission."

With obvious effort, Picquart calmed himself. He nodded for Welles to continue.

"Have you compared Esterhazy's handwriting with that of the *bordereau*?" Welles asked. "If the hand is the same, surely that would provide what you need to pursue the man."

Picquart leaned back against the windowsill, folded his arms across his chest.

"They are similar, I will grant you that," he said. "Just as I can find similarities in the hand of several of the men. Including Alfred Dreyfus, Monsieur Welles." Picquart shook his head. "At the trial, the testimony of the handwriting experts was useless. *The similarity of the loops in these letters make it certain that Dreyfus is the author of both*, says one. *The differences between the loops in these letters show that Dreyfus cannot have written the bordereau*, says another." He spread his hands, a gesture of helplessness. "Useless, as I say. If you wish to indict Major Esterhazy, you'll have to have more."

Welles had thought it would be enough to point the finger at Esterhazy and the handwriting evidence would do the rest. Now he understood that Picquart had anticipated him; that he already knew the hand was similar but would not be convinced by that kind of evidence. What else could he tell the man?

"You are a curious man, Monsieur Welles," Picquart said. "You have involved yourself in this affair, you and Mademoiselle Seigneur. You are allies; indeed, I would guess you are more than that. She trusts you, yet you repay that trust by betraying her father's confidence."

Picquart raised his eyebrows, inviting reply, but Welles had none. Picquart continued.

"Mademoiselle Seigneur's motivation is transparent: She believes Dreyfus is the victim of prejudice, and her nature demands that this injustice be righted. You, on the other hand, do not strike me as a crusader for justice."

"I am as committed to justice as the next man," Welles said. "I abhor prejudice in any form."

"Yes, I'm sure you do," said Picquart agreeably, but without conviction. "But tell me, Monsieur Welles, what is the nature of your association with Major Esterhazy?"

"I am not at liberty to say," Welles said. "I fear you must trust me."

Picquart snorted. He moved away from the window, circled his desk and sat behind it. He leaned forward, elbows on the desktop, hands clasped together before him.

"Let me explain the situation to you, Monsieur Welles," he said. "My superiors already know that I suspect Esterhazy, and why. They know he had the necessary access to the secret materials the spy gave to the Germans. They know his handwriting is similar to that of the *bordereau*. Knowing these things, they persist in their insistence that Dreyfus is guilty. If you mean to change their minds, you cannot do it by repeating what they already know."

"How, then?" asked Welles. "What will it take to convince them that Esterhazy is a traitor?"

Picquart shrugged.

"That is the wrong question," he said. "I venture to guess that if they were to catch Esterhazy in the act of spying, they might arrest him; but still they would not budge one inch from their conviction that Dreyfus is also guilty. No, Monsieur Welles, if you mean to free Dreyfus, it is not enough to point the finger at another man. What is needed is to destroy the case against Dreyfus."

"I tell you, colonel, that I know with certainty that Dreyfus is innocent," Welles said. "Esterhazy framed him to avoid being caught himself. The evidence in the dossier is false."

Picquart regarded Welles with a look of suspicion.

"Tell me how you can know that," he said.

When Welles did not reply, he went on.

"In Seigneur's home," he said, "I told you that I had a number of men followed. Esterhazy was one of them. It's true that he never led us to any suspicious encounters. On several occasions, however, the men following him lost his trail. It was never clear whether he deliberately evaded us or if it was just bad luck. Now I confess I find myself wondering something."

He looked at Welles expectantly. Welles nodded for him to go on.

"I wonder whether, if my men had not lost sight of Esterhazy, he would have led them to you?"

Welles tried to hold Picquart's eyes but failed.

"I see," said Picquart. "I thank you for coming to see me. But I had much to do today, and you have given me more, so I fear I have no more time."

Welles stood. "What will you do?"

"I must communicate your suspicion to someone else before I leave. Not someone in the Army; that will do little good, I fear. We must bring pressure from outside, from the government. I know a man in the Senate; I think he can be trusted to seek the truth."

"Will you use my name?"

Picquart walked around the desk, stood close to Welles.

"If I were free to do as I ought," he said, "I would arrest you this instant. I think that would be the quickest way to get to the bottom of this matter. As it stands, I can't, and if I were to denounce you to my colleagues, I fear they would do nothing. And I think it would not help my case to mention your name."

Picquart gestured to the door. He did not offer his hand. Welles took his hat from the table where he'd left it, crossed to the door. There he turned to face Picquart.

"Tell me something," Welles said. "If you can. How is it that you intercepted the *bordereau* in the first place? And the other things in the dossier. How did you get them?"

Picquart eyed him warily.

"Why do you want to know?" he asked.

"It may be important," Welles said. He shrugged. "Call it a professional courtesy."

Picquart hesitated, then seemed to come to a decision.

"The woman who cleans von Schwartzkoppen's office, at the embassy. A Madame Bastian. She works for us, Monsieur Welles. Good day to you."

Chapter 25

London, 12 August 1898

"You gave Esterhazy up," said Lawrence without preamble. "And more, you gave *yourself* up. You've betrayed us, Welles. Betrayed your country."

Welles sighed, lifted his nearly empty glass, drained it. He stood — pistol in one hand, glass in the other — and retrieved the decanter. He refilled his glass. He had been sitting for hours, and his legs were stiff, so he took a turn around the room, examining the paintings on the wall. Green rolling hills, horses and riders, and always the small red figure of the fox.

"Yes," he said at length. "At the time, it seemed the only thing I could do. I knew Esterhazy was guilty, but I couldn't prove it without exposing my relationship with him. I thought that if I could confirm Picquart's suspicions, he would be able to find the evidence to bring down Esterhazy on his own."

"From a posting in Tunisia?" objected Bingham. "I don't understand you, Welles. You had the evidence in your hands. What more did you need? You had only to show it to someone."

"Picquart had convinced me otherwise," Welles said. "No, Mister Bingham, it was clear that there was a conspiracy at the highest levels of the Army, one intent on keeping Dreyfus in chains; and that this conspiracy would not be defeated merely by indicting Esterhazy. To free Dreyfus, it would be necessary to destroy the case against him."

"You might have told Miss Seigneur," Bingham said. "Or her father."

Welles shrugged. "What could I tell them? How would I explain it? I couldn't tell Georges I'd stolen those documents from her father's desk. I couldn't tell her about Esterhazy, and how I knew he was a traitor. I couldn't even implicate Esterhazy, for I felt sure that she would uncover the link between us. She might even discover the part I'd played in persecuting Dreyfus. Then I would lose her. She would never forgive me for that." He drank more brandy. "So, I resolved not to tell them. I was determined to expose Esterhazy, but not at the risk of telling Georges what I had done. I had to find another way. The next day I made a copy of the *bordereau*, then returned it to the folder in Seigneur's office."

Bingham regarded Welles with a look of pity.

"Your life is a lie, sir," he said. "A tangle of lies. You have made it so."

"So I have," said Welles. "I was a fool, and I have brought myself to the brink of ruin. Only I have not done it alone. These men here have helped me to do it."

"Helped you to do it?" The Prime Minister was incredulous. "You blame me for the ruin you've made of your life? Why, before this night, I had never even heard your name."

"Had you never, sir? You surprise me. But I think you may assume too much — or perhaps too little! — when it comes to Sir Reginald. He is your creature. You have let him off the leash. You must answer to those whom he bites."

Salisbury shot a glance at Lawrence, but the other man said nothing. Salisbury turned back to Welles.

"What has Sir Reginald to do with your predicament, Mister Welles?"

"I am coming to that, I assure you."

Chapter 26

The Journal of Lieutenant Andre Durand

Friday, 19 February 1897
Zongo
Congo Free State

We arrived in Bangui three days ago. It is a small outpost, dwarfed by its Belgian neighbor, Zongo, located just across the river in the Free State. The colonial administrator here — a Monsieur Rousset — is an industrious sort and has been of considerable assistance in helping to unload the Villes and prepare her for the return to Brazzaville. I will take her back myself, while Baratier remains in Bangui to organize the next stage of our journey.

From here the river is too shallow for the Villes. We will need canoes, as many as we can get, so I crossed the Ubangi this morning to visit Zongo, looking to buy them from the Company. Corporal Dialike came with me, along with a few men to row the canoes back.

A constant flow of canoes arrived at the Zongo dock from upriver, rowed by black men bearing baskets of the small gray balls of rubber. These men set out at once from the docks with their baskets balanced on their heads. We left our squad of men guarding our canoe and Dialike and I followed the natives into the village in search of the Company office.

Zongo might once have been a typical native village, but now it resembled nothing so much as a factory compound. The land rose rapidly as we got further from the river, so that soon we emerged into a large open space where the ground was more or less dry. There were a half-dozen raised, open-sided warehouses of the type I'd seen in Giri. Three score or more native men labored at forming the rubber balls into large blocks and stacking the blocks for shipment. They worked under the watchful eyes of native soldiers bearing rifles.

The men with baskets stood in line before a large table. A white man sat at the table and several others stood behind him. All the white men were armed. Each native in turn presented his basket for inspection. After the balls of rubber had been counted and weighed, the native took from around his neck a leather thong on which a metal disk had been threaded. The white man scrutinized the disk then made a notation on a tally sheet. Payment was made in the form of a bundle of goods wrapped in a short length of cloth, which the native accepted without a word.

We approached the table and I introduced myself, asking where I might find the manager of the settlement. One of the men pointed the way and I thanked him. We headed across the factory compound in the direction he'd pointed.

'Did you see the payment?' I whispered to Dialike. 'Some cloth and beads. A knife. A bit of food. Why would men do this work for such a poor reward?'

'They have no choice, Monsieur' he replied. 'They must work or die.'

Just then we heard a shout. Two native soldiers were dragging one of the men away from the table. We watched as they tied him to a wooden frame erected at the side of a shed. They stepped back and a third soldier began to flog the man with a chicotte, a length of braided leather invented for this purpose. The native screamed, a piteous sound. I shouted an objection. I took a step toward them, then another; but Dialike grabbed me by the arm, arresting my progress.

'No, Monsieur,' he said. 'Look at them.'

He indicated the white men, who had heard my shout and now watched us warily. Seeing their faces, I knew that these men would not permit us to interfere. Indeed, I found it easy to believe they would kill us if we tried. The whipping continued; the sharp crack of the lash accentuated by the howls it produced.

We turned our backs on the scene and continued our journey across the compound. At the far end we found a trail that disappeared into the gloom of the bush. Dialike took the lead, and we made our way for perhaps a hundred yards to a second clearing. On the far side stood a small house of whitewashed planks, raised on pilings above the damp ground.

To our right was a long, low rambling structure. Several white men sat idly in chairs on the wooden porch, and as we watched, another emerged from the darkened doorway to look our way. The barracks, then, I thought. A curl of wood smoke rose into the treetops from somewhere behind the structure, and I could smell the aroma of meat cooking.

Dialike touched my shoulder, pointed to the left. Here was a third building of unpainted wood, in many places already marred by dampness and rot. Like the other two buildings, it was raised above the ground, but there was no shaded porch. Instead, from one end of the building stretched a cordon of stakes and wire, penning a large area of damp ground into something like a corral for livestock. Beyond the wire I could just make out indistinct shapes moving in the shadow of the tree canopy overhead.

'The women,' said Dialike.

Unable to stop myself, I walked toward the pen. Several black soldiers stood guard, and one watched me as I approached. The women in the enclosure clustered in small groups, chained together by their ankles. It was difficult to count them in the gloom of their prison, but there must have been more than a hundred of them. Then I smelled the stench of the pen — there seemed to be no accommodation for sanitation at all — and I halted in my tracks. Dialike was beside me.

'Monsieur, we are here for canoes,' he said.

He nodded his head in the direction of the white cottage.

'The manager will be there.'

I turned away from the pen, started toward the cottage. A white man approached from the barracks. He nodded to me, touched his cap as he passed. I turned to watch him. He stopped before one of the guards, spoke to him quietly. The guard nodded, turned, and walked to the pen. He took a ring of keys from his pocket, unlocked the gate, and entered the enclosure. He approached a group of women, who shrank from him. He shouted at them and they were still. He selected a key from the ring and used it to separate one woman from the group. He took her by the arm and led her out, locking the gate behind him. Other than his shout, the whole thing happened in silence.

He stood before the white man, presenting the woman. Again, the man spoke quietly. The guard stripped her of the cloth she wore. She stood nude, her feet and legs coated with the filth of the pen. Another guard brought a bucket of water and doused her legs with it, washing most of the muck away. The white man nodded, grabbed her by the arm and led her toward us.

I felt a hand grip my own right wrist, hard, and looked down to see that my fingers had curled around the grip of my pistol. Dialike's hand held my arm tightly, preventing me from drawing the weapon. For a moment I was angry. I struggled to free my hand, but his grip was strong.

'There is nothing for us here, Monsieur,' he said, his voice low but urgent. 'We will find canoes elsewhere. Let us leave this place.'

The man reached us, dragging the woman by the arm. He nodded to me as he passed. I tried to meet her eyes, but she turned her head, sent her gaze to the ground, whether in fear or shame I cannot say. They climbed the porch and disappeared into the dark interior of the barracks.

Dialike released my arm. He nodded in the direction of the river. We turned to go that way, then I stopped. My nose was filled with the smell of the cooking meat. Something had occurred to me quite suddenly, and I walked quickly toward the side of the barracks. Dialike was behind me, calling to me, but I ignored him and went on, guided by the trail of smoke rising into the sky.

I stopped abruptly, tried to make sense of the scene before me. Someone had dug a wide, shallow pit, built a strong fire, then scattered the hot coals across the pit and covered them with piles of wet moss and leaves. Smoke billowed from the pit, rising into the hot, humid air and blowing over a kind of wooden trellis that had been erected behind the pit, leaning away from it at an angle. Cuts of meat had been hung on the trellis, to be preserved in the smoke; but the ones near the bottom were too close to the cinders and were being roasted by the heat. Something about the picture was odd, though, and I took a few steps closer and saw it was not meat they were smoking; the rack was filled with the fresh-cut hands of men, *being preserved against rot by the smoke. There were more than a hundred of them. The trellis, I understood, was like an abacus. A means of balancing the books, bullets issued against bullets used. An accounting.*

I reeled, nearly fell to the ground. My cap fell off, but Dialike was beside me and he picked it up, put it back on my head. He took me by the arm, led me away from the fire. We passed an open window. From somewhere inside the barracks I heard the native woman weeping, her sobs rhythmic and punctuated by the sound of a man grunting.

I am in a kind of hell, a hell I begin to fear has been made by men like me.

Chapter 27

London, August 1897

The carriage dropped Welles on Horse Guards Road, at the foot of the stairs leading up to King Charles Street. He paid the driver and climbed the stairs. To his left was the long stone facade of the Foreign Office. He walked quickly along the pavement, past the entrance to the India Office to the main entrance, about halfway down the block.

He passed through the portal and into a courtyard: a long, open space rising three full stories and covered by a glass roof. To either side, a series of slim columns rose to graceful arches, each framing a window, and the pattern was repeated on the floors above. Midway across the courtyard on either side, two broad, shallow stairways each led up to doorways. Welles walked purposefully to the one on his right, climbed the short flight of stairs, and passed into the lobby. He presented himself to the man behind the reception desk.

"Percival Welles, to see Sir Reginald Hull."

He waited while the man checked the appointment book.

"Through that door, up the stairs, at the end of the hall."

He took the stairs two at a time, then walked briskly down the corridor to the end, where he found himself in reception room. The clerk at the desk looked up.

"Mister Welles? You're late. Sir Reginald is waiting."

The clerk rose, ushered Welles to the door. He opened it and pronounced Welles's name. Welles stepped into the room and the clerk closed the door behind him.

"Percy," said Hull, from behind his desk. "How very nice to see you. Please, do sit down."

Welles sat.

"I'm afraid I don't have much time," Hull said. "What did you want to see me about?"

"It is about Dreyfus," said Welles. He saw the look on Hull's face, went on quickly. "I have discovered he is innocent."

"Are we going to talk about Dreyfus again? I thought you understood. It's no business of ours, Percy. It can't conceivably help us. We are not interested in Dreyfus."

Hull was still smiling, but his tone was impatient. Undaunted, Welles went on.

"I'll grant that it was no business of ours before," he said. "But that has changed. When we forged a letter that ended any chance of a reprieve for Dreyfus, we became responsible for his plight."

"That is one view," Hull said, dismissively. "What makes you think he is innocent?"

"I know he is innocent," said Welles. "It wasn't Dreyfus who sold secrets to the Germans. It was Esterhazy."

The smile vanished.

"What do you mean, it was Esterhazy?" Hull demanded.

"He's the traitor, not Dreyfus. He spies for the Germans, just as he does for us."

"Where is this coming from, Percy? How can you know it was our man, not Dreyfus?"

"I've seen the *bordereau*. That's the document the French recovered from the Germans, the one that first put them on to the spy. The handwriting is clearly Esterhazy's. I saw it immediately."

"Handwriting?" The smile returned, accompanied by a roll of the eyes. "You can't be serious."

"I've been looking at Esterhazy's handwriting for more than a year and a half, Sir Reginald. I know it when I see it."

"Perhaps," said Hull. He regarded Welles with curiosity. "But tell me, Percy," he asked. "How did you get your hands on this *bordereau*? The one Esterhazy gave the Germans, I mean."

"From a man named Picquart. He was the head of counter-intelligence in Paris, the man charged with reviewing the Dreyfus case."

"I don't understand. Why should Picquart give these things to you?"

"He didn't give them to me," said Welles. "He gave them to Georges Seigneur, Miss Seigneur's father."

Welles explained the meeting at the Seigneur house, and how he had sneaked a look at the documents Picquart left with Monsieur Seigneur. How he'd taken the copy of the *bordereau* and compared the writing with Esterhazy's own.

"Does Picquart know you have it?"

"No," Welles lied. He had no intention of revealing his conversation with Picquart. "And I don't have it anymore. I returned it to Seigneur's office before it could be missed."

"And you've told no one else about this? No one, Percy, not even Miss Seigneur?"

"I have told no one except you."

"That was wise," said Hull. He shook his head as if in appreciation. "Well, isn't our Count the scoundrel."

"You never suspected?"

"No, Percy, I had no idea. How could I know he was playing a double game? He must be cleverer than I thought. In any event, you've done fine work here. It's good to know about him. We may be able to use it to our advantage."

"Use it?" asked Welles, dumbfounded. "Esterhazy is finished, surely."

"Finished?" Hull's voice was quiet, but his eyes revealed his barely repressed impatience. "What are you talking about, man?"

Welles opened his mouth to speak, then closed it. He paused, searching for the right words.

"If Esterhazy is guilty, then Dreyfus is innocent," he said. "If we had not interfered, the poor man would be free by now."

Hull said nothing. The two of them sat in silence for some time, each waiting for the other to speak.

"We are responsible," said Welles at last. "We must do something to help Dreyfus."

"Do something?" repeated Hull. "What did you have in mind, that we should deliver Esterhazy up to the French? No? Then how do you propose to help Dreyfus?"

Welles said nothing. In fact, he had meant to propose precisely that.

"Listen to me, Welles," said Hull. "Esterhazy is our best-placed source. He's providing us with invaluable material, things we can't get from anyone else. Your job is to help him; to protect him. I warned you once before about your obsession with Dreyfus."

Something seemed to occur to Hull, and he nodded at the thought.

"It isn't your obsession, though, is it?" he said. "It's that Seigneur woman. She's addled your brain. Get hold of yourself, man."

"Georges has nothing to do with it." Welles was angry now. "We have a responsibility—"

"*What is that damned Jew to us?*" Hull roared, his hand slapping the desktop for emphasis. "If he isn't a spy, then surely he is some other kind of villain. Why should we care what happens to him? Our responsibility is to Her Majesty's Government, Percy. That is the profession you've chosen. We make hard choices for the good of our country. If you aren't up to it, then say so now."

Of all the things Welles had imagined Hull might say, this had never occurred to him. For a moment he thought he would walk out. Yet he stayed in his seat, because he knew that if he were to quit now, he could do nothing for Dreyfus. He took a deep breath, trying to slow the racing of his heart.

"Yes, I see," he said. "Of course, I'm being foolish. Please accept my apologies."

Hull eyed him with a look of cold appraisal, searching his face as if trying to read his thoughts. Then, apparently satisfied, he dismissed Welles.

"Good. Then you'd best get back to Paris, hadn't you?"

Somehow, he was in the reception room again. The clerk said something to him but he took no note of it. There was a droning sound in his ears, a kind of buzzing. He walked numbly across the room, opened the door, stepped out into the corridor. He descended the stairs to the lobby, turned toward the entrance. Then something occurred to him. He turned back to the stairway, but instead of climbing the stairs he descended to the basement. He walked along an empty hallway, through another door and found himself standing before an empty counter. He rang the bell. A moment later a clerk appeared.

"I'm Welles," he said. "In from Paris. I need the Esterhazy file."

"Esterhazy?"

"Yes, Esterhazy. Marie Charles Walsin-Esterhazy, Paris."

"A moment, sir."

The clerk disappeared into the file room, returning a few minutes later with a file in hand.

"This one is restricted access, sir. Did you say Welles?"

"Yes, Percival Welles."

The clerk opened the file, read the first page.

"Yes, very well, sir. But it can't leave the premises."

"Of course," said Welles. "I just need to see it for a few minutes."

The clerk nodded. He placed the file on the counter, opened a ledger, made an entry.

"Sign here, sir."

Welles took the offered pen, signed the ledger.

"The reading room is through there."

Welles stepped around the counter, took the file, and followed the clerk into an adjacent room. There were several small desks in the room, one of them occupied. The man looked up at Welles, then back to the file open on the desk before him. Welles chose the desk farthest from the man, where he sat and opened the file.

It was arranged in chronological order, newest item on top, each page punched and bound to the folder by a thin metal clasp. He flipped through the file, page after page of reports he'd sent, documents he'd gotten from Esterhazy and passed on to London. Then he reached something he hadn't seen before, and began to read in earnest, turning the pages slowly.

Thirty minutes later, he had reached the end. He looked up from the file. The other man was intent on his own reading. Quickly, Welles flipped back through the file until he found the page he wanted. He tugged gently but steadily on the page until it tore free of the binding. He lowered the page into his lap, folded it twice, then slipped it into his jacket pocket.

At the counter he returned the file. The clerk made a note in the ledger, then picked up the file. Welles turned to go. At the door he paused, looked back. The counter was deserted; the clerk had taken the file to the archive. Welles stepped quickly to the counter, turned the ledger around, examined it. Then, without pausing to think further, he tore the page from the book He stuffed it into his pocket and departed.

Chapter 28

Paris, September 1897

A woman at the next table stepped gracefully onto her chair, then from there onto the table. As her dinner companions scrambled to move glasses and plates out of the way, she struck a pose: one leg before the other, the knee slightly bent, the foot pointed and only the toes touching the table, palms resting on her thighs. Slowly, she drew her hands up her body, the front of her dress rising with them to expose her legs. When her hands reached her hips, she paused, held the pose. Her eyes slowly surveyed the room, seeming to make contact with the eyes of each member of her audience before moving on to the next. She released her dress, raised her hands above her head, brought them together in a sharp clap; once, then twice. Then she was dancing, a slow, seductive movement. The orchestra caught the rhythm and began to play. Everyone clapped in time to the music, even the waiters. The woman closed her eyes, moved as if she were alone, dancing for her own pleasure. It was a thoroughly sensual experience, and Georges overheard one man say to another *My God, I feel as if even my thighs are blushing.*

The danced ended and the room erupted in cheering. The woman smiled and bowed deeply, her breasts nearly spilling out of the top of her dress, and the cheering grew even louder. One of her companions offered a hand and she stepped lightly down, first to a chair and then to the floor. A waiter appeared to reset the table, the other waiters sprang into action, and dinner went on.

"I told you that you would like Maxim's," said Max, seated next to Georges.

On the other side of Max was Alessandro Panizzardi, the Italian military attaché who was, Georges believed, Max's lover. Beside him was Panizzardi's wife Francesca, the Countess of Acerra. She was a striking woman, a few years older than Georges but a good deal younger than her husband. The Countess was engrossed in conversation with the man to her left, one Emile LeBlanc, a stockbroker rumored to be among the wealthiest men in Paris. Over the course of the evening it had become clear that he, in turn, was her lover. Between LeBlanc and Georges was another couple, an American writer and his wife whose names Georges had been told but now could not remember.

"That was extraordinary," said Georges. "Who is she?"

"She calls herself La Belle Otero," said Panizzardi. "From Spain originally, I think, though she is thoroughly Parisian now. She dances at *les Folies*."

"She is a courtesan, my dear." This from the Countess Francesca. "Though hardly a common one. They say she keeps company with the Prince of Wales."

"Does she do this sort of thing often?" asked the American. His face was flushed, and his wife's face was bright pink, the blush extending to the top of her bosom.

"Yes," said Max. "Monsieur Cornuche encourages it. He has an idea of the kind of place he wants Maxim's to be, the people he wants to attract. The right sort, mind you, but those who want to have fun. Not above a bit of bawdiness, but never crass or vulgar. Beautiful people." He smiled, raised his champagne glass in a toast. "People like us!"

They laughed, everyone drank, and Max called for another bottle.

She had seen a good deal of Max and his friends in the last year. At first, she had hoped to learn something from him, but he never brought up Dreyfus. On the few occasions when she had, he had simply laughed and said he knew less about it even than she did. She stopped asking. She liked Max, enjoyed his company and that of his friends, and her evenings with him had become a welcome respite from the unsettled tension of the nights she spent with Percy.

Something in their affair had gone badly wrong and she was hard-pressed to understand what it was. She had begun to wonder if Percy had another lover. There were the nights when he declined her company, citing one excuse or another, but never really managing to be convincing, so that it seemed to her that he led another life, one he kept from her. She had looked for signs of another presence in his flat. He'd given her a key, months ago, and sometimes she went there unexpected, dreading what she might find. But there was never anyone there with him; and, truth be told, she could not be certain whether she was relieved or disappointed by the failure.

They made love now with a kind of quiet urgency, as if they were consciously trying to bridge the divide between them. One time, afterward, she had felt so alone that she was moved to tears. She tried to cry quietly, lying in the dark, but Percy heard her. He was beside himself, anxious to know what was wrong, but she could not bring herself to confront him about his secrets. They lay awake for hours, in each other's arms but — somehow — she remained desperately alone.

"Are you well, my dear?"

It was Max, leaning close and speaking in a whisper. With a start, Georges realized that she'd slipped away. She took his hand in one of hers, caressed it with the other, forced a smile.

"I think you know, Georges, how fond I am of you," Max said, returning the smile. "It pains me to see you so melancholy. Your Percy, he is a beast, I think."

"*Cher* Max," she said, squeezing his hand. "You are too kind to me."

"No more than you deserve, my dear," he said. "You must tell me if there is anything I can do."

She wondered then if he might finally be willing to tell her the truth about his involvement in the Dreyfus affair, then felt ashamed at the thought. She was, she realized, unworthy of his friendship. She felt the sadness come over her in a wave. Then the Countess was trying to get her attention, something to do with gowns, and with no little skill — for it was plain to Georges that the woman had sensed her distress — drew her back into the conversation. There was more champagne. Panizzardi told a long and rambling story, but one with a good payoff, and then they were all laughing. The American told another, not so long, but even more funny, and she laughed until she thought her gown would split. She looked across at the Countess, caught her eye, smiled her gratitude. The Countess smiled back, nodding almost imperceptibly.

The party went on until the early hours of the morning. Time passed in a blur of champagne and laughter, until with a start she realized that the American writer's hand was on her leg. It had been there for some time, slowly inching up her thigh, bringing her dress with it. She shot a look at the man's wife, hoping for rescue from that quarter, but she saw that the woman was already watching the hand, intent on it, mouth slightly open, breathing deeply, her face flushed and the crimson once again spreading down her neck to color her bosom. Georges leaned in, close to the American, breathing deeply into his neck. She brushed her lips against his cheek, at the same time taking his hand firmly in hers and lifting it from her leg.

"Put it there again, *cher*," she whispered softly into his ear, "and I'll cut it off."

He pulled the hand away, smiled sheepishly. She turned to Max.

"It's late, Max," she said. "I really should be going."

He looked at his watch, raised his eyebrows in mock surprise.

"My God," he said, "it *is* late. I'm afraid, my friends, that I must see Georges home now."

They objected loudly, but he insisted, and, with good grace and cheer, the party broke up. She kissed Panizzardi on the cheek, and LeBlanc, and then hugged the Countess tightly. The American offered his hand, which she took. His wife did the same but could not meet her eyes. Then they were out the door, through the bar and into the street where Max's carriage was waiting.

In the carriage, Max took Georges' hand.

"I'm afraid I have bad news, my dear," he said. "I will be leaving Paris soon."

It was as if she had been struck a blow.

"Leaving Paris? Why? Where are you going?"

"To Berlin," he said. "I have been recalled, Georges. I am to leave next month, once my replacement has arrived." He smiled sadly. "It is to do with this Dreyfus business. There has been too much public speculation about me, about my role in the affair. The Foreign Ministry feels my position here has been compromised. I have tried to convince them otherwise. It has bought me more time here — I love this city, Georges — but they have at last decided."

"Then it is my fault," said Georges. "I have done everything I can think of to keep the story alive. To free poor Dreyfus."

"It is no one's fault. These things happen, Georges. You cannot blame yourself."

"I do," she said. "But what does it matter? I could not have done other than I have done. Oh, Max, what will I do without you?"

She turned in her seat to face him.

"You must know that, when I first began to see you, it was only to do with the affair," she said. "But we have become friends. I shall miss you terribly."

"And I shall miss you."

He took her hand in his. They rode together in silence until the carriage came to a stop in front of her father's house. The lamps by the door were lit and the butler waited on the doorstep. Max looked at her for a long moment.

"Georges," he said, "I have come to a decision. I want to tell you something. I shouldn't, but it will make no difference to me now and perhaps it will be of help to you." He held her hand in both of his. "I swear to you, Georges, that whatever else I have done, I have never in my life met Captain Dreyfus. I have never had dealings of any kind with him. Until he was arrested, I had never even heard the poor man's name."

She searched his eyes.

"That is nothing new," she said. "You have always denied having anything to do with the affair."

"That is one kind of telling. This is another."

He was telling her that he knew Dreyfus was innocent, she thought. *Knew it because he was involved. He knew who the real traitor was.*

"Oh, Max," she said. "Can't we at last put an end to the secrets between us? Tell me what you know, I beg you."

He released her hand, opened the carriage door, stepped out onto the pavement. He reached up to help her down. He held her by the shoulders, kissed her lightly on the lips. Then he released her, climbed into the carriage, closed the door. The carriage started forward, then stopped abruptly. His head appeared in the small window of the carriage.

"I can't tell you what you want to know, Georges," he said. "But I can give you some advice."

"Advice?"

"I think, my dear, that you must ask your questions of Percy."

For a moment, she was speechless.

"Of Percy?" she said, barely able to make the words audible.

"Yes. I shall miss you, Georges. Goodbye."

She watched the carriage pull away. It had started to rain. The butler appeared at her side, holding an umbrella over her head. She climbed the steps to the front door, paused there while he closed the umbrella.

"I am going upstairs to change," she said. "Then I'm going out again. Have the carriage brought around to the front, please."

***

It was nearly dawn, cold and raining. Welles had spent the evening following Esterhazy, something he'd begun to do whenever time permitted since he had returned from London. He hoped that Esterhazy would lead him to one or more of the other conspirators, or otherwise provide him with evidence of complicity he could share with Georges. So far, he'd accomplished nothing. Esterhazy spent most nights out, dining, drinking and gambling, and tonight was no exception. Welles had waited for hours outside the Press Club for the Count to emerge, until the owner of the bar in which he waited finally lost patience, tossed him out, and locked up for the night.

He let himself into the lobby of the building. He removed his hat and coat, shaking them vigorously as they shed water onto the stone floor. Madame Hebert would not be pleased. Wearily, he climbed the stairs, one flight after another, until he reached the top. He fumbled with the coat, trying to get his key from the pocket. Freeing it at last, he unlocked the door, turned the knob.

He stopped on the threshold, startled. The lamps were lit, and a fire burned in the grate. Georges was seated at the table. She was dressed casually, wool trousers and a heavy wool sweater, and her cape hung on the coat rack in the corner. There was an ashtray on the table, full of cigarette ends. Beside the ashtray were an open bottle of whisky and two glasses. One glass was half full, the other empty. A blue haze of tobacco smoke hung in the room.

"Good evening, *cher*," she said. "Or should I say good morning?"

"Georges," he said, weakly, for he was suddenly out of breath. "I wasn't expecting you."

"Sit down. Have a drink with me."

She reached for the bottle, poured whisky into the empty glass, then topped up her own.

"It's late, Georges, and I'm really very tired," he said. He pulled the door closed behind him.

"Percy," she said. "Sit down. We need to talk."

He hung his coat and hat on the rack, then sat. She slid a glass across the table to him. She raised hers, waited. He sighed, lifted the glass. They drank. She replaced her glass on the table.

"I don't ask you where you go when you're not with me," she said, "because I don't want to make you lie to me. But you tell me anyway; so still, I get the lies. What other lies have you told me, I wonder?"

"What are you talking about, Georges?" he asked.

She stared at him for a long time, her face hard, unforgiving. Then she took something from her lap, placed it on the table. He recognized the envelope. Suddenly, his throat was dry. He watched as she removed a few pages, laid them on the table and smoothed them with her hands.

"These were hidden in your chair," she said. "I searched for some time before I thought to look there."

She raised her eyebrows as if to invite a response, but he had none. She sighed, shook her head. She held up one of the pages, began to read from it:

"A personal letter, hand-written, containing a list of five secret military documents. Several letters to D from creditors. Letters of an intimate nature from three different women. Two notes between foreign diplomats stationed in Paris, naming D as the source of secret documents."

She paused to look over the page at Welles.

"What is this, Percy?"

He licked his lips. "It is a summary of the contents of the Dreyfus dossier." The words came out in a croak. He swallowed, went on: "I wrote it after out meeting with Picquart. I wanted to have it down on paper."

"With your memory?" She laughed, but her laughter had a hollow quality. She went on: "And, after writing it down, you hid it in a chair?"

He had no answer to this.

"There are things here that Colonel Picquart never told us, Percy. Much more. Almost as if you had seen the file."

"I have seen it," he said, filled with dread. He went on in a rush: "I looked at the file, after Picquart left. When I went back to your father's office for my cigarette-case, you remember?" She said nothing. "I'm sorry, Georges, I couldn't help myself, I had to see it. I should have told you, but I was ashamed." Still she said nothing. "I wrote it down as a precaution," he said, "in case something were to happen to the file."

She leaned forward, held the paper up for him to see.

"Do you think that after all this time I do not know your hand as well as my own?" She shook her head. "You never wrote this. Really, your lies are pathetic, Percy. You must think me an awful fool."

He could think of nothing to say. The contempt on her face was plain to see. She set the page aside, held up another; the photocopy he'd made of the *bordereau*.

"And this?" she asked.

"It is a copy of the *bordereau*," he said. "I took Picquart's copy from the file. I made my own, then put it back."

"Are you the author of the *bordereau*, then?" she asked. Her tone was acid. She held the two documents up before him. "These were written by the same person, Percy. Who wrote them?"

He could not hold her eyes, looked away. She waited in silence. When it was clear that he did not intend to answer, she laid the pages on the table. She took another drink, then set the glass down.

"Now I am asking you," she said deliberately. "Where do you go when you're not with me? What have you been doing all this time, Percy?"

He tried to think of something he could tell her. He might tell her about the work he did for Sir Reginald, about Esterhazy; but each answer would lead to another question. Could he, he wondered, avoid revealing his own role in persecuting Dreyfus? There might be a way, but he needed more time to think. And she was here, before him. There was no time.

Abruptly she stood, stalked to the coat rack and grabbed her cloak. She returned to the table, regarded him. She dropped something on the table, turned and walked towards the door. He looked down at what she'd dropped. It was her key. He leapt to his feet, dashed across the room, took her by the arm.

"Georges," he said, "I can explain everything, I promise—"

She whirled, struck him across the face with her closed fist. The blow stunned him and, reeling, he released her arm. She turned away from him, opened the door. She left it open behind her. He heard her footsteps, first in the hall, then down the many flights of stairs, then across the lobby. The front door slammed. Then there was only the sound of the rain.

Chapter 29

The Journal of Lieutenant Andre Durand

Wednesday, 10 March 1897
On board the Villes de Bruges
Congo River
French Congo

We departed this morning from Brazzaville for the return run to Bangui. Paké-Bô is ill again — another spell of malaria — and they carried him aboard on a stretcher just after first light. I tried to put him in the main cabin where he might rest, but he refused. The Villes is packed to the railings with the rest of our provisions, and there is hardly any space for the men, so he and I will bunk in the pilothouse and the men will use the main cabin.

The Villes rides very low now, lower than she did on our first passage to Bangui. I told Paké-Bô that I feared we would not make it, but he only shrugged.

'Either we will run aground, or we won't, Dédé. In any case, we must get to Bangui, even if we have to walk there.'

For this reason, we steam at full power. The Villes shudders and shakes, her stern paddles pushing the weight of vessel and cargo and men against the sluggish current of the Congo, and the sound of protests from her

shaft, linkage gears and the paddle wheel itself must be heard to be
believed. But we are in a race now, a race to reach Bangui before the
Ubangi is too low for our passage, and we must make the best time we can
while we steam in the deep, open water of the Congo. We will steam day
and night for as long as we can, although of necessity a good deal more
slowly after sundown.

Wednesday, 17 March 1897
On board the Villes de Bruges
Ubangi River
French Congo

We left the Congo yesterday, and our progress now seems interminably
slow. The river is not so low as I feared. Despite that, we make no better
than one-quarter speed as we pick our way among the rocks, searching for
a clear channel deep enough for the Villes to pass. Paké-Bô has grown
steadily stronger and takes his turn in the bow, pointing the way and
shouting commands, appearing in every respect to be having the time of
his life. At Dialike's suggestion we have put most of the men ashore to
lighten the vessel; and as we inch our way up the river, a line of tirailleurs
marches on the left bank, keeping pace with us throughout the day.

When night falls, the men return to the Villes, arranging themselves as
they can atop the stacked crates that we have labored so hard to bring this
far into the wilderness. The weather has been surprisingly clear and even
those men with a berth inside the main cabin seem to prefer the company
of their fellows under the bright stars of the African night. We eat a meal,
then Paké-Bô wanders among the men, stopping to talk with one soldier
or another, as is his way. Mangin accompanies him on these rounds,
though he has little to say to the men.

Several times I have thought to join them, but always I hold back, for I
would not know what to say or how to say it; and, truth be told, I try as
best I can to avoid Mangin's company. I busy myself in the pilothouse,
marking our progress on the chart and trying to estimate that of the next
day. Occasionally I hear the men laughing, Paké-Bô's own laugh loudest
of all.

Tuesday, 30 March 1897
On board the Villes de Bruges
Ubangi River
French Congo

Our good fortune ended today, only twenty miles from Bangui by my reckoning. The Villes ran aground shortly before noon and no amount of effort has served to get her afloat again. This is probably for the best, for on close inspection we found several hull plates sprung on the starboard side. The damage is not so bad that she cannot return to Brazzaville for repairs, but not with the weight of cargo she carries now.

Paké-Bô dispatched Mangin and Dialike with a squad of men to make their way on foot to Bangui. They will march all night and the soonest we can expect help from that quarter is tomorrow. We put the men to work today unloading the Villes; whatever tomorrow may bring, our supplies will go no further on board the Villes. The tirailleurs do not like the work, for they consider themselves soldiers, not bearers. But their discipline is excellent, and they took to the task without complaint. I believe they would do anything for Paké-Bô.

Our delay gave me time to consider what I had avoided thinking about for some time: The problem of General Kitchener at Dongola. Since I first heard about it at Christmas, I have watched my comrades carefully, searching for any sign of apprehension or decline in their confidence about our mission. I have seen nothing. It's true that I have spent most of my time with Baratier, who is eternally enthusiastic, so it would be a shock indeed to see him in any other state. But even confined in such close quarters with Paké-Bô and Mangin, I have seen no signs that either of them is worried about the possibility that we must confront Kitchener and his tens of thousands.

Now that Paké-Bô and I are alone, I resolved to broach the subject. We were in the pilothouse, Paké-Bô busy writing a dispatch to be sent from Bangui. The men toiled below, on deck or knee-deep in the river. I cleared my throat once, then again. He looked up at me and laid his pen down.

'What is it, Dédé?' he asked.

For a moment I could not think how to begin. But Paké-Bô must have taken note of my reluctance, for with a smile and a nod he encouraged me to speak. At last I let out the misgivings I'd harbored for some time. I was committed to our mission, I said; only, how could we hope to prevail against such a force as Kitchener commanded?

'I cannot tell you how pleased I am that you joined us, Dédé,' he said. 'A cadre such as ours requires a diversity of men. What officer has ever been so blessed with three such as I have been given to lead? If something impossible lies before us, then Baratier is the man to do it. If, on the other hand, it is something unthinkable, then that is a job for Mangin. Yes, I know,' he said, seeing my reaction, 'you do not approve of Mangin, but he is a man of courage, nonetheless. It is of a different kind than Baratier's, or yours, but you must trust me when I say we have need of it.'

'What courage have I, then?'

'Why, the courage to persevere, Dédé,' he replied. 'Even when in your heart you believe we will fail. That takes courage too, and that is the rarest kind of all. Baratier goes on because he believes we will win. Mangin because he believes we must win. You go on even when you believe we can't win.'

'And you?' I asked. 'Do you believe we can win against such numbers?'

'It may not come to that,' said Paké-Bô. 'Between us and Kitchener stands the Khalifa, with a hundred thousand fighting men of his own. Kitchener will have to destroy them to reach us. It is by no means certain that he will win through.'

'No,' I said. 'But if he does, we cannot face him alone.'

Paké-Bô stood, turned away from me. He looked upriver, almost as if he expected to see Baratier and his rescue party, but there was no chance of that, not before midday tomorrow at least. I waited in silence. At length, he turned back to me.

'We shall not be alone, Dédé,' he said. 'I cannot tell you more than that, but this much you should know: If we must stand against Kitchener, we will not stand alone.'

Saturday, 2 April 1897
Bangui
French Congo

Baratier came to our rescue just before noon on Thursday, leading a fleet of canoes bearing fifty tiralleurs and an army of laborers. These he put to work immediately, loading our cargo onto the canoes. Once a canoe had been loaded, there was room only for a few rowers and an armed soldier. The remaining bearers were assembled on shore and put to work cutting trees under the watchful eyes of our soldiers. They would carry to Bangui on foot whatever could not be borne by our canoes. For now, they made the tools they would need for the task they must accomplish before setting out on their long march.

It was late afternoon and only a few canoes remained to be dispatched when another arrived, bearing men from the colonial office at Bangui. Among them were a Belgian engineer and his assistant, who would take the Villes de Bruges back to Brazzaville to be repaired. These two men waded into the river and circumambulated the grounded vessel, inspecting every inch of her hull, until they pronounced her safe enough for the journey. Then the engineer boarded her and lit the boiler, detailing a native to feed wood into the firebox and to keep it full as she built up steam.

Now the hard work began. Even unburdened by cargo the Villes de Bruges displaces fully sixty tons. Shifting her off the riverbed and into deeper water was a to be a herculean task. Lines were tied to strong points all along her deck, then passed under the rail to teams of bearers standing in the shallows near the far bank. More laborers were ordered into the river, where they used long wooden poles as levers to shift the Villes while those on the ropes pulled.

It was backbreaking work, being done by men who had rowed the twenty miles from Bangui, then loaded crates weighing sixty pounds each into canoes, then cut and shaped dozens of poles from the dense growth of the Congo forest. I watched in amazement, sure that they must fail. But slowly, inexorably, the Villes began to move, creaking and groaning as she did. The engineer, who had taken up station with those at the ropes, shouted at them, imploring them to pull harder. Baratier, in the shallows on the port side of the vessel, ran from one group of bearers to the next, pointing to the spot where they should fix their levers to maintain the ground they had gained.

Then, with a tremendous shrieking of metal on rocks, the Villes broke free and slid rapidly towards the middle of the river. When he sensed that the ship was afloat, Baratier called his team of men off, and they backed away from her. On the far shore, however, the men at the lines continued to pull, for they had not yet realized that the Villes was moving freely. Those men in the river — between the Villes and deeper water — shouted in fear, turned and tried to flee. The water was too deep and despite their peril they could move only slowly, stumbling over stones on the river bottom. Several of them fell, then struggled to regain their feet as the Villes bore down on them.

From the pilothouse, I watched in horror as she slid over one man, then another. Their screams were sharp and terrible, then cut off abruptly as their heads were forced under the water, drowned or crushed beneath the weight of the ship.

The engineer shouted at the men on the far shore, lashing at them with a chicotte, and at last they stopped pulling. He made two lines fast to trees, and another pair of lines were run out to the near shore, so that the Villes was held fast against the current in the deep channel of the river.

The bearers who had managed to escape death staggered from the water and collapsed on the bank, trembling and exhausted from their ordeal. Almost immediately Dialike was among them, shouting and kicking at them until they struggled to their feet and staggered to join their fellows at the lines which ran to the near shore. The engineer came aboard, and I surrendered the pilothouse to him, grabbing my gear and disembarking.

I watched as teams of men at the ropes on both sides of the river slowly and carefully turned the Ville about so that her bow now faced downstream. The engineer blew the whistle, the lines were released and taken in, the great paddle wheel at the stern began to turn and the Villes slowly pulled away, heading for Brazzaville. The wheel churned up the river bottom, and for a moment I thought I saw bloody pieces of men in the roiling muddy water, but when I closed my eyes and opened them to look again, they were gone. Even now I cannot be sure that I saw them at all.

It had been an exhausting task, but the bearers were far from finished. Now our soldiers prodded them into a line and marched them past the great pile of stores for which there had been no room on Baratier's canoes. There, each man was burdened with a sixty-pound parcel. This he balanced on the top of his head, then set off to follow the man ahead of him to carry his load the twenty miles to Bangui. Mangin led them, taking Dialike and most of the tirailleurs with him to keep the bearers at their task. When the last load had been lifted to the head of the last bearer, the three of us — Paké-Bô, Baratier and me — climbed into the last canoe. The few remaining soldiers joined us, took up oars and propelled us up the river.

Thursday, 20 April 1897
Bangui
French Congo

Paké-Bô says that the next stage of our journey takes us to Ouango, five hundred miles to the east along the Ubangi. Baratier has assembled a fleet of seventy dugout canoes and we still have the boats he purchased at Loango and dragged all the way to Brazzaville. And we are to have another vessel, the steamboat Faidherbe. She is under the authority of the administrator Rousset, who does not want to part with her, so Paké-Bô has commandeered her. Rousset is not pleased, but by the time his complaint can make its way back to Brazzaville, we shall have left Bangui far behind.

We went to look at her today. She is much smaller than the Villes de Bruges, perhaps fifty feet long and narrow of beam. In truth, she is little more than a large boat, her single deck open to the air and fitted with vertical spars to support a canvas canopy for shade. Her boiler and engaging gear occupy fully a third of the deck, so that there is little room for cargo. She is fast, however, and shallow of draft. Her engine drives a single propeller shaft rather than paddle wheels, so she can navigate in even the shallowest of waterways.

Paké-Bô means to use her to ferry men and supplies to Ouango, and from there she will scout ahead of our main party, who will follow more slowly in canoes and on foot. With any luck, he says, we shall be able to steam all the way to Lake No and from there into the Nile. And, once we have reached Fashoda, she will give us a degree of mobility for reconnaissance and communication back along the path we have come.

If Paké-Bô and Baratier seem excited about the prospect of a French-flagged vessel on the upper Nile, Mangin is less so.

'She will be of some use getting us to Ouango, and perhaps even as far as Zemio,' he said. 'But from there she will become a burden. We shall have to carry her. I imagine her boiler alone weighs two tons.'

'If we have to move her over land, we will take her apart,' said Paké-Bô, undaunted.

Mangin walked a few steps along her deck, peering closely at her hull.

'Is she designed to be taken apart?' he asked.

'She was put together,' Baratier replied. 'If she has been assembled by men, men can take her apart.'

Mangin raised his eyebrows at this but said no more. We disembarked and headed back to our camp, walking along the north bank. When we reached a bend in the river, Mangin paused to look back at the Faidherbe. He snorted.

'She is an ugly thing,' he said, 'a highly risky contraption. Imagine how much worse she'll be after we've hacked her into pieces.'

Tuesday, 25 April 1897
On board the Faidherbe
Ubangi River
French Congo

Baratier and I have taken the Faidherbe. We make for Ouango with a cargo of supplies and ten of our tirailleurs. After what we have endured to reach this stage of our journey, it seems a serene and altogether pleasant journey. Paké-Bô was right: With the Faidherbe at our disposal, we will make short work of ferrying our expedition to Ouango and beyond.

How different our undertaking seems now when compared to what has gone before. At last this is the expedition Paké-Bô described from the start — a small band of intrepid explorers moving rapidly, almost invisibly through the waterways of equatorial Africa. I have been filled with *misgivings about all I have seen and the things we have done; but now I am resolved to put them behind me.*

<u>*Monday, 17 May 1897*</u>
<u>*Ouango*</u>
<u>*Bomu River*</u>
<u>*French Congo*</u>

Paké-Bô called a conference today. We met in the hut which serves as the office of the colonial administrator here. Paké-Bô spread his map on the table and nodded to Baratier, who has only just returned from a scouting mission upriver.

'We are here, where the Bomu river flows into the Ubangi,' he said, indicating a point on the map. 'The Bomu is deep enough that we can use the Faidherbe as far as Zemio, a distance of nearly two hundred miles,' he said. 'From there, the river may be too shallow. We shall have to break her apart and carry her.'

Baratier pointed to the map.

'If we are forced to leave the river here, we have a portage of some one hundred fifty miles until we reach the Mere river. There we should find enough water to float her again.'

Mangin snorted. 'One hundred fifty miles. Why not?'

'What do you propose instead, Charles?' Paké-Bô asked Mangin.

'We can use the Faidherbe to reach Zemio,' Mangin said. 'If the river is too shallow from there, we should abandon her. We can proceed by canoe.'

Paké-Bô shook his head. With one hand he traced a line east from Zemio to the Mere, then beyond, until his finger rested on the mark of an outpost.

'This is Tambura,' he said. 'It lies on the Sue river. The Sue flows north, then east, through the marsh of the Bahr-al-Ghazal.'

He moved the finger again, tracing the route as he spoke.

'From there, the marsh flows east to Lake No.'

He stopped again, raised his head to look at us each in turn.

'We have only to get the Faidherbe to the Sue,' he said. 'From there we can steam to Fashoda.'

'Perhaps,' said Mangin. 'Provided we get to the Sue before the dry season sets in. By October, at the latest. If not, we'll be stuck in Tambura for six months waiting for the rains.'

'Then we must reach the Sue before the end of October,' Paké-Bô replied. 'With the Faidherbe.'

Mangin shook his head again. 'Look at the route. We'll have to carry her from Zemio to the Mere.'

'Perhaps not,' said Baratier.

'Very well, perhaps not,' said Mangin. He placed his finger on the map. 'But we certainly will have to carry her from the Mere to Tambura. One hundred miles through the bush; then another hundred and twenty through the marsh. It cannot be done, not in five months.'

'It will be difficult, Charles, but we must try,' said Paké-Bô. 'The Faidherbe will be too valuable where we're going to leave her behind.'

'I agree,' said Baratier.

The three men turned to me.

'I agree also,' I said.

Mangin scowled at the three of us. I thought he would continue the argument, but he did not speak again for the rest of our conference.

Chapter 30

Paris, November 1897

Georges never returned to the office on Boulevard Haussmann. The day after she'd stormed out of Welles's flat, some men arrived for her things, loaded them onto a cart and drove away. He let a week go by, then went to her father's house and knocked on the door. She would not see him.

His business slowly died. He went to the office every morning, but there was less to do with each passing day. Most of the sources on whom they had relied were hers, as were the writers they had used. He quickly realized that without her he was little more than an itinerant journalist himself, desperately scribbling a few lines and hoping to sell them for pennies a word.

He stopped going to the office. He no longer met Esterhazy, no longer even went to Barre's shop. Instead he drank until he was unconscious, starting earlier each day until one day blurred into the next and he lost track of them. The drinking seemed to help him to forget and for a time he surrendered to the welcome oblivion. Then, in the early hours one morning, he was suddenly awake, lying sprawled across the bed and still partly dressed. For the first time in weeks he was sober. He lay in bed and remembered in excruciating detail every moment of that last meeting with Georges.

In the early morning light, he sat at the table in his flat, staring at the stack of cables from Sir Reginald he had not bothered to decrypt. He thought perhaps he ought to read them. He rose from the table and went to the bureau, then changed his mind. Instead, he took his hat and coat from the hook and went out the door.

He walked a few blocks in a cold rain, then ducked into the post office. At the counter a clerk gave him a slip of blue paper. He wrote carefully, worried that his trembling hand might render the message unreadable, then passed the slip back to the clerk along with a few centimes.

Two days later, he was waiting in the fitting room at Barre's shop when Esterhazy arrived in response to the *petit-bleu*. It was bad tradecraft, Welles knew, but he no longer cared if they were observed together. Indeed, he wanted that: he hoped that Esterhazy would be caught.

The two men sat in plain wooden chairs facing each other. Welles adopted a brisk, businesslike tone.

"I've not heard from you in weeks," he said. "Our masters are impatient. What do you have for us?"

The Count held his hands out, palms up, to show he had nothing.

"The wolves are at the door, Percy. I'm being watched all the time. It was all I could do to shake them in order to come here."

It had begun, Esterhazy explained, with the familiar feeling that he was being watched. He soon confirmed it. A man waited outside his flat each morning and followed wherever he went. A different man took his place in the evening. He had only taken the risk of coming to this meeting because he had no other choice. He feared, he said, that he would need Welles's help again.

For his part, Welles assumed that Esterhazy's predicament was the result of Picquart's having communicated his suspicions to the unnamed Senator before he left Paris. He realized at once that this was an opportunity.

"Very well," he said, though with a marked lack of enthusiasm. "I'll cable London, see what can be done. But I wouldn't get my hopes up. They'll want something in return."

"I don't understand, Percy," said Esterhazy. "What are you saying?"

Welles shifted in his chair, crossed one leg over the other.

"I think they mean to cut you loose. You're a risk — an expensive one — and lately, you haven't given us anything worth what we're paying."

Welles meant to put Esterhazy in an impossible position. If the Count tried to produce anything of use to London while he was being so closely watched, he was sure to be caught. If, on the other hand, he did not make the attempt, he could expect no help from Welles or anyone else.

"Be reasonable, Percy. I can't get you anything now."

Welles shrugged.

"You know how they are," he said. "They won't do anything out of kindness. You'll have to give them something."

He waited while Esterhazy digested this.

"All right," The Count said at length, without any hint of his usual warmth. "I'll get them something. But I need more money, Percy."

"How much?"

"Twenty-five thousand francs."

It was a huge sum, at least a thousand pounds. Esterhazy read the look in Welles eyes, and his own expression grew hard.

"Tell them," he said. "Twenty-five thousand pounds, or they get nothing."

"They won't pay it," said Welles.

"They will for Marchand. Bring the money here, Percy. Shall we say next week?"

***

To Welles's surprise, the Count was right: London would pay a fortune for news of Marchand. After a rapid exchange of cables, the money appeared, in a thick leather wallet delivered by a man from the British Embassy. For Welles's part, he hadn't cared whether London agreed to pay or not. It was enough for him that Esterhazy thought they might and, so thinking, would take the risk of trying to obtain secret information under the watchful eyes of the French authorities. With any luck at all, he would be caught in the act. Thus, Welles went to the rendezvous on the appointed day half expecting that Esterhazy would not appear.

He had been waiting alone in the small room for nearly an hour when there was a knock on the door. He slid the bolt, opened the door a crack, then stood back from the doorway and opened it wider. Esterhazy slipped in. He closed the door behind the man, threw the bolt. He returned to the chair he'd taken, but the Count remained standing.

"Do you have the money?" Esterhazy asked without preamble.

"I do," said Welles. "What do you have for me in return?"

"Let me see it."

Welles drew the wallet from his pocket. He opened it, showing Esterhazy the wad of bills.

The Count produced an envelope, held it up for Welles to see.

"A report on Marchand, as requested," he said. "He's camped in a place called Tambura. It's on the Sue river, in a region called the Bahr al-Ghazal."

"And where is that? What is it?"

"It's a marsh. Two hundred thousand square miles of pestilential wetlands which divides the French Congo from the Sudan."

"What does Marchand want there?"

"A good many things, as it happens. He wants artillery, a battery of 42-mm guns. He wants a battalion of men. And he wants an armored steamer, a gunboat. Mostly, though, he wants rain."

"Rain?"

"Yes. The marsh is nearly impassable in the dry season. The water is too shallow to float a vessel, and the grass too thick to hack your way through. The place is rife with malaria. He doesn't want to sit and wait any longer than he must. He wants to get to the other side."

"What's on the other side?"

"If he can make it through, he'll reach deep water at Lake No. That's on the Nile, Percy."

Welles was stunned.

"The Nile is British," he said, echoing what Sir Reginald had told him so many months ago.

"That is a matter of some dispute, I'm told. In any event, that's where he means to go."

Welles opened his mouth to object, closed it. It was pointless to argue, and, in truth, he no longer cared where Marchand was or what he meant to do.

Esterhazy held out the envelope. Welles took it. He stared down at it, lost in thought, until the Count cleared his voice.

"I'll have the money, Percy."

Welles handed him the wallet. Esterhazy held it open and leafed quickly through the stack of bills. Satisfied, he closed it and slipped it into a pocket.

"I believe our collaboration has come to an end," he said. "It is probably for the best. I have been relieved of my duties pending court-martial."

"Court-martial?" repeated Welles. "On what charge?"

"Espionage. The trial will be next month. Even if I am acquitted, I think they will insist that I retire."

"Why should you be acquitted?" asked Welles pointedly. "We both know that you're guilty. It was never Dreyfus."

Esterhazy regarded Welles in silence for a moment, then his face broke into a broad smile.

"No, it wasn't," he agreed. "I wondered if you would ever work that out."

He turned to go.

"Why Dreyfus?" asked Welles. "Why choose him to take the blame?"

"Because he's a Jew," said Esterhazy. "That made it simpler. We knew it would be believed, and no one would look very hard for another answer."

He was at the door. He turned the knob, opened it, then paused.

"I really will miss you, Percy," he said. "You have treated me well, probably better than I deserve. It pains me that it may go hard for you now that I'm out of the game. So I'll give you this, my parting gift: there may be a way to find out what Marchand means to do. One of Marchand's men is coming home. An officer named Durand. Andre Durand. We've been asked to organize transport for him from Loango back to France. It will be months before he is home, but he might tell you what you want to know. If he can be persuaded. You're good at persuading, aren't you?"

Then he was gone.

***

Welles sat at the table, a stack of blank sheets of paper before him, a bottle and a glass on the table. He filled the glass and drank, then set it aside. He took up his pen and began to write. He filled one page, then another. He refilled his glass, drank, then took up his pen again. Evening fell as the pen nib scratched across the paper. He rose to light the lamps, then returned to his seat and continued. When he was finished, he had five sheets of paper filled with his crabbed hand. He read through them once more, then aligned the pages carefully and folded them into thirds. He slipped the papers into a heavy envelope and sealed it. On the outside of the envelope he wrote a name: *Monsieur Mathieu Dreyfus*.

He slipped the envelope into his pocket, then took his coat and hat from the hook. He turned off the gas and locked the door behind him.

In the street, he pulled his coat tight around him against the cold and waved at passing cab.

"Avenue de Trocadero," he shouted to the driver, pulling the door closed behind him. The carriage lurched into motion.

Chapter 31

London, 12 August 1898

Salisbury stared at Welles, his face aghast.

"Marchand's objective is on the Nile?" he asked, incredulously.

Welles, who had paused to wet his throat with some brandy, nodded in reply.

"I don't believe you," said Lawrence. "If you got that from Esterhazy nine months ago, why didn't you tell Sir Reginald then?"

"I never had any intention of passing it on to Sir Reginald," said Welles. "I never sent him another report. That man could go to hell as far as I was concerned. So could you all."

"When will he arrive?" the Prime Minister asked, ignoring Welles's comment. "And where?"

"A place called Fashoda," said Welles, "in the Sudan. An old fort on the west bank of the river. As to when, I imagine he is already there. Might I have more brandy, Mister Lawrence?"

Lawrence glared at him, but he brought the decanter and poured. When he had returned to his seat, Welles went on.

"It is difficult to be certain. The last information I have is some six months old; but, barring the unforeseen, Marchand has most likely reached Fashoda. He will have raised the flag, claimed the Sudan for France."

"He can raise any flag he likes," said Salisbury. "The Sudan belongs to Egypt and, by extension, to Her Majesty."

"You know as well as I do that no European power recognizes British dominion over the Sudan. Egypt — and Her Majesty — abandoned the Sudan thirteen years ago. Since then, it has been under the control of the Mohammedans. First the Mahdi, then his successor, the Khalifa."

"General Kitchener will shortly put paid to the Khalifa," said Lawrence.

Welles laughed.

"He may, Mister Lawrence," he said, "but I am a journalist after all, and you should assume I read the papers. Mister Churchill's dispatches make good reading and, as I recall, Kitchener is encamped at Atbara, two hundred miles north of the Khalifa's stronghold of Omdurman. With, I should add, one hundred thousand dervishes — maybe more! — between him and it."

He paused to take a drink, then went on.

"And even if he were to take Omdurman and reoccupy Khartoum, he has twice again as far to go to reach Fashoda, presumably fighting all the way. No, gentlemen, I fear that Marchand has presented you with a *coup de main*. The French have staked a claim to the upper Nile. They will likely have months to reinforce that claim."

"If Marchand has reached Fashoda, he cannot hope to hold it with such a small force," said Salisbury. "The Khalifa will surely try to drive him away. And if he survives that, then Kitchener will — in the end — send him packing. We have only to give the order, and he will move with all haste to reclaim what is ours."

"If that is true," said Welles, "then we must agree that Marchand is a fool for having made the effort. That the French are fools for having sent him with so little, setting him a task which you say he cannot achieve."

Welles leaned forward, elbows on the table, and gestured at Salisbury with the pistol.

"Is that what you think, sir? That the French are fools? That they cannot count heads, or cannon?"

Salisbury digested this in silence. Welles leaned back in the chair, fumbled with his cigarette case, lit a cigarette. It was nearly gone when Salisbury spoke.

"You wish me to believe that Marchand is not alone," he said.

"The conclusion is inevitable, is it not?"

Welles drew on the cigarette, blew out smoke, extinguished it.

"In any event," he said, "I know he is not alone. And if he is not alone, then you must discover who his allies are, and where they are. Otherwise, if Kitchener were to do as you say, and move with all haste to Fashoda, he might be doing exactly what Marchand hopes he will do."

"Why should we believe that?" asked Lawrence. "Merely because you say so?"

"It's true that I have been a liar, Mister Lawrence," Welles said. "But I swear to you that I have told only one lie since I entered this room."

"Only one lie? Then you have hardly kept up to your own standards, sir!" Lawrence laughed: a harsh, mocking laugh with no joy in it at all. "Which was the lie?"

"It was when I came through that door, and pretended not to know who you were," said Welles. "I marvel that you still believe you attend my meeting with the Lord Salisbury by some unhappy accident."

Lawrence, who had continued to laugh while Welles was speaking, abruptly stopped. He eyed Welles now with a look of suspicion. Welles ignored him. He returned his attention to Salisbury.

"What do you think, Prime Minister?" he asked. "Do you believe that I have come here in this fashion, at great danger to my life and freedom, in order to tell you a lie?"

The room was silent as Salisbury considered the question. He sighed, shook his head.

"No, Mister Welles, I do not."

"Then, sir, will you at last agree that I know something that you would like to know?"

Welles raised the pistol, muzzle pointed at the ceiling, carefully released the hammer, and laid it on the table before him.

"Will you hear me out?" he asked.

"Do you intend to tell me what you know about Marchand and his allies, Mister Welles?"

"I do," said Welles. "Provided you meet my terms."

Salisbury sighed. "Very well. Continue your tale. I will listen, and hear your terms, and then we will see if we can come to an agreement."

Chapter 32

The Journal of Lieutenant Andre Durand

<u>Sunday, 1 August 1897</u>
<u>Zemio</u>
<u>Bomu River</u>
<u>French Sudan</u>

The village of Zemio is ruled by a self-styled Sultan, a man who fancies himself the descendant of the Mohammedans who rode out from Mecca and conquered all of northern and eastern Africa. To me, he looks no different from the Zande people he rules, and he speaks no more Arabic than I do; a remarkable achievement, given that I speak none at all. Still, he has taken great pains to show us hospitality, and has provided us with the bearers we need. Paké-Bô for his part treats the man with civility and respect.

The bearers came at a high price. When Mangin heard how many rifles and bullets the Sultan demanded for the men he was giving us, he spat in disgust.

'These petty kings,' he said, shaking his head. 'They add to the shortcomings of black rulers all the vices of the Turks.'

Still, we are well fed, and well supplied with men, and in good form to continue. It seems to me that the Sultan has treated us far better than we might him, were he to lead a force of men uninvited into a village along the Marne. I imagine it takes some skill for a ruler to survive in Zemio, with the Khalifa's realm to his north and east, and the great powers of Europe pressing him on every other front.

And we have at last had some good luck. Baratier reports that the rains have been heavier than usual, so the way is open to us along the Bomu, perhaps as far as to where the Mere joins it. Paké-Bô is exuberant.

'At this rate, we shall be on the Nile by Christmas,' he said when Baratier had given us the news.

I saw Mangin looking at our leader as if he were mad, but he said nothing. Paké-Bô seemed not to notice.

Friday, 10 September 1897
Mere River
Sudan

The flow of the Mere has grown more feeble each day and we can go no further. From here we must walk. One hundred miles of wet grassland and forest lie between us and the outpost of Khojali, on the Sue river. What we will find there depends on the rains. If our luck holds, the river will be deep enough to carry us from there.

Paké-Bô has gone ahead with Mangin to Khojali, leading a small column of bearers. The rest of the bearers remain with us, but we will need many more than we have now if we are to carry the Faidherbe. Mangin will bring them from Khojali. Baratier and I have begun the difficult work of taking our little steamboat apart, with the help of Corporal Dialike and a few of his men.

Monday, 13 September 1897
Mere River
French Sudan

Without wanting to admit it aloud, I have begun to suspect that Mangin is right about the Faidherbe. She resists our efforts to break her down into pieces that can be carried. Baratier is a genius with such things, and my own training as an engineer makes me an able assistant, but she was never built to be taken apart in this way.

We began by removing her boiler, an exercise which at once conveyed to me the difficulty that lies ahead of us. Even after removing the bolts which held the two halves of the boiler together, we found it difficult to lift it clear of the boat. Each piece weighs nearly two thousand pounds.

We built a hoist over the Faidherbe. Then we wove a net of many ropes in which we managed to entangle one of the halves, whereupon twenty bearers took up lines and pulled for all they were worth. Even then, we were only able to raise the great weight high enough to clear the gunwales of the Faidherbe; whereupon we swung it away from the hull and dropped it to the ground. It immediately sank into the soft, damp earth.

'We must build a road,' said Baratier. 'We will never be able to drag these weights over ground as wet as this.'

He gave the order, and Dialike took a team of laborers into the forest to begin cutting trees for the road.

We are building a mound of the hull plates, ribs and keel pieces of the vessel. Each section is carefully marked by Baratier, so that we shall know how to put them together again. All told, we will need two hundred men to carry the pieces to the Sue. I don't know how many will be needed to move the boiler, or even how we will move it. I asked Baratier, but he refused to venture a guess.

Wednesday, 22 September 1897
Mere River
Sudan

Our road is 15 feet wide, a bed of logs laid into the earth to give us a solid foundation over which to drag the boiler. In nine days, the road has advanced four miles; an astonishing achievement, a tribute to the sheer determination of Corporal Dialike and to the efforts of the two hundred men who labor to build it. Still, I have calculated that at this rate it will take more than eight months to reach Khojali, by which time the matter of the Nile will almost certainly have been settled and we shall have failed.

I said as much to Baratier, but he only shrugged.

'Mangin will return any day,' he said. 'He will bring more men.'

With nothing more to be said, we returned to weaving a net of thick ropes around one of the boiler halves. This took the better part of the day, not least because of the fussiness with which Baratier approached the effort.

'The weight must be evenly distributed,' he said, 'with no part of the net weaker or under more stress than any other, else the ropes will break from the stress.'

It was not until late afternoon that we were ready to try to drag the heavy weight along the road. Twenty men took their places on the lines. At Baratier's command, they planted their feet on the rough sureness of the road and began to pull with all their might.

Nothing happened. The team of black men groaned and strained, the muscles of their backs and legs and arms swelling, their perspiration mingling with the steady rain and streaming from their limbs to fall onto the road, whereupon their feet began to lose purchase. Dialike shouted, and more men joined the others on the ropes, until there was no room for any more hands.

The iron weight shifted slightly, groaning as it slid over the wooden surface of the road, and then one of the ropes tore apart. The report was like a gunshot and the split end whipped past my head, sounding for all the world like a bullet flying past. The men tumbled over each other onto the ground, where they lay exhausted and groaning.

Baratier looked at me and shook his head.

'We must build a sled,' he said.

Friday, 24 September 1897
Mere River
Sudan

The sled works. We built it by lashing together four of the dugout canoes, then used the hoist to lower one half of the boiler onto it, where we tied it securely in place. We pulled it with teams of twenty men at a time, changing them frequently, and over the course of twelve hours we managed to move the sled nearly three miles. It can be done. The problem now is the road. We need more men.

Sunday, 26 September 1897
Mere River
Sudan

Mangin has returned, bringing with him a column of laborers that stretched more than a mile behind him. They arrived early this morning, and the line of men continued to stumble into our encampment for nearly an hour. They had walked all night to reach us, but there was to be no rest for them. Dialike collected them in groups as they came, then sent them off at once to work on the road.

'Where did you find them?' I asked Mangin.

'In Tambura,' he said. 'The sultan was pleased to provide them in return for the usual payment, and the promise of good relations with France.'

I remarked on the general amicability of the local rulers, how it boded well for our mission. Mangin looked at me in wonder, then laughed.

'You don't understand, Durand,' he said. 'The sultan cares nothing for France or our mission. If it were the Khalifa's men who arrived in Tambura, he would be every bit as amicable and accommodating. Indeed, I wager that if Kitchener himself were to arrive there tomorrow, the sultan would offer our enemies the same friendship he has already offered us.'

'Of course,' I said, chafing at his tone. 'It is only to be expected. The sultan must make the best of things, surrounded as he is by greater powers. I imagine we would do the same.'

'I can readily believe you would,' he said.

We went to watch Baratier and his team lifting the second boiler-half onto a sled. We stood in silence as they lowered the weight, then lashed it securely to the canoes. Then the hauling team took up the ropes and began to pull. Seeing how slowly they moved the sled over the rough log road, Mangin shook his head, then turned and walked away.

'We shall have to work them day and night,' he said that evening as we sat around the fire.

'We will kill them, Charles,' Baratier objected. 'This is arduous work, and they must have proper rest to do it.'

'Three hours rest per day, no more,' said Mangin.

'It is not enough. We need them. If they die, what will we do then?'

'Oh, they will certainly die,' said Mangin.

He did not raise his voice, but I could tell that he was angry.

'Do not delude yourself on that point, Albert,' he said. 'The challenge will be to ensure they die slowly, so that we get from them what we need first.'

'You are a cruel man, Mangin,' I said, shaking my head in disgust.

But he was not shamed. Instead, he rounded on me, his voice a quiet fury.

'If it were up to me, we would leave this damned boat here,' he said. 'With the canoes and the men we have, I could be at Fashoda by Christmas, and few need die in that effort. It is you who will kill them, you and Albert here, and Paké-Bô. We must have the Faidherbe, you say. We must reach the Sue before the rains end, you say. And in so saying, you condemn these men to suffering, even to death.'

'Don't pretend you care about them,' I shot back, but my reply was hollow; his words wounded me, for I knew there was truth in them.

Mangin ignored me.

'I will take charge of the road crew. Albert, the boiler advances too slowly. If we do not reach Khojali in three weeks, we may as well never arrive at all. You must make six miles a day at least. I don't care how you do it. I'll make sure the road is ready for you and give you what men I can spare from the road crew.'

Baratier regarded him with a cold stare. Then he nodded abruptly, got to his feet, and went in search of Dialike.

'You are with me, Durand,' Mangin said. 'The road crew is spread out over too much of the bush for one man. I'll need you there.'

He fixed his fierce eyes on me until I, too, nodded my understanding. Then he turned without another word and stalked away. After a moment, I followed him.

Friday, 1 October 1897
Sudan

The first of the road crew died today, crushed beneath a tree trunk that slipped from the grasp of his fellows as they tried to maneuver it into place. It is the fatigue that killed him. The minds of the laborers have been dulled by the lack of sleep, and their limbs made heavy by constant effort. The trees are slick from the constant humidity, and weary hands lack the strength to hold.

They stood in a group around the dead man, heads down, unmoving. The length of tree lay at a diagonal across a section of completed road. A man's lower body and legs protruded from beneath the tree; the rest of him lay out of sight underneath it.

'We must lift it,' I said.

They looked at me, uncomprehending. I knelt beside the trunk, wrapped my arms around it and tried to stand. It was ridiculous, I couldn't move it at all. But the example was what was needed. One of the men knelt beside me, then another; and then they all took a hand, and we raised the trunk up to the vertical, where it could be held up with little effort. Seeing that it was secure, I bent down to examine the man. But it was no use; his head had been crushed.

'Come away, Monsieur.'

I looked up and saw Corporal Dialike standing nearby. His voice gave no hint of alarm, and though his rifle was in his hands, he carried it casually, the muzzle angled towards the ground. His eyes, however, conveyed a warning. My own followed his gaze to the men looming over me, balancing the heavy trunk on its end and, for the first time, I saw in their faces something other than dull fear. It was, I realized, hatred, a malignant animosity directed at me that might erupt at any moment. I scrambled to my feet and backed away from the dead man.

Dialike barked an order. Two of the men cautiously released the trunk, taking care to be sure the others held it steady. Then they took the dead man by the legs and dragged him away from the roadbed, leaving behind a smear of bone and tissue and blood.

Dialike spoke again and the men holding the log began maneuvering it into place. I watched as one man stumbled; their burden teetered for a moment, but he regained his balance. I looked down and saw that he'd slipped in the bloody grey and white remains left on the road. Then they positioned the trunk carefully and lowered it to the ground. The road advanced another foot.

<u>*Tuesday, 5 October 1897*</u>
<u>*Sudan*</u>

We leave a trail of dead and maimed men behind us. Axes slip, or the ax handles break. Trees fall in an unexpected direction. I don't know which men I pity more; those we drag lifeless into the bushes, or those we leave sitting at the side of the road, staring in shock at the ruin of an arm, or the stump where a foot used to be. We leave them a little food and water. Not much, for we have little to spare.

We work the men until nearly midnight each day, then release them to collapse and fall into an exhausted, restless sleep. We wake them again at three in the morning. Each day, we change their work. Those who have labored on the road are assigned now to carry supplies; while those who carried, now work on the road. The portage loads are heavy but, once a man has lifted one onto his head, it is a matter only of walking and keeping one's balance. We advance so slowly that it is a kind of cruel rest for them, the only additional rest we can give them. I tell myself that we sleep no more than they, and that I walk beside them through the long days and nights; but it is not the same and I know it. I am tired beyond thinking. I cannot imagine their suffering.

Dialike is everywhere now, watching, waiting. He can sense the mood of the laborers. He says that such men can endure much, but there is always a point beyond which they would rather risk death than continue. He has stationed our soldiers around the perimeter of the working party and along the line of march of the bearers. Two tirailleurs now accompany me wherever I go. I told Dialike it was unnecessary, but he dismissed my objection. He assures me that Mangin goes similarly guarded.

<u>*Sunday, 10 October 1897*</u>
<u>*Sudan*</u>

The break came today. I was at the head of the road watching a team working another trunk into place when I heard a shout, followed by others. Instantly I turned towards the noise, my hand on the revolver at my belt.

The line of bearers had been taking a rest to the north side of the road, perhaps a hundred yards away. Now they were in full flight, at last making their bid for freedom, abandoning our supplies and the unwieldy pieces of the Faidherbe where they lay on the ground.

I watched them run for their very lives, and it came to me that, rather than the fear and dread I ought to be feeling at our party being left — abandoned — in the wilderness, next to a great pile of food and wine and ammunition we had no means to carry ourselves, the emotion I felt was of another kind entirely. It was, dare I say it, elation. I held my breath as I watched the furthest of the fleeing men reach the shelter of the far tree line. In my mind, I was cheering him on.

'Go!' I wanted to shout aloud. 'Run for your lives!'

Then the firing began. Corporal Dialike, ever watchful and ready for action, had quickly organized a squad of tirailleurs. Now, under his direction, they took a knee, raised their rifles, and began to shoot the fleeing men. They are well-trained, their aim true, and it was like shooting the defenseless beasts we used for fresh meat. A shot, and one man fell; another, and a bullet found its mark in the back of a defenseless fleeing man. Soon a score of dead and dying men lay in the long grass. Some of the bearers stopped in their tracks, raising their hands in surrender rather than being shot. Others, further away, continued their flight to the tree line.

The sight brought me to my senses, and I ran to where Dialike's men worked their deadly magic. I reached the line of soldiers just as the man at the end lowered his rifle to work the bolt. He raised it again to his cheek, sighted along the barrel, took aim. I struck the rifle with my hand, knocking the barrel down so that the bullet he fired kicked up dirt only ten yards or so to his front. I grabbed the rifle, wrenched it from his hands.

'Stop!' I shouted, 'Cease fire!'

Several men near me heard my cry and lowered their rifles, turning their faces to me in confusion. But the gunfire further along the line drowned out my voice, and the shooting continued. I ran along the line, shouting and slapping each man on the shoulder to get his attention. Slowly the firing stopped. Then Dialike stood before me, his face registering surprise and, I saw, not a little anger at what I'd done.

'Monsieur, what are you doing?' he demanded in a hoarse whisper. Even in his anger and confusion, he sought not to be heard rebuking me before the men.

'They are defenseless men, Dialike,' I said. 'We cannot shoot them in cold blood.'

'Defenseless men?' he repeated, apparently dumbfounded by my words. 'And when they kill us in our sleep, Monsieur, what shall they be then?'

'They won't stop running until they are far away,' I said. 'We have nothing to fear from them.'

To my astonishment, Dialike took hold of me with both hands. Such was my surprise that he easily spun me around, so that I was facing back towards the roadworks.

'What about them, Monsieur?' he hissed, his face close to my ear. 'What do you think they will do now?'

Indeed, the work on the road had entirely stopped, interrupted by the spectacle we had created. Everywhere I saw the sullen faces of black men worked beyond the point of exhaustion. They were the faces of men who had begun to ask themselves which was the greater hazard: to be worked to death, or to risk death for a chance at freedom?

'We live only because they fear us, Monsieur,' Dialike whispered in my ear. 'If ever they should lose that fear, they will kill us."

I turned to look at him. His was the face of a man I had come to trust in all things; the face, I thought, of a friend. Despite his anger, his eyes met mine with concern and kindness, and I saw that, as always, he meant to help me, to show me the way to my duty.

'They are men, Dialike,' I said. 'Men like you and me. How can we treat them so?'

It was like a curtain had come down between us. His face was suddenly cold, expressionless.

'They are black men, Monsieur.'

I did not heed the warning in his words.

'As are you, Dialike,' I said. 'You must try to imagine what they might be, had they only been given your good fortune, or mine.'

'They are not like us,' he said. 'We are French.'

Then he turned away from me and shouted an order. The soldiers, who had been watching us in confusion, took up their rifles again. Dialike spoke to the soldiers rapidly in Senegalese. Some returned to the road, shouting at the laborers as they went, putting them back to work. The rest spread out across the field, rounding up the bearers who still stood in the field, their hands raised over their heads.

<u>Tuesday, 12 October 1897</u>
<u>Khojali</u>
<u>Sudan</u>

At last the road has reached Khojali, a small village perched on the edge of a marsh which flows slowly east and north until it becomes the Sue. Here the need for our road ends, and with it the murderous labor of building the damned thing. The marsh is not deep, but it is choked with grass. We will have to cut our way through. Mangin says it should be possible to float the Faidherbe from here to our camp at Tambura on the Sue, where Paké-Bô waits for us. Whether we can proceed from there is far from certain; already the level of the Sue will have begun to drop, and it may soon become impassable to us until the rains come again in the spring.

Mangin has been trying to piece together the parts of the Faidherbe which arrive in a steady stream on the backs of the bearers. Already he is frustrated with the complexity of the task. I tried to help him, as I had helped to take her apart; but soon it became clear that, without Baratier's genius to guide us, we would make little progress. So Mangin has ordered me back down the road. I am to take command of the team dragging the two halves of the boiler to their reunion with the rest of the vessel. Baratier will return to see that she is ready to receive them.

Corporal Dialike is to come with me. I am of two minds on that. On the one hand, I am grateful for his help and guidance; but on the other, we have not spoken as friends since the incident two days ago. I fear that I have insulted him beyond any possibility of pardon, and I am at a loss as to how I might heal the breach.

I meant only to help him see our bearers as human beings. Instead, he has heard me compare him to them; heard me deny his own superiority. Dialike in his pride is a Frenchman, the equal of any in the Republic; while for him the Zande are a lesser people, meant to be ruled. I begin to *think that we have thoroughly corrupted these fine Senegalese men. They are better soldiers than any poilu I have commanded in France, but we have made of them copies of our own vain selves. I fear what will become of them when they discover that France will never treat them as white men.*

Chapter 33

Paris, January 1898

The court-martial of Major Marie Charles Ferdinand Esterhazy began on the tenth of January and was over by the following morning. The judges of the court pronounced him innocent of the charge of espionage and ordered him returned to duty. This was not to be, however. As soon as he emerged from the courtroom to face the throng of shouting reporters, Esterhazy announced his immediate retirement from the Army.

As word of the verdict spread, rioting broke out across the city. Enraged bands of so-called *Dreyfusards* — a coalition of leftists, socialists, and Jews — clashed with nationalists and those of the far right, who had taken to the streets to celebrate the verdict. The violence peaked on the afternoon of the twelfth, and then began to subside.

By the morning of the thirteenth, an uneasy calm had settled over the city. Welles donned his heavy wool coat and hat and descended to the street. He walked along the Boulevard Haussmann toward the Arc de Triomphe until he found an open café. He hung his coat and hat, chose a table by the window. The waiter came and he ordered coffee and breakfast.

Traffic on the street was unusually light. Across the boulevard, he saw a man on the sidewalk in front of another café. The café windows were shattered, and the man was sweeping broken glass from the pavement into a dustpan.

The waiter brought his breakfast. Welles had not eaten at all the day before and he attacked it with urgency. He ordered more coffee. The waiter had only just delivered it when something at the window caught Welles's eye. He turned in time to see several people run past the café.

Alert to the possibility of more violence, he stood to get a better view. A mob of people at the corner of the next block were milling around a man selling newspapers. Welles tossed some money on the table, wrestled himself into his coat, grabbed his hat.

Outside, he sprinted to the corner. He forced his way through the crowd to reach the vendor. He handed the man a coin and grabbed a paper from the pile, then ducked out of the crowd and took shelter in a nearby doorway.

Paris, 13 January 1898

I Accuse...!
Letter to the President of the Republic
By Émile Zola

In disbelief, people wonder who Major Esterhazy's protectors are. I accuse Major Du Paty de Clam of being the diabolical creator of the miscarriage of justice — without knowing, I have wanted to believe — and of then defending his harmful work by the guiltiest and most absurd of methods. I accuse General Mercier of being an accomplice, at least by weakness of the mind, in one of the greatest iniquities of the century. I accuse General Billot of having held in his hands the unquestionable evidence of Dreyfus's innocence and of suppressing it, making him guilty of this crime against humanity and justice, with a political aim, and as a way for the compromised High Command to save their reputation. I accuse General de Boisdeffre and General Gonse as accomplices of the same crime; one undoubtedly because of religious prejudice and the other perhaps due to this esprit de corps which makes the War Office into an infallible holy body. I accuse the first court martial of violating the law by convicting the accused on the basis of evidence that was kept secret, and I accuse the second court martial of covering up this illegality and of committing the judicial crime of acquitting a guilty man with full knowledge of his guilt.

Zola's letter took up the entire front page of the paper. Welles read it carefully. It was like nothing he'd seen before, an appeal to the President of the country for justice, made publicly for all to see. Zola laid out the entire conspiracy in detail: Esterhazy as the real culprit, Du Paty as the persecutor of Dreyfus, the complicity of senior officers first in convicting Dreyfus, then in refusing to yield to the obvious fact of his innocence. Welles realized with a start that Zola must have got everything from Mathieu Dreyfus; from the envelope he, Welles, had delivered to the Dreyfus home this past November.

He heard the sound of glass shattering. Up the street, people were throwing stones at the windows of the café he'd just left. An empty *fiacre* was passing, heading in the other direction, and he waved to the driver. The carriage slowed and he dashed into the street, leapt onto the stair and settled himself in the compartment.

"*Ile de Saint-Louis*," he called to the driver.

Behind him, over the sound of the wheels on the cobblestones and the hooves of the horse, he heard more glass breaking.

In contrast to the growing commotion he'd driven through, the narrow lanes of the Ile de Saint-Louis were deathly quiet. The cab pulled up in front of Georges' house. Welles paid the driver, descended to the street, then climbed the stairs to the front door and rang the bell. After a moment, the door opened. The butler eyed him with an expression of contempt.

"Mademoiselle will not see you, Monsieur," he said.

"Take this to her, please," he said, offering the paper. "I'll wait."

The butler took the paper, stepped back, closed the door. Welles waited on the doorstep, his heart racing.

The door opened. The butler extended his hand, offering something. Welles took it without thinking. It was a coin.

"Thank you for the paper, Monsieur," the butler said. He closed the door.

Welles threw the coin to the pavement. He stalked away from the house towards the Pont Philippe. He stopped at the midpoint of the bridge, stood at the west parapet. The twin towers of Notre Dame rose above the leafless trees, a dirty white against the gray sky.

His eyes were drawn to the river below him. The current was swift, a rush of water the same dull gray as the sky. For a moment he was seized with the desire to jump. It was cold, colder than he could remember Paris ever being, and the shock of the water would probably stun him. The coat was heavy, and once the wool was soaked with water, it would drag him down even if — in the end — he were to struggle against it.

He lifted one foot from the ground, as if to climb up onto the wall. Then he lost his courage; the idea of the cold water suddenly terrified him. He lowered the foot, turned up the collar of his coat and continued across the bridge.

There were no cabs in the Quai de l'Hotel de Ville. He walked west several blocks, then turned right on the Boulevard de Sebastopol. Still there were no cabs. He resigned himself to walking and continued north along the boulevard until he spotted a large crowd ahead, approaching him. Some carried placards, but he could not make them out. He slowed, momentarily undecided. Then he saw the distinctive tri-color shield of a *gendarmerie*, a police station, midway between him and the approaching mob. He stepped out briskly, closing the gap so that he would have the protection of the police should the need arise.

Closer now, he could read the signs the men carried. *Viva L'Armee*, said one. *Mort au traitre Dreyfus*, another. One was more direct: *Mort aux les Juifs*. The men were shouting. It seemed to Welles that they were working themselves up, feeding on each other's rage, until they could find a suitable object on which to vent it. Many carried improvised clubs.

The police station was just ahead, on the left. Two *gendarmes* stood on the pavement in front of the station, arms crossed, watching the approaching mob. Welles considered turning around, going back the way he'd come, then rejected it. Instead, he walked briskly towards the *gendarmes*. He had taken only a few steps when he heard a shout.

"*Juif!*"

A man at the front of the mob was pointing at him. Another shouted, then more took up the call. The mob surged forward. Alarmed, he broke into a sprint, calling out to the *gendarmes* for help. They stood impassively as if they did not hear him; as if they did not hear the mob or see it. Then the vanguard was upon him.

A man hit Welles with his shoulder, knocking him to the ground. A sharp blow landed on his ribs; an ax handle, he thought, but the heavy wool of his coat absorbed much of the impact. Instinctively, he drew his legs up into the coat, curled into a ball. Another blow struck him on the shoulder; it hurt, but again the coat protected him.

Then someone kicked him in the head with a heavy boot. Stunned, he nevertheless had the sense to bow his head, chin to chest, covering as much of it as he could with his arms. He closed his eyes, braced himself as the blows fell.

His ears were ringing, so that the sound of the mob was muffled, as if it were far away. There was another sound, also far away, yet oddly piercing, and he recognized it as a *gendarme's* whistle. He heard a shout, very near: "*Assez!*" Another voice repeated the shout. The blows slowed, then stopped. He felt rather than heard the mob stepping over him, around him, continuing on their way.

He opened his eyes. A *gendarme* bent over him. Another stood a few feet away, between Welles and the mass of the approaching crowd, so that the mob split, like the current of a river as it met the pylon of a bridge, passing to either side of him as it continued down the street. Still he lay on the ground, until the last of the mob had passed.

"Are you injured, Monsieur?" asked the policeman.

"Injured?" he said, still stunned. "What the devil do you mean, am I injured?"

"Stand up," said the policeman. When he didn't move, the man nudged him with foot. "Stand, if you can."

Welles got to his feet with difficulty. He hurt in a dozen places, but nothing seemed to be broken. He felt a burning sensation on the side of his head, put his hand to his ear. He pulled the hand way to find it covered with blood. The policeman took hold of Welles's chin, turned his head to the side to see better.

"Not so bad," the policeman said, releasing him. "You'll live."

Welles heard a crash, turned to look down the street. The mob were breaking the windows of the shops they passed. He turned back to the policeman. The question was unspoken, but the man understood it well enough. He shrugged. He was powerless, the gesture seemed to say, or perhaps indifferent.

"You should get off the street," he said, "before you really get hurt. It's not safe for Jews today."

Welles opened his mouth to say that he was not a Jew, then closed it. The denial was irrelevant, craven even, and he was ashamed to have thought it. He looked around for his hat, spied it in the gutter, crushed flat. He limped to where it lay, bent down to retrieve it. He was suddenly dizzy and nearly fell but managed to maintain his balance and right himself. The hat was ruined, but it would protect his head from the cold, so he manipulated it into something approaching its original shape and put it on his head. He looked again at the policeman. The man waved him on, in the direction from which the mob had come. Welles took his handkerchief from a pocket, pressed it against his ear, and walked away.

***

Madame Hebert drew in a sharp breath when she saw him. "Monsieur," she said, alarmed. "What has happened to you?"

She came around the desk, stood close to him, examining his face. Like the policeman, she took hold of his chin, turned his head to one side. He still held the handkerchief to his ear. She took him by the wrist, pulled his hand away, looked closely. She made a clucking sound with her tongue.

"Come with me," she said.

He protested, but she held him by the arm, pulled him, and he did not resist. She led him past the staircase to the flat she occupied at the end of the hall. The flat was simple: a main room that served as a kitchen and sitting room, and another where she slept. A fire burned in the iron stove, and Welles felt warm for the first time in hours. She led him to the small table, sat him in a wooden chair. She poured water from the kettle on the stove into a pan, placed it on the table. She disappeared into the bedroom, returning a moment later with a clean cloth, which she soaked in the pan. She pulled another chair closer to him, sat, and began to clean the side of his face. The cloth was hot against his face, and his ear burned at the contact. He closed his eyes.

"There," she said. "It is clean now, Monsieur."

He opened his eyes to find her looking at him with genuine concern. She made the clucking sound again, then stood. She put the cloth into the pan, carried both to the sink. From a cupboard she took two glasses and a bottle. She removed the cork from the bottle and poured a strong measure into each glass. She sat, took one of the glasses, slid the other to Welles.

"Medicinal, Monsieur," she said, and drank.

He raised the glass, knocked it back in one go. The cheap brandy burned a fiery course down his throat, and he stifled an involuntary cough. His ribs ached with the effort.

"I worry about you, Monsieur," she said. "You are no longer working, I think. I miss the sound of the typing machine."

She smiled, shook her head.

"You come and go at all hours, but I think you do not eat enough. You have become so thin."

He said nothing. She lifted the bottle, poured more into his glass. She hesitated, then shrugged, poured herself a another.

"Mademoiselle does not come any more," she said. "Not to work. Not for anything."

He gave her a sharp look.

"I am not a fool, Monsieur," she said. "I have lived a life. You would not believe it to see me now, I know, but it is true."

For the first time, Welles saw the young, vibrant person who had become imprisoned behind the lined, doughy face. It was something to do with her eyes, he thought.

"I can readily believe it, Madame," he said.

He raised his glass in salute to her. She raised her own, and they drank.

"Mademoiselle will not return?" she asked, hesitantly.

"No," he said. "I fear she will not."

She took his hand in hers, shook her head sadly.

"You must be strong, Monsieur," she said. "This is how life is. Love comes, it goes. You must go on."

"Yes," he said, abruptly. He stood. "Thank you for your kindness, Madame."

She followed him from the flat into the hallway, stood at the bottom of the stair, watching as he started to climb. He had reached the first landing when she called to him.

"*Mon dieu!*" she said. "I have forgotten, Monsieur. A man came to see you today, while you were out. He came several times."

"A man?"

"An Englishman. He said it was urgent. He was so insistent the last time, I told him he could wait for you."

Welles turned to look at his office door, then back to her. She nodded.

"I told him he could wait," she said again. "I hope that was all right."

Hull had made himself comfortable in Welles's absence. The lamps were lit, and a fire warmed the room. He was standing when Welles entered, but Welles could see he'd been sitting at Welles desk. He had helped himself to Welles's whisky; the bottle was on the table beside a half-empty glass.

"There you are!" Hull exclaimed.

He crossed the room quickly to take Welles's hand, but stopped short.

"Good god, man, what's happened?"

Welles touched the side of his face.

"A demonstration in the street," he said, by way of explanation. "Bad luck, really. Wrong place, wrong time."

He was exhausted, and the thought of a session with Hull was almost more than he could bear. He struggled to remove his coat. Hull moved to help him, which was just as well, for Welles found he could barely lift his arms. He nodded his thanks, hung the coat on the rack beside Hull's own. He took off his hat. He meant to hang it on the rack, then changed his mind. It was almost shapeless now, and one side was stiff with dried blood. He dropped it into the wastebasket.

"Is that my whisky?" he asked. "Pour me a drink, would you? I won't be a moment."

He lit the lamp in the bathroom, closed the door. He fumbled with his trousers, relieved his bladder, then looked at the results. The urine was very dark, nearly brown, but there was no obvious trace of blood in it. He sighed, fastened his trousers. There was a mirror on the stand by the basin. He held it up, examined his face. It was a mass of bruises, in some places already purple and turning to black. The ear was badly lacerated, but had stopped bleeding, so he didn't think it needed any stitching. He looked for dried blood on his face and in his hair, but Madame Hebert had done a good job cleaning him up. He put the mirror down and took a deep breath, steeling himself. Then he turned down the lamp and opened the door.

Back in the office, Hull was waiting, glass in hand. Welles took the offered drink, nodded his thanks, then sat, choosing the chair opposite the desk. Had he been asked, he could not have said clearly why, only that it seemed to him a way of rebuking Hull for the easy liberty he'd taken with Welles's office. He waved his hand at the other chair, his chair, and Hull sat.

"They're fighting in the streets," Welles said. "All over the city. It was bad for a few days, then less so. Now Zola's letter has blown the lid clean off. Those on the left demand freedom for Dreyfus. Those on the right call him a traitor and defend the Army. It was the latter I ran into."

"But why should they assault you?"

"They thought I was a Jew." Welles shrugged. "They were primed for it. They'd worked themselves into a frenzy, and all they wanted was a Jew they could beat."

He sipped the whisky. They sat in silence, Welles waiting for Hull to say why he'd come. The other man waiting, too, but for what, Welles couldn't say. It was dark outside now, and the gaslight lent a golden hue to the room. The fire warmed him, and the whisky warmed him further, numbed the ache in his ribs, his arms, his legs. He was content to wait forever. Eventually Hull understood that.

"We've had nothing from you for weeks," he said.

Welles nodded. "You'll get nothing more. Esterhazy is finished."

"And the money?"

"I gave it to him. I expect he'll be needing it."

"See here, Percy," Hull said. "This isn't funny. This Dreyfus business has gone too far."

Welles nodded agreeably. Hull bristled.

"You've made a hash of everything," he said. "You were supposed to protect the man. It was your job, Percy, and you have failed. What have you to say for yourself?"

"For myself? Nothing."

"If there's no Esterhazy, there's no job," said Hull.

Welles put the empty glass on the table. He leaned forward, elbows on the desk, hands clasped before him.

"Yes, I worked that out on my own," he said. "But I have a proposal for you anyway. Give me the Esterhazy file. He's no use to us anymore, but I can use the file."

"Use the file?" Hull looked at him in wonder. "Use it for what?"

"To free Dreyfus, of course," said Welles. "There's no need to persecute the man further, surely? Why not help me free him now?"

Hull was suddenly angry.

"Help you? After what you've *done*?"

He got to his feet, approached Welles, stood over him.

"I'm not a fool, Percy. I know it was you who put them onto Esterhazy. You've thrown away the best agent we have ever had, and for what? For *Dreyfus*? You've betrayed your country for a *Jew*?"

He waited for an answer, but Welles did not respond.

"And now you want me to help you? Have you taken leave of your senses?"

Welles slumped in his seat, sighed.

"I'm tired, Sir Reginald, and sore. If I am no longer in your employ, then I see little reason to subject myself to your company any longer. I shall do what I must do without your help. Please go."

"I am going," said Hull. "But first, I want to be very clear, Percy."

He leaned forward, his head near Welles's, his voice low.

"You may not understand it, but when you agreed to take this job, you took an oath, to serve Queen and country. If you break that oath, the consequences will be dire."

"I don't care about the consequences," said Welles. "I expect the government to denounce me, even to prosecute me. Do your worst."

There was a long silence. Then: "I think you underestimate me, Percy. I promise you, the consequences will be very grave indeed, and not only for you. You should think about the others who have involved themselves in this affair."

Welles was suddenly alert.

"What do you mean, others?"

He struggled to his feet, stood face to face with Hull, only a foot separating them. They stared at each other. Then Hull turned away, went to the rack to collect his coat. He put it on, crossed the room to the door. There, he turned to face Welles.

"Do give my regards to Miss Seigneur."

Chapter 34

The Journal of Lieutenant Andre Durand

<u>*Friday, 22 October 1897*</u>
<u>*Khojali*</u>
<u>*Sudan*</u>

Mangin and Baratier labor day and night to reassemble the Faidherbe. I can hear them at their work. From time to time it occurs to me that I ought to join them. Instead, I remain here. Lying on my back, I have conducted a meticulous inspection of the condition of the canvas roof of this tent and, as a result, I admit that I hope it does not rain, even if it spells doom for our mission.

When, from time to time, I bestir myself, it is only to open this journal, and to read with new eyes the words I have written here. I can scarcely believe them now. What a fool I have been. I think of my father, and I wonder what he will make of my tale. In the end it is this thought that propels me from the cot. I am spurred to action; but not the action which duty demands. No, instead, I carry this journal to the desk. I sit, and take up my pen, and try to find the words to tell my story; to pick it up where I left off, and to recount the events which have brought me to this tent.

It has been nine days since we relieved Baratier on the road. We sent him back to Khojali with a few soldiers and took charge of the effort to move the boiler. Rather, I should say, Dialike took charge for, once he had begun, there was little for me to do save watch the behemoths on their slow progress eastward.

This is how it was:

A team of bearers took up the ropes, dug in their heels, and pulled with all their might. The sled began to move, slowly at first; but as it moved the men on the ropes began to step backward, to brace themselves again, to pull. The sled picked up speed. The men had learned through trial and error that, once the sled was moving, it was easier to keep it moving than it was to get it started in the first place. Thus, it seemed almost that they meant to run before the sled, though in truth they never succeeded at any pace beyond a slow, labored walk. And eventually — because the road was not straight, nor level, nor smooth, and because men on different ropes pull in different directions — the sled began to drift towards one edge of the log road or another. It drifted closer, and closer, and then they had to stop pulling; for if they were to allow the sled to slip off the road, we would lose the better part of a day lifting it back onto the road surface. Those on the ropes fell where they stood, then lay where they had fallen, spent. Another team of bearers, using lengths of strong wood as levers, slowly shifted the sled until it was aimed once again down a stretch of road. Then the tirailleurs shouted, and the spent men crawled out of the way of a fresh team of bearers, who once again took up the ropes.

There were two halves of the boiler to move, the second one perhaps three hundred yards behind the first. When the first one came to a halt, and the men began to wrestle with their levers to right its aim, Dialike would fall back to the second, just in time for it to be dragged into motion. When it eventually stopped, he would hurry forward to begin the lead one again. This, I began to understand, was how Baratier had spent his days and nights while we labored to build the road, and I was filled with a new appreciation for the man. And for Dialike, who showed every sign of following Baratier's lead.

After the first day had ended and the bearers lay exhausted around us in the night, I convinced Dialike to let me take charge of one of the sleds. If it seems strange to say that I — a lieutenant — convinced a corporal, that is the right word, for he no longer makes any attempt to pretend that it is I who commands and he who obeys. He was at first reluctant to trust me with such a difficult and delicate operation, but at last he saw the wisdom of dividing our efforts and agreed that I should take the lead sled. In this way, he said, he would be pursuing me, and better able to gauge the progress I was making and intervene should it be necessary. I bristled at this, and reminded him of our respective ranks, but he merely regarded me with his blank, expressionless face and waited until, exasperated, I consented to his plan.

In this way we proceeded for several days. The work was hard, even frustrating, for at times it seemed to me that we moved at a snail's pace. But when we conferred each night, Dialike pronounced himself satisfied that we had done enough. I confess now that I took a ridiculous pride in this weak and barely implied approval; so much so that I determined to do whatever was necessary to increase the pace of my progress.

I began to take risks, forcing the laborers to pull the sled further and further before stopping; ever nearer to the edge of the rough log road, not calling for a halt until the hull of the canoe which made up the outermost runner of the sled was balanced precariously at the very edge. Then I would exhort the men with levers to quickly right the sled and we would be off again. The laborers became exhausted at this pace, but I was not dissuaded. When they seemed to me too slow to take up the ropes, I shouted to my soldiers, who whipped them. Thus encouraged, the men took up the ropes with the fierce strength which comes from unreasoning fear and pulled as they had never done before.

In this way I began to pull ahead of Dialike and his team, so that he lost sight of us for longer periods of time. This had the strange effect of encouraging me to even greater recklessness. I see now that it was a kind of madness, one that was always bound to end in disaster.

So it did. I turned from watching the progress of the sled to observe the men at the ropes. It was only for a second, as I had done a thousand times or more before, but when I turned back, I saw that the tip of the outermost canoe had now left the road entirely, and the sled was veering further to the right. I shouted for the men to stop, and they did; but by that time, nearly half of the canoe was suspended in the air. The sled itself rocked and teetered as it shed its momentum and from its wooden joints came the most ominous of sounds: the creaking of the ropes which bound it together, and the cracking of the wood as it splintered under the unevenly distributed weight of the iron it bore.

I saw right away that we could not simply lever the canoe back onto the track. What was needed most urgently was to get a solid base under the canoe, something that would restore the distribution of weight essential to preventing the boiler-half from crushing the ramshackle wooden construction that was the sled. I directed the men to get a strong lever under the canoe, at a point just forward of where it had left the road; and to seat it firmly on the logs of the road itself, and then lift it to support the canoe. It took several men to lift the lever and hold it long enough for others to stack timbers underneath to take the strain. Then we moved forward a few feet and repeated the process again, until gradually we had built a kind of platform to restore stability to the sled.

Then I was able to take stock of the situation. I moved around the sled, inspecting it for any signs of damage or strain which might give when we tried to move it again. I could see nothing to alarm me, but there was much I could not see, not without climbing onto the sled and clambering over it to get a closer look. This would have involved exposing myself to the danger of being crushed should the thing suddenly collapse, but I had convinced myself that it needed to be done and was preparing to mount the sled from the rear when I heard a shout.

I turned to find that the second sled was now just fifty yards or so behind us. It was Dialike who had shouted. I waved him off angrily — for once I did not want his help — and determined then and there to get the sled moving again. He came on, ignoring my dismissal, but I turned my back on him and called for the laborers to bring more levers. This they did, and applied them, and began working them to shift the sled back onto the road.

It would not budge. Angrily, I called for more men with levers, placing them between the temporary supports we had built. I shouted for them to lift, all of them. Still the sled would not budge. I approached the men, exhorting them to greater effort. My eyes fell on one of the laborers. He had probably been straining with all his might, to no avail, but by chance, I looked at him just as he let up. It seemed to me he was making no effort at all. I pointed at him, and a tirailleur stepped forward with the chicotte and struck him across the back.

The man cried out and stumbled, falling against the stack of timber on which the support rested. It collapsed, taking the support with it. The sled rocked. There was a sharp crack as the next support broke, and the sled lurched towards us. The men shouted in fear, dropped their levers and fled. I heard another loud report and realized with a start that one of the ropes binding the joints of the sled had snapped. The weight of the iron bore down on the fragile wood framework, and it had begun to collapse.

The man who'd fallen lay on his back, his eyes wide with terror, as the outermost canoe slid towards him. Without thinking, I grabbed a lever and dashed forward. I wedged it into the soft ground and pressed it against the canoe, trying with all my might to arrest its progress, but it was hopeless. I looked down at the man on the ground, shouted at him to get clear; but I saw now that his leg lay trapped beneath the collapsed support.

I could not hold the sled back. I shouted for more men to aid me, but no one came. I put my shoulder to the lever, trying to use my whole body to hold it, but it forced me inexorably down. I heard another rope snapping, and the sled lurched towards me, driving me to my knees. I screamed at the man lying beside me. He began to move, scrabbling at the ground like a crab, twisting his body in an effort to free his trapped leg. I realized then that it was too late, that either I must run to safety myself or be crushed alongside him.

Then another lever joined mine, and the collapse of the sled was arrested. I turned to see Dialike beside me, his shoulder, like mine, under the lever, the strain of the effort evident on his face.

'Get away, Monsieur!' he snapped at me.

'We must help him, Dialike,' I said, indicating the trapped man.

'We cannot help him. Get away, now!'

In response, I tried to force myself to my feet. It was no use. The two of us had done no more than slow the collapse of the sled.

'I can't leave him here,' I said.

'Then drag him away, but quickly,' he shouted. 'I can hold it, but only for a moment.'

'No,' I said, 'you cannot hold it alone.'

'Do as I say, damn you!' he raged.

There came a sound of splintering wood. Dialike was shouting now, an incomprehensible torrent of Senegalese. I scrambled in terror from beneath the lever, found myself crawling over the man I'd been trying to save. The sight of his face brought me to my senses. I got to my feet, grasped him under the arms and began to drag him backward, away from *the collapsing sled. He screamed as his leg came free of the trap, then we were both scrabbling in the dirt with no thought but to get away. The sled collapsed in a cacophony of snapping ropes and splintering wood. The boiler-half tilted towards us, then began to slide, and before I could open my mouth to shout a warning, Dialike was gone, crushed beneath its great weight.*

Chapter 35

Paris, March 1898

It was a local bar frequented by the tradesmen, shop clerks and laborers who made their homes in the warren of narrow lanes and dead-end alleys which comprised the Montmartre neighborhood. The wine was cheap, sour, and brought to you in clay jars. Welles sat alone at a table near the front. He had chosen the table for its view of the entry to the alley across the street, but he had not reckoned with the decades of tobacco smoke, spattered wine, and other grime with which the inside of the window was coated. Now, he surreptitiously rubbed the glass with the sleeve of his coat, hoping to clean a large enough patch through which to see clearly. The result was better, though less than satisfactory. Outside, a steady rain was falling, and people hurried along the Boulevard de Clichy beneath the gas lamps that were surrounded by halos of light.

With little to do but wait, Welles was plagued by doubts about his intended course of action. He turned events over in his mind again and again, looking for some alternative but — as before — found none. The hopes with which he'd greeted Zola's accusation, a shout that had brought into public view the full ignominy of the Dreyfus affair, had been dashed by subsequent events. Instead of being shamed into action, the government and the Army had been defiant. Zola was accused of libel and quickly brought to trial, a proceeding which took place while mobs battled each other outside the courtroom.

Welles had watched from the gallery as Picquart, recalled from Tunisia, testified that there was no firm evidence against Dreyfus; that indeed, the evidence pointed to another man entirely. He felt sure that Picquart would have named Esterhazy had the judge not prevented him from doing so on the grounds that the person in question had already been acquitted of the crime.

He had watched as Major Henry rebutted Picquart's arguments. One exchange between the two men was so heated that they nearly came to blows, and only the forceful intervention of the judge prevented events from progressing to the point where they could only have been settled on the field of honor.

The next day a succession of senior officers had taken the stand, each categorically denying the claims Zola had made, while leaning heavily on the honor of their uniforms and their service. Last of all came the Chief of Staff himself, General de Boisdeffre. He testified to the certain guilt of Dreyfus and the equally certain falseness of Zola's accusations. Then he issued an ultimatum to the jurors: 'You are the jury; you are the nation. If the nation does not have confidence in the chiefs of its Army, in those who have the responsibility for national defense, then we are prepared to leave to others this heavy task.'

Following this statement, de Boisdeffre had refused to answer any further questions. The judge dismissed him from the stand even though he had not yet been cross-examined by the defense. As for the jury, it emerged that, on that very same day, each of their names and addresses had been printed in the pages of La Libre Parole, as open a threat to their well-being as Welles could have imagined.

The intimidation worked. On the 23rd of February the jury convicted Zola of libel. He was fined three thousand francs and sentenced to a year in prison. The guilt of Dreyfus had once again been reaffirmed.

Something interrupted Welles's thoughts. He peered through the window into the alley across the street. *There.* A light had gone out; the window at the end of the alley on the left was now dark. He checked his watch, noted the time. He lit a cigarette to wait.

Ten minutes later he crossed the street and entered the alley. He walked quickly to the end. He could just make out the sign over the door. He felt around in the dark until he found the chain, then pulled it. He heard a bell ring somewhere behind the door. He waited. When two minutes had passed, he rang the bell a second time. He was about to pull the chain again when he saw a flicker of light behind the curtained window. Someone grappled with the bolt on the other side. The door opened a few inches. A hand holding a candle appeared in the gap, followed by a face.

"Ah, Monsieur Smith," Leeman said. "It is quite late, Monsieur. I was in bed. Perhaps you might return tomorrow?"

"It is a matter of some urgency," said Welles. "I promise I'll make it worth your while."

Leeman sighed. He pulled the door open to allow Welles to enter, then closed the door behind him and threw the bolt. He led the way to the back room, holding the candle high so that Welles could see to follow him. He invited Welles to sit, then busied himself with lighting the lamp. That done, he excused himself and disappeared through another doorway. Welles sat in silence. The wait was not long. Leeman returned, having wrapped himself in a heavy dressing-gown against the cold. He took a chair opposite Welles.

"How may I be of service, Monsieur Smith?" he asked. "Do you require another rare document, perhaps?"

"Not this time," said Welles. "Although my need is related to that. I should like an accounting of all the *rare documents* you have provided to Basil and his associates for the last three years."

Leeman's face registered surprise at the request.

"Why should Basil need such an accounting?" he asked.

"It is not for Basil."

There was a long silence. Then: "Why should you want such an accounting, Monsieur Smith?"

"It is no business of yours," said Welles. "I will pay for it. That is all that need concern you."

Now Leeman smiled, a pained smile.

"Come now, Monsieur," he said, adopting a tone of exaggerated patience. "You know as well as I do that such an accounting is not something I would wish to make, or to put into the hands of another."

"Because it is a confession to a crime, you mean?" It was Welles's turn to smile. "Yes, I can understand your reluctance. But I need that accounting. You can name your price, and I will keep your name out of it."

"You are very kind. But I fear I cannot give you what you want."

Leeman raised a hand, palm up, as if he were weighing something.

"How can I trust you, Monsieur Smith?" he asked. "I don't know who you are. It's true that you came here before as a friend of Basil's, but now you return with a request which makes me doubt you are his friend. I feel sure that Basil would not approve."

"Then I offer you a choice," said Welles. "I will pay you for this accounting, as I have offered. If you do not agree, then I will return here in the company of the police; and you shall give your accounting to them, in return for nothing save the promise of prison."

"You would not do that, I think. You would be implicating yourself as well."

Welles leaned back in the wooden chair, his arms crossed over his chest.

"Nevertheless, I will do it," he said. "I would far rather pay you for what I want, but if you will not agree, then I am resigned to the alternative."

Leeman stood. Welles was suddenly alert, but the man only began to pace while he considered what Welles had said. After some thought he turned to Welles, hands clasped behind his back.

"What sort of accounting do you want?" he asked. "You understand that I don't keep records of these transactions."

"Don't take me for a fool," said Welles. "You would have required examples from which to manufacture your forgeries. When we did business before, you made careful notes of what I asked for, so that — you said — you would be sure to produce the letter exactly as I wanted it. When I paid you, you made an entry in your ledger. Those are the kinds of things I want. And the names of those who paid you for them."

"Any names will be of no use to you, Monsieur *Smith*," Leeman observed pointedly.

"Perhaps not," said Welles. "But I want them just the same."

The forger seemed to come to a decision.

"If I were to agree, I would need time to assemble what you want."

"How much time?"

Leeman shrugged. "Two weeks at least?"

Welles shook his head.

"Let us agree to one," he said. "That should be more than enough time. I shall return in one week to collect it and bring your payment. Shall we discuss the price?"

The forger hesitated, then nodded.

"Yes, let us agree on a price."

***

The night was clear and cold, and very quiet. Welles's footsteps echoed loudly from the close walls of the alley. He reached the end, where a faint light shone through the drawn curtains of Leeman's shop. He stopped and, in the sudden silence, thought he heard another sound. He looked back up the alley, standing perfectly still, holding his breath. Nothing. He turned to the door, found the bell-chain, tugged on it sharply. He looked up the alley again, still saw nothing. He patted his breast, seeking the reassurance of the thick bundle of bank notes in the inside pocket of his coat. He rang again, waited. He tried the doorknob, felt it turn, pushed cautiously inward. The door opened. In the dim light of a lamp on the counter he could see the main room. There was no one in sight. He stepped into the room, pulled the door closed behind him, turned to bolt it.

"Monsieur Leeman," he said, softly, then wondered why he was whispering. "Monsieur!" he called, louder this time. There was no response.

He made his way across the shop to the counter. He took the lantern, lifted it high, and moved around the counter to the dark doorway behind it. Leeman was there, seated at the table with his back to Welles. The man was slumped over, head resting on the table, as if asleep, or perhaps drunk. There was a jug on the table, and a cup; both were overturned and lay in a pool of spilled wine, shining and nearly black in the dim light of the lantern.

"Monsieur!" he repeated, at the same time kicking the back of the chair.

Still there was no response. Cursing under his breath, Welles stepped around the chair, placed the lantern on the table, grabbed the man by the hair on the back of his head and lifted it. Leeman had been lying in the pool of wine and, as his face came away from the table, long strings stretched from the table to his hair as if the cheap wine had congealed to a sticky and elastic consistency.

Welles peered into the man's face. It was covered with the same spilled wine which, as he watched, began to run down the man's cheeks and along his nose in rivulets, only very slowly, as if reluctant to flow. The eyes were closed. Welles shook him, shouted at him, but there was no response.

Welles drew the man's head further back. The eyes opened, staring sightlessly at the ceiling, as did the mouth, the chin slack; and then, to his horror, Welles saw another mouth yawn open, below the chin; a long horizontal slash of a mouth across the man's neck. Blackness gurgled out of the slash, spilling down the front of the man's clothes, already wet and dark, and Welles suddenly registered the odor he'd been smelling since he entered the room; the stench of an abattoir.

He gasped, released the man's hair, stepped back, noting absently that strings of warm, sticky blood stuck to his hand as he pulled it away. Leeman, free of Welles's grasp, fell forward again, his head striking the table sharply, and then the momentum toppled the body from the chair onto the floor, the chair falling beside it with a loud crash. Blood oozed slowly from the gash in Leeman's neck.

Welles looked down at his hand, covered in congealing blood. Without thinking, he rubbed the hand against his coat. His stomach lurched, and for a moment he felt he might be ill. He was seized suddenly by the urge to flee. He turned and half-ran through the doorway into the dark shop, leaving the lantern behind. He collided with the counter and nearly fell. He forced himself to be calm, walked slowly and cautiously across the floor of the shop to the door. There he stopped, felt for the latch, found it. Even as he took hold of it, he heard a sound behind him: a footfall. Then his head exploded in a sharp flash of light and pain, and there was darkness.

***

From somewhere he heard pounding. His head ached with a blinding pain. He groaned, opened his eyes. He could see nothing and for a moment thought he might be blind. He tried to move, succeeded only in rolling over and caught sight of the dim lamplight spilling through the door behind the counter. The pounding continued. It was coming from behind him now.

From the door, he thought. *Someone is banging on the door.*

"*Ouvre la porte!*" a voice called. The pounding stopped.

He managed to roll onto his hands and knees. A wave of nausea swept over him. He swallowed the bile, then gulped air as if he were drowning. Steeling himself, he got slowly to his feet. He stood a moment, trying to get his balance, then jumped and nearly fell again, startled by the sudden and loud crash on the other side of the door. Another crash, and the wood of the door protested.

"*Police!*" came the voice again. "*Ouvre la porte!*"

He suddenly recalled Leeman's body on the floor in a pool of blood. He'd discovered it, then fled in a panic. Someone had hit him from behind, and he'd lost consciousness. For how long? Was the person who hit him — who must surely be the murderer — still here?

He staggered away from the door on unsteady legs, peering into the gloomy shadows of the shop. He stopped on the threshold of the back room. The lamp stood on the table where he'd left it, in a pool of dried blood. Leeman still lay on the floor. Welles looked around the room, saw no one else. He reached for the lamp, then stopped in mid-motion.

Something was different. He stared at the scene, trying to call up a mental picture of how it had been before. Now he saw it: There was a knife on the floor beside Leeman's head. It had not been there before; he was certain of it.

Someone put it there, he thought. *Someone came here tonight and killed the forger, then waited for me to arrive. He knocked me senseless and left me here to take the blame.*

From the front of the room came a loud crash, followed by a splintering sound. He looked around in panic, searching for another way out of the shop.

There must be one. The killer bolted the door from the inside. He cannot have fled that way.

He took the lantern from the table, then walked quickly through the far doorway and found himself in a larger room which clearly served as an office and bedroom. There was a door in the opposite wall. He crossed the room. The door was unlocked and opened into a narrow corridor. He held the lamp high. The walls and floor of the passage were rough stone blocks, leading straight away into darkness.

He heard another blow from the shop, followed by the sound of wood tearing, and a loud crash that could only be the front door collapsing to the floor. He stepped into the passage, pulling the door closed behind him. At the end of the passageway he found another door. It was not bolted. He opened it and found himself in a dark, deserted alley.

He stepped into the alley, closing the door behind him. He extinguished the lamp. At the far end of the alley he could see the lights of the Boulevard de Clichy. He sprinted towards them. Just before he reached the street he stopped, placed the lantern in a dark doorway, adjusted his clothing as best he could. He stepped into the boulevard and walked briskly away.

Chapter 36

London, 12 August 1898

"They came for me the next morning," Welles said. "I thought they might, so I left my coat in a pile of rubbish on the way back to my flat. Once there, I packed a bag — nothing much, just some clothes, money, my passport. I meant to disappear, at least until I could determine if they were looking for me. Still, they very nearly caught me. I had just locked the door of my flat on the way out when I heard them in the lobby. I heard Madame Hebert, I should say, telling someone that Monsieur Welles wasn't at home, seemingly at the top of her lungs. To this day I don't know why she did that.

"I descended as quietly as I could, listening carefully and trying to gauge their progress up the stairs. There was an empty flat on the fourth floor, and I knew the door would be unlocked, as was Madame's habit. I slipped into the flat, closed the door and stood with my back to it, listening. When I heard the footsteps of the *gendarmes* reach the landing of the top floor, I slipped back into the hallway and then down the stairs.

"Madame Hebert was waiting at the bottom. She put one finger to her lips, took me by the arm and led me down the hallway to her flat. *There is another flic outside the front door, in the street,* she said. *Use the door at the back.* Then I was out the door, sprinting down the alley behind the building."

"You are a fugitive from the law, Mister Welles?" asked Salisbury.

"I am," said Welles. "I have been one since that night. Indeed, I suspect that now I am doubly so."

"Doubly so?" asked Lawrence. "What do you mean by that?"

Welles waved a hand impatiently. "I shall come to that in due course, Mister Lawrence. I knew the police would be searching for me. I could not remain in Paris; or, indeed, in France. I took a train to Brussels, then another to Antwerp. There I booked passage on a freighter bound for Southampton. Five days after fleeing my apartment on Boulevard Haussmann I was home, in the small flat I keep in London. There I barred the door and waited."

"Waited?" asked Bingham. "For what were you waiting?"

"For Sir Reginald. Or, to be more precise, for whomever he might send in his place to kill me."

"Don't be ridiculous, Welles," objected Salisbury.

"I am quite serious," Welles said. "There is no question of putting the events down to coincidence. Someone killed Leeman on the same night he was to give me the evidence of forgery. The killer waited with the body until I arrived, then knocked me unconscious. He left me there and sent the police to find me, dazed and confused, the dead man's blood on my hands and clothes. The conclusion is inescapable. Leeman must have talked to someone, told him what I sought; and this person had in turn determined to silence that unfortunate man and frame me for his murder."

"If Leeman talked to anyone, it was probably Esterhazy," said Lawrence.

"There is no reason to believe Leeman ever met Esterhazy," Welles said. "In any event, the idea is ridiculous. I have no doubt Esterhazy would kill to save his own skin, but he would surely bungle the job. No, I could not see him being the architect of such a plan, nor capable of carrying it out. As to whom Leeman would have spoken, the answer is obvious: It had to be the man Leeman knew as Basil."

"Mister Welles," objected Salisbury. "Do you expect me to believe that Sir Reginald killed this man in cold blood, and implicated you in the murder?"

"I expect you to look at the facts and draw the obvious conclusions," said Welles. "The police came to my apartment. *They knew my name.* How did they get it? Leeman didn't know it, I never used it with him. It can only have been the man who sent me to Leeman in the first place."

Neither Salisbury nor Lawrence had a reply to that.

"In any event," Welles continued, "that is what I believed at the time, and events have come to confirm my suspicions, as I will shortly relate."

"Then you have been in London since March?" asked Bingham. "Waiting all that time for a murderer to come for you?"

"No, Mister Bingham. When, after a few weeks, no one came, I decided that Sir Reginald no longer saw any need to kill me. Driven from Paris, I had been effectively neutralized as a threat. The evidence I'd hoped to gain from Leeman was now forever beyond my reach. Slowly, I began to live a normal life. At least, it was normal in the sense that I felt safe enough to venture out of my flat. But I was still obsessed with the plight of poor Dreyfus, and I spent my nights racking my brain to recall everything that had occurred, trying to find the loose thread with which I could unravel the whole conspiracy. But nothing came to me. It was galling, especially as I knew that everything I needed to free Dreyfus was but a few miles from my flat."

"Everything you needed?" asked Lawrence. "What do you mean?"

"I am coming to that," said Welles. "I spent my days and nights in search of an answer that would not come. Would not, I should say, until suddenly it did, spurred by a story I read in the *Times*, reprinted from one of the Paris dailies. Colonel Picquart had been dismissed from the Army. No reason was given, but the story hinted of suspicions that the colonel was a traitor to France; that he would in due course face charges to that effect. I was distraught at the colonel's plight, and I could not shake it from my mind; nor could I quite free myself of the feeling that there was something important I had forgotten. For a day and a night, it plagued me, and then in a flash it came to me. Precisely why that story should lead me to recall something Esterhazy had told me, I cannot say, but it did; and I knew then what I had to do. Despite the danger of arrest, I returned to France."

Chapter 37

Chartres, 19 July 1898

Hugo was barking. At first, Durand ignored him; probably a cart was passing on the road at the end of the long driveway that connected the farm to the rest of the world. But the barking grew louder, more insistent. He sighed, put down the mug of coffee. He walked from the kitchen, down the hallway past the empty front room, through the door and onto the covered porch.

His father had built the porch when he was a boy, so that his mother could sit on summer evenings and watch the sunset beyond the fields, the two mis-matched towers of the cathedral in the distance silhouetted against an orange sky. She had died two years later. Another of his father's plans that had gone wrong.

There was a cart; Durand could see it trundling on its way, away from the town. But Hugo was not barking at the cart. Instead, he stood on the gravel drive midway between the house and the road, facing the man who walked towards the house. *A foreigner,* Durand thought; then wasn't sure why he'd thought it. The stranger was dressed in a traveling suit, a bit dusty from the ride along the dirt road. The suit looked English. The man waved, kept coming. *Surely English.*

"Hugo. *Chut!*"

The dog stopped barking, turned and trotted to Durand, taking up a position beside him, seated but alert; ready for anything.

The stranger neared the house. He stopped, hands at his sides, as if uncertain how to proceed.

"That's a good dog," he said, in French, but with a poor accent. *Yes, English.*

"What breed is he?"

"A Briard," said Durand. "My father bred them for sheep. But the sheep are all gone now." *Like my father.* "What do you want?"

"*Pardon*, Monsieur. My name is Welles. Are you Andre Durand? Lieutenant Andre Durand?"

Close up, Durand could see it was a good suit, well-tailored, and that the shoes were good as well. But both were the worse for wear; over-worn, even, as if their owner had fallen on hard times.

"No," he said. "I'm not Lieutenant Andre Durand."

He was surprised to see the disappointment in Welles's face.

"Do you know him, then?" Welles asked.

The man's eyes darted around, taking in the doorway behind Durand, then the fallow fields beyond the farmhouse.

"I have been looking for Durand for some time," he said. "Isn't this his farm?"

Desperate, Durand thought. *Like an animal.* Something about Welles struck a chord, however, and to Durand's surprise he realized that he couldn't send the man away.

"*Lieutenant* Durand is no more," he said. "Now there is only Andre. Will you take a coffee, Monsieur Welles?"

He held the door open, beckoning Welles into the house.

It was a large kitchen, but the presence of a stranger made it seem small. Durand could not remember the last time anyone else had been in the house. He gestured to a chair. Welles sat. Durand took a mug from the cupboard, poured coffee, set the mug before Welles. He filled his own mug, returned the pot to the iron stove.

"There is cream," he said. "No sugar."

He sat at the table, added a little cream to his coffee, slid the pitcher of cream across to Welles, who declined it. The two men sipped coffee.

"Who are you, Monsieur Welles?" Durand asked. "What do you want from me?"

Welles lowered his cup to the table, cleared his throat.

"I am a journalist," he said. "I am in possession of some information, something which I believe will be of interest to my readers."

"And what is this information, if you please?"

"It has to do with an expedition in the Congo," Welles said. "A French expedition. Led by a man named Marchand."

Welles paused. Durand said nothing.

"I am told you were a part of the expedition," Welles continued, "and that you have only recently returned to France. I hoped to speak with you about it."

Durand raised his mug slowly, swallowed coffee, put it down.

"How interesting," he said. "I wonder, Monsieur Welles, if you can tell me where you heard such a fantastic tale?"

"Fantastic? Surely not fantastic. Intriguing, I would say. For I know with certainty the tale is true. As I think you do, *Lieutenant* Durand."

Durand waved this away as if shooing a fly.

"I asked how you came to hear the story."

"I am not at liberty to tell you," Welles said. "But I can say that the person who told me about Marchand also told me that you had returned to France. So, I came looking. You are real enough, it seems; which makes me believe the rest of the story is true."

Durand made a face.

"Whether it is true or not, why did you suppose you would learn anything from me? If it is true and a secret, then I am bound by my oath to keep the secret. If it is a fantasy, then I can tell you nothing more about it. In either case, I would deny the story and tell you nothing. I fear you have made a long journey for nothing, Monsieur Welles."

"Perhaps," said Welles. "Yet here you are. Lieutenant Andre Durand. Though, as you say, no longer *Lieutenant* Durand. You have resigned your commission. Why have you done that, I wonder?"

"For reasons that would be of no interest to your readers." Durand was impatient now. He stood. "Finish your coffee, then. I'll see you to the door."

Welles did not stand. Instead, he clasped his hands before him on the table. His chin fell to his chest, his eyes intent on the hands. Was he praying? Durand did not think him the praying type. Again, he was struck by a sense of desperation in the man, an impression Welles gave of being trapped, like an animal in a snare. Durand sighed. From a cupboard he took a bottle and two glasses. He filled both, put one on the table near Welles's clasped hands, returned to his own seat. He sipped the brandy.

"The answer to your question is simple enough," he said. "I received a letter from home. It had been carried eight thousand miles to reach me, to tell me that my father had died. After that, I had no heart to continue."

Welles raised his eyes to meet Durand's. He held them a long moment, then shook his head.

"It is a terrible thing to lose a father," he said. "Still, it happens to us all. I'm sorry for your loss, but I do not believe you would abandon your duty because of that."

Durand shrugged. "Believe what you like; it is nothing to me, Monsieur Welles."

"Where did the letter find you? Was it in Tambura?"

Durand could not stop himself from reacting to that, and he saw immediately that Welles had noted the reaction. Neither man spoke for some time. Durand finished his brandy, refilled the glass. Welles had still not touched his.

"My father wanted me to be a farmer," Durand said, as if to fill the silence. "From the time my mother died, this was his whole world. This farm, his dogs. Me. In that order."

He took another drink, holding the glass in both hands.

"I hated the idea, of course. I wanted to be a soldier. We argued about it constantly. But when the time came — when I was accepted by the Ecole Militaire — he drove me to the station and put me on the train to Paris. I imagine he felt it was his duty. He had a great regard for duty."

"He must have understood at least that you meant to do yours," said Welles.

Durand smiled, but his eyes were sad.

"He did not understand it at all," he said. "My father fought the Prussians in the last war. He was there at the end, at Sedan. It changed him, I think, though I was too young to know what he was like before." Durand refilled his glass. "He believed we owed a duty to the people around us; family, friends, even strangers we meet on the road. But never to a country. *'What is a country?'* he said to me once. *'You can't take it by the hand. It will never embrace you. But it will kill you, if you give it half a chance. Or it will make you a killer, which is worse.'*"

He drank.

"He was full of advice, my father, but I never heeded it. In the end, I had to go to the end of the world to learn he was right."

"Why did you go?" asked Welles. "What were you doing?"

"I was killing," said Durand. "Killing good men, for no reason I can explain now. Men no different than we are, you and me. As my father said I would."

He took a deep breath, then began to talk. He spoke for nearly an hour, describing the things he had seen and done. Explaining why, in the end, he had decided to come home. Welles listened without speaking. When Durand finished, he felt drained, exhausted. He refilled his glass, nodded to Welles.

"Your turn, Monsieur Welles," he said. "Why are you here?"

Welles unclasped his hands. He lifted his glass, drank. His hand shook as he lowered it, spilling brandy on the table. Absently, he wiped it, then rubbed his palm on his jacket.

"There is a man," he said. "A man wrongly accused, sent to die in prison. I want to help him if I can."

"Why?" asked Durand. "What is he to do with you? Why should you want to help him?"

"Because," said Welles, lifting the glass again, "I might have freed him once, but instead I helped to keep him there. It is only because of me that he languishes there still." He drained the glass.

Durand pushed the bottle across the table.

"Start at the beginning," he said.

***

Welles slipped the strap of the satchel over his shoulder. They shook hands, then Welles turned and walked up the dusty lane towards the road. Durand watched him go. Hugo nudged his hand. Absently, he petted the dog. Welles reached the road, turned right, heading into the town.

Durand looked at his watch. The train to Paris departed in just over three hours — if it were on time — so Welles would make it with time to spare. As he watched, Welles stopped, turned to look back at the house. Welles waved, shouted his thanks. Durand waved back. Welles walked on.

Durand watched until he was out of sight. He looked at his watch again. He cursed quietly, under his breath. Hugo stood, alert, his tail wagging. Durand looked at the dog, sighed.

"*Pas bouger!*" he said.

Hugo obediently sat, waited. Durand went into the house, climbed the stairs to the upper floor. His father's room was on the left, his own on the right. He had been unable to break the habit of a lifetime, and he still slept in his old room, on the small bed he'd used for as long as he could remember.

He took a leather kit bag from the top of the bureau. It was the same one he'd taken with him on the *Thibet*. He laid it on the bed, began to stuff it with clothing. From a dresser drawer he took a wallet, drew out a wad of bills, counted them. Enough, he thought. He stuffed the money back into the wallet, slipped the wallet into the bag. He closed the bag, buckled the straps. He took a cap from the top of the bureau, put it on his head. He lifted the bag, looked around the room one last time, then went out the door and down the stairs.

Hugo waited on the porch. Durand closed the front door, locked it, put the key in his pocket.

"*Viens*, Hugo," he said, starting up the lane. "Madame Bonnard will look after you for a while. But we must hurry if I am to make the train."

Hugo sprang to his feet, barked once, then fell into step at his side.

Part 4

"It is unlikely that the world will ever learn the details of the subtle scheme of which the Marchand Mission was a famous part."

— *Winston Churchill, <u>The River War</u>, 1902*

Chapter 38

Paris, 6 August 1898

The elevator came to a halt and the attendant opened the door. The car was not full — aside from Welles, there were only a half-dozen other passengers, workmen by the look of them — and in a moment he was standing on the second platform of the tower. The elevator delivered him to an enclosed space dominated by the two large elevator cages at the east and west corners, and a smaller cage in the center of the space. The workmen he'd arrived with crossed quickly to this cage and filed into another elevator that would carry them to the top of the tower. On impulse, Welles approached an attendant and asked him what the men were doing. The attendant shrugged.

"They are installing something at the top," he said. "An *antenna*, they called it. Some madness to do with sending messages through the air."

He raised his eyebrows at the absurdity of the idea.

"It must be important if they are working so late at night," Welles said.

"They work at night so as not to disturb the visitors, Monsieur."

The man produced a watch and made a sound with his tongue against the roof of his mouth.

"We close soon," he said. "If you miss the last elevator you will have to walk down the stairs. It is a long way, Monsieur."

Welles nodded, then crossed the lobby and passed through a door into the open air. The viewing gallery was deserted. He stood for a moment at the railing, looking down at the city of light which spread out below him in every direction. As he turned away, a workman came through the door. He glanced at Welles, looked the other way down the gallery, then turned around and went back into the lobby.

Welles continued to the next corner. Hull was seated on a bench, halfway along the gallery, a small leather valise in his lap. Welles hesitated a moment, then walked resolutely towards him, coming to a stop in front of the bench. Hull acknowledged him with a nod but said nothing. Welles shifted the satchel off his shoulder, sat beside Hull, then held the satchel on his lap.

"Did you bring the file?" he asked.

"Of course," said Hull. "And you?"

Welles patted the satchel with one hand.

"We'll have to hurry," he said. "They're closing soon, they'll clear the platform."

"No," said Hull. "I'll want time to examine what you've brought. We'll wait until they're gone."

He stood, gesturing for Welles to follow, then led the way along the gallery to where a small door was set in the wall. He opened the door. Welles peered into the small closet.

"Quickly, man," said Hull.

Welles stepped inside and Hull followed him, closing the door behind him.

The two men waited in darkness for what seemed like an eternity. At last Hull edged past Welles and unlatched the door. He opened it slowly and peered out, looking in both directions. He motioned for Welles to follow. They sat side by side on the bench. Welles clutched the satchel to his body. Sir Reginald placed his own valise on the iron deck between them. Welles eyes were drawn to the bag.

"I've seen the file before," he said. "If you've left anything out, I'll know."

"It's all there," said Hull. "As we agreed."

"Let me see it," said Welles.

"Not yet. You first, I think."

Welles hesitated, then realized he had no choice. He unbuckled the straps, opened the satchel and drew out the leather-bound volume Durand had given him. Hull took it, laid it on his lap, opened it. He flipped through the pages, peering at them in the dim light, until he came to the page where the journal ended. He scanned the last entry, then turned to the previous page. He read for several minutes.

"Very good," he said, closing the journal. He eyed Welles with curiosity. "How did you get this?" he asked.

"Durand gave it to me."

"Why would he give it to you?"

Welles shrugged. "I don't know." He nodded at the valise at Hull's feet. "Your turn."

Hull crouched beside the valise. He opened it and slid the journal in along one side. When his hand emerged, it held a gun. He rose to his feet, one hand clutching the valise, the other pointing the gun at Welles.

"Stand up."

Welles stood, the empty satchel sliding from his lap and falling to the deck. He opened his mouth to say something, then closed it. There was nothing to say. He should have realized that Hull would never give him the file; that he always meant to take the journal by force. That's why Hull had chosen this meeting place, this hour; so that there would be no one to witness the meeting, or to stop him from getting what he wanted. Welles understood suddenly that Hull meant to kill him. He ought to be frightened, but instead he felt a kind of strange detachment, as if he were standing off to one side watching Hull point the gun at someone else. From what seemed a long distance away, he heard Hull's voice.

"Move to the railing."

Welles didn't move. Hull gestured with the gun.

"Move to the railing, Percy," he said. "I'd rather not shoot you. It would be so much simpler if you were to jump. A man who has lost his job? Lost the woman he loves? A man wanted by the police for murder? Easy to believe he'd jump."

He raised the pistol, aimed at Welles's head. With his thumb, he drew back the hammer until it locked into place.

"But I *will* shoot you if you don't move. Now."

Welles took a step towards the railing, then another. Hull tracked his progress with the gun. Another step, and another, and then Welles was at the railing.

"Climb over," said Hull.

Welles looked down. The framework of the tower had been fitted with electric lamps, strings of lights lit the legs that sloped downward and away; and arc lights had been placed around the base, shining up at him. He could not make out the ground below — the glare from the lights robbed him of that view — but further away he could see the lights of the seventh *arrondissement*.

"Climb over," said Hull again.

Keeping the gun trained on Welles, he lowered the valise to the floor, then stepped closer.

"Listen to me," he said. "If you cooperate, make this easy, I'll spare the woman."

"The woman?"

"Miss Seigneur," said Hull. "They're on the way to her now, but there's still time for me to stop them."

He gestured towards the rail with the gun.

"But you have to cooperate. Do it now."

As if of their own volition, Welles's hands gripped the rail. He stared down at them, stunned by their betrayal, and then one foot lifted itself and settled onto the low iron step on which the rail was mounted. He felt his weight shift forward in preparation for throwing the other leg over the top of the rail. Then he heard a shout.

"*Que faites-vous ici?*"

A man in workman's clothes stood at the end of the gallery, facing them, his hands on his hips. It was the same man Welles had seen earlier. With a start, he realized it was Andre Durand.

Hull turned to face Durand. The three men stood motionless for a long breath. Hull looked down at the gun in his hand, then back to Durand. His shoulders sagged, and Welles thought he might drop the gun. Then Hull stiffened. He raised the gun, aiming it at Durand.

He will kill us both, Welles thought. *He thinks he has no choice now that Durand has seen the gun.*

Even as this thought was coalescing in his mind, he gripped the rail tightly and pivoted, swinging his free leg rapidly around in an arc to connect with the back of Hull's knees. The man crumpled just as the gun went off. Welles saw a spark as the bullet struck an iron girder at the corner just above where Durand's head had been an instant before. Durand himself had ducked to the floor and was scrambling on hands and knees to the safety of the corner.

Hull hit the floor, rolled onto his back, faced Welles and brought the gun around to bear on him. Welles released the railing, grabbed the valise and swung it wildly, catching the gun, sending it flying. It struck the rail, then the floor, then slid along the gallery towards the corner where Durand had taken shelter. Hull kicked out with both feet, catching Welles in the midsection and groin. Welles doubled over, fell to the deck. The blow brought tears to his eyes and he struggled to breathe. He saw Hull roll onto his knees, get to his feet and stumble after the gun. Welles tried to shout, to warn Durand, but the words came out in a breathless whisper. He rolled onto his hands and knees but could not muster the strength to rise any further.

Hull picked up the gun. He looked at Welles, who was crawling on the deck and gasping for breath, then turned away. He raised the gun and walked slowly towards the corner, looking for Durand. He was nearly there before Welles, drawing on all his strength, staggered to his feet and set off at a run, shouting a warning to Durand as he came.

Hull turned at the shout. He hesitated, uncertain whether to go on or turn back to deal with Welles. At that instant Durand leapt from behind the corner and grasped the gun hand with both of his own. Hull twisted towards Durand, driving his shoulder into the man's chest. Durand staggered backwards into the rail, releasing Hull's hand and grabbing the rail to prevent himself from toppling over. Hull brought the gun down hard against Durand's head, and Durand slumped to the floor, dazed. Hull aimed the gun at Durand's head, drew the hammer back with a loud click. Then Welles hit him at a full run, driving his shoulder into Hull's torso and straightening his back as he did, lifting Hull off the deck of the platform and propelling him into the railing.

It seemed to happen with a ridiculous lethargy. The gun, knocked loose by the impact, tumbled gracefully through the air. Hull was driven against the rail, then up and over it. His hands grabbed for a hold, but slowly, so that first one hand missed the rail, then the other. His head and shoulders were past the rail now, hanging over the abyss, and his legs spun slowly in an upward arc, like the hands of a clock moving inexorably towards midnight. Welles's momentum carried him into the rail, knocking the air from his body for a second time. His knees buckled and he crumpled, half lying on the deck, his cheek pressed against the metal of the rail. Through it he saw Hull's face; his eyes wide, his mouth open in bewilderment. Then — without having made a sound — Hull was gone.

Welles struggled to catch his breath. The platform was strangely silent until, without any warning, the gun struck the iron deck beside him, the impact jarring the hammer loose. The shot was loud, very close, and for a moment Welles felt sure he'd been shot, but the bullet passed harmlessly into the night.

Welles's head and shoulders slid down the rail until he lay on his side. The iron deck was cool and hard, but he wanted nothing more than to lie there; to sleep. He drew his knees up to his chest, closed his eyes.

"Get up."

Something prodded him on the shoulder. He opened his eyes. Durand was leaning over him. He grabbed Welles by the shoulder, shook him.

"Are you shot?"

"No," said Welles.

"Then get up." Durand was insistent. "Someone may have heard the shots. We should go before they come."

He took Welles by the arm, helped him to his feet. He looked around, saw the gun, picked it up. He held it out to Welles. Welles ignored it, walked instead along the gallery to retrieve Hull's valise. He looked inside. Durand's journal was there, and some clothes. Hull's wallet and passport. A box of cartridges for the gun. But no file. Nothing he could use. Durand was beside him now. Welles was suddenly angry, angry at Durand, though he could not say why.

"What the devil are you doing here?" he demanded.

"I followed you."

"Followed me? How did you even find me?"

Durand shrugged. "I have been following you for days. Since you left the farm. It was easy enough; there was only one train to Paris."

"But why? Why would you do that?"

Durand looked down at the gun in his hand. He held it out to Welles. When Welles didn't take it, Durand slipped it into the valise.

"Forgive me, Monsieur Welles, but it seemed to me that you were lost. Desperate. So I gave you the journal. Why not? It no longer held any importance for me. But then I thought perhaps you would do something stupid."

He looked around the empty gallery, back to Welles.

"Though, in truth, not anything quite so stupid as this," he said. "You must tell me who that man was, why you came here to meet him. Why he meant to kill you. But later. Now, we must go."

Why he meant to kill me, Welles thought. Because of what he knew. With a start, he recalled Hull's words: *I'll spare the woman.*

"Georges!" he blurted out. "Yes, we must hurry!"

He lifted the valise, sprinted to the door. He had reached the nearest elevator when Durand caught up with him and grabbed his arm.

"Listen," Durand hissed.

Now Welles could hear the elevator machinery.

"They're coming," said Durand. "This way."

He led Welles to the opposite corner of the lobby, opened a gate, and they were on the stairway. Welles looked at the stairs, then back to Durand.

"Only seven hundred steps, Monsieur," Durand said.

Chapter 39

Paris, 7 August 1898

Quite suddenly Georges was awake. She lay in bed, listening to the sounds of the house in the night, her body still and her mind focused. She listened for a long time but heard nothing. She realized that she was holding her breath. She let it out slowly, rolled onto her side, clutching a pillow in her arms. It must have been a dream. She closed her eyes, then opened them again. *There.* A sound that did not belong. Someone in the hall below her. Not a housekeeper or a maid; it was the sound of someone trying to move quietly who had been betrayed by the creak of ancient floorboards.

She slid quietly out of bed, put on her dressing gown. She listened at the door, then opened it and slipped into the hallway. She stood near the banister, peering down into the entry hall. The house was dark, but light from the street shone dimly through the windows, casting shadows across the floor below. One of the shadows moved. A dark figure made its way through the murky gloom towards the stairway.

She stepped lightly along the hall, away from the stairs. She passed the library, stopped before the door to her father's bedroom. She opened it and slipped inside. She could hear her father breathing, the heavy regular sound of someone deep in sleep. In the dim light from the windows she could just make out his sleeping form. She moved silently to the bureau opposite the bed, opened a drawer, and drew a large revolver from inside. She pressed a release, opening the cylinder to check that it was loaded. She closed it again with an audible snap. Behind her, she heard her father stir. She waited without moving until his breathing became regular again.

Back at the door, she dropped to a crouch, opened the door only a tiny crack, and peered through the gap. In the darkness of the hallway, she saw a dark figure appear at the top of the stair. She watched the figure move along the hallway. He — she assumed it was a man — stopped at each door, opened it carefully. He peered into each room, then closed the door and continued, moving inexorably closer with each step. He reached the door to the library, opened it, and was briefly illuminated by the light from the library windows. Yes, a man; she could just make out short hair and a beard as he opened the door wider, stepped into the library, and closed it behind him.

She slipped into the hallway and moved as quietly as she could to the library door. She put her ear to the door and listened, but she could hear nothing. She was torn between entering the library to challenge the intruder and retreating to her father's room to wait until the man left. She was afraid, but also angry, and her anger won out. She tightened her grip on the pistol, took hold of the latch and threw open the door.

"Who are you?" she demanded. "What are you doing in my house?"

Bright light reflected from the white cathedral walls shone through the windows and illuminated the intruder, who was bent over her father's desk. Her eyes were drawn to the large envelope he now held in one hand. She raised the gun, pointed it at him.

"Whatever you have taken, put it back," she said.

Instead of complying, the intruder slowly came to an erect position, facing her, his hands at his sides, still holding the envelope. She pulled back the hammer, cocking the pistol.

"Put it back," she said.

The gun shook in her hand and she raised her other hand to steady it. As she did so, something moved at the edge of her vision.

Startled, she turned her head towards the movement. Another man was there, at the top of the stair. She could just make him out, saw that his hand was extended; saw that there was something in his hand. She dropped to the floor just as the shot rang out, and she heard the bullet crash into the wood of the door frame. She pointed her father's gun at the intruder on the stair, squeezed the trigger. The revolver bucked in her hand, but she held it tightly, brought it back on target, squeezed the trigger again, and then again. The intruder on the stair cried out, then toppled backward and vanished from sight.

From her father's room she heard a shout, and more cries from the staff rooms on the floor above. She was suddenly nauseous, and a dry retching racked her body. She struggled to control it, taking deep breaths, and had barely managed to get to her feet when she remembered the first intruder, just as he crashed into her, knocking her to the floor again. She lost her grip on the gun and it spun away from her, sliding across the floor and through the banister, then fell to the floor below.

She looked up at the man standing over her. He still held the envelope he'd taken from her father's desk. She watched as he switched the envelope from his right hand to his left, then drew a knife from inside his coat. The sight of the knife brought her to her senses, and she kicked out at him, striking his shin. He muttered an oath, something that sounded strange to her ears. She scrambled backwards away from him. He dropped the envelope, but not the knife. Holding it before him, he advanced slowly. She retreated, scrabbling across the floor. She heard a loud pounding, and more shouting; someone was at the front door, hammering on it. Then her father was in the hall, behind her, calling her name.

Her assailant hesitated, then spun around and ran to the stairs. She struggled to her feet, meaning to give chase, but her father was beside her now, wrapping his arms around her. She peered over the banister, saw the intruder in the hall below heading for the back of the house. Then he stopped, bent over, picked up something that was lying on the floor. *The gun,* she thought, as she threw her weight against her father behind her and propelled them both back, away from the railing. She heard the gunshot, heard the crash of the bullet striking overhead. Then the front door splintered and gave way.

"Georges!" someone shouted, then again: "Georges! Where are you?"

Percy!

"I'm here," she called out, though when the sound emerged it was barely a whisper.

"We are here," shouted her father.

She leaned against the wall, then slowly slid down until she lay on one side. She drew her knees up, hugged them to her chest, her body shaking uncontrollably. She closed her eyes. She heard footsteps rushing up the stairs, then along the hall. Someone placed a hand on her upper arm.

"Georges," said Percy, from what seemed very far away. "Are you hurt?"

She could not answer. The hand gripped her arm, pulled, forcing her over onto her back. Then another hand was on her, feeling her abdomen, her sides, her chest.

"I don't think she was hit." Percy again.

"Are you sure?" That was her father.

"Can someone bring a lamp?"

Her father shouted for a lamp. The hands continued their probing, running along her legs now.

"Take your hands off me," she shouted; but again, it was barely a whisper.

Nonetheless, the hands stopped. Then she felt one against her cheek.

"I'm sorry, Georges," he said. "I just want to see if you're hurt."

She opened her eyes. Welles's face hovered over hers, staring at her intently. Beyond it, she saw her father's face. Shadows danced on the walls, then her father was holding a lantern. He held it above her while Percy resumed his inspection, this time with his eyes.

"Nothing," he said, the relief evident in his voice.

"There is a dead man here, on the stair," said an unfamiliar voice. "Shot twice. And his neck is broken, it must have happened when he fell down the stairs."

She pressed her hands against the floor, raised herself up and twisted until she sat with her back to the wall.

"I shot him," she said. "I think the other one ran when you broke down the door."

"The other one?" Welles said, his voice urgent. "There were two?"

"Yes," she said. "He was English."

"English? How do you know?"

"When I kicked him, he cried out," said Georges. "He swore. In English." She repeated the obscenity. "Sorry, Papa."

She smiled, as she always did when she'd said or done something to shock her father, and she saw that his eyes were filled with tears. She reached out, took his hand in her own, caressed it.

"I am all right, Papa."

A stranger approached Percy from the stairs. He was dressed in the clothes of a laborer, but something about his bearing belied his garb.

"I searched the dead man," he said to Percy. "Nothing. No identification or card, not even any money. He was lying on top of a gun. I assume it was his."

He looked down at the floor, then bent over and retrieved the envelope.

"He must have dropped this," he said.

"It was the other man," said Georges. "He took that from your desk, Papa."

"Took it?" asked Seigneur. "What is it?"

"I suspect it is the envelope that Picquart gave you," said Welles. "His copy of the Dreyfus dossier."

Georges turned to him, searched his face with her eyes.

"Why should you think that, Percy?" she asked, sharply. "How would they even know to find it here?"

Welles ignored the question. He took the envelope from Durand.

"We should make sure that the intruder has fled," he said. "And do something to bar the front door."

Durand nodded, turned towards the stairs. He had reached them when Welles called out to him.

"Durand!" The man paused, turned. "The police will be on their way. If they find me here, they will arrest me."

"Arrest you?" repeated Georges. "Why would they arrest you?"

Again, Welles ignored her question.

"I will have to leave soon, go to England," he said, speaking to Durand. "There is something I must do there. I wonder if you can stay here, with Georges and her father? Keep an eye on things?"

"That isn't necessary," snapped Georges. "We are quite able to look after ourselves."

Durand looked at Georges, then back to Welles. He shrugged.

"I'll stay. Hopefully with Mademoiselle's permission. But I will stay in any case."

He nodded to Georges, turned, descended the stairs.

"What in God's name is going on here, Welles?" demanded her father. "Who is this man?"

"His name is Durand," said Welles. "You can trust him. Please believe me when I say that you are in danger, and it would be good to have a man like him around."

"Why are we in danger, Percy?" asked Georges. "Who were these men? And why have you come here?"

Welles handed the envelope to her father.

"Keep this safe, Monsieur," he said. "Put it somewhere more secure than your desk drawer, if you can. It may be of vital importance to Captain Dreyfus."

He turned to Georges, offered her his hand. She hesitated, then took it and he helped her to her feet.

"I cannot answer your questions now, Georges," he said. "There is no time. But I promise I will tell you everything when I return."

Chapter 40

London, 12 August 1898

It was Lawrence who spoke first.

"Sir Reginald is dead?" he asked, the disbelief evident in his voice.

"Yes," said Welles. "I killed him. He left me no other choice."

"I don't believe you. You say it happened nearly a week ago? We would surely have heard by now."

"I imagine they still haven't identified the body. His wallet and passport were in the valise I took. I used them to get out of France."

Welles reached into his jacket, drew out a thin leather wallet, tossed it carelessly onto the table. The sound it made when it landed was like a slap to the face.

"By now they will have worked out that he was British," he said. "From the labels on his clothes. His shoes. They'll be canvassing hotels, looking for someone who's gone missing."

"Mister Welles." This from Salisbury. "Do you expect me to believe that Sir Reginald tried to kill you? That he sent men to kill Miss Seigneur, to murder her in cold blood?"

"It is impossible," agreed Lawrence. He appealed to Salisbury. "You knew Sir Reginald. Can you imagine him doing these things?"

"I knew him," said Salisbury. He addressed Welles: "Why would Sir Reginald kill the forger?"

"To conceal his own role in the affair."

"What role was that, Mister Welles?"

"Think, man," insisted Welles. "Leeman knew Sir Reginald as Basil; had done work for him before. Why did Hull employ a forger in the first place, if not to provide Esterhazy with false evidence to use against Dreyfus?"

Welles saw this argument strike home. Salisbury pivoted to stare at Lawrence, a look of apprehension on his face. Then he turned back to Welles.

"Even assuming that Sir Reginald helped to implicate Dreyfus — which I do not for a moment grant, Mister Welles — that is far short of murder. Why should he wish to kill you?"

Welles sighed in exasperation.

"He knew that I suspected what he'd done," he said, "that I was trying to prove it by blackmailing Leeman. He killed Leeman to silence him and tried to pin the murder on me. When I escaped, he thought that was the end of it; that there was nothing more I could do to threaten him. But then I demanded the Esterhazy file. Worse, I told him that I had already seen it."

"What is in that file, Mister Welles?"

"Proof of the connection between Hull and Leeman," Welles said. "He knew I could implicate him in the murder."

"And the lady? Why would he send men to kill her?"

"He couldn't know how much I had told her," said Welles. "Better to be sure. Better for him. Better for England. He believed in the things he did, you see. He was that kind of fool. I imagine it was easy enough for him to see eliminating me as his duty."

Here Welles paused, and fixed the Prime Minister with a questioning look.

"His duty?" Salisbury was indignant. "I hope you don't mean to say that Sir Reginald acted on my instructions, or even with my implicit sanction. We are men of the world, and the world is a dangerous place; but there *are* limits, I assure you."

"Are there? I should like to think so." Welles turned to Lawrence. "Do you say there are, sir?"

"What are you getting at, Welles?"

The news of Hull's death had worked a change in Lawrence, Welles saw. Something in the man's face gave him pause. Casually, without hurrying, Welles reached out and picked up the gun. He leaned back again, crossed his arms, the gun cradled in the crook of his elbow. He did not feel the need to point it at anyone. It was enough to have it in his hand, should he need it. He returned his attention to Salisbury.

"It may be that Hull was acting on his own," said Welles. "But this much is clear: he paid Leeman to provide false evidence against Dreyfus, in order to protect Esterhazy. He killed Leeman to cover up what he'd done and tried to frame me for the murder. When that failed, my own life was forfeit, for Hull knew that I would know he had done it."

"Why have you come here, Mister Welles?" asked Salisbury. "What is it that you want?"

"I want the Esterhazy file, and the freedom to use it as I see fit."

"You intend to prove that Esterhazy was the traitor?"

Welles shook his head.

"If proving Esterhazy's guilt was enough to free Dreyfus, he would already have been released," he said. "No, what I mean to do is impeach the evidence used to convict him; to show that it is a fraud, concocted by foreign adventurers to protect the real traitor."

Lawrence was apoplectic.

"You can't imagine we'll give you that," he said. "It would do tremendous harm to the Government."

He was looking at Welles as he spoke, but Welles understood that he was speaking to Salisbury. The Prime Minister did not react to Lawrence. Instead, he seemed to be considering Welles's request.

"Suppose I were to agree," Salisbury said. "What would I get in return?"

"You would have what you want," said Welles. "The truth about the Marchand mission. How he means to defend the French claim. You understand, sir, there isn't much time. If you're going to prevent him from being reinforced, you will need to act quickly."

Salisbury shook his head.

"We know it is King Leopold who means to help him," he said. "That was clear to us as soon as we knew the Belgians had loaned Marchand the *Villes de Bruges*. You told us that when you got it from Esterhazy, more than eighteen months ago. We know who Marchand's ally was; what we lacked was his objective. Now we know it is Fashoda, on the Nile. You've told us that, too. You've nothing left with which to bargain."

Welles looked from Salisbury to Lawrence, then back again.

"In that case," he said, "there is nothing further to discuss. You gentlemen are free to go."

As if to underscore his words, Welles released the hammer on the pistol carefully, lowered it to the table, and then slid it across the wood surface to Lawrence. The latter snatched it up as soon as it came within reach, then stood and pointed it at Welles.

"I shall summon help, Prime Minister," he said, moving towards the door.

"Wait a moment, if you please." Salisbury's voice was sharp. His eyes were on Welles, a look of calculation on his face.

"What are you playing at, Welles?" he asked.

"I came here to bargain with you," Welles said. "If what I had to bargain with was the news that the Belgians were in league with the French, then I would hardly have given that information away in return for nothing."

The room was silent as Salisbury considered this at length. Then he nodded.

"No, you would not," he said. "How can Marchand defend Fashoda? Do you know?"

"I do," Welles replied. "I'll tell you in exchange for the Esterhazy file, and your promise to let me do with it what I must."

"What will you do with the file?"

This was the moment for which Welles had been laboring for hours. He went on to explain, choosing his words with care, making the best case for his plan that he could. Still, when he had finished, Salisbury said nothing. It seemed to Welles that the silence was complete. He could hear nothing of the activity which must surely be going on — even now — elsewhere in the Travellers Club. He tried to read the expression on Salisbury's face, but could make nothing of it. The man might be undecided or might already have rejected Welles's proposal. There was no way to know. Everything now hung in the balance. He thought that, with a word, he might yet bring Salisbury around. But he could think of nothing more to say.

In the end, it was Bingham who broke the silence

"Mister Welles," he said. "You will recall that, some hours ago, I said you might have need of my services before the night was over. I confess I said it in jest, but I am in earnest now. It may be that you will face charges for holding us here, or even for murder — for this Leeman fellow, and for Sir Reginald — but I should like you to know that I stand ready to represent you."

"Mister Bingham," said Welles, "if it comes to that, I should be glad to have you."

"Then I am at your service, sir."

Bingham turned to address Salisbury.

"I would have you know, Prime Minister, that should you agree to Mister Welles's proposal — as I sincerely hope you will — then I will stand witness to the agreement, and I will hold you to your part. After all, as you say, there *are* limits."

Salisbury stared at Bingham for a full five seconds. Then he looked away, his eyes darting around the room as if searching for something. Then he sighed, looked along the table at Welles, nodded.

"Prime Minister!" objected Lawrence.

He took a step toward Welles, the gun ready. Salisbury raised a hand.

"Put down that gun, William," he said.

Lawrence hesitated.

"Put it down, I said!"

Lawrence slowly lowered the pistol. Salisbury turned to Welles.

"We are agreed, Mister Welles."

Chapter 41

The Journal of Lieutenant Andre Durand

<u>*Wednesday, 3 November 1897*</u>
<u>*Tambura*</u>
<u>*French Congo*</u>

A letter has come for me from my father, a letter that has followed me for months and has only overtaken me now because of the predicament in which we find ourselves. Despite all we have sacrificed to come so far, it seems we have arrived too late. The rains have ended, and the dry season is upon us. The river has fallen so far that the Faidherbe is useless to us. We shall not be able to move her for another six months. We are stranded here, only five hundred miles from our objective.

This afternoon Paké-Bô showed us a dispatch he has just received, one that came in the same packet as the letter from my father.

'Kitchener is at Abu Hamed,' he said, 'below the fifth cataract. Within three hundred miles of Omdurman.'

We must make a dash for it now,' said Mangin. 'The sooner we get there, the more time we have to prepare. If we wait for the rains he may be there before us, and all our efforts will have been wasted.'

'And the Faidherbe?' asked our leader.

'Leave her here. She can follow when the water rises.'

*They argued then. For once, I found myself agreeing with Mangin. The
steamboat has become an encumbrance to us, as he said it would. If we
had left it behind in Zemio, we would doubtless have already reached our
objective, and much would be different. When I thought of all the
suffering and loss we might have avoided, for a moment I was moved to
take his side. But I held back, for I had made my choice.*

Paké-Bô became angry.

*'It is I who commands, Captain,' he said, sharply. Then he seemed
embarrassed by the words. 'Come, Charles, let us not quarrel. The news of
Kitchener changes things, but not in the way you think. There has always
been the possibility of his defeating the Khalifa and confronting us at
Fashoda; and there is a contingency plan to deal with that possibility.'*

*From the little table he used for a desk he took a piece of paper, then held
it up before us.*

*'I have received the news for which I have long waited,' he said. 'It is
the answer to the question we have all asked ourselves countless times in
the last two years: How we can hold Fashoda against Kitchener and the
forces at his command.'*

*He lowered his voice as if imparting a close-held secret, so we three
drew closer.*

*'Minister Hanotaux has always understood that we may have to face
the British,' he said. 'Even as we were sailing from Marseilles, he put in
motion a plan to deliver to us the allies we would need to do it.'*

*'The Belgians?' scoffed Mangin. 'They have been little enough help and
will abandon us at the first sign of a fight.'*

*'No, Charles, not them,' said Paké-Bô. 'We want an ally, not a rival;
someone with as much to gain as we in forcing the British out of Egypt.
Someone already on the scene, so to speak. That is why Hanotaux sent a
man to Addis Ababa last year.'*

'Addis Ababa!' exclaimed Baratier.

*'The Emperor Menelik wants to rid himself of the Italians,' said Paké-
Bô. 'We have supplied him with the guns and ammunition he needs. In
return, he has agreed to support our cause. An relief force is being formed,
Abyssinian soldiers led by the Marquis de Bonchamps. They will be ten
thousand; more than enough to hold against Kitchener, and with any luck
enough to dissuade him from attacking.'*

'Then I repeat my counsel,' said Mangin. 'We must hurry to Fashoda now, before Kitchener can beat us to it.'

'Kitchener doesn't even know we are coming. And in any case, de Bonchamps will not be ready to advance to the Nile before September of next year. So, you see, we would not gain much more advantage by reaching Fashoda before the summer. In any case, we will need the Faidherbe; her speed may make the difference in locating de Bonchamps in time.'

I saw from the expressions of my fellows that he was right. We had long labored under the threat of Kitchener and his host, and we had been given no inkling of what Marchand meant to do should they oppose us. Now all was made clear. The conversation turned to more practical matters. Paké-Bô began to apportion to each of us the duties of maintaining and improving our camp. When he turned to me, I spoke before he could give me my assignment.

'Will you be sending a reply to Paris tomorrow?' I asked. When he indicated that he would, I went on: 'Then I should like to carry it.'

'Carry it?' he repeated, as if he had not heard me correctly.

'Yes,' I said. 'I mean to return to Paris, and there resign my commission. I shall have to return the way we have come, so I might as well carry the message for you. It is the least I can do.'

The three men looked at me with astonishment. I had not meant to explain myself, not to them, but I realized now that I could not leave it at that.

'My father has died,' I said.

Comprehension dawned in his face.

'The letter you received?' he asked. When I nodded, he went on. 'I mourn your loss, Dédé, but as your friend, I must counsel you not to be hasty. The news is a shock to you, but your father must have died many months ago. There is nothing you can do for him now.'

'Not for him, no,' I said. 'But perhaps for myself. The letter was from him, you see; he wrote it on his deathbed. He recalls me to my duty.'

'Your duty?' said Mangin, brusquely. 'Surely your duty is here, Durand. You took an oath.'

'I was a fool to take it,' I said. I addressed myself to Marchand. 'I regret to tell you that I no longer believe in this mission. I have seen what

307

France does in pursuit of her ambition for empire, and I have no further wish to be a party to it.'

'What did you think we were about?' demanded Mangin. 'Did you think that the people of these lands would welcome us, and thank us for becoming their masters? Did you imagine that we could conquer a people without subjugating them?'

'I had no thought for them at all, to my shame,' I said. 'But I cannot claim that now. I have seen them and can no longer offer the excuse of ignorance.'

Mangin snorted contemptuously, then stormed out of the tent. Baratier looked as if he meant to say something, but Marchand caught his eye; so he only nodded to me and followed Mangin, leaving me alone with Marchand.

'I beg you to reconsider, Dédé,' said Marchand. 'To resign under these circumstances would be a grave dishonor. People will think you a coward. It will end your career, and quite probably any chance of another.'

'I know it,' I said. 'But if I stay, I will become like Mangin.'

'You wrong him, Dédé.'

'Perhaps,' I admitted. 'He is the perfect machine for this enterprise: you could have no better. But I will not be remade in that image. If this is what it means to be a coward, then I will be one.'

He shook his head slowly, a sadness in his eyes.

'No man who knows you as I do could ever think you a coward, Dédé. You have never been one to choose the easy path. You must do what you think right, my friend. But I shall miss you.'

Chapter 42

Paris, 21 August 1898

Picquart turned the pages of the file, studying each one carefully. Welles paced the floor of Picquart's study, smoking one cigarette after another as he waited. At last Picquart closed the file. He took a deep breath before addressing Welles.

"You are a British spy."

"I am," admitted Welles.

"This file," said Picquart, tapping it with a finger. "It belongs to your Foreign Office. How did you get it?"

"I took it from there," said Welles. "I went to London to get it."

"Why bring it to me?"

"To whom else could I go?" asked Welles. "I need someone who is familiar with the Dreyfus dossier, someone who can compare this file to that one. Someone with contacts in the Army who can help me use it. But it must be someone who is not part of the conspiracy, someone not already committed to Dreyfus's guilt. And," he added, almost as an afterthought, "someone who already knows about me and would know that this file is real. That leaves only you."

Picquart opened the file again, turned the pages until he found the document he wanted.

"This Leeman, he was the forger? The British paid him to produce evidence against Dreyfus. He produced it, then gave it to Esterhazy?"

"Not directly," said Welles. "Someone else collected it from Leeman, then passed it to Esterhazy."

"Someone else," said Picquart. "Not you?"

Welles shook his head.

"Not at the start," he said. "I wasn't involved at that time, and my masters kept me in the dark about what they had done."

"Who killed the forger, then?" asked Picquart.

"I don't know," said Welles. "Someone wanted to silence the man. Leeman could expose them all."

Picquart turned the pages, chose another.

"Here is a record of a payment to Leeman, made in October of 1896," he said. "The annotation says it was for a letter, handwritten, from Colonel Panizzardi — the Italian military attaché — to von Schwartzkoppen."

He held the document up so that Welles could examine it. Welles nodded.

"What would Esterhazy do with such a thing?" asked Picquart. "It's true, we frequently intercepted notes between those two men. They were secretly lovers. The German was careless: he tossed Panizzardi's notes into his wastebasket, from which Madame Bastian retrieved them for us. But Esterhazy wouldn't have known any of that."

He paused, as if waiting for Welles to comment.

"Esterhazy cannot have done it alone," said Welles. "He never worked in the counter-intelligence section."

"Indeed. He could not have conceived of the idea of forging such a letter, much less have introduced the forgery into the process."

Picquart laid the document on the desk, leaned back in his chair.

"It doesn't make sense," he said. "Esterhazy wouldn't even have known that we had evidence there was a spy. Wouldn't have known that he was one of the men we suspected."

"Unless someone told him," said Welles.

Picquart did not reply to that. Instead, he crossed his arms, regarded Welles with a look of appraisal.

"I don't trust you, Welles," he said. "Not one damned bit. How can I?"

"You don't need to trust me," said Welles. "It is this file that matters."

"It *seems* genuine," Picquart admitted. "It matches things I know to be in the Dreyfus dossier. But I will need to verify it. I want to retrieve my copy of the dossier from Monsieur Seigneur. Compare it with this, see how things line up. Will you leave this with me? Only for a few days."

Welles nodded. "Very well, if you insist. You can reach me at the Embassy." He made a face. "Not where I'd prefer to stay, but I can't risk a hotel."

Picquart stood to show Welles out.

"They will line up, I assure you," Welles said at the door. "What then?"

"If what you've brought me is genuine," Picquart said, "then it is enough to break open this case at last. In that event, I believe I shall require your help. I must warn you, however: I have no authority to carry out an investigation in the ordinary manner. What we do, we will do as private citizens. It may even be that we must skirt the law."

Welles could not keep himself from smiling at this.

"I have been a spy and am now accounted a murderer. I doubt you can lead me any further astray than I have already gone on my own."

Chapter 43
Paris, 30 August 1898

Major Hubert Joseph Henry arrived promptly at eleven o'clock in the evening. Picquart met him at the door — he had dismissed his household staff for the evening — and led him down the hallway to the office. Henry entered the room, then stopped when he saw Welles, his eyes drawn to the gun in Welles's hand.

"What is the meaning of this?" he demanded.

"I regret the inconvenience, Hubert," said Picquart, "but I would like to discuss something with you. Monsieur Welles intends only that you should hear me out."

Welles indicated a chair for Henry. Welles took another, slightly behind and to the right of henry. Picquart sat behind the desk. He took a file from the drawer, laid it on the desk, closed the drawer. He opened the file and began to read, turning the pages slowly, as if Henry were not there. From time to time he made a note on a sheet of paper beside the file. At length he sighed, looked up from the pages before him.

"I must ask you some questions now, Hubert. If you answer them to my satisfaction, you will be free to go."

"You have no authority to question me," said Henry. "You are not my superior: you are no longer even an officer."

Picquart nodded, conceding the point.

"Nonetheless, I will ask my questions," he said. "I would like you to think back to the fall of 1894, Hubert. Madame Bastian found a document, the *bordereau*, in the office of the German military attaché. She sent it to you. You recognized it as evidence of treason. What did you do then?"

There was no reply.

"I imagine you reported it immediately to your superior, Colonel Sandherr," Picquart continued. "He, in turn, would have advised General de Boisdeffre. "

Still nothing.

"The Chief gave the matter over to Du Paty. You were assigned to assist him. Is that how it happened?"

Henry hesitated, then, grudgingly, grunted in the affirmative.

"How did you and Du Paty proceed?"

When Henry did not respond, Picquart smiled agreeably.

"Come now, Hubert, I'm only repeating what you've told me before. How can it harm you to affirm it again?"

"We analyzed the contents of the *bordereau*, then reviewed the service records of officers on the General Staff," said Henry. "We were looking for men who had a range of past assignments that would have given them access to the secrets listed in the document."

"With what result?"

"We compiled a list of six men who could have been the authors."

"And Dreyfus was one of those men?"

"Yes."

Picquart picked up a document, studied it. He made a note on the sheet.

"And tell me, who first suggested Dreyfus as the natural suspect? Was that you?"

Picquart spoke casually, without looking up or setting down his pen.

"Not me," said Henry. "That was Du Paty."

"Major Du Paty," said Picquart. "Not Major Esterhazy, then?"

"Esterhazy?" said Henry. He seemed confused by the question. "Why would it have been Esterhazy? He wasn't involved in the investigation."

"Well, he was one of the suspects, wasn't he? One of the six men who could have written the *bordereau*?"

"Yes," said Henry.

"Were any of the men told they were suspects?"

"No," said Henry, "of course not. Major Du Paty wanted to investigate Dreyfus first. Said he was the obvious suspect, not a proper Frenchman."

"Because he was a Jew, you mean?" Picquart looked up from the file, fixed Henry with his eyes. "Did you agree with him?"

"Someone had to be first," said Henry. He tried to hold Picquart's gaze, but couldn't, and lowered his eyes. "It made no difference to me who it was."

"Of course," said Picquart. He turned a page. "So then Du Paty summons Dreyfus to his office, is that right? He acts out that absurd pantomime of the injured hand, gets Dreyfus to write something down for him. Were you present for that?"

"Yes," said Henry.

"I wonder that you managed to keep a straight face, Hubert." Henry flushed but did not rise to the bait.

"Dreyfus writes what Du Paty tells him to write," said Picquart. "Then Du Paty takes the paper, looks at it. The handwriting is the same. Dreyfus is arrested. Is that the way it happened?"

"Near enough."

"Then what? You've caught your man. Only you can't convict a man for treason on *handwriting*, can you? Even Du Paty knew that. So, you set out to find the evidence you would need."

"It wasn't like that," objected Henry. "We had enough to charge the man. One always wants more for a trial."

Picquart stood. He lifted a page from the file, rounded the desk, and held the page before Henry.

"Do you recognize this, Hubert?" he asked.

Henry scanned the pages, nodded.

"Yes," he said. "It is a letter to Dreyfus from the manager of the *Cercle de la Press*, demanding payment of gambling losses in the amount of twenty thousand francs."

Picquart returned to his seat, laid the page before him on the desk.

"As I recall, Monsieur Demange — Captain Dreyfus's attorney — called the manager to the stand. He testified that he had never written any such letter. I believe he said that, to his knowledge, Dreyfus had never even set foot in the club. How do you account for that, Hubert?"

"I can't account for it," said Henry. "Maybe the man lied. Dreyfus is a rich man, from a rich family."

"Indeed," said Picquart. "A rich Jew, but apparently unable to pay his gambling debts." He turned the page. "There is a good deal of this kind of rubbish in the Dreyfus dossier, Hubert. Debts, mistresses. None of it held up at trial. I wonder, where did you get these letters?"

"The police found them. The men who searched Dreyfus's office. They collected all of his correspondence and turned it over to us."

"And if I were to tell you that I can prove these letters are forgeries — prove it, I say — then what would you say to that?"

"I have nothing to say to that," said Henry. "They were among his things. We found them there. If you want to know where Dreyfus got them, you must ask him."

Picquart fixed Henry with a look of frank disbelief. He shook his head, then returned his attention to the file before him.

"I ask you again, Hubert: Are you quite certain that no one told Esterhazy he was a suspect?"

Henry seemed surprised by the question. He moistened his lips before answering.

"I never told him," he said cautiously, treading with care. "I suppose it is possible someone else did, though I can think of no reason why they would. Why do you keep asking about Esterhazy, anyway?"

Picquart ignored the question.

"I'm going to read something to you, Hubert," he said. *"Mon cher ami, I am sorry not to have seen you before leaving. In any case, I shall return in a week. I am including the twelve master plans for Nice which that scoundrel Dreyfus gave me for you."*

He looked up from the page. Henry's face had gone quite red.

"The letter is signed *Alexandrine*. Who is that, Hubert?"

"You know very well," snapped Henry. "Where did you get that letter? It is an official secret, Picquart, from a sealed file in the counter-intelligence archives. If you removed it from there, you are a traitor yourself."

"Alexandrine is Colonel Panizzardi, the Italian military attaché," Picquart said, addressing himself to Welles. "He often wrote to von Schwartzkoppen in this manner. They were lovers." He returned his attention to Henry. "When and how did you come by this letter, Hubert?"

Henry hesitated. He cast a sideways glance at Welles.

"Oh, you needn't hold back," said Picquart. "Mister Welles knows all about Madame Bastian. When did she discover this letter?"

"As I recall, it was in late October," said Henry. "October of 1894, I mean."

"After you had arrested Dreyfus, but before his arrested was made public?"

"Yes."

"Did that not seem remarkably convenient to you, Hubert? You are looking for evidence against Dreyfus, and — obligingly! — this letter appears, naming him as a traitor? Had you ever before intercepted any communications naming Dreyfus?"

Henry did not respond.

"Of course not," said Picquart, answering his own question. "If you had, then you would have already known Dreyfus was a spy. His name only appears in the correspondence *after* you and Du Paty decided he was the man you were looking for."

"What are you getting at, Picquart?" Henry demanded.

"Take me through it, Hubert," said Picquart. "Madame Bastian found this letter in von Schwartzkoppen's wastebasket. Then what?"

"You know how it works." Henry was impatient. "She took the letter to the post office, deposited it in a numbered postal box. Later, one of our men visited the box, retrieved it. He would have brought everything in that box to us."

"To whom, exactly?"

"To me," said Henry. "All the material from von Schwartzkoppen's office comes directly to me. In order to limit the number of people who know about Madame Bastian."

"You personally attest that this letter is genuine? It was brought to you with the other things from the postal box?"

"I do."

"Very well," said Picquart. He set the letter aside, took another page from the folder, began to read: *"Mon cher ami, I have read that a deputy is going to ask a question in the chamber about Dreyfus. If they ask for any new explanations in Rome, I will say that I never had relations with this Jew. That's understood. If anybody asks you, say just that, for nobody must ever know what happened with him."*

He looked up from the page.

"Also from Panizzardi. Tell me about this letter, Hubert."

Henry shrugged. "There is little to tell. Madame Bastian took it from the wastebasket, deposited it in the postal box, and it came to me."

"When was that?"

"That would also have been in 1894. Near the end of the year, I think. As we were preparing for the trial."

"There are more letters like those two in this dossier," Picquart says. "More than enough to convict Dreyfus. He is sent into exile; erased from our memory, never to be thought of again. Time passes. Colonel Sandherr dies, and I take command of the counter-intelligence section. Life goes on until suddenly, in the summer of 1896, we read that Dreyfus has escaped. It is a hoax — you have Mister Welles to thank for that — but it reignites interest in the affair. Questions are asked. Doubts about the evidence raised. I decide to review the case. What happens then? Why, you bring me this."

He took another page from the folder, held it up so that Henry could see it.

"Yes, the secret message from Dreyfus to his accomplice," Henry said. "The one in invisible ink. Most ingenious. Dreyfus is not without cunning; we must give him that."

"Indeed," agreed Picquart, dryly. "A *cunning* Jew. Tell me how this letter came to you."

"Everything to or from Devil's Island goes by military transport through Paris. They set aside Dreyfus's mail, send it over to us for inspection. When we're done, it goes back to them for delivery."

Picquart laid the page on the desk. He fixed Henry with purposeful stare.

"Military transport," he said. "Fourth bureau?"

"Yes."

"Esterhazy's posting?"

There was a long silence. The side of Henry's face Welles could see was suffused with concentration, as if the man were considering a difficult calculation.

"Yes, Esterhazy," said Henry at last. "Why do you keep asking about him? Do you doubt the letter, or how it came to us?"

"I don't doubt it," said Picquart. "I know it to be false. It is a forgery. Do you know a man named Leeman, Hubert? Moise Leeman?"

"Leeman?" repeated Henry. "No, I don't know anyone by that name. Who is he?"

"He is the man I paid to forge that letter," Welles said, as they had rehearsed.

Henry twisted in the chair, trying to get a better view of Welles, who went on to explain.

"I asked Esterhazy for a letter from Dreyfus, one that hadn't been delivered yet. I took that letter to Leeman, and he forged a message in invisible ink between the lines Dreyfus had written. Then I gave it back to Esterhazy to give to you."

"Preposterous," said Henry. "Why would you do such a thing? Why would Esterhazy help you?"

"Because he wanted the Dreyfus inquiry ended," said Welles. "I wanted that too. As long as the case was open, Esterhazy knew he was in danger of being exposed."

"Exposed? What do you mean, *exposed*?"

"Esterhazy is the traitor," said Picquart. "He wrote the *bordereau*, gave it to von Schwartzkoppen."

Henry's eyes went back to Picquart.

"That is not possible," he said, but the words were ragged and faint, as if he were short of breath.

Picquart took a page from the top of his desk. He stood, approached Henry and held the paper before him.

"What is this?" asked Henry.

"It is a receipt from Leeman," said Welles. "He gave it to me when I paid him for the letter."

Henry twisted around to look at Welles.

"Why would you care whether Esterhazy was a suspect?"

"Because he was in my charge," said Welles. "Esterhazy was selling secrets to us — to the British, I mean — as well as to the Germans. It was my duty to protect him."

Henry's face registered first shock, then dismay. He opened his mouth several times to speak, then closed it again, as if the words would not come. Finally, he turned to face Picquart again.

"Esterhazy has played us for fools," he said. "Release me, Picquart. We must arrest him and the forger Leeman at once."

"Leeman is dead, Hubert," said Picquart. "Murdered, almost certainly by someone who wanted to conceal his role in the forgeries."

He half-sat on the edge of the desk in front of Henry, pivoted to drop the receipt on the desk and retrieve another page. He held it up for Henry to read.

"Here is another receipt from Leeman. Dated October of 1894. Can you read what it is for?"

There were tears now in Henry's eyes. He peered at the document, and his lips moved, but no sound emerged.

"It is a receipt for the Alexandrine letter," said Welles. "The one that mentions Dreyfus by name."

"You see the problem, don't you, Hubert?" Picquart laid the page on the desk behind him, crossed his arms. "The letter is a forgery. Leeman must have had another Alexandrine letter to consult, so he could reproduce the hand. The style and tone. How did he get it? Esterhazy never worked in counter-intelligence. He could not have known about the letters. Even if, somehow, he had, he couldn't get his hands on one. No, it must have been someone else, you agree?"

No answer. Picquart went on.

"And once the forgery was done, how did the letter get into your hands? Are we to believe that Esterhazy took it to von Schwartzkoppen's office and put it in the man's wastebasket? Esterhazy, who should have known nothing about Madame Bastian?"

Picquart shook his head, sadly.

"No, it must have been someone in the counter-intelligence section itself who helped the forger," he said. "The vital question is this: Did you deal with Leeman directly, or was Esterhazy the go-between?"

"Neither," said Henry, through clenched teeth.

"I don't think that is the way to play your cards, Hubert," said Picquart. "If you will not tell me who dealt with Leeman, then I will have no choice but to take this evidence to the Court of Cassation, leaving it to them to sort out who killed the man. No doubt the Court will conclude the same thing that I have: that they cannot prove Esterhazy's role in the affair, but they can prove your own. You claim the documents came from Madame Bastian, *that you took delivery of them from the courier yourself*; but, in fact, they are forgeries, so this is certainly a lie. Either you or Esterhazy could have commissioned them from Leeman, but only you could have provided him with the samples he needed. Only you could have introduced them into the intelligence flowing to us from the German embassy. They will blame you, Hubert. What else can they do? And once they decide that you were the one who employed

Leeman, then surely you must also be the one who killed him to keep him quiet."

Henry's face betrayed his indecision, but still he said nothing. Picquart breathed a weary sigh.

"I had hoped we could keep this mess quiet, Hubert," he said. "Inside the Army. But it seems not." He turned to Welles. "Let him go. He won't help himself. He'd rather hang for murder."

Welles stood. He slipped the gun in his waistband, moved to the door, opened it. Henry twisted in his chair to look at him, then turned back to Picquart.

"It was Esterhazy," said Henry. "After we arrested Dreyfus, I told him about the *bordereau*. Told him that we'd caught the Jew."

"Why did you tell him?" asked Picquart

Henry shrugged.

"No one could stand Dreyfus," he explained. "He was a model officer, always correct. A real prig, but one with a bright future. It was intolerable in a Jew. We all hated him, wanted to see him fall. The Chief wanted someone convicted, the affair put to bed, and Dreyfus would do. When he was arrested it was only natural that we talked about it. But we needed more evidence. The trial was approaching, and we had nothing but *handwriting*. Esterhazy said he could help. He brought the letters. The first ones were useless — debts, women — so I told him the kind of thing we needed. I gave him some samples of the letters we had obtained from von Schwartzkoppen's office. I never met the forger, didn't even know the man's name."

He seemed suddenly to become aware of the expression on Picquart's face.

"Dreyfus was guilty, Picquart. We knew that," he said. "We just needed more evidence to put him away."

"And when his guilt was called into question? When the case was reviewed? You did it again?"

"Yes," said Henry. "We had to. We knew the evidence would never stand up to serious scrutiny. So, we made more."

"The letters to Dreyfus in prison?" asked Welles.

"Yes, those. And other things. We just kept adding to the dossier. We wanted to be sure that anyone who looked at it would see overwhelming evidence of the man's guilt."

"Major Du Paty knew what you were doing," said Picquart. "Who else?"

Henry's face twisted into a sneer.

"Everyone knew. The War Minister, General Mercier. General de Boisdeffre, and his vice General Gonse. We never told them openly, but they're not idiots. Du Paty warned me once that Gonse had questioned one of the fabrications, said it was suspicious. *'You must take care, Henry,'* Du Paty said, *'Your papers have a bad smell about them.'* They all knew what we were doing."

Picquart bent over Henry, laid a hand on his shoulder. He spoke softly, confiding in him.

"Hubert, listen to me. Your only chance to survive this scandal is to admit your part in it. Your career is finished, but they might permit you to simply retire rather than punish you for what you've done. After all, the false evidence you used against Dreyfus is secret. This file I have can remain secret, too. You have only to tell them that you got the evidence from Esterhazy. That you knew it was false. They can announce a review of the case. In due time, they say that Dreyfus is innocent, that the whole thing has been a mistake. This, without ever having to admit what they did to the poor man. But — and I tell you this as someone who was your colleague — if you will not admit your part, and this file becomes public? Then they will surely try you, and convict you, and you will go to prison. The blame will be yours alone: they will sacrifice you in order to save themselves. You see that, surely?"

Henry's expression was that of a cornered animal, his eyes darting about the room, seeking a means of escape. There was none. He began to weep. He bowed his head, and his body shook with the sobs.

"To whom can we take him?" asked Welles. "Who has not been corrupted by this affair?"

"There is an officer, Captain Cuignet," said Picquart. "He has been asked by the new War Minister — Monsieur Cavaignac — to undertake yet another review of the Dreyfus case. Cuignet is a good man, thorough." He turned to Henry, put a hand on his shoulder. "All right, Hubert?"

Henry raised his head, looked up at Picquart. His face was wet, and tears still flowed from his eyes. Nonetheless, he nodded.

Chapter 44

Paris, 1 September 1898

On the evening of September first, a postman delivered a *petit-bleu* summoning Welles to Picquart's home. He left immediately and arrived just as Cuignet was knocking on the door. Picquart let them in and they retired to his office.

There, without preamble, Cuignet announced: "Major Henry was found dead in his cell this morning."

"Dead? What do you mean, dead?" demanded Picquart. "How did he die?"

"His throat was cut with a razor," said Cuignet.

"A razor? *He had a razor in his cell?*" Picquart was incredulous.

"Not when I put him there, colonel," said Cuignet. "They say he asked for one so he could shave."

Picquart collapsed in his chair. He blew out air, making a rude noise, as if to convey what he thought of that explanation.

"Yes, I know," said Cuignet. "I find it difficult to believe as well. If he wanted to shave, they should have given him a barber, not a razor. It was a terrible mistake."

"I think you are too charitable," said Welles, "to call it a mistake."

"You cannot believe that he has been murdered, Monsieur Welles!" Cuignet seemed stunned by the intimation.

"Why should they stop at murder?" asked Welles. "Leeman was murdered, after all."

In truth, Welles didn't like Cuignet, and the feeling seemed to him to be mutual. The Captain had reacted badly to Picquart's explanation of Welles's role in the affair, and had it not been for Picquart's considerable skill at persuasion, Welles thought he might have found himself in the cell next to Henry's.

"Enough," said Picquart. "We shall likely never know the truth of poor Hubert's death. It does no one any good to quarrel about it now. The important question is this: Where does his death leave us?" He directed his question at Cuignet. "You have his confession, don't you?"

"He admitted everything," said Cuignet. "Esterhazy gave him forged documents to use as evidence against Dreyfus. But I have nothing *by his hand*. He was to sign a confession today."

"Who knew that you'd arrested Henry?" asked Welles. He could not leave the question of the man's death so easily.

"The three of us," said Cuignet. "The prison commandant and the guards. And I told Minister Cavaignac, of course."

"Good God," said Welles. "Why would you tell him?"

Cuignet drew himself up to his full height.

"I could hardly keep this secret from him," he declared.

"No doubt Monsieur Cavaignac felt that he, in turn, could not keep this secret from General de Boisdeffre," said Welles. He spoke patiently, as if explaining to a child. "The good general will undoubtedly have had others from whom he could not in good conscience keep the secret. We can assume that everyone knew."

Cuignet took a step towards Welles. Then Picquart was between the two men.

"*Messieurs!*" he barked. He directed a glare at Welles, who returned it for a moment, then retreated to a chair and lit a cigarette. Picquart turned his attention once more to Cuignet.

"What do we do now?" he asked. "Who can we trust? Shall we go and see Minister Cavaignac together?"

"Cavaignac has left the city," said Cuignet. "He has gone to Le Mans to see General Mercier."

"Mercier?" asked Picquart. "Why would he go now to see Mercier?"

"Mercier was the War Minister when Dreyfus was prosecuted," said Welles. "He's part of it, he has to be. If Cavaignac is going to see him, then he's part of it, too."

"We can't know that," objected Picquart. "When will he return?"

This last was directed at Cuignet. Curiously, the man blushed. He took a handkerchief from his pocket and patted his forehead.

"It would not be wise for you to try to see Cavaignac," he said to Picquart. "Before he left, he signed an order for your arrest."

Picquart gaped at Cuignet.

"My arrest? On what charge?"

"On the charge of stealing military secrets," said Cuignet.

Picquart turned away. He walked around his desk and sat. He covered his face with his hands and rubbed vigorously for a moment. Then he dropped his hands to his lap.

"The Dreyfus dossier," he said. "I made a copy and took it with me when I left the counter-intelligence section."

"And shared it with others," said Cuignet. "Even with a British spy."

He turned to Welles. With barely disguised satisfaction, he said, "There is also a warrant for you, Monsieur Welles. On the charge of espionage."

"I have become accustomed to arrest warrants," said Welles dryly.

"Have you come to arrest us, Louis?" asked Picquart.

"Me? No, certainly not. I advised Cavaignac against ordering your arrest, but he would not be dissuaded. I have come to warn you, colonel. And to tell you that what you have done has not been in vain. I will not rest until the truth of this affair is revealed, no matter what it may be."

Welles snorted derisively. He stubbed out his cigarette, got to his feet.

"I'll take the files, colonel," Welles said. "The one I brought you, and your copy of the Dreyfus dossier."

He waited, his hand outstretched. Picquart made no move to surrender them.

"I'll need them," Welles said. "They're no good to you now."

"You cannot give them to this man, Picquart," said Cuignet. "How can you trust him?"

He took a step towards Welles, who produced the pistol from inside his coat. Cuignet stopped, stared at the gun.

"You can say that I stole them," said Welles, speaking still to Picquart. "That I held you at gunpoint and compelled you to give them to me. It's true enough."

Picquart looked from Welles to Cuignet, then back to Welles. Without speaking, he opened a drawer, took two files from it and handed them over. Welles took them. He nodded to Picquart, then backed to the door, keeping the gun pointed at Cuignet. He stood on the threshold.

"Come with me," he said to Picquart. "We may as well both be fugitives."

Picquart smiled.

"I cannot," he said. "I wish you good fortune, Welles. Do what you must to free him."

Welles turned to go, but Picquart wasn't finished.

"Welles," he called. "If I should die in my cell while shaving, or in some other ridiculous manner, you at least will understand that it was not by my own hand."

Welles nodded, then walked briskly through the hall to the front door.

Chapter 45

Paris, 2 September 1898

True to his promise to Welles, Durand had stayed in Paris to watch over the Seigneur household. At first, he'd been unwelcome, so he kept watch on the house from the street and followed Mademoiselle Seigneur whenever she ventured outside. This went on for several weeks until one morning when the Mademoiselle — exasperated to find him, once again, huddled miserably in the rain across the street from her home — invited him into the house. The old man quickly warmed to Durand and took to treating him as a member of the household staff. The exact nature and extent of his duties were not entirely clear, even to Durand, who understood only that Monsieur Seigneur wanted the assurance of his presence in the house. A crisis occurred the first time Seigneur tried to pay him; if it were not in the old man's nature to rely on a man without compensating him, no more was it in Durand's nature to take money for doing some days as little as reading a book in the library. Indeed, his situation in the Seigneur house left him in little need of money. In the end, they had arrived at an understanding, whereby Durand was treated more or less as a guest in the house. He, however, was unable to resist the impulse to earn his keep, so he took upon himself the task of answering the door after dark, and he continued to shepherd Mademoiselle Seigneur whenever she ventured out of the house.

For her part, Georges Seigneur endured his presence in the house and in her carriage with ill-concealed bad humor. She barely spoke to him and, on more than one occasion, she contrived to escape his escort, disappearing into a crowd or ducking out of a shop through the back door, leaving him with no other recourse than to return home and wait for her. Her father upbraided her, but she remained defiant. She refused, she said, to return to the state of captivity in which she'd spent her childhood. Durand wisely avoided these rows, and he made a point of apologizing to her whenever he joined her at the door, his hat in hand, ready to accompany her. Gradually, she began to soften, so that he did not feel so much an intruder in her life. This was a relief to him, for — he had to admit — he had fallen entirely under her spell and could not abide the disdain with which she had at first regarded him.

Tonight — as was his custom — he had waited up, reading a book, until Georges and her father had gone up to bed. Then he made the rounds of the ground floor, checking that all the doors and windows were locked and turning down the lamps as he went. He was approaching the front door when he heard a knock. He stood by a window, moved the curtain slightly to peer out; then opened the door.

"Welles!" he said, surprised. He had not known the man was back in Paris. "It's late. Georges has gone up."

"You'll have to wake her, Andre. And her father, too."

They met in the library, Seigneur and his daughter in dressing gowns. The old man was polite, welcoming Welles and inquiring after his health and well-being; but Georges was cold. She neither addressed him nor took his offered hand. She chose a chair away from them, one with a high back and upholstered armrests. She folded her legs underneath her, laid both arms on one armrest, rested her head on her arms, and regarded Welles with indifference.

Welles resolved to ignore her. He laid both files on the table before him.

"I have just come from Colonel Picquart's home," he said, addressing himself to Seigneur. "He is to be arrested."

"Arrested? What for?"

Welles tapped one of the folders.

"For stealing state secrets and revealing them to others. To me, as it happens. But that's not the worst of it."

Quickly Welles related what had occurred at Picquart's home.

"Then Cavaignac is with them," said Durand. "Maybe not from the start, maybe he wasn't one of those who framed Dreyfus. But he will protect them against exposure."

"My thinking exactly," agreed Welles. "Picquart tells Cuignet about Henry. Cuignet arrests Henry, then he informs Cavaignac. Henry dies the next day, and Cavaignac orders Picquart's arrest. Thus, the breach is sealed."

Seigneur looked from one of them to the other.

"I cannot believe that," he objected. "That a man like Cavaignac — a gentleman — would stoop to murder."

"I find it easy to believe," said Welles. "But let us assume you are right, that it wasn't exactly murder. Maybe Henry killed himself after all. But," —here he tapped a finger on the table for emphasis— "someone brought him the razor."

"Yes," said Durand, "Henry would know what it was for. Any officer in his position would know."

Durand stood, went to the bar. He held up a decanter, raised an eyebrow. Seigneur declined, but Welles accepted; and, to his surprise, so did Georges. Durand poured, brought a glass to Georges, then returned with his own and one for Welles. He sat, took a drink, then went on.

"With Henry dead, who else knows what he did?"

"Picquart knows," said Welles. "So Cavaignac orders Picquart arrested, knowing that will keep him quiet, at least for now. Maybe he has worse in mind for him, too."

"And for you, my friend." Durand took another drink. "If they have contrived the death of an officer like Henry, they will have no compunction about killing you."

Welles waved that away.

"They will certainly pursue me," he said. "If they find me, they'll also find these." He tapped the folders again. "I can't let that happen."

"What is it you have brought to my house, Monsieur Welles?" asked Seigneur.

"This is Picquart's copy of the secret Dreyfus dossier, the evidence on which he was convicted," said Welles.

"And the other file?"

"It contains documents which prove that the evidence against Dreyfus was forged."

"Forged?" asked Seigneur. "Forged by whom, for what reason?"

"By a man named Leeman. He did it for money. Those who paid him meant to divert attention away from a certain Major Esterhazy, who was the real author of the *bordereau*." Welles saw Georges react to the mention of Esterhazy, but he ignored it and went on. "Leeman forged the documents and gave them to Esterhazy," he said. "Esterhazy gave them to Henry. Henry and Du Paty used them to build the case against Dreyfus."

"But why should those officers — Henry, Du Paty — why should they wish to protect Esterhazy?"

"They didn't know they were protecting him," said Welles. "They had convinced themselves that Dreyfus was the traitor because he was a Jew. But they lacked the evidence to prove it. When Esterhazy offered to provide what they needed, they were eager to accept his help."

"Where did you get this, Monsieur Welles?"

Seigneur pointed to the file on the table. Welles looked at it, then at Georges. She was suddenly alert, sitting upright, her attention fixed on him.

"I took it from the Foreign Office in London," he said. He held Georges' eyes as he said it.

"London?" asked Seigneur, confused. "Why would they have such a file there?"

"It was the British who helped Esterhazy to concoct the false evidence. They introduced him to Leeman. They paid the forger's bill."

Realization dawned in her face; not only realization, Welles saw, but a kind of growing horror at what she was hearing. Nevertheless, he continued.

"Esterhazy was a British agent," he said. "He sold secrets to both the Germans and the British. When he came under suspicion, his British handlers helped him to divert that suspicion by incriminating Dreyfus instead."

"How do you know that, Percy?" Georges asked. Her voice was low, almost a whisper.

Welles could hold her gaze no longer. He turned instead to Seigneur.

"Because I was Esterhazy's handler," he said. "Not at the beginning, not in 1894, that was someone else. But from the time I came to Paris, it was my job to protect him."

He braced himself for her reaction, but when it came, it was not directed at him.

"You knew," she said, her eyes on Durand. "I can see it in your face. You knew."

Durand looked a question at Welles, who shrugged.

"Yes, I knew," he said to Georges. "Percy told me when we met. He wanted something from me, something he could offer his masters in exchange for that file."

"Something," she said, repeating the word with emphasis. "Secrets, you mean. The kinds of things a spy wants."

"Yes." Durand stood, took his glass to the bar, refilled it. He turned to face her, glass in his hand. "I could have refused him," he said, "and left Dreyfus to rot in a cell for the rest of his life. After all, what is the life of one innocent man against the affairs of the state?" He drank, went on: "For me, it was an easy decision to make, Georges."

"You never told us, Andre," she said. "Not any of it. You're no better than he is."

"Georges, please." Seigneur held his hand up. "I confess, Monsieur Welles, that I don't entirely understand all of this. But if what you say is true, then we must find this forger, this Leeman. We must find him at once."

"Leeman is dead," said Welles. "I had the same idea. I went to see him. I forced him to confess his part in the affair. He agreed to give me what I wanted. But when I returned to collect it, he was dead. Murdered." He looked at Georges. "The police believe I killed him. That is why I had to leave Paris."

The old man regarded Welles with a look of frank astonishment.

"Death attends you like a herald, Monsieur Welles," he said. "Leeman. Henry. The men who came here, who meant to do us harm."

He paused for a response, but Welles had none.

"Perhaps you can explain why you have brought these things here? What you expect us to do with them?"

"Keep them safe, Monsieur. Beyond that, I cannot say; at least, not yet. I had hoped we could use them to expose the conspiracy against Dreyfus, to force Henry to confess. Now that he's dead, I don't know how to proceed."

Seigneur regarded Welles in silence. Then he shook his head and stood.

"It is late, Monsieur Welles. I shall give this some thought, and we can talk again in the morning. I will have a room made up for you."

"A room?"

The old man had been making for the door. Now, he turned to meet Welles's eyes.

"I insist," he said. "You tell me that men have been killed over this matter; that others search for you even now, mean you harm. And you imagine that I will let you go back out into the streets? No, Monsieur. You will stay here, at least for the night."

"Thank you, but that won't be necessary." Welles stood to take his leave.

"Must you always be such a damned fool, Percy?" Georges' voice was surprisingly loud, the tone biting. "What good will it do anyone if they arrest you? Or kill you?"

The three men were startled by the outburst. They looked at Georges, then at each other. Finally, Durand broke the silence.

"She's right. Do as she says. Stay the night."

Reluctantly, Welles relented.

***

In the early hours of the morning, Georges tapped lightly at Welles's bedroom door. There was no answer. She turned the knob slowly, pushed the door open. The bed was neatly made, the covers turned down; it had not been slept in.

She found him in the library. He was standing in the dark near the window, staring out into the night, his face illuminated by the light reflected from the cathedral across the river. She tried to close the door quietly behind her, but the hinges creaked, and he turned from the window at the sound.

"Why are you here, Percy?" she asked, her back to the door. "There's nothing for you here."

She wanted to see his face, to see what he was thinking — his face had always been transparent to her — but, with the light behind him, he was only a dark silhouette.

"I'm here for Dreyfus," he said.

"You never cared about Dreyfus," she said. "You only agreed to help because you wanted me."

"That's not true," he said.

He sounded tired. *More than tired*, she thought. *Defeated.*

"You know it is true."

"Yes, all right," he said. "But it isn't that I didn't care about the man. It's only that I knew it would be a mistake for me to get involved. Given my responsibility."

"Your responsibility," she said. "Protecting that man, Esterhazy. You lied to me, Percy. Not only from the beginning. You never stopped lying. Even when you knew that he was the traitor; that he was the one who framed Dreyfus. Even then, you lied to me."

"I couldn't tell you. By then, it was already too late."

She felt a rush of anger. She took two quick steps toward him, then managed to stop herself.

"Too late?" They had been speaking in whispers, but her voice was suddenly loud. "Too late for what?"

He looked away, out the window, and now she could see one side of his face, a pale white apparition in the murky dark.

"Too late for what, Percy?" she whispered.

He took a deep breath, let out a sigh.

"I had become part of it," he said.

He went on, without turning from the window, as if it were easier to tell his truth to the night. With the gleaming white buttresses of Notre Dame before him, he confessed his own treason. How Esterhazy had come under suspicion, and how he'd needed to clear the man. How he had been ordered to do it. How Esterhazy had given him the letter from Dreyfus — poor Dreyfus, chained to his iron bed in a kind of hell on earth — and how he had taken it to the forger, so that Leeman could add the secret writing to it. And how he had given it back to Esterhazy to use against Dreyfus.

"And it worked, far better than I had expected," he said. "Picquart's investigation was shut down and he was sent away."

"Sent away to *die*, Percy!"

She had always known there was something, some shameful secret he had kept from her; but she had never imagined this.

"*Mon Dieu*, you are a wretched man."

"I told myself that Dreyfus was guilty anyway, that it would do no more harm to him," he said. "Then I saw the *bordereau*, the copy Picquart left with your father. I knew immediately that Esterhazy had written it; I've seen his hand so many times, I could reproduce it myself. That's when I knew what I'd done. I had ruined Dreyfus's best chance."

He turned from the window. She could feel his eyes on her. Somewhere, far away, she heard the wheels of a cart on the cobblestones.

"I don't know who you are, Percy," she said at last. "I don't know how I could ever have loved a man like you. You betray everyone with such ease."

"No," he said. "Not with ease."

But even to his own ears, his objection lacked conviction, as if it were really a kind of surrender.

"In any case, that is why I am here," he said. "I mean to make amends for what I have done. I've betrayed my own country to free Dreyfus. I've killed a man to do it."

"Killed a man?"

She found it hard to breathe, even to move. What else had he done that he hadn't told her?

He described his meeting with Hull on the tower: why he went there, what he had meant to do; what had happened instead.

Georges had several times asked Durand why he had come to her house that night in Welles's company, but the former soldier always declined to answer, saying only that the story was Welles's to tell. Despite herself, she felt sick with fear now when she thought of Percy climbing up on the rail, Hull's gun prodding him over. If Durand hadn't intervened, Percy would be dead. He would never have come to her house that night, so perhaps she would be dead, too; she, and her father.

She moved through the darkness of the familiar room, found a chair near Welles, sat. She saw regret in his face, and something else: Fear.

"I never thanked you for coming to rescue us," she said. The words nearly stuck in her throat.

"Don't thank me," he said. "It was I who put you in danger in the first place. And, as I recall, you seemed more than equal to it."

It was nearing dawn now, and she could make out the clouds overhead, tinged with a faint orange light to the east. They waited in silence as it grew lighter: he standing, she sitting, and each holding back in the hopes that the other would speak. Finally, she could stand the silence no longer.

"What will we do now, Percy?" she asked.

"Do?"

His eyes found hers, and she saw something bright behind the fear, as if she'd given him hope. She moved quickly to crush it.

"About Dreyfus," she said.

"Ah, Dreyfus," he said. "Of course. I think the time has come for an end to secrets, Georges. An end to lies."

Chapter 46

Paris, 10 September 1898

From the moment of his ascendancy, Henri Brisson had known that he was living on borrowed time. He had taken the reins of power only ten weeks earlier, after the collapse of the Meline government, and had immediately found himself and his cabinet mired in the Dreyfus affair. Although he had his own doubts about the case, his first instinct had been to try to quash the scandal: so, he had appointed Cavaignac as Minister of War. The choice came as a surprise to many. Cavaignac was a favorite of the generals, and one of the few Radical party members who was liked and respected on the right.

He had charged his War Minister with reviewing the case and establishing, once and for all, that Dreyfus was guilty. By all accounts, this had backfired badly. Rather than confirm the facts of the case, Cavaignac's investigator had found evidence of a conspiracy against Dreyfus. An officer thought to be part of that conspiracy was dead; it was said by his own hand, though no one who said so seemed entirely certain of it.

Cavaignac had immediately taken himself to Le Mans to consult with his predecessor, General Mercier. Brisson was acutely aware that the affair had begun on Mercier's watch, and he had been filled with dread at the thought of what Cavaignac might learn from that quarter. He still did not know. Upon his return, Cavaignac had declined to say what Mercier had told him. Instead, he simply resigned from the cabinet, leaving Brisson with the difficulty of finding a replacement for him.

That was why Brisson had chosen to receive Mathieu and Lucie Dreyfus alone at his home rather than in the office of the President of the Council. Alone, because he wanted the freedom to discuss the affair without any witnesses; and in his home because he hoped to avoid the kind of frenzy with which the papers on the right would treat such a meeting.

The Dreyfuses, however, did not come alone. The wife and brother of the convicted man were accompanied by two other men: one older, well past sixty, short and broad-shouldered, with a stiff brush of white hair; and the other younger, tall and lean and, Brisson thought, oddly striking. Mathieu introduced the two as Monsieur Georges Seigneur, an attorney, and his daughter, Mademoiselle Seigneur. Brisson, who had just extended his hand to the girl as he might any man, blushed with embarrassment and managed a perfunctory bow. For her part, Mademoiselle Seigneur — who was unaccountably dressed in what he could only describe as a man's casual suit — merely nodded without comment.

At Brisson's invitation, Mathieu took the lead. He thanked the Premier for receiving them, then drew an envelope from his pocket.

"Monsieur, this is a formal request to your government," he said, extending the envelope. "We ask that the case of my brother, Captain Alfred Dreyfus, be referred to the Court of Cassation for review."

"It is your right to make this request," said Brisson, accepting the envelope. "Though there was no need to bring it to me personally."

"We had hoped to discuss it with you," said Mathieu. "We should like to know that, when you discuss it with the Cabinet, you intend to recommend that the request be approved."

Brisson raised his eyebrows at this.

"I regret that I cannot commit to such a position, Monsieur," he said. "I can only promise that we shall give it a fair hearing."

Mademoiselle Seigneur snorted. Brisson turned his attention to her, but she said nothing.

"If that is all," he said to Mathieu, "then I bid you good day."

"If I may," interrupted the older Seigneur. "I think that, under the circumstances, it would be best if you gave your assurance, Monsieur."

"Do you?" Brisson was angry now. "To what circumstances do you refer, Monsieur?"

"I refer to the confession of a certain Major Henry," said Seigneur. "And to the subsequent matter of his death, under what can only be described as suspicious circumstances."

Brisson regarded Seigneur in silence for ten long seconds.

"I do not know how you came by this intelligence, Monsieur Seigneur, but I beg to inform you that you are mistaken," he said. "It's true that Henry was questioned in this matter, but there was no confession. If there had been, I assure you that I would already have acted on it."

"It is not we who are mistaken, Monsieur," said Mademoiselle Seigneur. "I fear you have been deceived. Henry confessed, and there are witnesses to this confession."

Her voice was low — unremarkable, Brisson would have said — yet, somehow, he found his attention riveted on this strange woman. He stared at her, expectant, but it was her father who spoke.

"And there is the question of Colonel Picquart," he said.

"Picquart?"

The name was familiar, but Brisson could not quite place it.

"Colonel Picquart has been arrested," said the young woman. "A strange sequence of events, do you not agree? Picquart uncovers evidence of a conspiracy to persecute Captain Dreyfus. On his own — for he was expelled from service for his past efforts to exonerate Dreyfus, was he not? — on his own he confronts one of the conspirators, Major Henry. He extracts a confession from Henry, then turns Henry over to Captain Cuignet. Cuignet questions Henry, who admits everything. Cuignet reports this to Monsieur Cavaignac. What happens next?"

She leaned forward in her chair, as if to emphasize a point.

"Why, Henry is found dead in his cell, and Picquart is arrested for treason. On the orders of War Minister Cavaignac, who promptly resigns from his post."

The room was uncomfortably warm. Brisson took a handkerchief from his pocket, dabbed his brow. The woman continued.

"Did you know, Monsieur, that Major Esterhazy has fled the country?" she asked. "He left last week, only a few hours after Cavaignac learned of Henry's confession. Another coincidence?"

Brisson turned to the older Seigneur.

"Monsieur, you would do well to instruct your daughter to take care. As a man of the law, you will understand the legal jeopardy in which she places herself with these insinuations."

To his surprise, Seigneur laughed, a full-throated laugh.

"My daughter studied law at the Sorbonne," Seigneur said, when he had regained his composure. "I doubt there is anything you or I can teach her about it, Monsieur. In any event, I gave up the idea of *instructing* her many years ago." He paused, smiling at Georges with evident affection. "In any event, she has only recited the facts as we know them. If you are unaware of them, then I submit that you are being poorly served by the men you have placed at the head of the Army."

Brisson had no more patience for this man and his strange daughter. He took the envelope from the table, slipped it inside his jacket.

"You have delivered your petition, Monsieur," he said, addressing himself to Mathieu. "I assure you that the cabinet will give it careful consideration."

He stood, signaling an end to the interview. The others, reluctantly, got to their feet. Brisson shook hands with Mathieu, then Seigneur. He took Lucie Dreyfus's hand lightly and bowed. He turned to Mademoiselle Seigneur, intending to do the same. To his surprise, she gripped the hand he offered tightly and would not let it go.

"Monsieur, I think it only fair to give you a warning," she said, in that same oddly entrancing voice.

"A warning, Mademoiselle?" he echoed.

"Yes." She drew him closer. "You should know that we are in possession of evidence which will prove beyond any doubt that Captain Dreyfus is a victim of a conspiracy. This conspiracy began with a few officers but has spread until it has ensnared the entire high command."

"Remarkable," he said, feebly, trying to extricate his hand from her surprisingly strong grip.

"Yes, remarkable," she said. She smiled, but it was a chilling smile. "If you do not believe me, you may ask Major Picquart, or Captain Cuignet, about the nature of this evidence. But do it soon, Monsieur. I give you two weeks to refer our appeal to the Court of Cassation."

"And if I do not, Mademoiselle?" he asked.

"If you do not," she said, releasing his hand, "then I shall bring your government down myself."

Chapter 47

Fashoda, 19 September 1898

The two men were impossibly neat, their khaki uniforms clean of mud and dust, their black faces freshly shaved and gleaming, and the red of their fezzes bright in the early morning sun. They had appeared at dawn on the far bank of the river, and Marchand had obligingly dispatched a boat to ferry them across to the fort. Once in his presence, they snapped to attention and rendered a sharp salute. Only after he had returned it did they drop their arms to their sides, whereupon the shorter of the two handed him an envelope. Inside, Marchand found a brief letter:

18 September 1898

To the Commander of the European Expedition at Fashoda:

Having captured Khartoum and restored it to the care of the Khedive of Egypt, I embark today to reclaim the rest of His empire in the Sudan, of which Fashoda forms a part.

Sir Herbert Kitchener
Sirdar

Brigadier General
Anglo-Egyptian Army

He folded the letter.

"I should like to send a reply," he said.

"There is no need, sah," said the shorter man. "He comes now."

Marchand inspected the two men again. Even their boots were clean, highly polished and carrying only the light layer of dust they would have picked up in the walk from the jetty up to the fort.

"How did you come here?" he asked.

Neither man replied. Marchand sighed.

"Nevertheless, I should like to send a reply. Will you carry it for me?"

"Yes, sah."

Marchand crossed to the camp table he used as a desk, took pen and paper, wrote quickly:

19 September 1898

To Brigadier General Sir Herbert Kitchener:

In the name of France, I am pleased to receive you at Fashoda; which, as you know, has been taken from the savage dervishes by feat of arms and is, along with all of south Sudan, French by right of conquest and possession.

Major Jean-Baptiste Marchand
French Colonial Army

He folded the note and handed it to the soldier, who put it inside his jacket. The two men saluted in unison, their heels striking the ground to emphasize the movement. He returned the salute. The two executed a neat turn and were escorted from his office. He followed them out the door, then stood on the gun platform of the fort to watch them return to the jetty.

The town of Fashoda was an unimpressive place, a poor cluster of huts clinging to the outside of a bend in the river. The huts were mud brick, the same dull red as the mud of the riverbank and, from the heights of the fort, they were nearly impossible to make out. The fort was made of the same bricks, though at some time in its long and obscure history someone had coated the surface with a layer of whitewash. It had been long abandoned, though, and the merciless sun had taken its toll, so that when Marchand had at last approached it from the west, he'd thought for a moment it was a crumbling bluff of pink stone rather than a man-made structure.

His men had worked wonders in the two months since they'd occupied the place. They had cleared the fort of years of debris, repaired roofs and reinforced the walls, using timber taken from their supply crates. They had made the place livable, even comfortable. The thick walls offered them a cool respite from the heat of the day. From where he stood, he could look down on the garden they'd planted, one which already supplied them with fresh vegetables, and the river brought them fish and game. Baratier had found an old cave just above the river and fashioned a rude cellar there, so the wine they'd carried with them from Loango was cool and refreshing. They were as healthy and strong as they'd been the day they had set out on their long expedition.

The tricolor of France hung limply from the flagpole they'd erected at the top of the fort. The mountain guns had been placed at the old embrasures in the walls, from which they had a commanding view of the river to the north and south. They had suffered two attacks since arriving, by forces presumably sent by the Khalifa to expel them from the fort; but both had been driven off with no casualties on the French side. In all respects, they were well situated here; all, that is, except for one. They'd had no word from France since their arrival. Indeed, they'd had no contact of any kind with the outside world since they had departed Tambura at the beginning of June. Marchand had dispatched messages, but he could not even be sure that anyone knew they had reached their objective. While they did not lack for food, they were short of ammunition, and they were too few to repel any serious effort by the British. Their relief force was overdue. Two days before, he'd send Baratier and the *Faidherbe* steaming south to Sobat in search of de Bonchamps.

"Look at them," said Mangin.

His face was impassive, but his tone registered disbelief. Marchand followed his gaze, across the river to where the boat was pulling away after depositing the two soldiers on the far bank. Marchand watched them, waiting for them to begin the long walk north to return to where they'd come from; but they made no move. Instead, they simply stood, facing the river and the fort, their hands clasped behind their backs.

"What are they doing?" asked Marchand.

"God knows," said Mangin. "Waiting for Kitchener, I suppose. They're good soldiers, those two. I hope all his men aren't like them."

They watched for ten minutes, but the two men never moved. Marchand took his watch from his pocket, examined it. It was half past eight in the morning, and the sun was already unbearably hot.

"Keep an eye on them," he said. Mangin grunted. Marchand retreated to the cool darkness of his office.

He was writing in his journal when he heard distant gunfire, a single cannon shot. He walked quickly out into the sunlight. Mangin was at the parapet, looking to the north. Marchand joined him.

North of the fort the river described a wide curve, first to the east, then to the west, where a high stone bluff blocked any view further north. Now a riverboat had come into sight, steaming south against the current and making good speed. The vessel was long, perhaps one hundred and fifty feet from bow to stern, and low to the water. The main deck was flat and bore a superstructure of three decks mounted in the middle third of the vessel. The walls of the superstructure were curiously flat and featureless, with only a row of very small square ports high up on each deck, so that Marchand understood immediately that the walls were, in fact, armor plates. The forecastle was dominated by a round gun turret, the two guns pointed up and away from the fort. As he watched, a puff of smoke appeared at the muzzle of one of the guns, and seconds later he heard the report. The entire vessel was painted white, so that to look at it for any length of time in the bright sunlight was painful to the eyes. From a mast behind the forecastle flew two flags: the standard of the Khedive of Egypt and the Union Jack.

"Fire a salute," said Marchand.

Mangin hesitated a moment; they were dangerously low on ammunition. Then he shrugged.

"One shell won't make any difference," he said, and went to see to it.

Marchand watched as the gunboat approached, then steered to port, hugging the far bank of the river. The turret had now rotated to aim at the fort, though otherwise the British had made no threatening move. The vessel dropped anchor and, shortly thereafter, deployed a small boat to retrieve the two soldiers from the riverbank. When the boat had returned and the two men had been taken aboard, he checked his watch, noting the hour for his journal. It was just after ten in the morning.

"Prepare a boat," he said to Mangin. "We shall row out to meet them."

***

The iron plates of the vessel — the *Dal*, it was called — radiated heat like a furnace, and for a moment Marchand feared that the officer who met them at the ladder meant to take them into one of the compartments; which must, he thought, be like an oven. Instead the man led them aft along the main deck, past the superstructure to the aft deck, where a canvas had been rigged to provide shade for a group of chairs and a table of refreshments. An intermittent breeze carried cool air from the river across the deck, so that it was almost pleasant.

Two men waited for them there. Kitchener was a tall man, well over six feet. He had a cast in one eye and an impressively thick mustache which, in combination, lent him a fierce aspect he used to every advantage. His hair was still dark, but the mustache had been bleached white by the sun. Like Marchand, he wore field khakis, though the general's were in a much better state of repair.

Marchand executed a neat bow.

"Major Marchand, French Colonial Army, at your service," he said. He indicated Mangin. "I present Captain Charles Mangin."

"Kitchener," the man replied tersely. "*Sirdar* of His Highness the Khedive. I regret to inform you, Captain, that my instructions are to take possession of Fashoda in the name of His Highness."

"Your master gave up the Sudan thirteen years ago, left it to the mercy of the savages," said Marchand. "My orders are to occupy Fashoda and the other parts of the upper Nile abandoned by Egypt, and thereby lacking a legal owner." He tilted his head slightly, as if confiding a secret. "You have come too late, Monsieur, but I offer you the hospitality of France."

Kitchener glared at him. The silence stretched. Then the *Sirdar* turned away, walked to the starboard rail and stood facing the fort across the river, hands clasped behind his back. Marchand turned for the first time to the other officer: a short, slight man in his mid-twenties, dressed in khakis and wearing the boots of a cavalry officer.

"Churchill," the man said, introducing himself with a slight bow.

Marchand bowed in return. The *Sirdar*, still at the rail, cleared his throat. Churchill nodded in his direction, and Marchand belatedly realized that Kitchener wanted that he join him at the rail. He nodded his thanks to Churchill, then walked to the rail, where he stood beside the general.

"I will not argue these diplomatic points with you, sir," said Kitchener, in a low voice meant only for him. "Instead, I ask you to take note of the forces I have at my disposal and consider the weakness of your own position. You have done well to come so far, but you are outmatched."

"We have come far indeed, Monsieur," said Marchand evenly. "I beg you to understand that, having come this far, we will not willingly give up what is ours."

At this Kitchener sighed.

"I have some discretion," he said. "I don't mean to precipitate a war between our two countries." Here he paused, turned towards Marchand. "I mean *our* two countries, yours and mine," he said, and Marchand understood that he was speaking now not as the *Sirdar* of the Khedive, but as a general in the British Army. "If there is to be a war, I don't wish it to be started here."

"Nor I, Monsieur."

"Good," said Kitchener. "But I am commanded by His Highness the Khedive to raise the flag of Egypt over Fashoda. To do that this day, sir."

Marchand shook his head.

"I regret that I may not permit you to raise any flag over the fort." Kitchener stiffened at this, but Marchand went on. "However, if you wish, you may raise it over the *town*."

The two men looked at each other in silence. Finally, Kitchener nodded his agreement.

"That will satisfy my obligation to the Khedive," he said. "Shall we leave the larger matter of your presence to the frock coats in London and Paris? I intend to steam further south to Sobat, then return to Khartoum. I will cable London from there. I can convey to your government whatever message you see fit to entrust to me."

"I thank you, but that will not be necessary," Marchand lied. "I am in communication with my own government. But in any event, I agree, let us leave this matter to our masters."

"Very well, major," said Kitchener. "Will you and Captain Mangin join me in a drink?"

***

On the spur of the moment, Marchand invited the two men to come ashore to lunch with him and enjoy a tour of the fort. The *Sirdar* accepted, so Marchand sent Mangin ahead to make the necessary preparations to receive their guests.

Lunch was a buffet table laden with cold roast game and smoked fish, supplemented with fresh vegetables and herbs from the garden, served on fine china in the dark and welcome coolness of the largest room in the old fort. They washed it down with crystal glasses of the champagne they'd brought with them from France. The wine was cold and refreshing in the heat of the afternoon.

Afterward Marchand offered cigars. They smoked in convivial camaraderie until the *Sirdar* announced that it was time to take his leave. He stood, shook hands with Marchand and Mangin, nodded to Churchill, and left the room. Marchand, who had expected Churchill to follow Kitchener, looked at the young lieutenant with some puzzlement. Churchill had brought with him a large leather dispatch bag which he'd carried on one shoulder all afternoon. Now he opened the bag and drew a sheaf of papers from it.

"The general asked me to give you these," he said. "Papers from Paris, only a few weeks old. He thought you might like to read the news."

He handed the stack of newspapers to Mangin, who accepted them with thanks. Then he addressed Marchand.

"Might I have a word in private, sir?"

"Very well," said Marchand.

He led Churchill out of the dining room and down a narrow passage to the chamber he used as his office. There, the young man reached into the bag again and withdrew a fold of paper.

"I am instructed to give you this," he said. "It is in English, I'm afraid; I hope that won't be a problem?"

Marchand shook his head. Churchill extended his hand. Marchand took the paper, unfolded it, and began to read:

14 August 1898

From: Field Marshall Viscount Wolseley, Commander-in-Chief of the Forces
To: Brig Gen Kitchener, commanding the Anglo-Egyptian Army, the Sudan

1. Have recvd reliable intelligence from Paris that armed French force aims to occupy Fashoda in the Sudan and claim it for France. This force estimated at 150 men lightly armed and may already have arrived.
2. Second force has embarked from Abyssinia. This force consists of ten thousand Abyssinian soldiers led by French and Abyssinian officers. Will reach the Nile south of Fashoda some time in the latter half of September. From there will move north to reinforce the garrison.
3. Foreign Office view is that if you can get between Fashoda and this relief column with sufficient force they will decline to fight their way through and the Fashoda garrison will be isolated.
4. Urgent therefore that you defeat the forces before you at Omdurman and move with all dispatch and in force to isolate Fashoda.

Marchand read the telegram through twice, then lowered the paper to his side.

"You are betrayed, sir," said Churchill. "You have made a heroic journey, but it has been for naught."

"We are here, in possession," said Marchand. He thrust the telegram at Churchill. "This means nothing."

Churchill took the telegram, returned it to the bag.

"Some men will come ashore," he said, "to raise the flag over the town. As you agreed."

He bowed to Marchand and took his leave. Marchand watched him go, then returned to the dining room. Mangin sat in a corner, reading one of the newspapers Churchill had given him. Several more lay on the floor around him.

"They know about de Bonchamps and the Abyssinians," said Marchand.

Mangin did not respond.

"Did you hear me, Charles?"

Mangin looked up from the paper.

"They have gone mad," he said. He shook the paper he was holding. "The government has fallen."

"Fallen? When?"

"In June," Mangin replied. "Just after we left Tambura. Meline is out. And Hanotaux."

It was Gabriel Hanotaux who had sent them to Fashoda in the first place. Of all the men in Paris, he was the one most committed to their goal of taking the Nile and driving Britain from Egypt.

"Who has replaced him?" asked Marchand.

"Brisson has formed a government," said Mangin. "Delcasse has the Foreign Ministry now."

Marchand was still reeling from the impact of the telegram. He walked on unsteady legs to a chair, sat.

"How did this happen?"

"It's all to do with that Dreyfus fellow," Mangin said. "The Jew, the one they caught spying. You remember?"

Marchand nodded.

"Well, apparently it is a great scandal now. *The Affair*, they call it. Some people say he's innocent. Others say it's a plot by Jews and Socialists to undermine the Army. They're fighting each other in the streets. Not only in the streets — fights have broken out in the Chamber of Deputies."

He folded the paper, handed it to Marchand, who took it and scanned the front page.

"Kitchener has arrived at the worst possible time," said Mangin. His tone was bitter, resigned. "They say this Brisson government won't last, either. It must be chaos there. They won't give a damn about us."

Marchand opened his mouth to rebuke his friend, but they were interrupted by a shout. The two men reacted instinctively, running from the dining room into the bright sunlight, where they stood at the wall. The *Dal* had weighed anchor, and she moved slowly to the south, against the current, black smoke belching from her stack. As she pulled away from the shore, the far bank behind her was revealed. Two men ran along the bank to the north. Their khaki uniforms were all but invisible against the dry and dusty ground, so that Marchand could make them out only by the red of their caps. For no reason he could explain, he knew that these were the same two soldiers who had brought him the letter from Kitchener. *Was it only this morning?*

A second gunboat appeared from the north, steaming into view as it rounded the bend and came towards them. It was a larger vessel than the *Dal*, and Marchand could just make out the mass of men in uniform which filled the deck from stem to stern. The troop carrier came on and, behind it, another gunboat appeared. Marchand's eye was drawn to some movement on the shore. He shielded his eyes with his hand to get a better look. A troop of cavalry moved along the far shore in tandem with the gunboats, their banners fluttering in the breeze of their passage. Behind them were the first ranks of an infantry regiment, row upon row of black-faced men in khaki, the red of their fezzes marking them out with geometric precision. A third gunboat came into view.

"We are finished," said Mangin.

"They aren't coming here," said Marchand. "Not yet. They're going south, to intercept de Bonchamps."

He told Mangin what he'd learned from Churchill.

"The bastards." Mangin removed his cap, rubbed his head. "They've betrayed us. They mean to abandon us here."

"They will not abandon us," said Marchand. "I will not permit it."

Chapter 48

Paris, 26 September 1898

CRISIS AT FASHODA
French Forces Under the Command of Major Marchand Lay Claim to The Upper Nile

At the Cabinet Council today the Minister for Foreign Affairs, M. Delcasse, read a telegram from General Sir Herbert Kitchener, the British Commander on the Nile, which had been communicated to the Foreign Office by the British Ambassador Sir Edward Monson. It was worded as follows:

"Met at Fashoda Sept 19 Marchand flying French flag. Marchand arrived July 10 with 3 officers and a company of Senegalese tirailleurs."

In the dispatch, General Kitchener declares that Marchand's position "is as impossible as it is absurd." General Kitchener is said to oppose Marchand with a force of some 15,000 soldiers and artillery and a flotilla of armored gunboats. Ambassador Monson has protested the presence of French forces on the White Nile in the strongest possible terms. M. Delcasse stressed that, while no orders have as yet been sent to Marchand, it is the position of the French Government that the territory of the Sudan from the town of Fashoda on the White Nile south to Sobat and west as far as Wau are French by the right of conquest and occupation.

***

Paris, 7 October 1898

ARMY OFFICER CONFESSES TO USING FALSE EVIDENCE AGAINST DREYFUS
Major Henry Found Dead in His Cell Under Mysterious Circumstances

A person in authority who is familiar with the matter has revealed that Major Joseph Henry, an officer of the General Staff, provided several important pieces of secret evidence in the infamous Dreyfus dossier which he knew to be fraudulent. Major Henry confessed his guilt to a certain Captain Cuignet, the officer charged by the Minister of War, M. Cavaignac, with reviewing the affair. In yet another strange turn of events, Major Henry was found dead in his cell shortly after his arrest and confinement in the fortress of Monte Valerian. Another officer, Major Esterhazy, who has previously been acquitted of espionage and treason, has fled the country and is said to be residing now in England. This sequence of events, our informant says, led to the decision by M. Brisson's cabinet to grant the request of Madame Dreyfus to refer the case to the Court of Cassation, and it was this decision by the cabinet which in turn caused M. Cavaignac to resign from the government in protest. M. Cavaignac was replaced by M. Chanoine, who by all accounts surprised the government by immediately ordering thousands of troops into Paris. A rift has formed between the government and the high command, in which cabinet ministers accuse senior officers of complicity in the conspiracy against Dreyfus, while those officers in turn accuse the government of attacking the honor of the Army. This discord has had a profound negative effect on the ability of the government to develop a response to the Fashoda crisis.

***

London, 10 October 1898

GOVERNMENT DENIES FRENCH SUDAN CLAIMS

In recent days the French Ambassador, Baron de Courcel, has made public statements which call into the question the resolve of Her Majesty's government in the matter of the French intrusion into the Sudan. These questions have been answered to the satisfaction of all by the Blue Book published today by the Prime Minister. Lord Salisbury made clear his refusal to consider France's claim, and insisted that the question of who is entitled to possess the Sudan has been settled on the battlefield of Omdurman by Lord Kitchener and his victorious Anglo-Egyptian force. Lord Salisbury expressed surprise that France should have acted in so unfriendly a manner towards Great Britain as to dispatch a secret expedition to seize a valuable strategic point in territory that came within the scope of British influence.

***

London, 14 October 1898

LORD ROSEBERY OFFERS SUDAN WARNING

Lord Rosebery, speaking yesterday in Surrey, issued a warning to the French they would do well to heed: "Great Britain has been conciliatory, and her conciliatory disposition has been widely misunderstood. If the nations of the world are under the impression that the ancient spirit of Great Britain is dead or that her resources are weakened or her population less determined than ever it was to maintain the rights and honors of its flag, they make a mistake which can only end in a disastrous conflagration."

***

Paris, 18 October 1898

BRISSON GOVERNMENT REJECTS BRITISH DEMANDS

M. Delcasse, the foreign minister, informed the British Ambassador to France, Sir Edmund Monson, in explicit language that France did not *regard Lord Salisbury's claim to Sudan by virtue of conquest as applying to Fashoda or the territory of South Sudan on the grounds that it is Major Marchand, and not General Kitchener, who has conquered those territories. M. Delcasse argued that France considered herself equally entitled with England to possession of any point occupied by French officers.*

***

London, 21 October 1898

WAR ORDERS DRAFTED

Her Majesty's government today announced a call-up of the Reserve Fleet. Lord George Hamilton, First Lord of the Admiralty, further revealed that war orders have been drafted for the Home Fleet, the Channel Fleet, and the Mediterranean Fleet.

***

Paris, 23 October 1898

RUMORS OF MOBILIZATION FROM THE COAST

It is reported in Cherbourg that orders have been received at the military and naval arsenals there to prepare for the arrival of a large body of troops tomorrow. The barracks are being hurriedly put in order for their reception. Despite this report, the Government refuses to confirm whether a general mobilization will be ordered.

***

London, 24 October 1898

FASHODA CRISIS THREATENS BRITISH INTERESTS IN EGYPT

The most recent French statement on Fashoda seems to indicate an intention of the French Government to utilize the Marchand affair as a means of raising the whole Egypt question. This impression is confirmed by the comments of most of the Paris papers this morning, which also report rumors of a general mobilization of the French Army. The Foreign Office admits the gravity of the situation, while declaring that it is impossible to consent to any negotiation until Fashoda is evacuated. As, however, the French minister M. Delcasse with equal firmness declines to withdraw Marchand without previous negotiations, the situation now has an ominous outlook. Events are made worse by recent revelations in the Dreyfus affair, revelations which have placed the Government of France and her Army at odds with one another. In such a climate, it is difficult to predict what may happen next.

***

London, 26 October 1898

FRENCH DEPUTIES IN SESSION FORCE GOVERNMENT TO RESIGN
The Session Was Followed by Street Rioting

The Minister of War, M. Chanoine, resigned his office in dramatic fashion, denouncing before the Chamber the Government's decision to refer the Dreyfus conviction to the Court of Cassation. His resignation provoked an uproar and led to a motion of no confidence in the Government. M. Brisson's Government has been defeated, and his Ministers have accordingly resigned. Widespread rioting broke out at the close of the session, and offenses against Jews and Socialists have been reported. Rumors persist that the Army will take power. President Faure is said to have prevailed on some Ministers to remain until a new Government can be formed. Notably, M. Delcasse is to continue in the Foreign Office, perhaps in consequence of the Fashoda crisis which now shows every sign of leading to war.

Chapter 49

Paris, 26 October 1898

It was fitting, Theophile Delcasse thought, that the Marchand matter would, in the end, be his problem. As France's colonial minister in 1893, he had launched the first French mission deep into the Congo, seeking a way to a French claim on the Nile, and Marchand's expedition was surely the spiritual child of his own. Nonetheless, when he'd taken over the reins of the Foreign Office from Hanotaux in June, he'd been shocked to learn of the scope of the adventure. In the months since, he'd secretly hoped that Marchand would fail; but the man was incapable of failure, it seemed, and now he sat in his fort on the Nile, awaiting the reinforcements and the orders that would propel France into open war with Britain.

He read again the cable he had received from Marchand yesterday. It had been carried by runner and steamer from Fashoda to Bangui, thence to Brazzaville, before finally reaching a telegraph outpost, and as a result it was already nearly three months old. The British lines of communication were far better, and there was little in Marchand's cable that he could not have learned from reading the London papers.

He set the cable aside, picked up another. This one came from Captain de Bonchamps, the officer commanding the relief force. In the matter of fact, clipped sentences that were the language of the telegraph, de Bonchamps spelled out what amounted to disaster. He had expected to reach the Nile at Sobat by the end of August but delays and a noted lack of cooperation from the Abyssinian officers in his force meant he did not reach the village until the 25th of September, nearly four weeks late. There, he found Sobat occupied by British and Egyptian soldiers camped under the flag of Egypt. He had deployed scouts for several days, seeking a way around the village, but encountered pickets at every possible crossing of the river. In the end, he had determined that there was no choice but to fight his way through or turn back. With no orders to fight, he had reluctantly withdrawn to Addis Ababa, a retreat which had taken another three weeks to complete. There, the Emperor Menelik had made it clear that he would lend no further assistance to the French as he had no intention of being drawn into a war with Great Britain. Marchand, it seemed, was on his own.

Now the problem was entirely his. Brisson had resigned, as he was required to do after yesterday's vote. President Faure had summoned Delcasse to the Elysee Palace last night, begged him to remain in his post in an interim capacity. With France on the brink of war, he'd had no choice but to accept. His inclination was to defuse the crisis by ordering Marchand to withdraw, but that was impossible. General de Boisdeffre had made clear that the General Staff preferred to fight for the Sudan. Now Paris was rife with rumors of an imminent military coup and, if he were to order a retreat, the Army might well refuse to carry it out.

Delcasse put both cables in the drawer of his desk. That done, he rose, crossed to the door, opened it.

"You may show the Ambassador in," he said to his clerk.

Delcasse was surprised to see that the Sir Edmund Monson had arrived with a companion, another man who carried a leather satchel. Monson introduced the man as Welles, an associate, but said nothing more about his role or why he'd brought him to the meeting. Delcasse considered objecting, then thought better of it.

He had a private word with his clerk, then invited the two men to sit.

He began without preamble, as if he and Monson were continuing a conversation already in progress; which, indeed, they were.

"I must again suggest that we discuss some suitable accommodation to resolve the situation in the Sudan," he said. "One which recognizes the interests of both our countries."

Monson adopted an expression which conveyed both patience and pain.

"As I have said before, Monsieur Delcasse, it is the position of Her Majesty's government that there can be no negotiations on this matter so long as Major Marchand remains at Fashoda."

Delcasse was indignant.

"Monsieur Ambassador, that is the question to be decided!" he said. "We cannot begin a conversation on the status of Fashoda by first ceding the question of Fashoda. Surely you understand that."

"There is no question of Fashoda. The Sudan belongs to the Khedive of Egypt."

"If that is the case, Monsieur, then why am I not addressing an emissary of the Khedive? Why is Fashoda surrounded by British soldiers?"

"Egypt is a weak country, as all the world knows," said Monson, "and His Highness the Khedive has graciously invited Her Majesty to protect His interests."

Monson crossed his legs, tapped the arm of his chair with a forefinger.

"I beg you to understand, Monsieur, that we are not prepared to entertain any conversation on the status of Great Britain in Egypt. There are already many in my country who believe that it was the purpose of Major Marchand — and of your government — to bring about a change in that status. If that is the case, then you have failed, and I regret to say that if you cannot recognize that, then there is nothing more to be said."

This seemed to Delcasse unusually blunt, and he bristled.

"I might as easily say that the ruler of the local people — the *Reth* Kur Abd al-Fadil — has signed a treaty with France, recognizing our presence and influence in the region. If we are to imagine that this is a dispute between the Khedive and the Reth, then I say, *let the Khedive and the Reth resolve it.*"

He mimicked Monson's gesture by tapping his finger on the table.

"Let us not be quite so naive as that, my dear Monson," he went on. "It is not the fleets of the Khedive that have been ordered into the Channel. Britain wants Egypt; France wants the Sudan. That is the heart of the dispute."

"The Nile is a British sphere of influence," said Monson. "This is a question which has long been settled between our two countries. That France now questions it — indeed, that France has violated that understanding by sending a secret expedition into the heart of our territory — is seen by many of my countrymen as an unfriendly act. Now, it is my own view, Monsieur, that this is simply a misunderstanding, one we may easily resolve between us; but not so long as the insult to Her Majesty remains. Remove Marchand, I urge you. If you do, then I believe we can be amenable to some broader understanding of our two spheres, one which will be to the advantage of both our nations."

"Impossible," declared Delcasse. "There is no question of removing Marchand. If you will only accept that, then we can proceed to this broader understanding of which you speak."

To Delcasse's surprise, Monson's companion cleared his throat.

"If I may, Messieurs," the man said, leaning forward in his chair as he did so, "you appear to be at an impasse; and not, I venture to guess, for the first time."

"Indeed, Monsieur—" Delcasse struggled to remember the man's name. "Ah, yes, Monsieur Welles. There is something you wish to say?"

"There is," said Welles. "Ambassador Monson is perhaps too polite to say so, but we are aware that your position in this matter is untenable. Whether or not you personally wish to abandon

Fashoda, your own generals will not permit it. They will drive you to war, Monsieur, a war you cannot win."

War was the one word Monson and Delcasse had labored to avoid. Both men were visibly dismayed to hear Welles speak it. Monson raised a hand to restrain Welles, but Welles brushed it away. Delcasse looked from one of them to the other.

"Who is this man?" he asked Monson. When Monson did not reply, he turned to Welles. "Why are you here, sir? What is your interest in this matter?"

"In truth, I have no interest in it at all," said Welles. "It is a matter of no importance to me who owns Fashoda, a place of which almost no one had ever heard until a month ago. If you wish to fight a war over it, then fight one, and be damned for it."

"Mister Welles—" began Monson, but Welles cut him off.

"I am here, Monsieur, on behalf of Captain Dreyfus," he said. "My interest is in justice. I would see him set free, for he is innocent of the crime for which he was convicted."

This declaration was so tangential that Delcasse could think of no reply. He turned to Monson for an explanation, but the Ambassador was silent, his face grim. Delcasse collected himself, addressed Welles.

"I confess I am unable to understand your purpose, Monsieur, or that of Monsieur Monson in bringing you to this meeting. I am not prepared to discuss the matter of Captain Dreyfus with you, other than to inform you — if you are so ignorant as to need informing — that the case has already been referred to the Court of Cassation for review."

Welles smiled at this.

"I am aware of the referral," he said, "just as I am aware that it was this decision by Monsieur Brisson that brought down his government. If the nationalists take power — or worse, if the Army does — then Dreyfus is doomed. They will prevent the review, or subvert it, and he will die on Devil's Island. That is where our interests align, Monsieur. You want to abandon Fashoda to avoid war, but the generals won't permit it. I want to free Dreyfus, but they won't permit that, either. So, you see, we have the same enemy."

Delcasse turned to Monson, his eyes wide in mock astonishment.

"Who is this extraordinary man, Monsieur Monson? What possessed you to bring him here?"

"Hear him out, please," said Monson. "He joins us today at the express wish of the Prime Minister. I grant that he is an unorthodox fellow, but I promise you it will be to your advantage."

Delcasse appeared to consider this, then turned to Welles, a doubtful expression on his face.

"Tell me one thing that will be to my advantage to know," he said.

"Very well. You will by now have received a communication from Captain de Bonchamps, in which he reports that his relief force was unable to reach Fashoda. He failed to reinforce Marchand because General Kitchener's forces at Sobat blocked his way. Kitchener's men were there because I told him de Bonchamps was coming."

Welles paused, his eyes fixed on Delcasse's own. Delcasse cleared his throat.

"And how did you know of de Bonchamps' mission? Indeed, how could you know anything about the Fashoda mission at all?"

"I have known about Marchand's mission for more than two years," said Welles. "I learned it from an officer of the French Army."

He lifted the satchel onto his lap, drew from it a sheet of paper, then half-stood to offer it to Delcasse.

"This is a copy of a cable sent to General Kitchener on the 29th of August, warning him of de Bonchamps and his purpose," he said.

Delcasse scanned the cable, then laid it on the desk.

"I ask you again: who are you, Monsieur?"

"I am an agent of the British Government," said Welles. "In that capacity I have had dealings with an officer of the General Staff: a traitor, Monsieur. I can offer proof of his treason."

He reached into the satchel again, produced a file which he placed on Delcasse's desk, just out of the man's reach. He kept his own hand on the file, as if to say *I have not yet given this to you.*

"In the course of my work," he continued, "I discovered that Dreyfus was innocent; that his conviction was the result of a conspiracy to blame him for the crimes of another man, a Major Esterhazy. I knew Esterhazy because he was in my charge. He was a traitor to France who supplied me with the first intelligence Britain had of Marchand and his mission. Esterhazy conspired with the late Major Henry and with another man, Major Du Paty de Clam, to shift the suspicion to Dreyfus, and to fabricate the evidence needed to convict him."

Delcasse fell back in his chair as though struck by a blow to the chest. He shot a look at Monson, as if looking to him for rescue.

"As bad as it sounds, Monsieur," Monson said, "I am afraid there is more to come. And it is far worse."

"Indeed," said Welles. "Henry and Du Paty persecuted Dreyfus because he was a Jew. They did not know that Esterhazy did so for another reason; that he was the true traitor and needed to shift the blame to save himself. And there was another thing they didn't know: that, in building this edifice of lies, Esterhazy had our help."

"Your help?" Delcasse asked.

"Yes, our help," said Welles. "The effort to implicate Dreyfus was aided by British agents here in Paris, acting on instructions from their superiors in London."

"That is impossible," said Delcasse. "I can believe that a terrible mistake has been made, Monsieur Welles. I can even believe that some officers, in their zeal, might have gone too far. But I cannot believe that the Army has been duped by foreign agents; duped into the worst crisis of our generation."

"You must believe it, Monsieur," said Welles. He patted the file with his hand. "The proof is here, in this file."

Delcasse made no move to take the file. Indeed, to Welles it seemed the man regarded it as if it were a snake. The three men sat in silence, each now waiting for another to speak, knowing that he who yielded first would be at a disadvantage. In the end it was Delcasse.

"How do you propose I use it, Monsieur?"

"The evidence I offer is a profound embarrassment to the Army," said Welles. "In particular to de Boisdeffre, Mercier, Gonse. All of them should have known from the start that the case against Dreyfus was absurd. If it were up to me, I'd use it to destroy them. Publish the proof of their malignant stupidity. Once they have been so discredited, you will be free to abandon Fashoda. And they will be powerless to interfere any further in the review of the Dreyfus affair."

Monson raised a hand to silence Welles.

"Monsieur Welles's idea has some merit, and would surely be gratifying," he said. "However, perhaps there is a less drastic way forward. It may not be necessary to humiliate them, Monsieur. You need only have their agreement to abandon Fashoda and recognize British influence over the entire course of the Nile. In return, let us say, for some similar accommodation on our behalf elsewhere in Africa?"

"And they must agree to let the Court of Cassation proceed unhindered," added Welles. "Some of the truth must surely come out, but the scandal can be limited to a handful of men. Esterhazy has fled, of course, and Henry is dead; but Du Paty is convenient, if they need someone to blame for the miscarriage of justice."

"Quite," said Monson. "So long as things proceed in the direction of justice, there should be no need to reveal our role in the affair, or the extent to which your generals have gone to protect their ugly secrets."

There was a discrete knock at the door, and Delcasse's clerk entered. Delcasse beckoned to him. The man approached, bent down to his ear, spoke a few words. Delcasse nodded. When the man had left the room, he turned to Monson.

"You were saying, Monsieur? Something about the lengths to which they have gone to protect their secrets?"

"Men have died," said Welles. "Major Henry is dead, for one, and under suspicious circumstances. Whether he was murdered, or coerced into taking his own life, the result is the same."

Delcasse hesitated, then reached out, took the file, slowly drew it across his desk until it was before him. He opened it, examined a page, then another. He sighed, closed the folder.

"This is inscrutable," he said. "What am I to do with it?"

"Colonel Picquart can explain it to you," said Welles. "He is in the military prison at Mont Valérian. Send for him. Sooner is better than later. While he still lives, I mean."

Delcasse stared at Welles, then shook his head. He turned to Monson.

"Even if I were to agree, even if General de Boisdeffre were to agree, I fear Marchand will not abandon Fashoda. He is a determined man. Having won his prize, he will not give it up."

"Then you must send someone to convince him otherwise," said Welles. "I have just the fellow in mind."

The three men spoke for another half hour before coming at last to an agreement on how to proceed. Welles was elated; he could hardly wait to return to the Seigneur home to give them the good news. Then, as he and Monson were taking their leave, Delcasse addressed him.

"Monsieur Welles," he said, "I'm told there is a warrant for your arrest."

Welles froze.

"Who is this Leeman?" asked Delcasse.

"He was the forger," Welles said.

"And you killed him?"

"No," said Welles. "Not I."

"Then who did?"

He waited for a reply, but Welles said nothing.

"How it is, Monsieur, that you are here in France?" Delcasse asked.

"I had the use of another passport," said Welles.

"That of a man named Hull?" Delcasse asked.

When Welles nodded, Delcasse made a clucking sound with his tongue.

"Another dead man!" he exclaimed. "Are there others?" When Welles did not reply, he went on: "Perhaps, Monsieur, it would be best if you were to leave France. Until the question of these murders has been cleared up."

Chapter 50

Fashoda, 24 November 1898

A whistle sounded. Marchand set aside the report he'd been writing and walked through the cool darkness of the fort into the light of day. A gunboat was steaming towards the fort from the north, one of the smaller ones that Kitchener used to run errands up and down the Nile. He watched as it approached the new wooden pier the British had built alongside the town.

Mangin and Baratier joined him on the platform. The latter raised field glasses, inspected the boat a moment.

"I cannot believe it," he said.

"What?" asked Marchand. "Who is it?"

"See for yourself."

Marchand took the glasses, raised them to his own eyes. The gunboat eased up to the pier. Crewmen made lines fast, then a figure wearing uniform khakis stepped up onto the dock. Marchand drew in his breath sharply.

"C'est impossible!" He lowered the glasses, turned to the others. "It is Dédé."

"Durand?" asked Mangin. "What the devil can he want here?"

"Who can say?" Marchand peered through the glasses again. "That British officer is with him. The thin, reedy one. What was his name? Ah, yes. Churchill."

He met Durand and Churchill at the gate to the fort. He embraced Durand and the two comrades exchanged greetings while Churchill stood politely to the side. Then the British officer stepped forward and offered his hand.

"It is a pleasure to see you again, Major Marchand," Churchill said.

"The pleasure is mine," Marchand replied. "You are in time for lunch, if you care to join us."

"I would be delighted to join you, once we have concluded the necessary business that brings me here."

Marchand led the two men into the courtyard. There, Durand paused, looking up at the walls.

"So, this is Fashoda," he said, turning around in place to take it in. "It hardly seems worth the effort. When did you arrive?"

"In July," said Marchand, indicating with a hand the entrance into the fort.

"More than two years to get here, then," said Durand, pointedly. "To think I left Paris only twelve days ago."

They passed into the fort, and Marchand led them down a dark passage to the narrow stairway which wound its way to the upper floor. The steps were old and uneven. Durand stumbled, placed a hand on the wall to steady himself. He marveled at how cool it was.

In his office, Marchand invited them to sit. Durand chose one of the two chairs set before Marchand's desk. Churchill took the other, carried it a few feet to the wall, then sat, as if to say he was not a principal in this meeting, but rather an observer. Marchand circled the desk and sat in his own chair.

"Well, Dédé?" he asked.

Durand unbuttoned the pocket of his tunic, withdrew a fold of paper and handed it across the desk to Marchand.

"I have come to order you home," he said.

Marchand took the paper, unfolded it, and scanned the lines of the text. He let the paper fall to the desk and fixed his eyes on Durand's.

"It is a mistake," he said. "They will soon change their minds."

"No, my friend, they will not. There will be no war between Britain and France over this place."

Durand stood and took a turn around the room, gathering his thoughts. He stopped at the small window and peered out, then turned to face Marchand.

"Do you know, it was only when I arrived in Cairo last week that I understood how mad we have been?" he said. "I do not speak now of the horrors we have done since we set out, Paké-Bô. No, I mean the folly that prevented us from asking one simple question."

"What question is that?" asked Marchand.

"*What in God's name we meant to do here*," said Durand. "Let us suppose that the British allow us keep it. What then? Will we trade in rubber? Ivory?"

"Why not?" asked Marchand.

"We will carry it across that wilderness, then?" asked Durand, gesturing with a hand to the west. "On men's backs? How long will that take?" He snorted. "For anything of value to reach France from this place, it must go down the Nile to Cairo. Did you not hear me earlier, Paké-Bô? *Twelve days* from Paris to here. Without the river, we might as well be at the end of the world. Do you think the British will agree to ferry us up and down their river? Now, after we have stolen this place from them? No, we cannot profit here. We cannot even supply it properly. That is what Monsieur Delcasse now understands. The mystery is that anyone ever thought otherwise."

"Delcasse does not matter," said Marchand. "General de Boisdeffre would never abandon us here."

"General de Boisdeffre has resigned," said Durand. "Others will surely follow. There is no way you can grasp it in this remote place, but the generals have nearly destroyed France with their madness about Dreyfus. One by one they will be exposed. In the entire service, there is no senior officer free of the suspicion of having thus betrayed France."

"I cannot believe that such men have abandoned their honor," objected Marchand, holding up a hand to block the bright light shining through the window so he could better see Durand's face. "Damn you, Dédé, come away from there!"

Durand moved away from the window, returning to his seat opposite Marchand.

"You must believe it," he said. "I have seen the proof with my own eyes. Dreyfus is innocent. He is a loyal officer wrongly accused by his fellows. There was never a shred of evidence against him, save for the forgeries concocted by those who meant to blame him."

He went on to explain how, at first, a small group of officers had conspired to frame Dreyfus; how the conspiracy had spread through the General Staff, until each man who came to know that Dreyfus had been wrongly accused was moved to suppress that knowledge for the good of the Army.

"They kept the secret these four long years," he said. "While Dreyfus wasted away in chains on Devil's Island. But no more, Paké-Bô. The secret is out. The new Premier holds the evidence of their crimes in his hands."

"Still, he will not use it," said Marchand. "He cannot. No Premier of France would wound her so. The Army *is* France."

"He has no choice," said Durand. "The Army has declared war on the government. They have already brought down Monsieur Brisson's cabinet. Chanoine did that: he denounced the inquiry into the affair as an attack on the honor of the service and resigned. Then he had the audacity to put himself forth as an alternative: the man on a horse who would save France. It is only because he is not much loved by the other generals that he failed. They did not answer his call, and he was made a fool. But you must understand that Premier Dupuy will do what he must to bring down any officer who will not submit to the authority of the elected government. He cannot do otherwise, or Republican France is lost."

He fell silent, giving Marchand time to consider all he'd said. At length, Marchand spoke.

"Be that as it may, Dédé," he said, "my duty remains clear. I must hold Fashoda for France. When the dust has settled, they will thank me for having done it."

He reached for a piece of paper and his pen.

"I shall give you my reply to Delcasse, explaining the situation here. You can telegraph it from Cairo. I am sure once he has read it he will agree with my view."

"I will not take it," said Durand. "Who are you, Jean-Baptiste?" It was the first time he'd used Marchand's given name. "I took you for a soldier of France. *She has ordered you home.* If you mean to betray her — to serve yourself rather than her — then I will not be party to it. You will become like those others: men without a shred of honor to their names. And you will have become a murderer."

"A murderer!" objected Marchand.

"Yes, a murderer," said Durand, "for, if you refuse this order, then Kitchener must rout you from this place. The men who brought you here will likely all die. Certainly, Charles will, and Albert, for do you imagine they will not be at the forefront of the action? And many of the others; men who followed you four thousand miles through the wilderness and made it possible for you to come to this place. You think it will be glorious, I know, but then you will be dead, all of you. And Kitchener will have Fashoda anyway."

"I'm afraid our Government will rather insist on it," said Churchill.

Marchand held the pen above the paper, his eyes fixed on Durand's own. The hand moved, an involuntary twitch. Then he slowly lowered it to the desk, laid down the pen.

"Excellent," said Churchill. "I am instructed to inform you that we will provide you and your men with transport to Cairo. It is the least we can do under the circumstances."

Durand saw Marchand's jaw tighten.

"Be quiet!" Durand snapped at Churchill.

The latter made a clicking sound with his tongue but said no more. Durand turned back to Marchand.

"That course is intolerable," barked Marchand. "If we are to go, we will go as we came. As soldiers, not passengers"

"*Mon Dieu!*" said Durand, the exasperation clear in his voice. "You cannot mean to march these men back to Loango."

"No, not that. We will go south to Sobat. From there, we can march east, into Abyssinia, then to Djibouti. They can send a ship for us there."

"That will take months, Jean-Baptiste."

"Perhaps. But we will not be carried home like prisoners."

"Her Majesty's Government has no objection if you choose to find your own way home," said Churchill. He stood. "I shall leave you gentlemen now to make your plans," he said, then crossed to the door. At the threshold he stopped, turned to face them. "But you must leave before the end of the year."

The two men sat in silence for some time. Then Marchand spoke.

"Why did you come, Dédé?"

"They thought I could convince you to accept their decision."

"Yes, of course, that is why they sent you. But why did you agree to come?"

Durand shrugged. "I suppose I felt it my duty. Not to France. To you. To Albert and Charles. And to the men who would die trying to hold this place."

"Only them? Or do you mean to save them all?"

"All?"

Marchand gestured with his arm; a sweeping motion intended to encompass the world.

"Or do you think that if you save these men here, you will have atoned in some way for what came before?"

Durand did not reply.

"It won't make any difference, Dédé," said Marchand.

There was a sadness in his voice, and a kindness, as if he meant to soften the blow.

"If we are not here, the British will be instead," he continued. "Or the Belgians. You know they will be no kinder to these people than we would have been."

"Perhaps," Durand said. "But it will not have been I who made that possible."

Marchand held his eyes for a moment, then nodded. He took up his pen and began to write.

***

Later Durand stood on the gun platform and watched the sun set over the wilderness. He was alone, aside from one sentry posted at the door. Marchand had given the order to withdraw and below him he could see men scurrying here and there, busy about the work of preparing for their departure. The *Faidherbe* lay alongside the old stone pier below the walls of the fort, but the British gunboat on which he'd arrived was nowhere to be seen. Churchill had taken it to Sobat, to prepare the way for the French exodus. He had promised to return in two days to take Durand back to the railhead at Khartoum.

A light flickered below him. Men were lighting the torches which stood along the interior walls of the fort. The sun disappeared below the horizon, and the sky passed quickly through a deep, dark blue to black. The first stars appeared.

He heard a sound behind him, turned to find a second *tirailleur* bearing a burning torch. On seeing Durand, the man came briefly to attention; then he moved quickly to light the torches spaced along the ramparts of the gun platform. A moment later he was gone. Durand's gaze returned to the sky, but the light from the torches ruined the seeing, and he struggled to make out more than a few of the brightest stars.

From somewhere came the smells of cooking, and he realized that he was ravenous. There had been a luncheon in the afternoon, ostensibly to welcome him back, and to honor Lieutenant Churchill; but the mood had been anything but celebratory, and as a result he'd eaten little. Mangin had been seated across from him, but he had somehow avoided meeting Durand's eyes and had not said a word throughout the meal.

Durand had wondered what might be going on behind that impassive mien. Of course, Mangin was angry. He was never, Durand knew, not angry. But at whom? Their masters in Paris, certainly. And as the bearer of the bad news, surely he, Durand, had been allocated his portion of the man's ire. But what he had found himself wondering was whether Mangin, stewing in his silent rage, had directed any of it at himself. Durand had recalled with some shame how he'd once thought Mangin a man with no human conscience at all; how stunned he'd been to realize, following Mangin's outburst on the road, that the cruelty of the man stemmed not from a lack of any conscience, but from the torment of a conscience weighed down with guilt for all the things he'd done.

After lunch he'd sought Mangin out, found him in the cool dark room which served as his quarters. The two men had regarded each other without speaking. Durand had come to apologize to Mangin, to say that he'd misjudged the man. He had wanted to offer the friendship and understanding he had never extended before. There was no evil thing Mangin had done that he, Durand, had not done himself. That Mangin did them with clear, open eyes and no hint of self-deception, while he'd done them as if against his will — as if he'd had no choice in the matter! — seemed now to make no difference at all. The dead lay dead behind them and cared nothing for the lies the two men told themselves.

But the words had not come. The silence became more uncomfortable.

"I am sorry," Durand had blurted out at last.

Mangin had not seemed to react to that at all; he had simply stared through Durand as if he weren't there. Despondent, Durand had turned to go. He had been at the door when Mangin called his name.

"It has all been for nothing," Mangin had said.

His voice was tight. The rage had come to the surface, had threatened to burst into the open.

"All for nothing!" Mangin repeated through clenched teeth.

"There was never any point to it," Durand had said. "Don't you see, Charles? We should never have come."

A sound behind him broke his reverie, drawing him back from his memories. He turned to see that a second *tirailleur* had arrived to relieve the sentry. The two exchanged places with a stiff formality, and the relieved man disappeared into the fort. Durand took a last look around the torch-lit platform, then turned and made for the door. The sentry snapped to attention as he approached. He nodded absently as he passed and was at the door when the man spoke.

"Monsieur."

Durand stopped, turned to look at the soldier. His face was familiar. With a start Durand realized it was the same soldier whose rifle he'd knocked aside when the bearers were fleeing the road, all those months ago.

"What is it?" Durand asked.

"I am wanting to know a thing," the man said. Durand waited.

"Why does the white man Durand say we must go?" the soldier asked. "This white man brought us here. He made us fight, and many men suffered and died so that we might win this place. Why does the white man take us away now?"

Durand could think of nothing to say to this. He turned towards the door, but the man went on.

"If this white man takes us away from here, what do I say to the wives of the dead? To their sons and daughters? Why did they die for this white man?"

Durand hesitated at the threshold.

"This white man cannot say," he said, then plunged himself into the darkness of the fort.

Chapter 51

London, 30 January 1899

Over brandy, Lawrence offered Welles a job.

They had dined at Lawrence's invitation, in the same room of the Travellers Club where Welles had held the man at gunpoint five months before. He wondered if it was a coincidence, or if Lawrence had arranged it out of some macabre sense of humor. He had not wanted to come. He had no desire for Lawrence's company. Still, he had consented, if only out of curiosity, for he assumed the man had something to tell him. He had been right, it seemed, but he'd never have imagined it would be this.

They had passed dinner politely, if not warmly. Lawrence had surprised Welles with the good news that he was no longer a wanted man in France. The death of the forger Leeman — it had been decided — was some mystery of the underworld which the man frequented, and the case had been closed as unsolvable. As for Hull, the French authorities had been convinced to treat his death as a suicide. From that start, Lawrence had made every effort to be a congenial host and, despite Welles's obvious coolness, he now launched into a lengthy appreciation of Welles's talents and his suitability for a permanent position in the Foreign Office.

"You've acquitted yourself well in this affair," he said. "Especially when one considers the odds stacked against you, when you found yourself in opposition to Her Majesty's government. Still, you found a way to turn the situation to your advantage."

Welles formed an objection, but before he could voice it, Lawrence waved a hand at him, cutting him off.

"Yes, I know it was a matter of conscience for you, so not only to your advantage, but to that of poor Dreyfus, too. Men must be governed by conscience; else we are no better than beasts."

Lawrence paused, inviting Welles to agree.

Welles thought of Sir Reginald, dashed into a bag of broken bones and torn flesh beneath the looming iron tower. In his mind's eye, he saw again the pallid face of Leeman, his lips, in death, drawn back into a smile echoing the larger smile that gaped below his chin. He smelled again the coppery stench of the black blood splattered across the table. He thought, too, of the things Durand had told him of his journey; the sheer inhumanity of it, and the growing horror with which the man had greeted each new day. And he thought of Dreyfus: poor Dreyfus, chained to an iron bed in an airless hut on Devil's Island while he, Welles, had done all he could to help the evil men who put him there.

"No, not beasts," he said, in a voice so low that Lawrence had to strain to hear it. "Surely we are not so good as beasts."

"Come, man! Look at what you've accomplished. The Court of Cassation has at last begun an inquiry. The wheels of justice turn slowly, but surely; and just as surely Dreyfus will go free. Marchand has been recalled and the Sudan is ours. All thanks to you."

Welles did not reply. After a moment, Lawrence went on.

"In confidence, I can tell you that there is to be an agreement, an Anglo-French Accord. We shall share Africa. We'll have our north-south axis: control of the Nile, a railroad from Cairo to Cape Town, and all the east. France will have the north and the west. We agree to support each other in these claims, to our mutual advantage."

"I imagine the Kaiser will not be pleased with that arrangement," said Welles.

Lawrence laughed.

"No, surely not. But even there, it is all to the good. We have felt for some time that a reckoning with the Germans is inevitable. With your help, we have, through this crisis, brought the French closer to ourselves, something I believe may serve us well in times to come. Her Majesty's government is well pleased with you. It is time to claim your reward."

"Reward?" Welles looked at his glass. He lifted it, then drained it and set it again on the table. "What would you have me do?"

"Become our man in Berlin. Manage and develop our intelligence resources there."

Welles considered another brandy, decided against it.

"I regret that I've wasted your time," he said. "I must decline."

"Decline? Why should you decline? You've a knack for this work, man. Born to it, I'd say. What will you do instead? Write articles about gardening, or horse races? You'll be bored stiff in a month."

Welles smiled: a poor smile, weak and sickly.

"Perhaps so. Still, I decline your offer. Let us leave it at that."

Lawrence leaned back in his chair, crossed one leg over the other. He watched Welles silently over his glass. His face betrayed nothing; he simply waited for Welles to go on.

"I don't like the uses to which you put people," Welles said. "I would not like to become accustomed to them."

The older man nodded, as if Welles had said something at once original and profound. He took a cigarette from his case, lit it, shook out the match. He blew out smoke, pointed at Welles with the cigarette.

"And you, sir? What of the uses to which you put people?"

Welles shook his head.

"No," he said. "You'll not judge me. Not you, after the things you've done."

Lawrence cocked his head.

"The things I've done? You mean Sir Reginald, surely. We had no idea how far he'd gone. The man must have lost his mind, cracked under the strain."

Welles reached into his breast pocket, withdrew a folded sheet of paper, unfolded it. He held it up to the light and read aloud:

Foreign Office Memorandum
Most Secret

It is a matter of vital importance to Her Majesty's Government that the intelligence source Esterhazy be protected from exposure. The Supervising Officer and Case Officer are authorized to take any steps necessary to protect this source and are further rendered immune to any legal cause of action which may result from their efforts in this regard.

So ordered, by my hand this Second of October 1894
William Lawrence, Director, Intelligence Branch.

He laid the paper on the table before him.

"The second of October 1894," he said, "a few weeks after Madame Bastian plucked the *bordereau* from a wastebasket in the German embassy. Henry tells Esterhazy he's under suspicion. Esterhazy runs to Hawthorne. Hawthorne cables Sir Reginald. Naturally, Sir Reginald comes to you for instructions."

Lawrence drew on the cigarette.

"You gave Hull a license to do what he did," Welles said. "You *ordered* it."

Lawrence expelled smoke, then stubbed out the cigarette.

"May I ask how you came by that letter?" he asked.

"I took it from the Esterhazy file," said Welles. "When I came to London to see Sir Reginald."

"Ah," said Lawrence. "I should have guessed. I checked the file before we gave it to you, but it wasn't there."

"What on earth possessed you to write such a thing?"

Lawrence shrugged. "Hull demanded it. He was worried that he would be left holding the bag should things go wrong."

"I would say he was right to worry."

From his jacket Welles drew the revolver, held it casually.

"This is Hull's gun," he said. "I took it from the tower. After he fell."

If Lawrence was frightened by the gun, he did not show it.

"After you threw him from the tower, you mean," he said. "Do you intend to kill me now?"

"I don't know," said Welles. "I think I came to kill you. God knows you deserve it."

He stood. With his thumb, he drew back the hammer, then pointed it at Lawrence. He held the pose, his finger tightening on the trigger. Welles wanted Lawrence to defend himself; to bolt from the chair or duck beneath the table. He wanted the man to plead for his life. Instead, Lawrence sat perfectly still, his face betraying no hint of fear as he waited to die.

Welles put his thumb on the hammer, released it carefully. He laid the gun on the table.

"Keep it," he said. "I'm sure Hull would want you to have it. Keep the memorandum, too. It's only a copy. The original is in a safe place. If something untoward should happen to me — or to Georges — then it will be published, along with an account of all that has occurred in this affair."

Lawrence studied his face a moment, then nodded.

Welles walked stiffly from the room. He descended the stairs with leaden legs. He brushed past the doorman in the hall and stumbled through the doors into the night, where he stood, gasping, sucking the cold January air into his lungs, tears streaming down his cheeks.

Chapter 52
Paris, June 1899

London, 3 June 1899

Dreyfus Verdict Set Aside!

The decision of the Court of Cassation on the Dreyfus case will not be given until Saturday, or even on Monday; but it is as certain as anything can be that the conviction of Dreyfus will be annulled, and that the Court will order that Dreyfus be retried by another Court-Martial. This is the course demanded by the prisoner's counsel, who declared that Dreyfus expressly asked to be tried again by his peers. The report of M. Ballot-Baupre, the official Reporter, was entirely in favor of the revision, and he distinctly declared that in his opinion the bordereau was not written by Dreyfus, but by Esterhazy. Yet Esterhazy cannot be prosecuted and punished, for he has been tried and acquitted already, and no man can of course be tried twice for the same offense. A ship has been dispatched to free Dreyfus from his island prison and return him to France. It only remains to be said that Colonel Du Paty de Clam was arrested at 7 o'clock on Thursday evening and lodged in the Cherche-Midi prison. The exact nature of the charge against him is not stated.

The *fiacre* bounced on an uneven section of paving, jarring Welles. He looked up from the newspaper he had been carrying with him for nearly two days. From the station in London to the port at Dover, from there by ferry to Dunkirk, and then by train to Paris, he had clutched it in his hand as if it were a passport. Now he laid it beside him on the bench and looked out the window.

It was the kind of day in Paris one always dreams of, the bright spring sun reflecting off brilliant white clouds as they drifted across an impossibly blue sky. It brought tears to your eyes if you stared at it for too long. He looked away, wiping his eyes, and saw that they had reached the Place de la Concorde. He held his breath as the driver skillfully navigated the chaos of carriages heading in every direction, so that they seemed always on the brink of collision, and then they were through to the other side. Momentum forced him toward his right as the cab veered to the left and, now, through the window, he saw the grey water of the Seine. A tourist boat was passing under the bridge, and the people on the deck waved to him. He waved back, then felt foolish for doing so.

Now the gardens were on his left and, ahead, he could see the ponderous grey immensity of the Louvre. Each street he passed brought him closer to his destination, and he ticked their names off in his mind as he would mile markers. His heart was racing, and his breath came in ragged gasps. He picked up the paper again, attempted to re-read the story for the hundredth time since he'd picked it up at the corner stand near his flat in Chelsea; but he found he was unable to concentrate, and put it down again.

He could not really say why he had come. He had last been in Paris in February, that bleak and dreary month when the whole city is trapped in a cold, grey drizzle, and the street cleaners must contend each morning with the ice and, occasionally, the frozen body of some hapless soul curled up on itself in an alley. He had gone to her house then. He had climbed the steps and rung the bell, only to be turned away. For several days he had watched the house, hoping for a sight of her, but had met only disappointment.

In the end, despondent, he had taken a train to Chartres and nearly froze to death on the long walk from the station to the farm. Durand was surprised to see him, but pleased. He had opened the door wide and invited Welles in, taken his coat and bag and offered him a bed for as long as he meant to stay.

Inevitably they spoke about Georges. After his journey to the Sudan, Durand had returned to the Seigneur home himself.

"They were very kind," he said, as the two men drank sour red wine from clay cups, sitting at the table in the kitchen where the iron stove burned so fiercely it nearly glowed. "They even seemed glad to see me. The old man did, at any rate. Georges said the right things, but I could see that she had not been happy for a very long time. In truth, I have never seen her happy."

"I have," said Welles.

He had avoided looking at Durand as they spoke. His eyes wandered around the kitchen, searching for something else to settle on.

"You and I, we have always told the truth to each other," said Durand. "So I must tell you something now, my friend. I went back there for her. I hoped that I could make her happy. I returned to that house for that reason, on the chance that I could at last make her notice me; and that, seeing me, she might love me as I love her."

"A blind man could see you loved her, Andre. I saw it the night you first met her. It is why I asked you to stay with them. I knew you would keep her from harm."

Welles reached across the table, lifted the jug, poured more wine. He drank, wiped his mouth with the back of his hand.

Then, though he dreaded the possibility: "And? Did she notice you, Andre?"

"No." Durand smiled a sad smile. "I don't think she notices anyone. She moves through life like—" he paused, searching for a way to express what he felt. "Like she is not part of the world. She touches nothing, and nothing touches her. It was too much for me to bear. And, in truth, there was really nothing for me to do there anymore. So, I left, came home."

He paused, smiled again to rob his words of any offense.

"You hurt her very badly, my friend."

"I was a fool," said Welles. "I have tried to make amends, God knows, but what can I do to atone for such a betrayal? I cannot even say that I have succeeded in freeing Dreyfus. The months go by, and the Court of Cassation hears one witness after another, but still the poor man lies chained to an iron cot on the other side of the world."

They spoke about the case for a while. Then Andre recounted what had occurred in Fashoda; how, in the end, he felt he had betrayed everyone. They sat together in silence for a time, each taking it in turn to refill the empty cups. At last the jug was empty. Welles shook it, upended it over Durand's cup, but only a few drops fell. Durand stood, took the jug and disappeared into the pantry. He reappeared a moment later, the jug full, and poured wine into their cups.

"Now what?" Welles asked, gesturing with one hand at the empty fields beyond the window. "Will you be a farmer after all, Andre?"

"No, not that."

"What will you do?"

"My father told me once that life was one disappointment after another," Durand said. "That the measure of a man was how he bore each one. Whether he let them grind him down into nothing or, instead, awoke each day strong and upright and expecting something better." He paused, shook his head ruefully. "I always thought he was a mad bastard, my father, but the longer I live, the more I appreciate the things he tried to tell me."

"He was a wise man," said Welles. "And so?"

Durand shrugged.

"I will wake tomorrow, strong and upright and expecting something better."

"Good God," said Welles, and both men laughed. Durand cut some bread and cheese, and a bit of hard sausage, and put them on the table, then took his seat across from Welles. They ate.

Later, Durand rose to light a lantern. Welles took a card from his pocket and passed it across the table.

Durand held the card up to the lamp.

"*Edmund Morel, Elder Dempster Line,*" he read. "*Liverpool and Antwerp.*" He laid it on the table. "Who is he?"

"A shipping clerk," said Welles. "I met him through a friend in London."

"And what is Monsieur Morel to me? Do you mean to find me a job, Percy? I would make a poor shipping clerk."

"A job, yes," said Welles. "But not a shipping clerk. Through his work, Morel has access to the records of all shipments between Belgium and the Congo. He is a curious man, and has detected some...*discrepancies*, I will call them."

"Discrepancies?"

"Between the public reports of trade issued by the Anglo-Belgian India Rubber Company, and his own records of the goods passing back and forth between the Free State and Belgium. You would be surprised at what one may learn if one has access to the cargo manifests of all the shipping in and out of Antwerp."

"And what has he learned?"

"Two things," said Welles. He counted them off on his fingers. "One. That almost no trade goods make their way from Antwerp to the Congo, even though the returning steamers bring back more ivory and rubber every year. Two. That, instead, the outbound cargo consists almost entirely of small arms. Rifles. Pistols. Ammunition." Welles lifted his cup, drank. "Morel asks himself questions."

"What questions?"

"If the Company engages in trade in the Free State, what do they trade? If they do not trade, how do they acquire such prodigious quantities of rubber and ivory? And what possible need could a few hundred Belgian traders along the Congo river have for an arsenal sufficient to arm one of the smaller European states? Naturally, when he related those questions to me, I thought of you."

"Why me?"

Durand drew back from the table, folded his arms across his chest, his face unreadable.

"Morel seeks men who have been to the Free State and are willing to talk about it," said Welles. "And, I should add, who are willing to return to it and report to him what they find."

"Why? What business is it of Monsieur Morel?"

Welles shrugged. "He strikes me as a man of conscience, Andre. His sense of justice is offended by the implications of the figures he has seen, and by the obvious answers to the questions they raise."

"I have no desire to return to the Free State, Percy."

"Perhaps not, my friend. I thought only that you should meet him. Tell him what you know. What harm can that do? Think about it, in any event."

Durand stared at him for a long moment. Then he reached out a hand slowly, took up the card. He looked at it again, then slipped it into his shirt pocket.

Welles stayed three days; days they spent walking the farm and through the surrounding countryside, Hugo running ahead of them. On the fourth day, Durand harnessed an old horse to the farm cart and drove him to the station. On the platform, they embraced.

"Go and see Morel," Welles said, clasping his friend by the shoulders. "He means to try to do some good, and he will need all the help he can get. Remember what your father said. Perhaps this is your *something better*?"

"Perhaps," Durand conceded. "I will give it some thought."

Welles released him, picked up his valise, stepped up into the waiting coach.

"Welles!"

He turned on the stair.

"I will write to her," Durand said. "Tell her that you were here. How you are. What you have tried to do."

"No, don't," said Welles. "It is over between us."

Durand smiled his sad smile, shook his head.

But Durand had written to her, he confessed, in the long letter he'd sent to tell Welles after Durand had gone to meet Morel. He would, he'd written, be returning to the Congo after all. Morel had it in mind to organize the Dutch and British missionaries who had begun to settle along the Congo, to use them to gather intelligence about what was happening in the Free State. By now, Welles thought, Durand would already be there, searching for his redemption. He hoped Andre would find it.

The *fiacre* bounced again, returning Welles to the present. Through the window he saw they were crossing the bridge onto the Ile Saint-Louis. *Nearly there,* he thought, and, for a moment, he was certain he would be sick. What would he say? He had rehearsed a thousand speeches in the past few months; even written them down, then stuffed them into envelopes and, like a madman, posted them to her. *Would she have read them,* he wondered? He hoped not. Better if she had tossed them into the fire unopened.

The cab jolted to a halt. For a moment he thought to tell the man to drive on, then he steeled himself, took up the paper, and stepped from the carriage. He paid the driver and the cab departed. He stood in the street a moment, gathering his courage.

He had brought nothing with him — no bag, no clothes, barely even any money. He had simply gone from the newsstand in Chelsea to Charing Cross station and boarded the next train for Dover. He had been wearing the same clothes for two days; they looked as though he had slept in them, and he badly needed a shave and bath. *You're an idiot,* he thought. Then he gritted his teeth and mounted the stairs and, somewhat tentatively, rang the bell.

He seemed to stand at the door for an eternity. He thought he heard footsteps approaching, then receding: a careful, measured tread, unhurried. But the door did not open, and he decided he must have imagined it. He waited, unsure if he ought to ring again, or whether it might be better to go in search of another cab. He cursed himself, and rang the bell, insistently this time. Again he heard footsteps approaching; only this time, it seemed to him, they sounded different, more rapid and clipped. *More urgent,* he thought, as if infuriated by his incessant ringing. He heard the latch being thrown, and he braced himself. The door opened.

"Hello, Percy," Georges said.

He gaped at her. She seemed taller than he remembered, and her hair had been cut quite short, an austere style that nevertheless seemed to suit the sharp features of her face. She was, he thought — for perhaps the thousandth time since he'd first laid eyes on her — more beautiful and graceful than any woman he had ever seen, and his heart quailed at the thought that she would send him away.

"*Mon Dieu*," she said, "You look terrible. You'd better come in."